Unleashed

DANCING WARRIORS TRILOGY ~ PART III

when Those of Grace hear again
the Unwilled One comes
times of great strife are His path
under the heel of a new Master the
Land will reel
as water divides so shall the People be
then by their own hearts will They be betrayed

KEVIN M DENTON

www.kevinmdenton.com

Published by New Generation Publishing in 2021

First Edition

ISBN
    Paperback   978-1-80031-389-7
    Hardback   978-1-80031-388-0
    Ebook   978-1-80031-387-3

Cover design by Nicholas Roberts

www.newgeneration-publishing.com

 New Generation Publishing

In the world of the sane,
being unable to recognise reality
is dangerous.
Being unable to doff its shackles
is catastrophic.

If I have erred, the fault is mine,
for everything I know of love
has come from those
who have loved me most,
God, and the parents He gave me.
The little that I return
is nothing compared to
that which has been received.

ACKNOWLEDGMENTS

Thank you to all those who have supported me during the
considerable number of years it has taken
to complete this endeavour.
A book such as this is never solely the product of the author, for so
many people contribute in so many ways.

Special thanks must go to Alison, Elaine, Debbie, Steve and Praful
for their excellent feedback. Their encouragement, as well as their
suggestions, have helped make this book a reality.

Glossary

A full list of character names,
geographical references
and miscellaneous terms
may be found at the end of the book.

1

A light breeze permeated the forest pines, lacking force enough to be bitter, yet boding only colder things to come. Winter's first dusting of snow had all but vanished under weak sunshine, leaving trees dripping as though rain were falling.

"Is Mitcha really the best place for us to be heading to, sir?"

Torrin-Ashur regarded his sergeant for a moment. With eyes that had sunk deep and stubble peppering his normally shaven chin, Nash wore a haggard look.

"Where else? Every place we've come across so far has been ransacked."

Nash seemed unconvinced. He tilted his head sideways.

"What if it's suffered the same fate as Tail-ébeth?"

"Gods, don't say that!"

"But we do seem to be trailing a sizeable force, sir," Nash persisted. He nodded forwards, drawing attention to the rutted forest track they were following. Churned mud and a lack of greenery in the middle suggested many hooves had passed that way in recent days. "And if we're heading in that direction…"

Torrin-Ashur closed his eyes for a moment, too drained to offer argument. If the Tsnath did have the same objective in mind, or if perhaps Mitcha had already fallen, then it was likely nowhere in the Territories was safe. That was a prospect he couldn't bring himself to contemplate just now.

"How are the young ones holding up?" he asked, changing tack to avoid having to think about it.

Nash glanced back at the handful of Tail-ébeth children old Cosmin had managed to save from the ravages of the Tsnath and let out a quiet sigh. "They're regular little soldiers, sir – brave faces and all. But behind that? Hard to say. Their whole world has been shattered."

They weren't the only ones still coming to terms with what had happened, Torrin-Ashur mused. The destruction of Tail-ébeth had dealt such a devastating blow that contemplating its fate with dry eyes was impossible. It was easier to allow anger to swallow the pain.

He thrust those thoughts aside and tried to concentrate on figuring out what was happening elsewhere in the Territories. Tail-ébeth's sacking was no border raid gone too far. It was a definitive move by the Tsnath, the start of whatever Daka had been planning all these months. Just ahead of winter, too. No one had expected that.

A churning in the pit of his stomach distracted him. As each day passed he was becoming more and more attuned to the *Sèliccia~Castrà* and the way it issued its subtle warnings. He recognised the signs now. His hand shot up, fingers splayed, sending the platoon and the survivors from Tail-ébeth scurrying into the trees.

No sooner had the last man made it to cover, than a cart crested the summit of a small hill a little way ahead of their position. It hurtled down the nearside at breakneck speed. The driver was a woman, her hair a wild cloud billowing out behind her, giving the impression of a banshee struck by lightning. Controlling the team of horses straining at their harnesses was a battle she seemed destined to lose.

Two men on the flatbed behind her unleashed arrows rearwards at a furious rate. Their target crested the ridge only moments later; a unit of Tsnath cavalry.

As the cart closed in on his position, Torrin-Ashur spotted children crouched behind the driver, clinging to the wooden sideboards for dear life as the contraption jolted over bumps, careering along the track at a catastrophic pace.

No matter what its speed, unencumbered stallions against burdened carthorses made for inevitable odds. The Tsnath were gaining ground at a frightening rate.

"Archers," Torrin-Ashur signalled.

Ashurmen on both sides of the track scrambled forwards, keeping within the cover of the trees. The second the fleeing cart passed his position, Torrin-Ashur dropped his hand.

Arrows spat out at the pursuing riders. Three of them went down instantly, ripped from their saddles by an unseen hand. A fourth doubled over, out of action but just managing to remain mounted.

The sudden transformation from predator to prey took the Tsnath by complete surprise. They slowed in confusion, a move that cost them dearly. Four more went down to another salvo before the remainder scattered from the track, aiming their horses towards the trees.

One of the riders ploughed into the scrub and headed straight for two of the Tail-ébeth children. Sword raised, he screamed a battle cry, either unaware or uncaring of the lack of threat they posed.

A dagger silenced him, the tip of its blade taking him though the side of the neck. His body slumped backwards in the saddle. As his horse veered round the stump of a tree he pitched over the side, tumbling to the ground like a sack of coal. He rolled to a stop not a yard from where the terrified children crouched. Bereft of rider, the stallion continued on, disappearing into the trees in moments.

Torrin-Ashur regarded his empty hand as though it belonged to another. In utter shock, he realised it had been his dagger that had felled the Tsnath. Two more riders heading his way prevented him from dwelling on the thought more than a moment.

The all-consuming might of the *Sèliccia~Castrà* flooded him with stunning force. His previous experience of its power was a mere fraction of what swamped him now. This wasn't the facing of an arrogant noble seeking First Blood. These foe were hell-bent on his annihilation. The War Song responded accordingly. His mind was inundated. Absolute obedience was demanded from every sinew of his being.

The first of the two Tsnath reached him in seconds. Torrin-Ashur's sword arched thought the air in a blur, severing the man's arm at the elbow. The rider let out no cry, his mind probably too shocked to register the blow. In a single instant he'd been deprived of both weapon and the means to wield it.

The second rider was more prepared. Storming forwards with sword raised above his shoulder, he tried to deliver a downward blow. Without shield to block the attack, Torrin-Ashur performed a pirouette in front of the horse, narrowly avoiding a crushing mêlée of hooves as he crossed its path. The rider had no time to adjust aim and his sword slashed nothing but air. Torrin-Ashur spun on the spot and delivered a jarring blow to the wing of the rider's poleyn. The armour protected his knee, but the Tsnath had been distracted. He failed to draw his horse short in time and rode into the lower branches of a tree a few yards further on.

In an athletic feat, he thrust himself backwards over the rump of the horse. He landed heavily but upright, swinging round instinctively. He raised his sword just in time to block Torrin-Ashur's blow, barely managing to deflect it.

Torrin-Ashur stepped back, pausing to fix his gaze on his opponent's eyes. Incensed, the Tsnath lunged forwards with a furious cry.

Without thinking, Torrin-Ashur whipped his blade around the oncoming sword and flicked the attack aside. He spun full circle and drew the tip of his blade in a long arc, slitting the Tsnath's throat from side to side. Stunned confusion appeared on the man's face. His legs gave way and he landed in a kneeling position, tottering there for a couple of seconds before his torso toppled forwards, burying his face in a carpet of damp pine needles.

Torrin-Ashur was hardly out of breath. Unlike the call-out with Borádin, there was no collapse now; he felt charged to the brim. He cast around for more of the enemy, yet by the way the power of the *Sèliccia~Castrà* was already receding, he knew there were no more Tsnath posing a threat.

He stepped over to the first of his kills and tried to retrieve his dagger. It did not come free easily. Standing on the dead man's head, he yanked harder on the hilt. Four inches of crimson blade slid free.

The sound of retching from one of the children brought him to his senses with a jolt. Sickening realisation of what he'd just done swamped him. He stared down at the body, the first person he'd ever killed, and was overwhelmed by an emptiness that nearly consumed his very soul. He went utterly numb.

Nash came up behind him and grabbed the edge of his breastplate. Uncomprehending, Torrin-Ashur flinched and tried to back away.

"Look at me, sir, look at me."

Torrin-Ashur' eyes refocused. He managed a nod.

"It'll pass, sir. I know what you're going through."

"I... I never killed anyone before."

Nash tightened his grip. "Try not to think about it, sir. This skirmish is over. But there will be more."

"Does it get easier?"

"Only if you're the one that dies, sir."

Torrin-Ashur smiled weakly, grateful for Nash's rather brutal candour. He turned towards to the children who were still huddled nearby, a boy and a girl. Squatting on his haunches, he tried to put on a reassuring face.

"I'm sorry you had to see that."

"You were amazing, my lord," Paulus blurted out, barely able to contain himself.

Torrin-Ashur's eyes widened. Revulsion he could have understood, even fear; he had not expected enthusiasm.

"Killing people is not something to be proud of," he said. He

4

turned his attention to the girl next to Paulus. She looked pale. She must have been the one who'd been sick. "It's Hallvor, isn't it?"

The girl nodded, but said nothing. Her eyes were wide with shock. She was shaking. Torrin-Ashur shook his head. What these young ones had gone through in the past few days was an injustice beyond words.

"Sir, you'd better come quick."

Torrin-Ashur glanced over his shoulder. "What it is, Corporal?"

Botfiár raised an eyebrow. "It's Tomàss, sir. Something's wrong with him."

"Injured?"

"Not exactly, sir. I think you'd better come and take a look."

Torrin-Ashur glanced back at Paulus. "Look after her," he said, flicking a finger towards Hallvor before rising to his feet. The young lad nodded and put an arm round her shoulder.

Torrin-Ashur followed the corporal to where Tomàss was lying on the ground. There was no obvious sign of why he was out cold; he just appeared to be asleep.

"Anybody see what happened to him?"

"I did, sir."

Millardis seemed hesitant to explain. "Out with it, M'Lud."

"Well, sir, he'd managed to get himself cornered – a case of his being in the wrong place at the wrong time."

"Something he has a knack for."

Millardis smiled. "Yes, sir. The Tsnath were forcing him towards that thicket over there. He had nowhere to go."

Torrin-Ashur glanced in the direction of Millardis's gesture. "And?"

"Well, sir, all of a sudden, instead of running away, he just turned and charged back at them. He killed them both in less time than it takes to blink."

An eyebrow edged its way up Torrin-Ashur's forehead.

"I've never seen anything like it, sir. Just as the two horses were passing either side of him, I swear he managed to jump at least his own height off the ground. He decapitated both Tsnath while he was in mid-air. Then straight afterwards, he collapsed in a heap right where he is now. I've checked him over, but there doesn't appear to be anything the matter with him."

Torrin-Ashur realised there was one possible explanation for what had happened, but he needed to speak to Tomàss to confirm it. "Keep an eye on him, M'Lud. Let me know the moment he comes round."

Millardis nodded.

"Now, what happened to that cart?"

"It's a little ways down the track there, sir," Botfiár answered. "It's come a cropper – one of its wheels has fallen off."

Torrin-Ashur wasn't in the least bit surprised. At the speed the thing had been going, it was bound to have fallen apart sooner or later.

He made his way out of the trees on to the track and was immediately confronted by a pair of wary strangers, one of whom was taking aim at him with a longbow that was nearly as tall as he was. He raised his hands, prompting the archer to drop his guard a little. The bow slackened off slightly.

"My name is Lieutenant Ashur. I command the troops that just ambushed the Tsnath that were chasing you."

"Much obliged," came a curt reply.

The bow slackened further and was reduced to pointing at the ground. Torrin-Ashur took that as sufficient diplomatic progress to risk closing the gap a little. He noticed the woman who'd been driving the cart hiding in the trees, surrounded by children. She hugged them close like a hen with her chicks. He smiled to put her at ease.

His attention moved to the cart. "Looks like its fighting days are over." The axle had dug a significant gouge out of the ground for several yards as the bed had slewed to a stop. Only the gods knew where the errant wheel had ended up. The horses were nowhere to be seen.

The burly-looking man with the bow finally relaxed and smiled.

"Those damned Tsnath would have had us for sure if you hadn't intervened."

"What are you doing all the way out here?" Torrin-Ashur asked. "Your accent puts you south of the mountains."

"My name's Elam," the slimmer-built of the pair replied, "and this is Mac. We came north looking for a change of scenery."

Torrin-Ashur didn't try hiding his surprise. "Travelling – at this time of year? With a young family?"

"Ida's my wife," Mac informed him.

"And the children – yours too?"

"So she tells me."

Mac flashed a wink. Torrin-Ashur returned a smirk. "Well, even so, you'd have been better off waiting until spring."

"Our departure from the south was, shall we say, an involuntary affair."

"Oh?"

"Seems we'd become a liability to our former employer," Elam explained.

"Former employer?"

"We're mercenaries."

"I see," Torrin-Ashur murmured, though he was still some way short of a full understanding of the situation. He let that slide for now. "So how is it you came to have the Tsnath chasing you?"

Elam puffed his cheeks out. "My fault. We heard the Tsnath approaching, so we got off the track and waited for them to pass. We thought they'd all gone, but I hadn't counted on a rearguard about half a mile behind the main column. Fortunately, there was a fork in the track between them and us, about a mile back. While they were coming down one leg, we shot off up the other. Not quite quick enough to escape being spotted, though. They gave chase and, well – the rest you pretty much know."

"And where were you heading for originally?"

"A town called Tail-ébeth. We heard it was a good place to stay."

Torrin-Ashur's heart sank at the mention of the name, and the reminder of the catastrophe that had been visited upon the place. "It would have been. The Tsnath have beaten you to it. There's nothing left there now."

"You've been there?" Elam asked.

"A couple of days ago. It was my home town. My father was the march lord."

Elam's eyes widened. "Survivors?"

"Not many." Torrin-Ashur shook his head as visions of the desolation filled his mind. "I need to ask you about the other Tsnath you saw. What strength and how fast were they moving?"

"Difficult to say how many," Mac said with a shrug. He un-nocked his arrow and returned it to the quiver on his back. He slung the bow over his shoulder. "They were moving at a medium trot and took quite a while to pass. A thousand troops, perhaps?" he said, glancing at Elam for corroboration. "Not a force you'd want to run into."

"Definitely not. We're only platoon strength. We were lucky with that lot chasing you. But if any of this other force come back looking for them, it could spell disaster for us."

"Whereabouts were you heading yourself, if you don't mind me asking?" Mac said.

"Mitcha. Our main army is camped there. Or at least, it was, before the Tsnath arrived. They've probably mobilised by now. But there's a walled town there, too. Some shelter at least."

"You've considered the possibility that the Tsnath are probably headed that way?" Elam said, unknowingly echoing Nash's earlier concerns.

Torrin-Ashur's shoulders heaved. "I've got little choice. I'm cut off from my chain of command. Besides, I've got survivors from Tail-ébeth to worry about. Children, five of them, and a few wounded. And an old man. I need to find shelter for them sooner or later. I know this region well, and one thing I can guarantee is, it's going to get a lot colder as winter sets in."

"There go the palm trees," Mac muttered under his breath.

Torrin-Ashur frowned.

"Private joke, Lieutenant," Elam advised with a grin.

Paulus approached from behind, drawing Torrin-Ashur's attention away. The lad had found himself a Tsnath dagger, which he'd tucked into his waistband.

"Millardis sent me, my lord. He says to tell you that Tomàss has come round."

"I'll be right with you." Torrin-Ashur turned back to Elam. "I'll send some of my lads to help with the cart, though I'm not sure there's much that can be done with it. There's very little left in the direction you were heading. You're free to go whichever way you see fit, but you're welcome to come with us if you want."

Elam gave him a nod. "My thanks. We'll discuss it."

Torrin-Ashur left it at that and followed Paulus back to where Tomàss was now seated, propped up against a tree.

"Lads, I'd like a moment to speak to Tomàss alone."

Nash herded the rest of the platoon away, issuing orders to some of them to round up the Tsnath horses that had wandered off into the trees. Several men were sent to help with the collapsed cart.

Torrin-Ashur dropped to his haunches. "How are you feeling?"

"A bit groggy, sir," Tomàss croaked. "Don't know what came over me."

"I think I do. Tell me, when you turned on those two Tsnath, what did you feel?"

Tomàss's forehead creased into a frown. "It was odd, sir. One minute I was fleeing for my life, the next I felt like I was invincible."

"And everything seemed as if it was mired in tar?"

Surprise widened Tomàss's eyes. "Yes, sir."

8

"I've experienced the same thing myself. First time was during the call-out with Borádin. I think I need to explain this to the whole platoon. Sit tight. The giddiness will pass."

Torrin-Ashur beckoned Nash over. "Sorry about this, Sergeant, but get the lads back together again. There's something I need to tell them."

It took the men a few minutes to reassemble, some having only just gone off to round up the stray horses. Cosmin appeared and shuffled up beside Torrin-Ashur with a look of interest enlivening his wrinkled face.

Elam and Mac, with Ida and her little flock, loitered at the periphery of the gathering.

"Lads, there's something going on which I need to try to explain to you as best I can. During his investigations, Brother Jorra-hin discovered the existence of something which in A'lyavine is called the *Sèliccia~Castrà*."

"The what, sir?" Silfast interrupted.

"In our language it translates as the *War Song*, Corporal. It is an ancient magic, once given to the people who lived in this region. They were called the Dendricá back then, although they became better known as the Dancing Warriors. They and the War Song both disappeared over a thousand years ago, and as far as we know, this magic has remained dormant ever since. Until just very recently. In fact, until the day I had that call-out with Borádin."

Murmurs flurried amongst the men. Torrin-Ashur didn't miss the curious look Elam shared with Mac.

"The War Song enables those who can hear it to fight far beyond themselves. It defends them and helps them anticipate their enemy's moves. It gives them tremendous endurance and speed. During the call-out with Borádin, I didn't know what was happening to me. Now we know it was the *Sèliccia~Castrà* resurfacing."

"This Seleecha whatsit, this war song thing, is it something you can actually hear, sir?" one of the men asked.

Torrin-Ashur sighed as he tried to figure out how to articulate something he wasn't fantastically clear on himself. "Not quite. The best way I can describe it is, it's like imagining that you can hear it." That merely seemed to add to the men's confusion. "Look, I know this sounds strange – you'll just have to trust me." He turned to Tomàss and beckoned him forwards. "I believe Tomàss has just had his first experience of the *Sèliccia~Castrà*. It takes a lot out of you when you're not expecting it. That's why he collapsed after his encounter, just like I did at the end of the call-out."

"That's a bit dangerous, ain't it?" Tick muttered.

Torrin-Ashur agreed with a raised eyebrow. "Fortunately, this effect reduces the more you become accustomed to what's going on."

"Sir, are you saying that any of us could get this thing?"

"It's possible, Tick," Torrin-Ashur nodded. He added a shrug, seeing as how he wasn't entirely sure. He wished Jorra-hin were here; an explanation from the Adak-rann would go a long way right now. "Brother Jorra wasn't able to tell me how I've managed to end up with this gift, though he thought it might be due to my family being descended from the Dendricá."

Tomàss let out a grunt. "I'm not even an Alondrian, sir."

Torrin-Ashur shrugged again. "The truth is, we have no idea how or why the ability to hear the *Sèliccia~Castrà* has resurfaced, or how it might spread. But it does appear to be doing so." He wafted a hand at Tomàss again as proof.

"Do you only experience this thing when you're fighting?" Silfast asked.

"Apparently so, Corporal. According to Jorra-hin, the mages that created the War Song wanted to limit how it could be used, so they made it defensive in nature. It awakens only when those it protects are in danger."

Torrin-Ashur caught sight of Paulus listening in at the edge of the gathering. There was a look of awe in the boy's eyes.

"Anyway, that's as much as I can tell you, really. I just wanted you to be aware that it might affect you too. So, unless you've got any questions…"

"Just one, sir," Nash said before anyone had had a chance to move. "You said something about Dancing Warriors?"

"Yes. The Dendricá. They became known as the Dancing Warriors because of the effect the *Sèliccia~Castrà* had on them. In battle they flowed so gracefully that it almost appeared as though they were dancing."

"I've never heard of these Dancing Warriors before. What happened to them?" This question came from Elam.

"Nobody knows. Apparently, they disappeared rather suddenly. But I do know this – after the mages gave the *Sèliccia~Castrà* to the Dendricá, they were never again defeated in battle."

Amid a certain degree of unspoken curiosity, Torrin-Ashur

dismissed the men to prepare to move out. They'd already remained too long. Every minute they delayed risked the return of more Tsnath. They couldn't afford to encounter significant numbers. Speed and stealth were their only defence at the moment.

While the men dispersed to prepare for departure, Elam and Mac sauntered over.

"We've decided there's safety in numbers, Lieutenant. The two of us have experience between us. We could prove useful if push comes to shove."

Torrin-Ashur shook Elam's proffered hand.

"Of course, being mercenaries, we normally get paid for fighting," Mac added hopefully.

"Not much chance of that, I'm afraid."

The burly man glanced at Elam and shrugged. "I guess we'll have to do 'staying alive' for free."

Torrin-Ashur smiled. Mac's easy-going temperament sounded like it could be useful for morale if nothing else, though his stocky build had undeniable potential in the pushing and shoving arena.

The cart was abandoned as a lost cause and several of the Tsnath horses were demoted to pack animals to carry its erstwhile load.

The growing platoon set off without further delay. At the crossroads Elam had mentioned earlier, Torrin-Ashur selected the longer route to Mitcha. The shorter one looked well trampled, suggesting the Tsnath had been down it. The last thing they could afford just now was to run into the back of a large enemy force.

As they settled into to the trudge, with no immediate danger apparent, Torrin-Ashur's mind drifted back to the *Sèliccia~Castrà* and its nature. The survivors from Tail-ébeth had mentioned that he would have been proud of his brother; that Eldris had fought bravely – not something he'd been renowned for. Had he, in his final moment of need, somehow also been protected by the ancient magic? As brothers, they shared the same lineage. Jorra-hin had been of the opinion that the ability to hear the War Song might be down to being a descendant of the Dendricá. On that basis, Eldris might have heard it too.

Yet there was still the question of why the *Sèliccia~Castrà* had resurfaced now. It wasn't as if facing adversity was a new thing; many an Ashur ancestor had been in battle. Some of them had died that way. Torrin-Ashur remembered fondly the stories his father had told of how his grandfather had been gathered to his forebears in the

Kilópeé War. So it clearly wasn't just being in need of protection that had triggered the ability to hear the War Song.

Cosmin drew up alongside. "Loyalty," he muttered out of the blue, appearing deep in thought. "If I was going to make a magic like you describe, I'd bind it to loyalty."

Torrin-Ashur smiled. It was almost as if Cosmin had heard his thoughts. He considered the suggestion for a moment. "You mean, because I have the ability, those loyal to me might inherit it, too?"

"I could be wrong," the old man shrugged, "I'm just saying, that's how I'd have done it if it had been up to me. After all, its spread would have to be limited somehow, otherwise everybody would have it. Then you'd get opposing sides protected by the magic – and where would that leave you?"

"Carnage," Torrin-Ashur mused.

Cosmin chuckled. "Or stalemate."

Loyalty made a certain amount of sense. Ever since the call-out, Tomàss had been intensely loyal. If that was the key to the spread of the *Sèliccia~Castrà,* then Torrin-Ashur could think of none other in the platoon more likely to have been the next to hear it.

2

"A h, Döshan, come, come."

Döshan bowed to the emperor from the far end of the hall and proceeded with haste, scuttling in what was probably an unseemly manner.

Omnitas was not seated on the dais, but standing beside a table that had been brought in and set up just before its step. He was dressed, Döshan noted with a slight frown, in garb rather more military than his usual attire, though he sported no armour or weapons. Then again, with the ever-present imperial guard lurking all around, neither was really necessary.

"Your Majesty," he acknowledged as he drew near, slightly out of breath. He had run most of the way from his quarters on hearing his presence was required.

Omnitas didn't glance at him, but simply wafted his hand over a map unfurled across the table. It was a large-scale representation of the Tep-Mödiss and had a number of small figurines placed across it at various points of significance, representing the current state of play regarding Daka's invasion forces.

"I want your assessment."

Again Döshan found himself frowning. Since the invasion had begun and Lord Özeransk's reports had been coming in, the emperor had been consulting his military advisors more than his political ones.

"Forgive me, Sire, but I don't quite understand."

Omnitas grunted and dithered his hand over the central portion of the map.

"She has moved quickly, has she not?"

Döshan noted the positions of the figurines. A serf stood over Nairnkirsh, a squire over Taib-hédi and a knight at Mitcha. A mounted knight rode at Halam-Gräth, with another further south at the Dumássay Gorge. The Am-gött had a little row of pikemen menacing its southern approach.

The charcoal smudge blotting out Tail-ébeth caught his eye. News of its fate had reached him the day before. Such a display of brutality

13

had been disheartening. The reasons for it escaped him. War was never pleasant, but it didn't have to be barbaric.

"Daka seems to have achieved many of her principal objectives, Sire," he said, stating the obvious for want of something better to say. He was still at a loss as to what the emperor really required of him.

"She has done well. A little too well, perhaps."

"Sire?"

"Her forces have covered most of the region. But she is not consolidating her hold as a proper commander should."

Döshan bent his thoughts towards the military perspective, not his usual stance, and tried to figure out what was on the emperor's mind.

"Does she have the manpower to do so, Sire?"

The emperor's head bobbed slightly. "The Alondrian army has been annihilated – at least, what remained of it after Kirshtahll was called south to deal with the Nmemians. Özeransk and Minnàk have crushed it in various engagements all across Ràbinth and Vickràdöthmore. That idiot Alondris sent up to replace Kirshtahll played right into their hands."

"Jàcos fragmented his forces trying to meet them wherever he could," Döshan acknowledged. "Has that not, then, dealt with the primary threat to Daka's invasion, Sire?"

"For now, yes," Omnitas murmured. "Which is why her continuing tactics baffle me."

The emperor's implicit questioning was having a similar effect on his advisor, Döshan mused.

"She is leaving almost nothing where she should. She barely has her little finger pressing down on her conquests, let alone her thumb. She has left but a tiny force in each of the towns she has taken."

"How is she maintaining control?"

"By intimidation," the emperor sighed. "She is using Tail-ébeth as an example to the others. She has also taken hostages, relying on threat to keep the Alondrian population in check. Non-cooperation costs the captives dearly."

While he did not countenance such tactics, Döshan still couldn't see what troubled the emperor so. With limited resources at her disposal, Daka probably had no choice but to conduct her occupation in such a manner.

"Could she be relying on the advent of your reinforcements to take over that role, Sire? With larger garrisons stationed at each town, perhaps the hostages could be released and some normality be restored. After all, if we are to retain the region, proper government will have to be established. Daka's coercive approach cannot go on indefinitely."

"That does not explain why she is keeping the bulk of her forces on the move," Omnitas muttered, now sounding a little annoyed. "Perhaps she does not have enough to truly control the whole region, but she has enough to do far more than she is. It's almost as if she is holding her men in reserve. The question is, why? What is there she still faces?"

Döshan considered the situation. Lord Özeransk had reported early snow, even in the lowlands. That meant the Mathian passes would be clogged and difficult to traverse, if they weren't already impassable. The Am-gött was being covered by Fidampàss and the Dumássay Gorge by Töuslàn. So the threat of Alondrian reinforcements coming up from the south was largely negated, at least until the spring. What Daka ought to have been doing, therefore, was consolidating her position and digging in for the winter.

The fact that she apparently wasn't doing that suggested the very thing they'd suspected for some time – that her objective wasn't the long-term retention of the Tep-Mödiss. Which left the Ranadar angle.

"May I ask, Sire, has there been any indication of Daka making a move towards the Mathian Mountains?" Özeransk had not mentioned it in his dispatches, but the emperor had other sources of report coming in, and it was always possible word had been sent via means that had not passed through Döshan's hands.

"Not yet. The currently reported position of her troops, here, just south of Mitcha, puts the mountains within easy reach. But she appears to have stopped."

"She is waiting for something?"

"We do not know."

Döshan saw the look of frustration on the emperor's brow. It was a pity that Özeransk's method of communication, relying on enthralled falcon, could only be used for him to send messages, not receive them. The bird could certainly carry its miniature scrolls both ways, but it was too dangerous. There was no guarantee that it would be Özeransk who received the bird when it got back to his camp, and they couldn't risk anyone else discovering that he was communicating with the emperor directly. So they were reliant on what messages he sent, as and when he could. It would have been nice to be able to ask a few questions by return.

"She must be intending to make her move on the Old Homeland

soon, Sire. She will not want to leave that until the very depths of winter, not with the entrances being high up in the mountains. And she won't want to leave it until the thaw – that would risk intervention by the southern Alondrians. Now is her moment, I feel, Sire."

The emperor nodded in agreement.

"And your view on her chances of success?" he prompted.

Döshan swallowed. The matter of Ranadar's treasure, the whole fabulous tale of it, was a perplexing one.

"Sire, I have conferred with a Dwarvish acquaintance of mine, Gorrack-na-tek." Omnitas shot him a suspicious frown. "He is a follower of Bël-Aírnon, Sire, as am I. His discretion may be relied upon, I assure you. I have known him for many years. He lives here in Jèdda-galbráith."

"That in itself is suspicious."

Döshan smiled. "But explainable, Sire. His taste in women runs to the tall and thin – traits somewhat hard to find amongst his own kind."

Omnitas nodded with a grunt. "So what have you learned?"

"That Daka's chances of actually obtaining Ranadar's treasure are very slim indeed. He does not think it exists, in point of fact."

"Does not exist?" Omnitas shot back, his eyes widening.

"To his people, Sire, the treasure is regarded as a legend, but one without much substance. It is a story they tell their children, but put little store in as adults."

The emperor whistled softly. A slight grin broadened his lips. "Then Daka could be in for some considerable disappointment."

"In which case, she will also be in for some trouble."

"Trouble?"

"As I understand it, Sire, her supporters are expecting to be paid a share of the bounty. If she doesn't come up with the goods, who knows what they'll do. They could turn on her."

Omnitas slipped into a contemplative mood for a moment. When he spoke again, something of a gleam had appeared in his eye.

"An opportunity, perhaps?"

Döshan dipped his head slightly. "If her support wavers, so might her hold on what she has already achieved."

The emperor's grin blossomed further. "It would be a shame for that to go to waste. Perhaps a few more of my forces should be readied at the border. To wade in and save her operation. She is playing into our hands, Döshan. I am sure of it."

Unfortunately, Döshan wasn't sure of anything. Daka was many things, most of all a vexing thorn in his side. But she was no fool. Suddenly he felt unaccountably worried.

3

Nash steered his charge through the trees, guiding him by the shoulder. The man wasn't the first lost and bewildered soul the platoon had encountered as they proceeded east, nor was he likely to be the last.

"Sir, got another one. A soldier – calls himself Massim."

Torrin-Ashur glanced up but was too tired to climb to his feet.

The newcomer before him looked beleaguered. His uniform was ripped in places and covered in a lot of blood. Whose, it was hard to say.

"Whose man are you, Massim?"

"Standing army, sir, based at Mitcha. Placed under Lord Mir."

"Mir?" There was a name that left a sour taste, Torrin-Ashur mused; Borádin's sycophantic second from the call-out. "So tell me – how is it you're not with the rest of your platoon?"

"I'm the only one left, sir."

"Explain…"

Massim gave a shrug. "A while back, some Tsnath bastard nicked the crystals from the camp's messaging tent, sir. Lord Mir ended up being the one what got sent out to track him down."

Torrin-Ashur shot Nash a glance. "The first strike – cut our lines of communication."

The sergeant nodded. "This has been a well-planned attack."

"That ain't the half of it, sir," Massim cut in.

Torrin-Ashur's gaze snapped back to the soldier.

"His lordship took us up north, beyond Taib-hédi, sir. That was where the trail led." Massim paused, clearly struggling with the memory of whatever he'd experienced. "Like lambs to the slaughter."

"What happened?"

"We was ambushed, sir. Marched right into it. Wham!" Fist slammed into palm. "Total chaos – nobody knew what was going on. We was massacred, sir."

"How many of you were there?"

"Five hundred."

"Five hundred!" Torrin-Ashur nearly came to his feet. "Who in the name of the gods put Mir in charge of that many men?"

"It were that new general, sir, the one what came up after Kirshtahll got called south."

"You mean Jàcos?"

Massim nodded. "Mir was always at his side – practically the man's shadow, he was."

That sounded about right; Jàcos and Mir were cut from the same cloth – both self-preening idiots. Still, that anyone, even Jàcos, had given Mir command of such a sizable body of men defied belief.

"You're telling us that, out of a battalion strength force, you're the only one left?" Nash challenged. He gave Torrin-Ashur a very sceptical glance.

"Well, I was the only one able to walk when it was all over. I got hit up top, see..." Massim gingerly lifted his fur hat, revealing a nasty gouge, still very red and raw. A whole chunk of scalp was missing. "I reckon the Tsnath left me for dead. When I came to, they'd all gone."

"Were there many others left alive?" Torrin-Ashur pressed.

The soldier carefully replaced his hat to keep out the cold. "Some, sir, but not many. Couldn't do much for 'em. I figured it best to go and get help. Only, that didn't work out, either." The man let out a bitter scoff. "Everywhere I went was just as bad. The following day I discovered another battlefield, somewhere west of Taib-hédi, I think. It was the same thing, all over again. More men, though. I lost count, sir, but it seemed at least double what we'd had."

Torrin-Ashur shook his head in resignation. Massim's news painted a bleak but not wholly unexpected picture. They'd heard similar stories from others they'd met over the last few days. "Sounds like you've had a rough time of it, Massim. Just one more question. Have you been anywhere near Mitcha since all this happened?"

"That's where I headed back to, sir. Get meself back home, I figured; someone there will know what to do. But even that was no good. The camp's a ruin."

"And the town?"

"Got Tsnath crawling all over it, as far as I could see."

Torrin-Ashur felt the ground open up and swallow him. That was the last thing he'd wanted to hear.

"Did you see the enemy, anything of their strength, perhaps?"

Massim shook his head. "It was them, though, sir. They've hung a load of our men on the walls as a warning."

"Hung?"

The soldier grimaced. "Looked to me like it was probably some of thems what the general left to guard the camp."

Nash launched into a diatribe against all things Tsnath, airing every expletive in the book. He finished with, "Haven't these bastards heard of taking prisoners?"

"Prisoners have to be fed," Torrin-Ashur muttered. He pushed down his own anger; after Tail-ébeth, it was a wonder he had any emotion left to quell. "Alright Massim, go find the cook and get some food down you. And have that head seen to. Ask around for Mage Cosmin – he'll make sure the wound doesn't fester."

Massim saluted and wandered off, led mostly by his nose.

"What do you think?"

Nash exhaled and dropped to his haunches, slumping his shoulder against the nearest tree. "That we're in trouble, sir."

"That much I can figure out for myself. I know Mir couldn't have fought his way out of a tavern brawl, but still, five hundred men wiped out – in just one encounter? Is our army really that ineffective against the Tsnath?"

"How many did Kirshtahll leave up here? Four, maybe four and a half thousand men?" Nash hazarded a guess. "Take away Mir's battalion, and let's say another thousand if Massim's report of that second battlefield is correct – that leaves three thousand out there somewhere."

"And that doesn't sound like nearly enough to counter what the Tsnath have thrown at us."

"No, sir. Whatever force hit Tail-ébeth, it was a sizable number. And not the only group the Tsnath have in play; Massim didn't run into the same bunch as we've been following these last few days – not unless the bastards have learned to fly. This is an all-out invasion, sir. They've probably hit us all along the border."

Torrin-Ashur closed his eyes as he tried to think. It was hard. Memories of the utter desolation of Tail-ébeth clouded his thoughts. He could still see the listless smoke curling up from between piles of rubble and charred roof beams.

The battle for the town wouldn't have amounted to much; a few street skirmishes perhaps, one or two desperate fights put up by the more able-bodied, his father and brother amongst them. Nothing that would have taxed the attackers too much, though. It was the sheer level of destruction the enemy had wrought afterwards that was hard to comprehend. Not a wall had been left standing. There must have been thousands of them, swarming over the place like ants.

So why hadn't the same devastation been inflicted on Mitcha? Why did it still have walls to hang men on?

"The question is, should we stick with our plan and carry on to Mitcha? Maybe take a look."

Nash sucked in a breath between his teeth. "What's the point, sir? The Tsnath will have it buttoned up tight."

Torrin-Ashur let his head flop back against the tree behind him. He stared up through its branches at the greying sky. Rain was on the way, perhaps even another bout of snow. "Our options are thinning fast. Mitcha may be lost to us, but we're going to need to find shelter and food somewhere."

"Could we still get through the mountains and make it south?"

"I doubt it. We've already seen snow down here in the lowlands. You can bet your last aldar the passes will be thick with it by now."

"What about the mountains themselves, sir? Any places to go up there?"

That thought had occurred to Torrin-Ashur, though until now he'd not given it any serious consideration. "The Mathians could offer a degree of protection, I suppose. There are plenty of caves we could use."

Nash nodded. "The Tsnath would find it difficult to track us up there, too."

By way of a welcome interruption, Mac threaded his way through the trees and arrived with several bowls of broth. "The cook said you'd probably be needing these."

"Indeed." Torrin-Ashur accepted one of the offerings from the stocky mercenary with enthusiasm. He warmed his fingers around the steaming bowl for a few moments before spooning a mouthful. The taste didn't exactly reveal what the broth was made of, but it was warm and would fill a hole.

"He also says to tell you that we're getting low on food."

"Aye. We were supposed to re-supply at Tail-ébeth, only we were too late. We've also just heard that Mitcha has fallen."

"Ah," Mac murmured. "Not good."

"Nash and I were just wondering about the possibility of going up into the mountains. We could at least shelter up there while we figure out what we're going to do."

"Doesn't get you round the fact that you still need to restock the larder."

"Food is only part of the problem," Torrin-Ashur replied, pausing as he considered the mounting logistical hurdles that faced them. "Up there, the cold is a killer. As things stand, we're not well equipped to survive a Mathian winter."

Mac broke out in an unexpected grin. "You know, I wasn't always the nesh landlubber you see before you now. Once, I was the scourge of the southern seas." He let out a small *argh* and started to walk away. "I'm going to get it in the neck from Ida if you make me return to me old ways."

Torrin-Ashur exchanged a flummoxed glance with Nash.

"Err – Mac?"

The burly man stopped and glanced back over his shoulder.

"You need supplies, right? So – the good ship Tsnath just sailed into port. She'll be fully loaded. Slip aboard and make off with her cargo." He started walking away again, but added, "Under the cover of darkness, of course."

*

Deep down, Torrin-Ashur knew they'd do well to steer clear of Mitcha, as Nash had advised. Yet Mac's idea had appealed to more than a few when aired amongst the men. What's more, they really didn't have a choice; their need outweighed the risk.

Mac assumed the role of advisor with great gusto. Compared to taking a ship at sea, sneaking up on an unsuspecting town in the middle of the Northern Territories presented slightly different challenges to those he was used to, but the principles were the same. There just wouldn't be so much water sloshing about, as he put it.

One advantage the raid did have in its favour, other than Mitcha not being able to raise anchor and sail away, was that the town had a series of holes below the waterline.

There was just one obstacle.

"Wrought iron grills that block the drainage tunnels, sir," Silfast explained. "We might be able to get round them, though."

"Oh?"

"They're designed to be swung out of the way to allow the pipes to be flushed."

"And how in the name of the gods do you know that, Corporal?"

"One of the few benefits of having been in the Pressed, sir." Silfast rolled his eyes up. "Cleaning duties. We's quite familiar with Mitcha's

22

underbelly, ain't we, lads?" He gave the rest of the platoon a leery glance.

"Corp," Tick piped up, "them grills can only be opened from the inside, remember."

Torrin-Ashur eyed Silfast for his response.

"Aye, sir, he's right. But someone small enough could get through, I reckon. They only need to be able to shift the locking mechanism. We could do the heavy stuff from the outside."

"I'll give it a go," Paulus offered, stepping forwards.

The corporal shook his head. "Too big."

"Sorry, Paulus." Torrin-Ashur saw the lad's crestfallen response. "But thank you for volunteering."

Paulus slumped back against one of the trees. He'd found himself a short sword to complement the dagger he'd picked up the other day. He'd be a walking armoury before long, Torrin-Ashur mused.

"What about my boys?" Mac suggested.

Quite how Ida managed to hold her tongue, only the gods knew, but hold it she did, along with a firm grip on the collar of her youngest squirming son. The other two escaped her clutches with ease and proudly arrayed themselves in front of their father.

Torrin-Ashur tried to quash any qualms he had about allowing such youngsters to be put in danger. They'd face the same risks as any man on the mission; the Tsnath wouldn't care that they were just children if this whole mad plan went belly-up.

*

As the distance to Mitcha reduced, the higher the risk of running into Tsnath patrols became. The final few miles needed to be taken with extreme caution. Their approach was punctuated with long periods of lying low whilst scouts probed forwards. Torrin-Ashur likened it to hunting deer, but without the excitement of the chase. Each interval became nothing but an opportunity for anxiety to run amok.

It wasn't until the onset of dusk that they finally reached the fringe of the forest and could see the town clearly. The ground surrounding it was bereft of vegetation larger than a grassy tuft, giving any watchmen the Tsnath might have posted an unobstructed view all the way back to the treeline. The plan was to launch the raid after midnight, when not only would it be as dark as it was going to get, but there was a reasonable chance that most inside the town would either be asleep, or drunk.

Torrin-Ashur crept up to the very edge of the treeline and nestled behind a pine sapling so that he could observe their target. There was little going on other than the occasional head disappearing and reappearing from behind the crenellations. With no obvious threats to divert his attention, his thoughts were drawn towards the bodies of the men hung around the walls. In the fading light they were indistinct and hard to make out, but if they were indeed men from the camp, then some were probably known to him. He thought it strange that that didn't engender much depth of feeling. After all that had happened over the last few days, he realised he was beginning to harden to the horrors of war. The only way to survive was to shut out the emotion and just face what needed doing.

Even so, there was no escaping the fact that what the Tsnath had done was truly an act of barbarism. Their grotesque display was a dire warning; resistance to their occupation would not be tolerated. That really rammed home the reality that this raid was going to be dangerous. Capture would almost certainly mean death.

More doubts about the wisdom of the plan surfaced. Mac and Elam had fighting experience, as did Nash, but for the rest of the Ashurmen, this was their first offensive action. They'd only clashed with the Tsnath twice thus far, both occasions having been rescues of sorts, Kassandra at the Ablath, and Elam and Mac a few days ago. Neither encounter had been deliberately sought. This time it was different. Now they were taking the action to the enemy, and it was an action they'd chosen to undertake, not one forced upon them.

He just hoped they could avoid getting embroiled. Get in, get what they needed, and get out again, that was the order of the day. No wreaking of revenge for Tail-ébeth; even though blood cried out for it. This mission was about staying alive, which meant procuring essential supplies in order to survive the winter. Revenge would have to wait.

Such thoughts churning round made the hours drag by. The only interruption was Elam kicking Mac when the burley mercenary fell asleep and began to snore. When the time finally came for action, it was a relief.

Half the platoon had volunteered to take part in the raid. They assembled in a huddle and checked their equipment one last time. Torrin-Ashur inspected each man as best he could, but with everything metallic or shiny covered in cloth, and faces smeared with mud or soot, he could scarcely see them. At least the Tsnath lookouts would face the same problem. Satisfied that they were as ready as they'd ever be, he gave the order to move out.

Taking the lead, he crept beyond the treeline. It felt terribly exposed after days spent with the forest providing cover. Nervous anticipation kept his heart pounding as he maintained a purposeful scuttle towards the base of Mitcha's southern wall.

His aim was slightly off; the darker patch he'd been aiming for was just a dip in the ground. Crabbing sideways, his nose soon told him he was closing in on his target. Moments later he slid down the embankment of the drainage ditch and landed in something unpleasant.

The rest of the men flitted across the open ground and slithered into position beside him.

"Right, Mac, you got us into this mess, so you can lead the way," he whispered.

The ghost of a grunt acknowledged the order.

The drainage tunnel stank. It was slippery and wet, though it was warmer than Torrin-Ashur had expected. That didn't make the thought of his lads having once had to work down here more palatable. A grimace thinned his lips.

Safely inside, Silfast lit two torches and passed them along the line. Mac took one and moved forwards with his two sons close on his heels.

The expected iron grill came into view in short order, flickering light illuminating badly rusted metal. It seemed a formidable barrier, its brooding hulk emanating its intent to keep them out. The entire mission depended on Mac's sons being able to get it open.

"Jess, you first," Mac whispered, handing the torch to Marro. He hoisted his eldest son up and fed him feet first through one of the square holes in the lattice. It was a tight squeeze at the hips, but a bit of diagonal wiggling prevailed and the boy squelched down on the opposite side, none too worse for wear. Mac passed him the torch. Marro, younger and smaller than his brother, slipped through with no trouble. "Right, boys, you know what to do. Quietly now…"

Jess and Marro slithered their way forwards a few yards, slipping in the thick sludge that covered the bottom of the curved channel. The release mechanism for the grill was nothing more than an iron rod with one end bent at a right angle, like the bolt on a household door, only vast by comparison. Held to the wall by several large iron straps, it first had to be twisted a quarter turn before it could be withdrawn from the eyelet in the grill.

The boys heaved mightily. Their grunts and puffs more than demonstrated that they were giving the mechanism everything they could muster. Torrin-Ashur imagined every man in the tunnel was pouring his will towards them, wishing they could lend their strength.

A few minutes of struggle produced nothing. "Alright, rest for a moment," Mac called out softly.

The boys collapsed to their haunches, panting hard. Mac glanced back at the rest of the men and nodded. "Don't worry, they'll get it done."

Torrin-Ashur wasn't so sure.

The boys got back to work. This time the corroded bolt creaked once before they had to stop for another breather. A glimmer of hope sparked into existence, countering Torrin-Ashur's earlier pessimism.

On the third try, the bolt gave up its resistance with a sharp crack. Working its end up and down repeatedly, each move succeeding in a slightly greater degree of twist than the last, the boys managed to get the bolt rotated through a quarter turn. Jess shoved his foot against one of the brackets holding it to the wall and leaned back with all his strength. Inch by tortuous inch, the locking end of the shaft crept clear of its eyelet.

Mac grinned with pride. "Told you."

Two men squeezed in beside him and helped lift the grill. The corroded hinges produced a wail of protest, sending alarm bells clanging right across Mitcha. Or so Torrin-Ashur imagined.

Mac herded his sons back down the tunnel. They were deluged with pats on the shoulders and many a whispered 'well done'. Their father sent them scuttling back across the open ground to the relative safety of the forest and their doubtless anxious mother.

Silfast took over the lead. Torrin-Ashur followed immediately behind him. After forty yards or so, the corporal paused beneath a vertical shaft that led to the surface. He closed his eyes for a moment, as though trying to imagine what was above. "Not this one," he whispered. "T'would bring us out in the middle of the road leading to the southern gate. Too exposed." He carried on, stopping at the next shaft. Without a word he started climbing.

The slime-filled foot holes cut into the shaft's walls were slippery in the extreme. He lost his grip almost every time he hauled himself up to a new position. Each slip heralded a stream of quietly hissed curses. Torrin-Ashur waited at the bottom, well out of the way; he didn't relish the prospect of being landed on.

At the top of the shaft, the grate covering the opening pushed up with a surprising lack of resistance. It made no sound as Silfast manhandled it out of the way.

"Just like I remembered, sir," he whispered back down. "It's the courtyard to one of the stable blocks."

Torrin-Ashur was glad their subterranean navigation hadn't gone awry. He relayed the message to the others. "Assemble in the stalls. We'll take stock from there. Try not to spook the horses."

Once up the shaft, Torrin-Ashur dashed straight for the nearest stall. The rest of the men followed, one by one rising from the deep like demons from a swamp.

As soon as they'd reassembled, Torrin-Ashur continued his briefing. "You all know what we're here for. Food and clothing. If you bump into any Tsnath, pretend you're a townsman and act submissive. Only fight if you absolutely have to. But whatever you do, do *not* lead them back here. This is our only route out. We protect it at all costs."

"Lieutenant," Mac interrupted, "if anyone does have to do any killing, the bodies should be brought back here."

Frowns indicated an explanation was required.

"Look," Mac huffed, as though dealing with idiots, "a man gone missing won't be suspicious until morning; a man turning up dead raises an immediate alarm."

"Good point. But remember," Torrin-Ashur said, glancing round at the rest of the men, "ideally I want us to get out of here without anyone knowing we've been. Let's not give the Tsnath any reason to carry out reprisals against the townsfolk."

With that the men paired off and slipped out into the alleyways like wraiths.

"Lieutenant, mind if I come with you?" Elam asked. "Mac's better on his own in situations like these."

Torrin-Ashur nodded and led the way out of the stable.

"So where to?"

"The mayor's house."

"Is that wise?" Elam challenged.

"I need information. For a start, I'd like to know how the Tsnath took the town intact, instead of levelling it. Also, the mayor might know what the Tsnath are doing elsewhere."

"Assuming he's not one of those hanging on the walls."

Torrin-Ashur grunted. He didn't need any more pessimism to add to the load he was already carrying.

They skirted the town square via several back streets before having to cross one corner of it to get to the mayor's house. They took cover behind a couple of ornamental bushes that stood either side of the steps leading up to the front door.

"We can't just knock," Elam whispered.

"Let's try round the back."

A small alleyway separated the house from the building next door. It was blocked by a high gate, which rattled as they scaled it, setting a dog to barking somewhere close by. They froze, waiting for things to settle down again. An annoyed shout silenced the mutt.

As soon as things had gone quiet, Torrin-Ashur made his way along the side of the house and climbed over the stone wall into the mayor's garden.

"There might be Tsnath inside," Elam murmured, crouching beside him.

Torrin-Ashur scrabbled about for a few small stones. "Stay here and keep out of sight."

He took up position where he could easily dive for cover and started lobbing the pebbles at what he hoped was a bedroom window. It was slightly ajar, suggesting that the room beyond might be occupied.

His first couple of throws brought nothing. The third stone miraculously sailed through the gap between the open pane and the frame. A face appeared above the sill. Torrin-Ashur took cover before being seen.

The window opened further. "Who's there?" a female voice called softly.

It wasn't the challenge a Tsnath soldier would have given, that much was certain.

"I'm an Alondrian," Torrin-Ashur whispered back. "I need to speak with the mayor. Is he there?"

"No."

"Where can I find him?"

The figure leaned out of the window a little further. "Stay there — I'll come down." The window closed.

To Torrin-Ashur, it seemed to take an age for there to be any sign of movement downstairs. But eventually a bolt was withdrawn and the back door to the house cracked open a fraction.

"Show yourself."

Torrin-Ashur stepped out of the bushes.

"My name's Torrin-Ashur. I'm from Tail-ébeth."

The door opened a bit further. "Anyone else with you?"

Elam rose from his hiding place.

"You'd better come in."

The young woman stood aside, allowing them to enter what appeared to be a kitchen, though it was illuminated only by a small night lantern with its wick trimmed down. Most of the room was shrouded in darkness.

"You stink," the girl noted, wrinkling her nose up.

"You can thank Mitcha's drains for that. Is anyone else here?"

The young woman shook her head. She had short, very curly hair, and quite possibly freckles, though it was hard to be sure in the dim light. "My mother was away when the Tsnath came." Worry added a tremble to her voice. "We haven't heard from her since."

"Is your father the mayor?"

"Yes. I'm Katla. The Tsnath have him and many of the other men under guard."

"Where?"

"In the town gaol mostly."

"So the town's only got women and children left in it?"

Katla nodded. "And the elderly. The Tsnath only rounded up those they thought might give them trouble. They're holding us hostage against each other. They threaten us to keep the men under control, and vice versa."

"Pleasant sods, ain't they?" Elam growled.

"How have they been treating you?" Torrin-Ashur asked.

"Me personally – not too bad. But I've heard of some women being raped."

That stirred Torrin-Ashur's anger. He pushed it back down; of all the lessons his father had taught him, keeping his temper in check was the clearest. His men depended on him being able to keep a level head now.

"Any idea how many the Tsnath have got in the town?"

"Not as many as you might think." Katla sighed and pulled a chair away from the table. She sank down. Elam went back to the door to keep watch. Torrin-Ashur remained standing, not wanting to sully the mayor's furniture with what he'd picked up in the sewer. "During the day their commander meets with my father and some of the other town elders to discuss organisational matters. I've been able to listen in sometimes. From what I can gather, they've only got between sixty and seventy men here."

Torrin-Ashur was surprised. "So how did they manage to take the town?"

"That's only what's left. There were thousands here a couple of days ago. Most of them have moved on."

"But still, Mitcha has fortified walls."

Katla cast a sullen glance at the table. "The Tsnath gave us an ultimatum – surrender or be sacked. They told us the whole Alondrian army had been wiped out, so no one would come to rescue us. The town elders decided we'd best not resist, not after what we saw them doing to those poor men left over in the army camp."

"The men hung on the walls?"

Katla nodded. "The Tsnath dragged them round the town behind their horses until the elders had made up their minds. Not many of them survived the ordeal. Those that did were hung anyway."

Torrin-Ashur was sickened to the core. He saw Katla tremble and reached for her hand.

"Your father is responsible for civilian lives, not fighting wars. He did the right thing."

"Did Tail-ébeth surrender?"

Torrin-Ashur's throat became choked. He had difficulty replying straight away. "They weren't given the same choice. Tail-ébeth has been completely destroyed. I've a handful of survivors with me, mostly children. Everyone else is dead."

Katla sucked in a breath. There was a moment or two of silence between them.

"Lieutenant, we ought not be too long."

Torrin-Ashur nodded to Elam. "You're right. Katla, aside from those in the town, do you know of any other Tsnath hereabouts? What about over in the camp?"

"There's nothing left of it. I don't think anyone's over there now."

Torrin-Ashur frowned. "I wonder where they've all gone, then?" he said, eying Elam.

The mercenary appeared to ponder the question for a moment. "You know, Lieutenant, it makes me think they're under strength."

"*Under* strength?"

"Think about it – you invade a territory, but don't have sufficient resources to control the whole region, so what do you do? You overcome any pockets of resistance by hitting them hard with your main force and then, before anyone realises your true strength, you establish a heavy martial law. Small garrisons are left to manage a subdued population, freeing up most of your army to continue the campaign."

Torrin-Ashur could see the logic of Elam's argument. "But they must know that once the south realises what's going on, a large force will be sent up. Quite apart from anything else, as soon as Kirshtahll hears of this, he'll march straight back up here with the other half of the Northern Contingent. Even if that means he has to come the long way round via the Am-gött."

"Who's Kirshtahll?"

Torrin-Ashur blinked in surprise. That anyone in the Northern Territories could not know who Kirshtahll was seemed extraordinary. But then, Elam wasn't from the north.

"Until just recently, he was the overall commander of all the Alondrian forces stationed up here."

"Was? What happened to him?"

"He was ordered to take half the army down to Colòtt. Some brouhaha with the Nmemians."

"Colòtt?"

Torrin-Ashur nodded.

"Lieutenant, there's something you ought to know. Colòtt is where Mac and me just came from. We had to get out in a hurry."

Torrin-Ashur didn't manage to make a connection and frowned.

"The last job we did took us into Nmemia," Elam explained, "to deliver a message."

"A message? About what?"

"I don't know. But what I do know is this – a couple of days later, our employer tried to have us killed. My guess is he's brokered some sort of deal with the Nmemian, and was trying to cover his tracks."

"So what is it you're saying?"

"I'll bet you every aldar in Alondris that the Nmemians are working with the Tsnath. Whatever's going on down south – I reckon it's a diversion for what's going on up here."

Torrin-Ashur was stunned. It felt as though a mule had just kicked him in the guts. "You're suggesting our own people have colluded with the Nmemians to draw our forces out of the Northern Territories?"

"I can give you a name if you like."

Torrin-Ashur's stare demanded it.

"Gëorgas."

"Minister Gëorgas?"

"The very same."

"Gods!" Torrin-Ashur hissed. He pulled out a chair and slumped down, dumping his forehead into his hands and staring at the lantern on the table.

It was bad enough that the Tsnathsarré Empire had invaded, destroying the army, laying waste to his home and killing thousands. But the notion that the Territories might have been betrayed by members of Alondria's own Grand Assembly was just too much.

Elam stepped up close and lowed himself to his haunches. "Are you alright, Lieutenant?"

"We have to get a message to Kirshtahll," Torrin-Ashur croaked. He glanced at Katla. "Does Mitcha have any means left of communicating with the south?"

Katla gave her head a forlorn shake.

"Gods. I wonder if anyone in the south even knows what's happening up here?"

Elam threw his hand up for silence. "Something's up," he said, dashing from the room. Torrin-Ashur exchanged a brief frown with Katla before following. He found Elam crouched beneath the sill of a window at the front of the house.

"What is it?"

"Not sure. I just caught sight of a Tsnath squad heading down that street over there." Elam pointed across the square. "They were in a hurry."

Torrin-Ashur's heart began to race. He knew in his guts that something was wrong.

"Katla, we've got to go. Will you be alright? You could come with us, if you want."

Katla shook her head. "I can't. My father – they might punish him if I disappear."

Torrin-Ashur nodded. Given the way the Tsnath were behaving, that seemed a very real possibility. "Well, I hope we haven't put you in any more danger. May the gods be with you."

Elam disappeared back through to the kitchen and out into the garden. Torrin-Ashur was close behind. They abandoned some of their earlier stealth and hurried back towards the stable block.

They weren't the first to return. Twelve others had made it back without running into trouble. They'd managed to gather quite a haul.

But no hastily thrown together mission such as this was ever going to go off without a hitch. Mac staggered in a few moments later, his arms supporting a huge mound of furs on one shoulder, and a dead Tsnath soldier on the other.

"Sorry to be the bearer of bad tidings," he puffed, unceremoniously dumping both his loads on the floor, "but three of our lot have just run into trouble."

"Where?"

"I'd have to show you. I saw them taken by a Tsnath squad a few minutes ago."

Torrin-Ashur didn't hesitate. Having heard from Katla how the men on the walls had ended up there, he wasn't prepared to leave his own men to share the same fate.

An idea struck him. It wasn't refined; there wasn't time for niceties. It was, however, just mad enough to succeed. He quickly outlined his plan.

"Draw swords," he ordered, heading for the stable door. "Archers, ready your bows. If it looks Tsnath, don't wait for the order – just shoot."

Mac led the way back across the town to where the three men had run into the Tsnath. There was little sign of any disturbance now. Only a few guttural shouts from a nearby street broke the nocturnal silence.

Flitting from door to door, alleyway to alleyway, they continued across the town, making it as far as All Man's Way without encountering any Tsnath. There their luck ran out.

The street ended at a junction with another running crosswise to it. On the far side was the town gaol. Six Tsnath guards loitered outside it, warming themselves around a glowing brazier.

Torrin-Ashur motioned for the lads to backtrack before they were spotted.

"Form up into a squad," he ordered. "Those of you with swords, hold them outside your scabbards. Archers, keep your bows nocked, but carry them lowered. We'll march down the street like we own the place – they won't be expecting that. As soon as the game's up, let loose with everything you've got."

The squad emerged into All Man's Way three abreast and four deep. Torrin-Ashur and Elam marched alongside. Mac kept hidden at the rear; his bulk made him stand out too much to be an ordinary ranker. Footsteps stomping on the cobbles made it clear stealth was not intended.

The ruse worked for a while. They advanced nearly half way down the street before the Tsnath thought to challenge. When the inevitable shout came, Torrin-Ashur raised his arm in a wave and dredged up as much phlegm as he could. He spat with considerable force. It was crude, but it bought them another ten paces.

The moon, up to that point largely hidden behind clouds, chose that moment to emerge from cover, turning the tide in the Tsnath's favour. Suspicions roused, one of them drew his sword. He cried out the moment he realised the approaching squad was not one of theirs.

"Now!" Torrin-Ashur shouted.

The front rank of the squad darted out of the way. The second and third ranks brought their bows to bear, loosing a volley forwards. With no time to aim, six arrows flew, but only one found its mark, taking a Tsnath guard in the belly. He went down writhing in agony.

Torrin-Ashur drew his sword and charged down the street towards the five remaining enemy soldiers. The rest of the Ashurmen were only a step behind.

For a few moments the Tsnath seemed paralysed. When their sense caught up with them, as one, they abandoned their fallen comrade and fled towards the gaol house door. Before they could get it bolted, four Ashurmen cannoned into it, brushing those behind it aside.

In the darkness of the interior swords flailed in confusion. Torrin-Ashur followed instinct rather than sight; how the others managed to distinguish friend from foe he didn't stop to consider. Somehow they managed. The Tsnath went down one after the other in the face of the Ashurmen's onslaught.

As shouts and the ring of steel on steel fell silent, Botfiár barged his way across the room. "Sir, I just saw a couple more Tsnath soldiers running off up the street."

"Then we can expect reinforcements at any moment." Torrin-Ashur glanced round. "The local militia armoury is in here somewhere. Find it – we're going to need more weapons."

"Aye, sir."

"The rest of you, follow me."

Torrin-Ashur advanced towards the archway at the rear of the room, beyond which lay steps that led down into an underground chamber. Mindful that more Tsnath could be lurking in the shadows, he pulled Tick out of the line of sight.

"Send a few arrows down there first," he ordered.

Four of his archers loosed a volley. No arrows came back in reply. The only response they did get was a cry of pain and the sound of a table tipping over.

A further three Tsnath guards occupied the deeper recesses of the gaol. One of them was dead already, his body sprawled over the remains of a table, two arrows in his chest. The others were too drunk to fight. One impaled himself on Nash's sword in an attempt to escape, the other fell to his knees begging for mercy. Someone, Torrin-Ashur didn't see who, knocked the man senseless with the handle of a torch. The mead-filled jar he was still holding shattered against the bars of one of the cells.

Mitcha's arrangements for incarceration reminded Torrin-Ashur of the night they'd gone to fetch Golan back in Alondris. A row of cages made out of iron grills embedded into stone arches lined either side of the central corridor. Designed to hold a couple of prisoners apiece, they were stuffed to overflowing now. A lack of amenities had turned the place into something resembling the sewer tunnels of recent acquaintance.

Nash retrieved a bunch of keys from the belt-hook of a dead guard and tossed them to Elam.

"Which one of you is the mayor?" Torrin-Ashur called out.

"I am." A short, portly man pushed his way through the throng of men clambering to get out of one of the cells.

"Lieutenant Ashur, from Tail-ébeth. Your daughter Katla said you'd be in here."

"Is she alright?" Torrin-Ashur could see where Katla got her curly hair from. Though the mayor's mop was considerably thinner on top. "The Tsnath haven't done anything to her, have they?"

"She's fine. But listen, we haven't much time. More Tsnath will be on their way. We need to be ready for them."

"Ready? What do you mean?"

"If you want your freedom, you're going to have to fight alongside us. Otherwise this gaol break is going to be the shortest in history."

"Why, how many men have you got?" the mayor shot back. He looked worried.

"I had twenty one when we came into Mitcha. Three have been taken by the Tsnath, and several others are still missing. I've got fourteen with me right now."

35

"Fourteen!" the mayor gasped. His worry dissolved into horror. The sentiment spread rapidly to his fellow townsmen. "The Tsnath will massacre us!"

"No they won't."

"But we're not soldiers. We're not trained in combat."

"Maybe not. But you *are* Alondrians. More than that, you're Northerners. The time for relying on others to keep you safe is over."

"But we can't take on hundreds of Tsnath," a man further back in the crowd called out.

Torrin-Ashur decided to err on the side of optimism. "There's only sixty Tsnath in the whole town. We've taken care of nine of them already. With you all armed, we'll outnumber what's left three to one." Fear still haunted the townsmen's faces, he could see that, but this was no time to pander to it. "So stop arguing and follow me."

Back out near the entrance, he found Botfiár directing an assault against the armoury door. A large table, upended for use as a battering ram, smashed against the oak planking around the hinges. Two hits later, the door collapsed inwards. It ended up at an odd angle as the last few rivets of the lower hinge grimly held on. A final kick flattened it.

There were more pikes than swords in the militia's arsenal, and not many shields. The place was quickly stripped bare and the weaponry distributed. There wasn't enough to arm all the men, so the most able were given preference. It wasn't easy to see who was who, but the sight of the mayor in the front row, shield and sword in hand, inspired Torrin-Ashur with renewed confidence in their chances.

"What's happening outside?"

Tick peered out of a grimy window. "Looks like about twenty Tsnath out there, sir."

"Archers?"

"Can't tell."

Torrin-Ashur nodded. "Botfiár, grab your battering ram. We'll use it for cover."

Botfiár and a couple of others hoisted the table up into a vertical position behind the gaol's entrance, using its legs as handles to propel it forwards.

Tick flung the door open. A flight of arrows immediately thudded into oak.

"That answers that, then," Torrin-Ashur muttered.

Botfiár and his two helpers manhandled the makeshift shield out into the street. The rest of the men tucked in behind it as best they could, edging their way out. More arrows poured into the tabletop.

As they cleared the entrance, the Ashurmen darted out, screaming their way towards the Tsnath. Archers became redundant as the gap between opposing forces closed to nothing. The fight dissolved into a mêlée of hand-to-hand combat. Townsman, emboldened by sheer weight of numbers, flooded across the street to join in the fray. Pent-up anger was quick to be vented on former captors.

The clash was loud and chaotic, more a disorganised brawl than a disciplined battle. Men hacked at each other in the dark. The Tsnath were swamped. The fighting was over in less than a minute.

Torrin-Ashur surveyed the scene and took stock. They'd suffered relatively few casualties. Tick was nursing a bleeding arm, Nash had a cut somewhere above his forehead that made him look like he'd been scalped, and one of the other men, Symon, had an arrow protruding from his thigh. Torrin-Ashur grabbed the shaft and pulled it free before the man even knew what was happening. He screamed a stream of obscenities.

"Sorry," Torrin-Ashur shrugged. "I know what it's like. Trust me, you didn't want this thing in you any longer." He flung the arrow away. "Get that bandaged, and Cosmin can sort you out later."

Some of the townsmen had come off a little worse; several were dead. One hadn't made it beyond the gaol entrance. He sat leaning against the doorframe, head drooped, sightless eyes staring at the haft of the arrow that had taken him in the chest.

The remaining Mitcha men were flushed with their success. A rush of zeal coursed through them. Torrin-Ashur wanted to exploit it before it went off the boil.

"Well done men, good work. Now all we need to do is find the rest of these bastards. By my reckoning there's about forty Tsnath left. Nash, are you fit to fight?"

"I've got a killer of a headache, sir, but nothing a night's rest won't cure."

"You can rest tomorrow. Take Elam and half the men and cover the south of town. I'll take the rest north. Bugle if you run into heavy resistance."

"Aye, sir."

After scavenging the dead Tsnath's weapons, the two groups took off in opposite directions.

As they ran back up All Man's Way, Torrin-Ashur called to Mac, "Where do you suppose the Tsnath have taken our lads?"

"The town square, most probably."

Torrin-Ashur nodded, not that the gesture could be seen as he ran down the street. He grabbed a townsman and had him lead the way by the shortest route.

They arrived at the southeast corner. Near the far side, a group of Tsnath soldiers, numbering somewhere between twenty-five and thirty, surrounded two men on their knees. The body of a third man was already sprawled on the ground.

At the very instant Torrin-Ashur emerged into the square the Tsnath commander swung his sword high above his shoulder and felled his second prisoner.

Torrin-Ashur skidded to a halt, almost bent double, his head pounding as if he himself had just been struck. He struggled for breath, supporting hands on his knees.

When he managed to straighten, the gods of thunder had lent him their countenance.

He let loose with a bloodcurdling scream that shocked those around him. He tore across the square without regard for life or limb, pure, unadulterated rage hammering through his veins, turning his blood molten and maddening him into something even a berserker would have fled from in terror.

He was half way across the square before the Tsnath had the wit to respond. Their commander barked a few orders and took refuge behind the rows of men that formed up in response.

Torrin-Ashur crashed into the first rank like an enraged bull, throwing the full force of his body behind a borrowed shield. It cannoned into a man on his left, knocking him clean off his feet. He relinquished the shield so that he could grip his sword with both hands. Using his momentum to pivot round, he swung his blade in a powerful arc that brought it scything across the chest of a soldier on his right. The Tsnath's first line of defence was breached in seconds.

Ducking as a weapon from the second rank pierced the air above his head, Torrin-Ashur snatched up a fallen sword to add to his own and hacked his way forwards, both weapons flailing at anything within reach. He had but one objective – the Tsnath commander. The gods themselves would have been fools to stand in his path.

The rest of the Ashurmen and the men of Mitcha flooded across the square. They numbered nearly a hundred. What was left of the Tsnath's first rank withered under a storm from soldier and townsman alike.

Torrin-Ashur burst through the third Tsnath rank. He flung away his second sword, reversed his hold on the one he had left, and stabbed backwards, ending an attack from behind without even looking. The remaining Tsnath soldiers were too busy dealing with overwhelming numbers from the front to spare a thought for their commander.

The Tsnath officer spat something that sounded nothing like a plea for mercy. Torrin-Ashur slowed his advance, forcing the officer backwards with each step. He held his sword with two hands up by his right shoulder, proclaiming his intent unequivocally.

The Tsnath commander knew he was going to die. It was in his eyes.

Torrin-Ashur let out another terrible scream and hurled himself forwards, curling his blade round to slice at his opponent's right arm. The hit was blocked. He pirouetted round and slammed into the Tsnath from the opposite side. Blow after blow knocked the enemy commander about like a rag doll. Unable to withstand the ferocity, the man stumbled. Torrin-Ashur instantly took advantage. He hammered down, sending the Tsnath's sword skittering across the cobbles. Defenceless, the man found himself with his back up against a wall.

"KNEEL!" Torrin-Ashur screamed.

The Tsnath officer slumped. He looked up at the dark spectra of death towering over him.

Torrin-Ashur's blade descended.

*

Katla stood on the battlements just above the north gate of the town, looking down under a cold grey sky at the solitary figure below her shovelling soil back into a grave. She hardly noticed as her father came up beside her.

"What's he doing?"

"Burying his men," she answered quietly.

"Not pyres? No, I suppose not. Too visible." Her father gazed down and pointed with his chin. "Couldn't he have got someone else to do that?"

"He wouldn't let them. His men, his duty, he said. Their loss seems to have hit him hard."

Her father sighed with a nod. He leaned against the stonework.

"He's young. Probably not very experienced. Last night I didn't realise just how young, especially not after what I saw him do in the square…"

Katla shuddered. She'd seen glimpses of the fighting from inside the house, but nothing of the detail. It had been the stories recounted afterwards that had sent shivers down her spine. Torrin-Ashur had decapitated the Tsnath commander with one slice of his blade. She found this image of him hard to reconcile with the one she had formed based on their encounter in her kitchen just hours earlier.

"He's lost everything. You've heard about Tail-ébeth?"

Her father nodded. "Bad business, bad business. These Tsnath have turned the world upside-down." He paused a moment, coming to some private conclusion about something. "Well, I hope yon lad doesn't take too long. We've got a lot to sort out. Can't stay here now."

"You've decided we should leave, then?" Katla retorted, not hiding her surprise. "A couple of hours ago you wouldn't so much as hear of it."

"Aye, well, the elders have had time to think on it now. Like the lad said, there's no telling whether the Tsnath might come back this way in force. For better or for worse, we're stuck with the way the dice have landed." He paused again, then added with a snort, "Not sure which is better; rotting in my own gaol, or freezing to death in the damned mountains."

"Father!"

He winked and kissed her a quick peck on the cheek. "Tell the lad when he comes in that we need to talk."

Katla nodded and returned her gaze to Torrin-Ashur. He was just patting down the last of the earth on the second grave. Out of the corner of her eye she saw the Tsnath survivors, only nine of them, digging a much larger hole under the watchful gaze of some Alondrian archers. Seventy six of their number had fallen; her estimate of how many there had been in Mitcha had been slightly under. In any event, theirs was to be a mass grave.

The bodies of the Alondrian soldiers that the Tsnath had hung on the walls had all been cut down and were to be buried separately. Townsmen had volunteered to attend to that grim task. Fitting, seeing as how it had been for their sakes that the soldiers had died.

Katla shook her head. So much death in such a short space of time.

Things had changed forever.

4

With fresh snow dressing the Mathian slopes, wind-driven into deep drifts in places, Jorra-hin was glad of the snowshoes purchased at Bythe-Kim, a trading post they'd passed through a few days back. Yet even with them on, the constant demands of striding from one sinking hole to the next was exhausting. The oversized footwear now felt like it was made of rock and lead rather than birch-lath and gut-string. Only a stubborn determination to reach his brothers at the Jàb-áldis monastery kept one foot heaving after the other.

A gust of wind buffeted down the valley. It knifed through his clothing, blowing recent memories of the summer heat in Alondris even further into the realms of the forgotten; it was hard to reconcile that these mountains even belonged to the same country. Equally blown away were Kirin's playful antics. Snow never touched Nicián shores, so when it had first transformed the landscape she had gleefully scampered through it, engaging in snowball fights and building her first snowman. The novelty had soon worn off. This high up in the mountains, the cold seeped into the bones and took the joy out of everything.

Even Elona, with her love of the countryside, had lapsed into a stoic, silent plod. Seth seemed to find their current exertions invigorating, an outdoors upbringing on his father's farm no doubt helping, yet of late even he'd become quite taciturn and hard to read. The only vociferous one amongst them was Pomaltheus; he'd taken up moaning with a vengeance.

"We'll stop there," Seth called out, gesturing towards a cleft in a nearby rocky outcrop. Uninviting though it looked, it would at least afford them respite from the wind. The group trudged over and huddled against the cold hard granite.

Pomaltheus unstoppered his canteen and tipped it to his lips. Nothing came out. "Bloody hell," he grumbled. After a moment's concentration, he murmured an incantation and sent a wave of thawing warmth into the container. It was a skill he'd had plenty of opportunity to master over the last few days.

"How much further?" Seth asked, gazing up the valley.

Jorra-hin's shrug was mostly lost under his furs. "I don't recognise where we are yet. I'm more used to looking down from the monastery rather than up at it."

Pomaltheus let out a grunt. "It had better not be far."

Kirin suddenly drooped forwards. Pomaltheus threw out a hand, propping her back up again.

"Are you alright?"

Kirin's eyes clawed their way open. She managed a thin smile.

At Seth's bidding the trudge resumed; a few minutes rest was all he allowed. Physically the most capable amongst them, he'd become the much needed driving force that kept their small party going. Out of necessity he was a hard taskmaster. The effort of wading through powdery snow, up ever steepening terrain, made for slow progress. They had supplies, but time was not on their side. Without shelter it was easy to die in the Mathians.

Those cheery prospects turned Jorra-hin's thoughts to what lay ahead. It sapped his will to know that the worst was still to come. The monastery was perched on a ridge just below the summit of Mount Jàb. The last few miles would be absolute torture. He tried not to think about what they'd do if the snow had already made the climb impossible. The southern approach to Jàb-áldis was rarely used, even in summer. Yet he stood by his insistence that they come this way. From Bythe-Kim, the normal route through the Kimballi Pass and then back along the Jàb-áldis Pass was more than twice the distance. It would have turned less than one week into more than two. Time he feared they might not have.

Seth was the first to notice when the monastery did finally appear in the distance. He stopped and pointed up the mountainside.

"Praised be the gods!" Jorra-hin exclaimed. His heart swelled at the sight. "Home. Hot soup. Bed."

He judged that Jàb-áldis was probably two miles further on, seemingly with half that straight up. The sight boosted his morale, but that could only reinvigorate him so much. The flight from Alondris had already been long and hard, hampered by the need to avoid the usual roads and easier modes of transport. His reserves of strength were dwindling fast as the cold and altitude took their toll. That he'd lived in this region his entire life didn't appear to be helping much.

The last mile turned into a gruelling ordeal. Discerning where the path lay was impossible; it had disappeared under snowdrifts that had sculpted and re-sculpted the mountainside at the whim of the wind. Jorra-hin blindly followed Seth as he led them in a zigzag back and forth, traversing the treacherous blanket by whatever contour offered the least resistance. One mile became two, ten, a hundred – it didn't seem to matter anymore; the monastery never got any closer. It just sat there, taunting them from on high.

"Won't be long before the sun sets," Seth noted on their latest pause. There was no mistaking the worry in his voice. He scanned the dimming skyline while Jorra-hin contemplated his navel. "Come on, we've got to keep moving."

Without rising, Elona glanced up at the ridge. "I don't see any lights up there."

"They'd better be in," Pomaltheus declared.

Jorra-hin found it within himself to manage a chuckle. "They'll be there. The Adak-rann haven't left the monastery vacant in eight hundred years."

"Move, you lot," Seth ordered. "We can't afford to get caught out here in the dark."

He set off, dragging Kirin to her feet as he went. Jorra-hin longed to help her, but he was barely able to propel himself, let alone anyone else.

Despite Seth's goading, darkness descended well before the exhausted group crested the edge of the small plateau on which parts of the monastery sat. They crawled on to the flatter ground on their hands and knees. It was the only safe way to proceed.

The monastery's stonework presented a black and unwelcoming façade. Jorra-hin felt unnerved that even he should find his home extending no more hospitality than the rocks of Mount Jàb.

He struggled to his feet and waded over to the wall. Groping his way along until his frozen hand found the indentation of an archway, he started hammering on a small, seldom-used door. The rest of the group joined him. Between them they maintained an erratic beat for more than half an hour before anyone inside noticed, giving Pomaltheus plenty of opportunity to air his views on Adak-rann vigilance.

The greeting hatch suddenly slid open.

"Hello?"

Jorra-hin recognised the voice. "Brother Valis, it's me, Jorra-hin. For the sake of the gods, let us in!"

The hatch slammed shut, bolts clanked back and the door creaked open, allowing a drove of snow to invade the monastery. Valis was swept aside by an influx of bodies that poured in with it.

Jorra-hin's relief overwhelmed him. He grabbed Valis and hugged him; the man was real, not just a fatigue-induced figment of imagination.

"You've no idea how good it is to see you," he gasped over the man's shoulder. Pulling away, he smiled and glanced round at the others. "This is Brother Valis. He's on the council of elders."

Brief introductions were made, Pomaltheus, Seth and Kirin all receiving a nod and a handshake. Anticipating a certain reaction, Jorra-hin left Elona for last. Valis was immediately beset by a bout of bobbing, punctuating everything he said with a bow. Being told that such deference wasn't necessary had no effect whatsoever.

"What in the name of the gods possessed you to come up the southern approach – at this time of year?" Valis eventually managed to ask.

"No choice, Brother. I must speak with Brother Heckart."

"Yes, of course. He's entertaining other guests at the moment, but he'll be delighted to see you."

"Other guests?"

"Yes. A couple of scholars from Höarst arrived this morning. I don't know," Valis chuckled, shaking his head, "we go practically the whole year without any visitors at all, and then two lots turn up at once! It's becoming quite an interesting day."

It's not over yet, Jorra-hin added silently. "Brother, it's urgent. The monastery could be facing great danger."

Valis' eyebrows rose. He nodded and gestured for everyone to follow him.

"Err – hot soup?" Pomaltheus mentioned hopefully.

*

The monitoring room was packed. The entire council stood before the Taümathakiya, holding the floating black teardrop with sceptical attention. Jorra-hin's revelations had shocked them into silence. Behind them, other brothers jostled shoulder to shoulder all the way back to the walls. Yet more peered in through the doorway, straining to hear what was being said.

Such was the press from behind that Elona's fur-clad boots were nearly invading the neatly tamped sand that surrounded the Taümathakiya. A meal and a chance to defrost had done wonders for her demeanour. Standing just beside her, Kirin still looked exhausted, though a little colour had returned to her cheeks. Despite suggestions of bed, she had insisted on being present, her desire to see the object that had put the fear of the gods into Jorra-hin overruling her need for sleep.

Pomaltheus and Seth had displayed no such curiosity.

"So, it's not a Taümathic indicator, then?" Yisson queried, his brow creased.

"No, Brother. The Vessel's movement under Taümathic influence is entirely coincidental."

"Makes us look like a bunch of idiots, doesn't it?" Heckart muttered, "I mean, watching it all these years."

"The Taümathakiya has proven itself useful, Brother, even if its true purpose has been misunderstood."

Brosspear's observation didn't appear to impress the head of the Adak-rann. "And this mage, Lornadus you call him, is to blame for the deception?" Heckart asked, glancing up from reading the scroll of Jorra-hin's Record.

"The bit I still don't understand," Yisson interrupted before a reply could be given, "is why this thing is a threat to us now. We've had it here for centuries."

"*It* isn't." Jorra-hin let out a quiet huff. Yisson's persistence in failing to grasp what everyone else seemed to have taken in their stride was becoming tiresome. "The danger comes not from the Vessel, but from those who might know of its true nature."

Yisson lowered his eyes and didn't meet Jorra-hin's gaze.

"And you believe that now includes the Tsnathsarré," Brosspear added.

"Yes, Brother. Baroness Daka has had men out looking for the six Vicar stones, the Menhir of Ranadar as they have become known to us. These stones form part of what controls the *Dànis~Lutárn*. While we can't be certain, it is possible Daka also knows this. We do know her men have found at least one of the menhir. In fact, I believe they have broken it."

"What makes you say that?" Heckart pressed.

"It's a conclusion I have come to based on something I read in the writings of Papanos Meiter," Jorra-hin replied. He flicked a finger towards the scroll Heckart was holding. "As I mention in my Record,

Brother, he was the Master Stonemason at the time of the *Dànis~Lutárn*'s creation. The mages employed him to inscribe the controlling spells on the six Vicar stones. According to Meiter's notes, the stones had to surround the Vessel at all times. He noted that the mages were terrified that he might cause damage during the course of his work. They seem to have been afeared of an uncontrolled release of Taümathic energy. That made me realise that if one of these stones was broken, it might be responsible for creating a significant Taümathic disturbance," Jorra-hin gestured towards the Taümathakiya, "one that could very well have had a dramatic effect on the Vessel."

Heckart's eyebrows rose. "You're suggesting that's what caused the movement we observed a few months back?"

Jorra-hin nodded. He threw a glance towards the wall where he'd knocked himself out cold. Sweeping one minute, crash the next – he still hadn't quite figured out the mechanics of that mighty leap.

"Surely this is conjecture, Brother Jorra," Valis challenged. "You told us earlier that the Vessel was designed to absorb power, so I can see that it might emit such a shockwave if it were broken. But why would the same be true of the Vicar stones?"

Jorra-hin acknowledged Valis's observation with a contradictory waggle of a finger. "Because Papanos Meiter was only employed to inscribe the A'lyavinical spells on to the Vicar stones, not to actually make them. Both the Vessel and the Vicars were brought to his workshop for him to carry out his work. His notes tell us that the Vessel had to be surrounded by the Vicars right from the start. Clearly these stones exerted some form of controlling power over the *Dànis~Lutárn*, even before the spells had been carved. For that to be the case, the stones must have been imbued with Taümathic power of their own, must they not?"

"I see." Valis's posture took a slump.

"Besides, we know nothing has happened to the Vessel itself – it's right here in front of us," Jorra-hin went on. "I suspect that the Tsnathsarré broke the menhir they found while trying to move it. After all, having remained undisturbed for twelve hundred years, I imagine it was probably stuck fast in its hiding place."

"Well, that appears to clear up one little mystery, then," Heckart sighed. "Congratulations, Jorra, you have done well in your Recordership."

"And then some," Brömin added, his pride sounding from the edge of the room.

Jorra-hin caught his old mentor's eye and bobbed his head in acknowledgement.

"Returning, then, to the danger that Daka may pose," he continued, "in my opinion there are only two possible reasons why she has an interest in the Vicar stones. The first is that she misguidedly believes there to be treasure buried in the Old Homeland and she is attempting to open the mines to retrieve it. The second is that she knows about the *Dànis~Lutárn* and wishes to obtain it for some purpose. If the latter is the case, she will know about the Vessel."

"And you believe that to be the more likely scenario?" Heckart prompted.

"I do. At least one other person has made some, if not all, of the same discoveries about the Vessel as I. During my investigation, it became apparent that I was following in the footsteps of another. Furthermore, that Baroness Daka even knew to look for these menhir suggests that someone has been feeding her information. I feel it is reasonable to assume, therefore, that she knows the truth behind what the Taümathakiya, the Vessel, really is."

"Which leads you to conclude that she might send someone to obtain it?"

Jorra-hin met Heckart's question with a silent stare, then shrugged. "What I can't say is whether she knows where the Vessel is. I recognised its description in Papanos Meiter's notes, as any brother of the Adak-rann would, so I knew immediately that it was the Taümathakiya, and therefore also knew its location. Whether someone from outside our order would be able to come to the same conclusion is hard to say."

"Hmm," Heckart mused, tucking his hands under the leather belt about his ample midriff, "prudence suggests that we assume they *do* know. Which puts us in a bit of a pickle."

"You can see why I felt it urgent that you be warned," Jorra-hin agreed. "Besides, I couldn't remain in Alondris – not after the ridiculous nonsense of my being denounced as a Natural mage."

"No, quite," Heckart murmured, a bemused smirk briefly touching his lips. He turned towards the Vessel and paused for a few moments as he considered matters. Drawing a breath, he went on, "Well, Brothers, as I see it, we are faced with two questions. The first is whether or not we should move the Taümathakiya to prevent it falling into Tsnathsarré hands. That raises some difficult issues for us as brothers of the Adak-rann. The second question is whether we should remain here at Jàb-áldis ourselves."

"Us, Brother?" Valis queried.

"Hmm. Moving the Taümathakiya is one thing, but whoever may come looking for it will more than likely still hold us responsible for handing it over, whether it's here or not."

"Couldn't we just destroy the thing?" Yisson suggested with a shrug.

"**No!**"

Jorra-hin shot Kirin a glance. Suddenly she didn't look tired anymore. As they'd both reacted at the same instant, surprised heads spun in both directions.

"The Vessel is a Taümathic construct, Brother," Kirin explained, pinning Yisson with a rather belittling stare, "designed to hold what Mage Yazcöp described as the single most powerful entity ever created. The Vessel absorbs the Taümatha from its surroundings, something it has been doing now for centuries. Even though it is empty of its original charge, any attempt to destroy it could be catastrophic."

All eyes refocused on the black teardrop floating serenely in the centre of the room. To Jorra-hin, it exuded a rather perverse kind of innocence. Despite knowing its true heritage, even now he found it hard to imagine that this familiar object, one the brothers had lived alongside for so many years, could unleash horrendous destruction if abused.

"In time perhaps, with the right preparations, it might be possible to release its energy safely," he suggested.

"But it could take months just to figure out how," Valis countered.

"Months we probably don't have," Heckart nodded. He let out another heavy sigh. "Brothers, I have to admit, my instincts are to avoid interference with the course of fate. That is, after all, the Adak-rann way. It strikes me that if we move the Taümathakiya, we risk changing what will be, to say nothing of endangering ourselves. If someone does come looking for it, what might they do to us in retaliation for our attempts to thwart them?"

Jorra-hin was stunned by Heckart's reasoning. It hadn't occurred to him that the Adak-rann might actually choose to do nothing, given what he'd told them. He found himself reeling from the realisation that for the second time in his life his sense of duty was at loggerheads with the tenets of his order.

"Brother," he began hesitantly, "with respect, I do not agree."

"You *must* act," Elona cut in. Her poise straightened and she became, perhaps unintentionally, rather more her regal self than the mere weary traveller she'd been moments before. "Brother Heckart, I understand your position. As the head of this order, I know it must be hard for you to act against tenets you hold so dear. But in this instance, you must."

"We have within our grasp the power to prevent a great travesty," Jorra-hin urged. "If the Tsnathsarré succeed in attaining the *Dànis~Lutárn*, they could do untold damage."

"Adak-rann aside, Brother," Elona resumed, keeping up the pressure, "you are an Alondrian. You owe it to our people to do what you can to protect them. You must act – if not for yourselves, then for your country."

"But Your Highness, we *are* the Adak-rann. We observe, we record, we keep the histories of the people. What we do not do is *make* history. Nor do we throw it off course."

Jorra-hin swallowed hard. He understood Heckart's quandary, the wrenching conflict of interests that was no doubt warring inside the man. He'd faced all the same questions and challenges in the aftermath of Emmy's healing. But just as then, he knew there was only one right path now.

"The question is this: faced with a choice between the tenets of an order and the path of a moral duty, which do we choose?"

His comment cut to the quick. There was silence in the room as every brother struggled with his own internal battle of conscience.

It was a long moment filled with awkward tension before Heckart eventually cleared his throat. "Look, it's getting late. I suggest we all get a good night's sleep and we'll figure out what to do about this in the morning."

*

With customary hospitality, the two visiting scholars from Höarst had been shown to their room for the night. Their needs were catered for with pleasant cordiality as befitted any a guest.

Genuine visitors of the Adak-rann would not usually have then bolted their door, thrown off their robes and laid out an array of weapons on the nearest bed. Which is exactly what Gömalt did.

Alber crossed to the small slit window and peered out. "Snowing again."

"Good. Less chance of us meeting brothers outside. We'll give it an hour or two, then make our move."

Alber nodded. "Do you think this lot will give us any trouble?"

"I know what they'll get if they do," Gömalt responded, airing little concern. "The only ones we need to watch out for are the mages amongst them. The baroness says they're mostly old men who haven't practiced magic in years, but they might still muster an attack between them, so be on your guard. If they don't comply, we'll take hostages. They'll have little stomach for risking their own brothers' necks."

"Why can't we just kill 'em?"

Gömalt afforded Alber a lopsided grin; clearly his right hand man thought wholesale slaughter was the best way of dealing with recalcitrance. Under other circumstances, he might have agreed, but the baroness had been quite specific in her orders.

"Because Daka doesn't want to anger the Adak-rann too much. There are many in Tsnathsarré who hold the order in high regard. Until she's seized power, she doesn't need any more enemies to add to the ones she's already got."

Alber returned his gaze to the scene outside the window. "Where do you suppose she gets all her information from?" he wondered. "She must have some high up Alondrians in her purse, surely? I mean, how did she even know to send us here?"

Gömalt let out a grunt. "That is a question I have asked myself many times. She must have a set of messaging crystals somewhere, like the ones the Alondrians use. That's the only way she could possibly get hold of some of the information she receives. I know she has a contact down in Alondris. More than one, probably."

"What about this mage making his way up to meet her?"

"He's the reason we're here; the one that told her we need this artefact."

"Be interesting to find out who it is," Alber mumbled.

Gömalt couldn't agree more. "We'll meet him soon enough, once this mission is complete."

They spent the next hour going over the plan. It was simple in detail, but the contingencies had to be catered for. This was a situation in which they couldn't just kill anyone they bumped into. Encounters had to be avoided if possible.

When he deemed it late enough that even the most insomniac monk ought to be asleep, Gömalt positioned himself by the door.

"Ready?"

Alber patted his various weapons, concealed once more under the scholarly robes he'd put back on, and nodded. Gömalt slid the bolt back and cracked the door open as quietly as it would allow. The corridor outside was dimly lit by a handful of lamps, token guides that did little but convey the gist of where the passage went. Satisfied that the coast was clear, he slipped out with Alber close behind and darted to the end of the corridor.

The door leading out to the main courtyard was at the far end of a short hallway. Gömalt was just about to head for it when a slight sound stopped him short. He flung his hand out across Alber's chest, shoving him backwards. They retraced their steps and slipped behind a pair of heavy woollen curtains that closed off the entrance to a side passage.

An unsuspecting brother trundled past, attending to his nightly duties. The monk paused at each lamp, replenishing its reservoir from a brass can with a long spout, as might a gardener feeding cuttings in a greenhouse. Gömalt watched through a crack between the drapes. The brother pottered on, never knowing just how close he'd come to a crack on the skull and a headache in the morning.

Gömalt waited until the brother had disappeared out of sight, then gave it another minute before stepping out of the side passage and making his way across the hallway to the courtyard door.

There would be no quiet opening of this exit, he soon realised. The hinges were old, the wood warped and the bolts jammed so tightly in their stays that the only way to loosen them was to jostle them up and down until they came free. He gritted his teeth as each twist of the metal emitted a screech. Alber scurried back across the hallway to keep an eye on the approaches in case the noise brought anyone along to investigate.

As the last bolt popped free, the warped oak sprang open with a crack. Frosty air blew in, giving Gömalt an unpleasant reminder of just how bitter the nights were up in the Mathians at this time of year. The warmth of an afternoon and evening spent in the monastery, albeit under false pretences, had been a welcome respite from the rigours of the journey up from Mitcha. He wondered how the rest of his men were getting on, enduring the cold outside the monastery's walls.

The snow was several inches thick out in the courtyard. Their footsteps left a telltale trail, the white blanket compressing beneath their feet with a crunchy, squeaking sort of sound as they hurried towards a hut that served as the gatehouse.

The brother on duty there was hardly a guard; more a doorman in case someone should arrive during the ungodly hours. He was lucky that it was winter; wrapped in so many blankets to ward off the cold, he was cocooned to the point of immobility. Gömalt overpowered the man before he knew what was happening. Summarily gagged, trussed, and dragged into a nearby storeroom, he was unceremoniously dumped in a corner where he couldn't cause any trouble.

"Well, that went smooth enough," Gömalt whispered. He flicked a glance at the gate. "Grab the other end of the crossbar."

Between them they lifted the oak beam that locked the two halves of the main gate shut. It rose out of its iron brackets without protest. Gömalt found it ironic that it should prove easier to open the main gates to the monastery than it had been the door to the courtyard.

"I'll wait here, you go and fetch the others," he instructed Alber. "Make sure they come quietly – I want to establish control before the monks get wind of us."

Alber nodded and trotted off down the snow covered track to find their frozen comrades.

*

Heckart came awake to the touch of a cold blade, a *very* cold blade, at his throat. Being a man to panic only after due consideration, he didn't make any sudden moves, which might otherwise have had undesirable consequences. With little more than grunts and gestures he was ordered out into the corridor, where he merged in with a stream of similarly bleary-eyed brothers.

They were herded, night shirts and all, into the dining hall, where their circumstances were explained to them with deadly simplicity. Surrender the Vessel, or die.

Wonderful options, Heckart mused. A day earlier and they wouldn't have known what these soldiers were talking about. He scanned the gathering, trying to see if everyone was present. It was impossible to tell. He did, however, note the absence of Jorra-hin, the princess, and the three young mages that had arrived with them. He turned his attention to one of his erstwhile Höarstish guests so as not to raise suspicions.

"Am I to presume, then, Gömalt, that you are not in fact a scholar?"

Gömalt smiled. "I am not afraid."

"I'm afraid not," Heckart corrected automatically. He only considered the wisdom of that after the fact. "So, what is this Vessel you're on about?"

"Playing me the fool is a dangerous game," Gömalt advised, still smiling. "You are knowing well enough what the Vessel is. Now, a brother will accompany me to show where it is kept. To fail will be uncomfortable."

Heckart decided it was best to play along for now. "Since the welfare of these brothers is my responsibility, it shall be me who accompanies you."

There seemed little doubt that the leader of these now obviously Tsnathsarré soldiers knew too much to be duped. His demand, specifically for the Vessel, calling it by its true name, made it clear that those who had sent him here, Baroness Daka it was to be presumed, knew exactly what it was and where it was kept.

Alber took over the supervision of the incarcerated brothers and Gömalt waved towards the door, prompting Heckart to lead the way. Unbidden, five other soldiers fell in behind as they left the dining hall.

They proceeded down the tangled web of corridors and flights of steps towards the monitoring room.

"Do you mind my asking you a question?" Heckart hazarded, putting on his most cordial and apparently unconcerned voice.

Gömalt shrugged.

"When you found the Menhir of Ranadar, did you by any chance try to move it?"

"Why you ask this?"

Heckart stopped to face him. "Did you break it?"

Gömalt didn't answer the question as such, but his expression, one of curiosity and a rising eyebrow, was enough to tell Heckart that he'd hit the nail on the head. Young Jorra had been correct in his assumptions. The Taümathic disturbance they'd witnessed all those months ago did indeed have its explanation. He chuckled.

"And how many menhir have you found so far?"

"No more questions," came a stern reply, accompanied by a prod to move on. The bemused smile had gone, replaced with a rather more frosty expression.

It had been worth a try, Heckart figured. He resumed course.

They came to the end of the passage and the room that housed the Taümathakiya. The door was already open. It was usually kept closed, if for no other reason than to prevent the various feline residents of the monastery from using the sand surrounding the device to make certain deposits.

Heckart's mild curiosity about the door was replaced by utter shock on discovering that the Taümathakiya wasn't sitting where it should have been.

"What the..." he spluttered. He was cut off by a blade withdrawn from its sheath. "Now wait a minute..."

"Where is it?" Gömalt demanded in very deliberate tones.

"I – I don't know. It was here last time I saw it, just a few hours ago."

Gömalt's blade touched the underside of Heckart's chin.

"What have you done with it?"

"Nothing, I swear. I know nothing of this. It *should* be here, I promise you. It's always here, never moved."

Gömalt remained frozen for several moments, staring Heckart in the eye. "Then I am advising you to find it."

Heckart nodded, though none too vigorously, given that a blade was hard up against his jowls.

5

Jorra-hin watched a Tsnath soldier, little more than two yards away, probe the dim recesses of the archive with the beam of a lensed lantern. Another rummaged about with his sword, using it to lift up books, move piles of paper and prod at anything that caught his eye. Between concealment and discovery stood nothing more than a bookcase stuffed with scrolls that had been hastily repositioned across the end of two other bookcases, forming a small enclosure. Jorra-hin was acutely aware of the negligible protection such a barrier offered.

As though his thoughts had been heard, the soldier with the lantern suddenly moved closer and pulled a scroll out from the shelf. A hole appeared not five inches away from Jorra-hin's head. His heart beat a manic tattoo. The document received but a cursory glance before being casually discarded. The gap it left received little attention.

Several more minutes went by as the Tsnath continued to poke about. Eventually they seemed satisfied that there was nothing of value to be had. They moved towards the door and disappeared into the corridor.

Jorra-hin blew out a long breath. "Ye gods, that was too close for comfort."

In the virtual darkness, Pomaltheus's raised eyebrow went almost unnoticed.

"Alright, what now?" Elona whispered.

"The escape tunnel isn't far, Your Highness," Valis assured her. "As I said, it was built for just such a situation as this. Not that I ever expected to need it. Who would have believed, in this day and age, that Jàb-áldis would come under attack?"

Amid Valis's incredulous tone Jorra-hin detected a note of excitement. He had to admit, it was hardly an average day in the life of the monastery. Though for himself, avoiding capture had become an alarmingly regular necessity of late.

"We can philosophise about the hand of fate later," Elona muttered, airing a degree of nervous impatience.

Valis nodded. He turned to the bookcase and heaved it aside. He slipped out of the makeshift hiding place and took up station near the door. Elona and Kirin joined him.

Seth and Pomaltheus manoeuvred themselves behind the Vessel and leaned into it with their shoulders. Though only the weight of a man, it seemed to possess the inertia of an elephant. Huge effort was required to get it going, but once moving, it then became exceedingly difficult to slow it down again. Getting it to turn was equally hard. Yet in a straight line, hovering as it did, it glided over the stone floor as smoothly as a knob of butter across a warm pan.

Jorra-hin guided from the front. He gripped handfuls of an old Adak-rann cassock that had been slipped over the Vessel and hauled sideways, trying to steer it round the end of the bookcases into the open. On its way towards the door the artefact clipped the edge of a heavy oak table, knocking it aside as though it were little more than a three-legged stool.

Once they'd reached the corridor, the monastery's abundant steps immediately presented a problem. Going down wasn't so difficult, but for every descent there was an ascent soon after, and those became back-breaking struggles. The confines of the corridors didn't allow for all six of the group to lend a hand at once. Thus headway was far from the rapid flight that Jorra-hin had envisaged earlier when they'd taken the decision to attempt to get the Vessel out from under the Tsnaths' noses.

It wasn't long before they paid the inevitable price of their ponderous progress.

"Back, back," Valis waved, hurriedly retracing his steps from the end of the passage. "Tsnath coming."

Jorra-hin slammed his shoulder into the Vessel. It nearly knocked him off his feet. The soles of his boots struggled for purchase on the smooth stone floor. Seth rushed round to lend his weight. Pomaltheus clawed at the cassock, pulling from a nearly seated position as though in a tug-of-war. Valis piled in, bringing the Vessel to a stop. It began to move in the opposite direction, though with frustrating disregard for any sense of urgency.

"Not fast enough," Valis hissed. He glanced round, frantically searching for somewhere to hide. There was nowhere within reach that they could duck into. "Look, you go on. I'll see if I can buy you some time."

"No." Seth suddenly let up from pushing and straightened. Pomaltheus stopped pulling. With its momentum regained, the Vessel blithely continued to drift on. "Leave this to us," Seth ordered, nodding at Pomaltheus.

He turned to face the anticipated Tsnath approach.

"You have a plan?" Pomaltheus wondered, joining him at his side.

"Fire."

Pomaltheus's brow furrowed. "I may have produced Mages' Fire back in the Cymàtagé, but I doubt I can summon it here. Not at such short notice."

"Not the kind of fire I was thinking of."

The two Tsnath soldiers marched into view. They came to an abrupt halt, frozen in a moment of surprise. It was only a moment. The pair went for their swords.

Seth advanced, one hand raised, palm forwards. Above Tsnath demands for him to stop, Jorra-hin heard the young mage begin to utter something in A'lyavine. Only it didn't sound right. Something jarred. He plunged his brain into action, trying to figure out what Seth was attempting to do.

"*séà* **eggatalis** *iccànciá*," he shouted.

Pomaltheus and Seth both shuddered at the words. They repeated the phrase, just as it had been demonstrated.

Flames from the Tsnath's torches instantly flared into a huge fireball. The conflagration engulfed the men. They hurled the torches away, but it was too late, their clothing was already alight. Shock gave way to screams. The pair flailed wildly, staggering back the way they'd come. Their cries quickly faded into the distance as they fled.

Kirin's face was a mask of horror. She stood rooted to the spot, staring as though she could still see the Tsnath in front of her.

"We've got to move quickly," Valis prompted, attempting to swallow with a throat gone dry. "That's bound to bring others."

The group heaved at the Vessel, struggling to get it to reverse again. Goading it down the passage as fast as they could, its momentum caused it to drift into the walls as they came to corners. There was no time to manoeuvre it gently now. Every time it hit the stonework, the dull thud made Jorra-hin cringe. If the Vessel cracked, the gods only knew what devastation might ensue.

"There!" Valis urged, pointing at the entrance to a side passage just a few yards ahead.

With no wall to arrest its momentum, the Vessel slid past the opening. Manhandling it back again cost valuable seconds.

"The entrance to the escape tunnel is concealed inside the storeroom just down the end there," Valis panted.

They were only part way along the new passage when a shout went up. There was no mistaking the guttural sounds of the Tsnathsarré language, particularly when laced with anger. A squad of soldiers appeared across the end of the corridor a moment later. It took them little time to size up the situation.

Valis shoved Elona towards the storeroom door. "Go!" He grabbed Kirin and herded her forwards too, then turned to Seth and Pomaltheus, who were still struggling with the Vessel. "Leave it! We gave it our best."

Pomaltheus turned towards the Tsnath and raised his palm forwards. Seth snatched him by the collar and yanked him back.

"There's too many of them!"

Jorra-hin cursed the hand of fate. A minute more was all they would have needed to reach the storeroom and get safely out of sight. A sudden surge of anger flooded through him. He grabbed one of the corridor lanterns and hurled it towards the Tsnath. It ricocheted off the wall and smashed, spilling burning oil across the stone floor. It did little to hinder the Tsnath. The first soldier to reach the flames simply jumped over them and charged. Jorra-hin lunged for the storeroom.

Valis tried to slam the door shut. A Tsnath sword jammed into the gap thwarted his attempt to get it bolted. Seth flung himself against the oak panelling and heaved for all he was worth.

"Jorra, over there," Valis urged between gritted teeth.

Jorra-hin followed Valis's nod. The Jàb-áldis escape tunnel did not feature in daily life at the monastery, but all the brothers knew what to look for. He scrambled over to an innocuous-looking cupboard and wrenched it away from the wall. Kirin thrust a torch into the black void revealed behind it. Rough-hewn rock walls extended away beyond where the light penetrated.

"Quickly, inside."

Kirin scurried forwards, with Elona close behind. Pomaltheus hesitated, torn between manning the storeroom door and escaping into the tunnel.

"They'll just follow us in," he protested.

"Go, just go!" Valis yelled. The monk pinned Seth with a stare. "You too. I'll hold them off as long as I can."

Seth didn't budge.

"Move, you bloody idiot!"

Seth's eyes widened. He hung on a moment longer, then gave Valis a parting nod and dived for the tunnel. Valis managed to hold the door shut for only a few seconds more before his resistance was swept aside and Tsnath spewed into the storeroom.

Jorra-hin grabbed a lever on the wall of the tunnel, something that resembled the sconce for a torch, and yanked down hard. An ominous rumble overhead was all that sounded.

One of the Tsnath soldiers snatched a handful of Valis's hair and flung him against the far wall. The plucky monk sprang back in defiance. He swiped a small clay storage jar off one of the shelves, sending it hurtling towards the intruder. The Tsnath batted the projectile aside and plunged his sword into Valis's guts.

"No...!" Jorra-hin screamed.

The Tsnath's attention snapped sideways. He took one step towards the tunnel and vanished from view behind a huge, smooth-sided slab of rock that slammed down across the entrance. More rumbles reverberated from the tunnel roof. Seth cannoned into Jorra-hin, flinging him backwards just as tons of rock cascaded down. The roar was deafening. Clouds of dust billowed up into the musty air.

The smaller bits of rubble took a while to eventually come to rest. The ensuing silence was muted, a deadened nothingness. The tunnel had been utterly cut off from the outside world.

Pomaltheus coughed amid the lingering dust cloud. "Was that supposed to happen?"

"No," Jorra-hin croaked, fighting off the urge to cough. Seth rolled sideways, allowing him to clamber to his feet. His back hurt; Seth had landed on top of him.

"Are we trapped?" Elona asked, a clear note of apprehension in her voice.

Nobody answered. Until the dust settled, it was impossible to tell how bad the cave-in had been.

Jorra-hin felt his strength suddenly wane. He slid to his haunches. The demise of Valis, the loss of a brother, assailed his thoughts. He couldn't shift the sight of the man going down, callously felled amid a valiant attempt to protect the rest of the group. He'd never lost anyone close before. It made him feel numb, bringing a hollowness inside that was almost painful. He began to tremble.

Kirin groped her way over and knelt down beside him, draping an arm around his shoulders. "I'm so sorry, Jorra. Valis was a brave man."

"He saved us," Seth added, nodding.

Silence took hold again. There was little else anyone could say.

The lull gave time for the lingering dust cloud to settle. Slowly the scale of the avalanche became apparent. Nothing of the drop slab was visible.

Pomaltheus pitted his strength against one of the boulders jammed between the top of the rock pile and the tunnel's ceiling. It didn't budge an inch. "We'll never shift this lot," he groaned, "not without picks and shovels, at any rate."

"So what do we do now?" Kirin asked.

Jorra-hin tried to pull himself together. The others were looking to him for leadership. Jàb-áldis was his part of the world, after all. The fact that he'd never even seen this particular bit of the monastery before didn't seem to matter.

Valis's plan had been simple; get to the tunnel and hide inside. The idea had been to pull the storeroom cupboard back into place from behind and drop the sealing slab. Then the Tsnath would have been none the wiser as to where they'd disappeared to.

"Jorra, can this tunnel be opened from outside?" Seth asked.

"No." Jorra-hin stepped over to the debris and tried to gauge how much rock had fallen. "This must be yards deep," he murmured. "The ratchet mechanism for raising the slab is not only buried, but probably destroyed. Somebody is going to have to hack their way through to get to us."

"That somebody might be the Tsnath," Elona intoned gravely. Not all rescuers could be relied upon to have benevolent intentions.

Pomaltheus shook his head. "Why would they bother? They've got what they came for. They're not going to waste their time on us — unless..."

"Unless what?"

Pomaltheus grimaced at Seth. "Unless they know who Elona is. She'd make a damned good hostage."

"The brothers won't give her identity away," Jorra-hin countered. "The bigger worry is whether they will be able to get through to us — if and when they are allowed to try. The monastery is not well equipped to cater for an excavation of this scale."

"Meanwhile, our food is limited and our water supplies almost non-existent. Time is our greatest enemy," Seth pointed out.

Jorra-hin shrugged. "Then we might as well explore this tunnel and see where it goes. It's meant to be an escape route, after all. It must go somewhere."

"What about these torches?" Elona said, waving hers about. "Our chances of getting out of here are non-existent if they die."

"Didn't Valis mention there should be fresh torches in here somewhere?" Kirin looked to Jorra-hin for confirmation. "Provided they haven't just been buried."

They began probing the immediate stretch of tunnel. It didn't take long to find a series of alcoves cut into the rock. Stone jars full of oil, piles of cloth strips and wooden brands sat waiting for an emergency to press them into use. At least his brothers had maintained some level of preparedness for the unthinkable, Jorra-hin mused. Though not recently, judging by the dust and cobwebs.

"Damn, these things are heavy," Pomaltheus gasped as he heaved one of the jars down. He inspected the top. It was plugged with some kind of a wooden bung and sealed with wax. Fishing out a small knife from his pack, he gouged his way through. The oil inside was old. It had thickened to the constancy of tar. While the others watched, he doused his torch, plunged it into the goo and gave it a stir. When he relit the torch, it flamed much brighter than before.

"Well, at least it burns." Seth turned and peered into the black as though he could see some distance beyond the torchlight. "I suggest we make an initial exploratory search of the tunnel. If it looks like going on a long way, we'll come back and stock up with more oil. There's no point lugging the stuff around if we don't need it."

He set off down the tunnel. The residual dustiness of the entrance quickly receded, leaving just the mustiness of stale air. Little broke the monotony of the hewn but otherwise featureless rock walls.

After a hundred yards, they came to a junction where the passage met another crossing it at right angles.

"Great. Now which way do we go?" Pomaltheus huffed.

"I don't understand," Jorra-hin murmured, more to himself than anyone else.

"What's to understand?"

"Well, if this is just an escape route, doesn't it seem strange that there's more than one tunnel? And another thing – why make it so big?" Jorra-hin glanced each way down the new passage. It had to be at least four yards wide. Far larger than was necessary to serve its purpose.

"We go right," Seth declared, unconcerned by Jorra-hin's observations. Pomaltheus gave him a quizzical glance. "It goes up hill," Seth shrugged. "Jàb-áldis sits at the top of Mount Jàb, so anything that goes up can't go far, can it?"

Jorra-hin couldn't fault Seth's logic. It was his luck that proved flawed. The tunnel ran a short distance and ended abruptly at a wall of ice.

"Any chance we can hack our way through?" Pomaltheus wondered, giving it a poke with the end of his torch. There was no give in it at all.

"What with?" Seth landed a hand on the ice, inspecting it close up. "This isn't fresh, it's packed solid. My guess is that if this is the way out, decades of snow building up from the outside has formed an ice plug that has pushed its way back down the tunnel. We could spend weeks trying to get through, with no guarantee of success."

"We don't have weeks," Elona murmured. "We have days at best."

Jorra-hin glanced back the way they'd come. "There's no point in us wasting our efforts here until we've at least explored our other options." He was all too aware that those options rather worryingly now boiled down to just one.

They returned to the junction and carried straight on.

In less than fifty yards it, too, came to an abrupt end. But not at a frigid wall of ice. This branch of the tunnel looked as if the diggers had simply abandoned their efforts, as though they'd suddenly decided they were going the wrong way. Not impossible, Jorra-hin supposed, but improbable.

"Some escape route," Pomaltheus grumbled. "Now what do we do?"

"This doesn't make sense," Jorra-hin muttered, shaking his head.

Seth disagreed. "It just means the other way *was* the way out — once."

Jorra-hin picked up a fist-sized lump of stone and began tapping the tunnel walls in various places.

"What *are* you doing?" Elona demanded.

"Testing a theory."

"Huh?"

Jorra-hin ignored Elona's confusion and carried on tapping, focusing on the sound it made, a dull thud, rock on rock. But then, a change in note, a less solid, slightly hollow sound. He concentrated his attention in the same area, tapping more frequently until he had defined the extent of the difference. Then he aimed at the centre of the patch and slammed his tapping stone against the wall. It produced a crack. It also shattered his makeshift hammer. He found a replacement and gave the wall another blow, loosening a triangular shaped shard. He wiggled it free with his fingers. A few more hits and a sheet of rock the size of a serving tray disintegrated and crumbled to the floor. He hopped back before his feet were pummelled.

"My friends, I give you one of the Menhir of Ranadar."

The rest of the group gawped at the hole. Kirin came to her senses first. She stepped forwards and ran her hand over the ancient relic. "My gods," she breathed, "one of the Vicar stones. How did you know it would be here?"

Jorra-hin smiled, feeling rather satisfied that he'd been right. "It was the nature of the tunnel that got me thinking. Why make it so big? My Adak-rann predecessors wouldn't have dug something so extensive as this if all they'd wanted was an escape route for use in dire emergencies. That made me wonder whether they were even the ones who had dug this tunnel in the first place. As it turns out, they didn't. The Dwarves did. This," he waved his hand at the apparent end of the tunnel, "is one of the entrances to the Old Homeland."

Seth joined Kirin and reached out to touch the menhir, just as she had done. "So, we may not have found a way out, but we may have found a way *in*?"

Jorra-hin nodded, though he immediately sighed and turned his attention to the end of the tunnel. "Yes. But with just one slight problem. According to Yazcöp, all the entrances were sealed with a glean." He flicked his hand forwards. "So the question becomes, how do we get through such a thing?" He was well aware that the burden of figuring that out would fall to him.

There was still more of the Vicar stone to uncover. Hoping that the rest of it might hold further clues, he commenced chipping away at the rock covering that had hidden the relic for nigh on twelve hundred years. The upper portion of the menhir contained the same text as he'd discovered back in the pattern room of the Stonemason's Guild. Papanos Meiter had carved that, before Lornadus and his mages had left Alondris for the Mathians on their murderous mission. But as he proceeded to uncover the lower section of the Vicar stone, he noticed a change in writing style.

"Interesting."

Kirin knelt down beside him. "What have you found?"

"A change in, for want of a better word, handwriting. Look..." He pointed at the bottom two lines of text. "*Jüsta licheránthé e bèdeöm*" he read out. "You see how neat and precise the words in the upper section are? That's Papanos Meiter's craftsmanship. These last lines have been added by someone else. In a hurry, judging by the crudity of the characters. My guess is one of Lornadus's mages chiselled this on when they re-tasked the Vicars to help bolster the gleans they left in place."

"So what does it mean?"

"A rough translation would be, *To pass, one must see the truth.*"

"How does that help us?" Elona asked.

Jorra-hin pondered that for a moment, sucking in his breath. "Well, as Kirin once told me, a glean is a form of illusion. Due to its Taümathic nature, it has substance, which is why this one has the ability to stop people getting through."

"But only if you believe in it," Kirin jumped in, excitement gaining ground. "To get through, you only have to *see the truth* – in other words, believe that there's nothing really there." She went and thumped the end of the passage. Her hand hit something that seemed very solid. A frown formed on her brow.

Jorra-hin smiled. "Nobody said it was going to be easy. The mind is a powerful thing. Convincing yourself that something you can see and touch isn't really there is going to take some preparation, I think." He glanced at Pomaltheus. "Would you like to try?"

"Why me?" the young mage shot back, suddenly wary of the consequences of being put forwards as a test subject.

"Because you've had the most Taümathic training. I'm sure Mage Mattohr has taught you techniques to help you clear your mind. Don't worry, I'll guide you on what to do."

Pomaltheus didn't look convinced, or indeed happy. It was with some reluctance that he took Kirin's place. He put his hand up against the rock.

"Wait!" Seth called out.

Pomaltheus snatched his hand back, almost as if he'd been bitten.

"Will he be able to return?"

"I would have thought so."

"But you don't *know* so?"

"No." Jorra-hin let out a sigh. "But given what a glean is, and how they are constructed, I believe this one only stops people entering the Old Homeland, not leaving."

"Why?"

"Because they are hard to make. The mages who put this glean here weren't trying to stop anybody getting out. They'd already trapped the Dendricá at Üzsspeck using the *Dànis~Lutárn*. Their purpose here was to seal the mines so that no one else could get in and discover the atrocity they'd just committed. There's no reason why they would have made matters more complicated than necessary."

Seth still wasn't satisfied. "Alright. But say, just for the sake of argument, that Pomaltheus manages to get through and can't get back again. What then? We'd have to follow him in. Are we sure that's what we want to do?"

Jorra-hin glanced round at the others, then returned his gaze to Seth and shrugged. "Do we really have a choice? You've seen for yourself — both our other exits are blocked. We can either stay here, waiting for a rescue that might never come, or we can push on and see where the mines take us. There are at least five other ways out of the Old Homeland."

"And a labyrinthine maze of tunnels to get lost in."

Jorra-hin shrugged again. "What can I say? Life's a risk."

Elona stepped forwards and put her hand on the apparent rock wall blocking the passage. "The Dwarves managed to live here for generations. It can't be that bad. I say we go, take our chances. If the hand of fate is truly against us, I'd rather die trying something than sitting around doing nothing."

After a moment for that dark thought to sink in, Pomaltheus huffed. "Well that's settled, then. So can we *please* just get on with it?"

Jorra-hin caught Kirin's eye. She nodded in agreement.

"Seth?"

Seth shrugged. "Seems I've been out-voted."

Jorra-hin smiled and turned his attention to Pomaltheus. "Alright, I want you to face the end of the tunnel and close your eyes. Clear your mind. Then imagine that the only thing ahead of you is an empty tunnel. I'm going to speak to you in A'lyavine, and all I want you to do is listen to my voice."

Pomaltheus complied with the instructions. Jorra-hin allowed him time to calm his mind and clear his thoughts. Then he began to repeat the phrase he had read from the menhir, coaxing Pomaltheus's mind to see through the superficially obvious to the real truth of what was in front of him. When the moment was right, he applied a gentle pressure to Pomaltheus's shoulders from behind, prompting him to step forwards.

The young mage shimmered for a moment, then seemingly dissolved into the rock wall and vanished.

Kirin gasped in awe. Elona stared, eyes wide with wonder.

If anything, Seth just seemed a little alarmed.

"It should be easier for the rest of us," Jorra-hin explained. "Now that we've seen it can be done, we shouldn't have so much trouble believing what's going to happen."

"Fine," Seth muttered, letting out a resigned sigh. "I'll go back and get the oil and the rest of the torch supplies. Just don't you all disappear without me."

6

Kirshtahll strode towards his makeshift quarters with Temesh-ai at his side. He set a brisk pace, holding the collar of his cape up on one side against a biting wind. Having just spent a futile hour atop the Great West Wall watching the Nmemians faffing about half a mile away, he was chilled to the bone.

"Captain!" he boomed in surprise the moment he caught sight of Agarma inside the tent. "My gods, man, you look like you died last week."

Agarma climbed to his feet and managed a smile along with a weary salute. "From you, sir, I'll take that as a compliment."

Agarma's normally immaculately trimmed beard was looking decidedly unkempt, and his fair hair, cut short, hadn't recovered from being under whatever hat he'd been wearing recently. The ride west from Alondris to Colòtt must have been a hard one, Kirshtahll judged.

He dispensed with the formalities and waved the captain back down. "Sit, sit. Tem, get the man a drink."

Temesh-ai crossed over to a small wood-burning stove on the far side of the tent. A kettle sat on the edge of the pot-bellied contraption, the water in it warmed but not quite simmering. He moved it over the hottest part of the stove and within just a few moments a whiff of steam began to curl from the spout. A fresh spoonful of leaves added to a pewter pot were soon mashing while a clean mug was sought. He had to inspect several before he found one that passed muster.

Kirshtahll removed the wolfskin from his shoulders and gave it a shake to shed the snowflakes that had settled on it. Winter down here in Colòtt would never truly arrive with quite the bite it did up in the Northern Territories, but things had nonetheless taken a decidedly chilly turn over the last week. He threw the pelt over the back of a spare chair before slumping down behind what passed for a desk in these otherwise temporary quarters.

"Well, Captain, what news of this brouhaha back in Alondris?" he asked, allowing a slightly bemused smile to cross his lips. "Is our wayward princess following on behind you?"

A tinge of worry added lines to Agarma's already haggard features. "Err – not exactly, sir. Elona's gone north with Jorra-hin and a handful of acolytes from the Cymàtagé."

"North?"

"To the Adak-rann monastery at Jàb-áldis."

Kirshtahll's eyes bulged momentarily, before narrowing under a frown. "What in the name of the gods is she heading up there for? And why aren't you with her?"

Temesh-ai decided the tea had had long enough, poured and handed Agarma a steaming mug. He handed another to Kirshtahll, before finding himself something of a more fortified nature.

Agarma took several warming gulps before launching into an explanation of his arrival. "It's a long story, sir," he began. "I suppose it all really started when Jorra-hin landed himself in trouble. He's been denounced as a Natural mage."

"I heard," Kirshtahll harrumphed. "A lot of nonsense, if you ask me. I cannot bring myself to believe he had anything to do with Mage Nÿat's death."

"If does seem unlikely," Agarma agreed. "But that's not the half of it, sir. The young monk's made some rather startling discoveries, some of which you need to hear about. That's why I'm here. Elona insisted I come and explain. She didn't think you'd take it seriously from anyone else."

One of Kirshtahll's eyebrows rose. As he sat listening to the captain's story, it rose further, his mind quickly beginning to reel. By the time the details about the danger posed by the discovery of the *Dànis~Lutárn* had come out, he was feeling positively sick. Partly because of the threat to the north, from which he'd been lured away by this ridiculous Nmemian flare-up, and partly because Elona was heading right into the thick of it. She was the closest thing he would ever have to a daughter and it worried him to the core that she might be in danger. Young, and too rash by far, she had already jeopardised her position by sticking her neck out for Jorra-hin. Midana could rant all she wanted, but if Elona tried any such nonsense with the Tsnath, they'd have her head from her shoulders.

"Did Jorra-hin explain what he thought Baroness Daka might want with this *Dànis~Lutárn*?"

Agarma's face soured. "He told me that the *Dànis~Lutárn* was what he called adaptive magic. He said that while its power was originally intended to subdue the Dendricá warriors, his research suggested that

that wasn't its ultimate purpose. Apparently, it can be re-tasked to perform other duties."

"Such as?"

"Well, sir, Jorra-hin believes that, in the right hands, the *Dànis~Lutárn* could be configured to do many things, including being turned into a weapon."

Kirshtahll sucked in a breath. "Against which, I dare say, we'd have no defence." He sighed gravely and leaned back in his chair. The less than comfortable perch creaked under the strain. "Our army might be able to defend against conventional forces, but not against a foe in possession of ancient magic. I doubt we could rely on our own mages, given what you've described of the power of this thing. We'd be as defenceless as the Dendricá – and *they* were the most formidable fighting force there's ever been."

"Not much hope for our lot, then," Temesh-ai chipped in dryly.

Kirshtahll swung back the rest of his tea and put the mug down. The infusion was renowned for being able to fix many things, but not, it seemed, concern.

"So let me see if I've got this straight. To control the *Dànis~Lutárn*, the Tsnath need these Vicar stones, which we've come to know as the Menhir of Ranadar?"

"Yes, sir," Agarma nodded.

"And Jorra-hin believes the *Dànis~Lutárn* can be moved, provided it is first returned to its Vessel for transportation?"

Agarma nodded again.

"Which explains his fear that the Tsnath might be on their way to Jàb-áldis," Kirshtahll concluded. "The *Dànis~Lutárn* is no use to them stuck where it is now."

He let out another worried sigh. If Daka managed to find the remaining Menhir of Ranadar, no small task, and somehow succeeded in reconfiguring the *Dànis~Lutárn*, there would be no stopping her from fulfilling her intentions. The question was, what *were* those intentions? How far did her ambitions go? If they extended south, then not even the Mathian Mountains would pose a problem to her in the long term. The heartland of Alondria might be under threat.

"I can see why Elona sent you over. She was right – from anyone else, I would not have believed it." Kirshtahll shook his head. "Gods, it's a mess. How much of this is known back in Alondris?"

"I don't know, sir." Agarma paused to let out a snort. "We had to get out of the city rather quickly. We couldn't risk Jorra-hin falling into Dinac-Mentà hands again, nor Elona into Midana's."

Kirshtahll's eyebrows shot up. "No indeed. This story would have been seen as the desperate invention of the condemned."

"Elona was hoping that if you were to explain, perhaps Midana might listen to you. The queen may not like you that much, sir, but she at least respects you. She dare not treat you as she does others."

"Because she knows damned well what she'd get if she did," Kirshtahll shot back. "Don't worry, Captain, we'll get this whole stupid mess straightened out one way or the other."

Agarma smiled thinly. "So, how's the situation here, sir? Are the Nmemians behaving themselves?"

"The Nmemians are being a pain in my arse."

Temesh-ai chuckled. Kirshtahll glanced at him and rolled his eyes up.

"They are camped, the whole damned lot of them, a couple of miles the other side of the border. All we seem to be doing is sitting on our respective sides of the fence, wasting each other's time. I'd damned well march in there and give them all a good kicking, if only it wouldn't start a war."

Agarma laughed. The tea seemed to have restored some colour to his cheeks. "No news on what they're up to?"

"None. That's the damnedest thing about it. They've made no demands, no threats, in fact they haven't even attempted to send over an envoy. They're just sitting there. At the start of bloody winter." Kirshtahll let out a noise that sounded almost like a growl. "That alone makes no sense. Now is not the time of year for an army to make such moves. Spring's the time for campaigning."

The flap of the tent suddenly flew open. Taken by surprise, Kirshtahll subconsciously went for his sword before he could stop himself. It was only Timerra.

"General, sir," the young lieutenant burst out, heaving for breath. He'd obviously just sprinted some distance. "Begging your pardon, sir, but you need to come right away. And if you would, sir, could you bring the major with you?" He flicked a nod at Temesh-ai. "He's needed urgently."

"What's happened, Lieutenant?"

"Messenger from the Northern Territories, sir. In a bad way."

Kirshtahll shot Agarma and Temesh-ai a look of anticipation. "Two messengers in one day! Action, methinks. Captain, if you're up to it, join us."

Temesh-ai grabbed his bag from behind Kirshtahll's desk and caught up as Timerra led the way to a large tent serving as a mess. The half-dead horse outside didn't bode well for the state of the messenger, to whom it obviously belonged. At least someone had thrown a blanket over the poor beast and was attempting to revive it.

Inside, the orderlies attending to a prostrate figure snapped to attention at Kirshtahll's entrance. They fell back to allow him access. With his usual propensity for getting suck in, Temesh-ai pushed past and got to work.

"I'll need warm water, hot, but not so hot you can't leave your hand in it, in four separate bowls. They need to be large enough to put hands and feet in. And bring me a bottle of Brock or something similar."

"Brock?" Kirshtahll murmured. "Is that wise? You're always telling me not to drink when it's cold."

"It'll be alright now, so long as we keep him warm." Temesh-ai gently lifted one of the messenger's hands. It was purple-blue in places, and black at the fingertips. "He has severe frostbite, Padráig. The alcohol will help to get the blood flowing near the surface of the skin again. It's the best way to defrost him. He'll be lucky to keep all his fingers and toes, though. He's suffered a lot in the last few days, that much I can tell you."

Kirshtahll nodded. The rest of the messenger was cocooned in a mishmash of garments, a mixture of uniform and civilian clothing cobbled together to ward off the cold. Ice still clung to his hair at the front, where it poked out from under a hat that was tied on with a scarf. "If he's just come over the Mathians at this time of year, I'm not surprised. Whoever sent him must have thought it extremely important." He moved over to the messenger and bent down. "My name is General Kirshtahll. Where are you from, son?"

The man tried to speak, but only managed a rasping hiss that Kirshtahll couldn't understand.

"Sir, he was clutching this when we peeled him off his horse."

One of the orderlies handed Kirshtahll a leather pouch. It contained a single folded sheet, a letter, not even sealed with wax. He straightened it out, perched on one of the mess benches and began to read.

Lt. Ashur, Torrin son of Naman, Lord of Tail-ébeth.

To General Kirshtahll, Lord of Kirsh, Commander Alondrian Northern Contingent.

Sir, greetings.

It is my fervent hope that this letter will find its way to you without delay, for your worst fears have been realised. The Tsnathsarré have invaded in considerable strength. Our army has been overwhelmed. Brigadier Jàcos is dead. Tail-ébeth has been completely destroyed.

"Oh, dear gods, dear gods, dear gods…" Kirshtahll gasped in a drawn-out hiss. He read on.

Similar fate has befallen other places, including Taib-hédi – the Brigadier was ambushed there. There is now no Alondrian military presence up here, other than a few scattered remnants such as ourselves.

I have temporarily liberated Mitcha from under Tsnath control – the enemy left only a small garrison there. The townsfolk told us that the Tsnath have incapacitated the messaging corps, so no word goes south.

I have some two thousand souls with me – Mitcha is no longer a safe place. We have come up into the mountains, southwest of the March of Ashur, sheltering in the caves hereabouts. So far no indications of Tsnath pursuit.

Sir, I have met a couple of mercenaries up here, whom we rescued from Tsnath attack. They recently had reason to flee from Lamàst, where I understand you to be camped. They were employed to make a secret incursion into Nmemia, to the town of Hamm-tak, to deliver a message to a Superintendent there called Gil-kott. Message content unknown, but after their return, the man who sent them there, Minister Gëorgas, tried to have them killed. They survived and fled north.

Sir, our own ministers are conspiring with the Nmemians in some way. It is perhaps presumption, sir, but it seems to us that whatever the Nmemians are up to, it is merely a pretext to draw you out of the Territories ahead of this Tsnath invasion. We have been betrayed by members of our own Grand Assembly. I do not know how rife this conspiracy is amongst the ministers, but the chances of further support from them are fading fast, unless Lord Vickrà can prove an effective ally.

Sir, the situation here is desperate. I beg of you, do whatever you can to return. We think the Tsnath currently do not have enough troops here to adequately control the whole region. But they will undoubtedly consolidate their foothold, with more men coming down from the Empire to reinforce their positions. We will do whatever we can to hinder them, though we are but one platoon and a few stragglers. We alone cannot turn this tide.

With the hope of seeing you again soon,
Yours,
Torrin-Ashur. Lt.

Kirshtahll sat for a long moment, hands shaking, his mind reeling from the devastating news. It beggared belief that they were up against a conspiracy; that their own ministers were in league with the Nmemians to keep him out of the Territories while the Tsnath rode coach and horse through his life's work of keeping the region protected.

He rose to his feet, his face a storm.

"What is it, Padráig?" Temesh-ai demanded.

"Just see to it that that man recovers."

He left the mess without another word. He strode back to the Great West Wall, mounted the steps up to the walkway two at a time and planted his hands firmly on the parapet, fixing his gaze on the Nmemians in the distance.

Someone was going to pay for this.

Nothing in this world was going to get in the way of him returning north, army and all, winter be damned.

7

For the men on the wall.

The words, daubed on Mitcha's north gate, held a certain poignancy. Not only were they written in Tsnathsarré, but in Tsnathsarré blood. As if that wasn't enough, impaled on the hilt of his own sword was the severed head of the erstwhile garrison commander. The blade had been crudely jammed between the cobblestones beneath the gate's arch.

Özeransk held his tongue, waiting for Daka to react. Such a sight ought to have been unnerving, but predicting the baroness was never easy.

"Who was he?" she eventually murmured, clutching the lapels of her fur cloak closed against the chill, though it might have been to ward against unpleasant thoughts.

"Sörrell. One of Minnàk's men." Özeransk added a shrug and turned to her. "Perhaps making an example of the Alondrians was not such a good idea."

There was a moment of silence. Daka didn't like being questioned. She was even less receptive of criticism. At Mitcha's fall, Özeransk had voiced his opposition to her treatment of the prisoners. The Alondrians had fought well. Their commander, a major by the name of Riagán, had been especially valiant in the face of overwhelming odds. Sadly, that had only led to his fate being more gruesome. Özeransk still felt a rill of shame at the memory of the man's demise. Rending him limb from limb between four horses had been a churlish display of Daka's intolerance, nothing more. As for the rest of the Alondrians, none had deserved to be hung from Mitcha's battlements.

And now the inadvisable brutality had come back to bite them.

"An example had to be made."

Daka's tone was icy, her indignation brewing. Özeransk had learned to read at least some of the signs of her mood since joining her retinue. She worked hard to hide her emotions, but if anything had the capacity to escape such tight control, it was her ire. He set himself on guard and held back from being antagonistic. In situations like these, she could be a dangerous woman; her predilection towards snap decisions taken in anger usually led to problems, which later had to be untangled with tact and diplomacy. He wasn't in the mood for either just now.

"I'm surprised the Alondrians managed to liberate Mitcha so quickly," he said, hoping to defuse the moment. "I know we didn't leave many men here, but even so... not good."

"One town, seventy men – hardly the end of our campaign," Daka retorted.

"One town, seventy men – dispatched swiftly and easily. Don't underestimate what has happened here, Alishe." He stared into her eyes, dark and impenetrable, trying to see into her soul. Addressing the baroness by her minor name, a tactic only he was brave enough to employ, seemed to have a certain ability to undermine her defences. "Resistance spawns quickly and spreads like a plague. An achievement like this will give the Alondrians hope. It will embolden them."

Özeransk was an experienced campaigner. He knew well enough the dangers of allowing foes to build success upon success. Momentum was easily gained by those fighting for their homeland. Once the Alondrians got the notion that their enemy wasn't the all-conquering invincible horde they at first appeared to be, the attacks would escalate, and Daka was spread too thinly to survive a sustained campaign of resistance before the emperor's reinforcements arrived.

"So what do you suggest we do?" she demanded.

Özeransk glanced round. The doors to some of the houses swung listlessly in the breeze coming in through the north gate. Items of clothing, the odd piece of furniture, even a partially loaded cart, had been abandoned in the street, all signs of the rapid exodus that had taken place. No food or livestock had been left. There was evidence, charred patches on the cobbles, a few broken barrels strewn around, that some supplies had been deliberately destroyed rather than be left for use by the invaders. Someone had been harsh with the pragmatism; only portable essentials had been taken. All of which suggested many of the townsfolk had left on foot.

"Unfortunately, there's little sign of where the people went. I've had men out looking. A lot of snow has fallen since and obliterated any tracks."

He couldn't help wondering who had led the uprising. An interrogation of the nine surviving soldiers who'd been found locked in the town gaol had revealed that the raid had been executed by a relatively small band, with the help of some liberated townsmen. He'd kept the details from Daka lest she take revenge on the survivors for having failed her. Minnàk would not appreciate having his men slaughtered for no good reason.

"The townsfolk will need shelter, though" he went on. "They aren't soldiers. Some, I suspect, will disperse to the surrounding hamlets. But not all. Mitcha must have had, what – fifteen hundred, maybe two thousand inhabitants? The majority will be hiding out somewhere, probably up in the mountains."

"Then leave them there. Let the winter be the end of them," Daka suggested.

Özeransk sighed, but silently. He did not entirely agree with that approach, though they had little choice. The people of Mitcha knew this region, it was their land. They knew how to survive here. He couldn't help but feel that winter alone would not be the end of them. Yet sending out patrols to scour the countryside would take up valuable resources, men they couldn't really afford to spare.

*

"Mage Nÿat, it is good to finally meet you in person."

Steaming a little, having just been in front of the fireplace, Nÿat surged across the room with some gusto, the billowing of his vermillion robes somewhat constrained by the sable fur cloak he had yet to remove. The man was no doubt a nesh southerner feeling the cold, Gömalt mused.

"Likewise, Baroness. Having exchanged so many communications, it seems almost strange to put a face to the words at last."

Nÿat took the baroness's hand and gave it a customary kiss, though in this case that amounted to no more than a brush with his beard. There was little fealty conveyed; the man seemed too full of himself for that.

With hand relinquished, the baroness gestured sideways. "This is Gömalt, my right hand. He may be trusted with our more secret affairs."

Gömalt gave Nÿat a curt nod. "A pleasure, sir."

So, *this* was the baroness's southern contact in Alondris, not to mention the very source of the secrets behind the true nature of their quest, Gömalt mused. He would never have admitted it to anyone, but the question of where the baroness's information had been coming from had irritated him for months. To be able to put the mystery to rest at last was gratifying.

While pleasantries weren't Daka's strongest suit, she made some attempt to be civil. Nÿat was no ordinary visitor. "So, your journey up, how was it?"

"Cold, very cold." Nÿat gave a mock shiver. "Fortunately, I know one or two means to ward off such things. I did in fact wonder about opening the mines from the southern side and coming through the mountains, instead of over them. I dare say it would have been a less frigid experience."

"You might never have emerged," Daka observed. "Our Dwarvish envoy, Roumin-Lenka, has the only maps of the interior."

"There is that," Nÿat acknowledged with an unconvincing nod. Gömalt suspected the mage may have had means of navigation he was not divulging. "Still, water under the bridge. I came over the top, like normal people do."

The mage's tone suggested normal people were somewhat beneath him. Gömalt took note of the arrogance. It could sometimes be a weakness. Knowing the chinks in a man's armour was always useful.

"Did you have any problems getting away from Alondris?" Daka asked.

"No, no. They think I'm dead, so no one is looking for me. By the time they discover the truth, it will be too late."

Daka's brow wrinkled. "I'm curious to know how you managed to fool your brethren?"

"A stroke of luck, as it happens." A smile fluffed Nÿat's beard. "I had the good fortune to receive a nocturnal visitor some while back, an enterprising young man come with the notion of blackmail in mind."

"Blackmail?"

"Yes!" Nÿat over-emphasised his incredulous reaction. "He was simply a thief who happened to overhear an exchange between messengers. Being something of an opportunist, he followed one of them, which led him to my residence. And can you believe it..." an expansive wave punctuated the tale, "the scoundrel had the notion he might demand payment for his silence!"

"The fool," Daka observed coolly, quite failing to match the mage's grin and enthusiasm.

"Quite. Well, naturally I divested him of such notions the moment we met. However, having realised just how close to discovering the truth that wretched young Adak-rann monk was getting, I knew it would be pushing my luck to remain at the Cymàtagé much longer, so I'd already started making plans for my departure. My little nocturnal visitor came in quite useful. At the appropriate moment, I dressed him in some of my robes, added a few of my more identifiable personal effects, and then incinerated him, giving my fellow mages the impression I'd gone the way of all flesh."

Gömalt hid his reaction well. Perhaps the former Deputy Chancellor of the Cymàtagé wasn't quite the nesh southerner he'd first assumed. The man clearly had a ruthless streak to him.

"In so doing, I managed to deal with Jorra-hin at the same time," Nÿat enthused, clearly enjoying the opportunity to revel in his own ingenuity, "playing upon his strengths."

"Oh?"

"Yes indeed, ma'am. He was quite a remarkable young man in many respects. Hidden talents, and all that. Only, my dull-witted colleagues largely failed to appreciate them. I, on the other hand, came to realise that all I had to do was denounce him to the Dinac-Mentà, playing on the idea that his abilities with A'lyavine were signs that he was a Natural mage. Over the preceding weeks I'd built up something of a case against him, making sure a few others knew of my *suspicions*. When the time came, Jorra-hin fell right into my trap."

"And the Dinac-Mentà were only too keen to believe that he was responsible for murdering you," Gömalt concluded.

"Precisely. I did slightly stack the deck by making sure he was found unconscious at the scene of my *oh so tragic* demise."

Gömalt laughed, appreciating the irony.

"When I left, as far as I know, the Dinac-Mentà were trying to figure out how to dispatch Jorra-hin safely. With luck they'll have rid us of any further interference."

Daka raised an eyebrow. "Oh, so you haven't heard?"

"Heard?"

"Jorra-hin has escaped. He was – *rescued*."

"Rescued?" Nÿat repeated.

This news took Gömalt by surprise. The baroness had yet more informants in Alondris?

Daka chuckled mirthlessly. "Yes. By Princess Elona, no less."

Nÿat's jaw literally dropped open in shock. "She never did!"

"She has committed treason. She forged a royal petition in the name of your queen and used it to gain access to him. I gather warrants have been issued for her arrest."

"My, my, my," Nÿat muttered, shaking his head. "We do seem to have put the fox in the henhouse." He paused for further thought and wandered back to stand near the fire. When he turned, he said, "Perhaps that may be to our advantage. The more Midana focuses on such internal concerns, the less she'll be keeping an eye on what's happening up here. Speaking of which, is it here yet?"

Nÿat's sudden change in tack didn't throw Daka for an instant.

"It is. Gömalt secured the Vessel for us a few days ago."

"Excellent." The mage turned to Gömalt. "Did the Adak-rann give you any trouble?"

"Hardly," Gömalt scoffed. "A small group did attempt to spirit the Vessel out of the monastery, but they didn't get very far."

A frown creased Nÿat's forehead. "Did they, indeed. Was this before or after you'd told the brothers what you were looking for?"

"Before." A twinge of concern cracked Gömalt's composure.

"Interesting. And the ones responsible – who were they?"

"I don't know. We secured the Vessel, but the perpetrators managed to flee into an escape tunnel. It was sealed shut with a large slab of rock – we were unable to pursue them."

Nÿat glanced at Daka. "Baroness, have you any news on the current whereabouts of Princess Elona and Jorra-hin?"

Daka shook her head. "Why?"

"Well, it's just that the Adak-rann have been ignorant about the true nature of the Vessel for the better part of a millennium. Yet their action in trying to keep it from falling into your hands suggests knowledge of the artefact's true significance. Someone..."

"Must have told them," Daka cut in. "Jorra-hin?"

Nÿat nodded. "Tell me, Gömalt, these ones you gave chase to, do you think they made good their escape?"

"No." Gömalt was quite emphatic about that. "I questioned several of the monks independently about where the tunnel led. After a little persuasion, each one gave me a similar answer. The tunnel was a dead-end, sealed shut by decades of snow. No way out."

"I see." Nÿat let out a sigh. "I think, Baroness, we just missed an opportunity to gain an extra feather in our cap."

"I don't follow," Gömalt said.

The baroness eyed him with a look of annoyance. "What Mage Nÿat is suggesting is that one of those attempting to escape may very well have been Princess Elona."

"Who would have made a very nice bargaining chip indeed." Nÿat paused for a moment, shrugged, and then added brightly, "So, moving on, would it be possible to meet this Roumin-Lenka I've heard so much about? She sounds rather interesting."

Gömalt suppressed a chuckle. There were many ways in which he could described Roumin-Lenka. Merely *interesting* wouldn't have been top of his list.

Daka nodded her consent.

"I'll go and find her," Gömalt responded. "She was making copies of the Old Homeland maps last time I saw her."

*

Özeransk found the baroness deep in conversation with the new arrival. Word had got around that an Alondrian mage had turned up. Not that that was why he had come looking. He needed to speak with her because of rather more disturbing news.

The baroness didn't rise from her seat as he entered the erstwhile mayor of Mitcha's office. The mage, however, did climb to his feet.

"Ah, Lord Özeransk, this is Mage Nÿat," Daka introduced. She turned her head to address the mage. "Özeransk is the commander responsible for annihilating the bulk of the Alondrian army at Taib-hédi."

"Ah!" Nÿat sounded far too enthusiastic about the slaughter of his own countrymen. Özeransk took an instant dislike to the man. "An impressive victory, I'm told."

"Hardly. They were badly organised and badly led. I would have been ashamed to have failed."

Nÿat stiffened at the putdown. Daka moved quickly to intervene. "You look disturbed, my lord. There is a problem?"

"Yes, Baroness. I've just received word from Minnàk's forces over in Nairn. One of their main supply columns has been attacked and plundered."

"Our losses?"

"Total."

Daka scowled. She knew as well as he did how much this might set them back.

"Minnàk will be going hungry shortly. His men were only lightly provisioned so that they could move fast."

Daka's face contorted into a grimace. "Then they'll just have to get what they need from the local population."

Özeransk sighed. It was a predictable response, the baroness's answer to everything. She seemed to have learned nothing from the Alondrian reprisals for what had been done at Mitcha. "We must be careful," he cautioned. "We cannot afford to have the people rise up against us. We need to track down the culprits and stamp out this resistance before it spreads. If fortune favours us, we may even retrieve our supplies in the process."

"You said we couldn't afford to go chasing small pockets of resistance all over the countryside."

"We can't. But whoever this particular group is, they're well organised and quite effective. They might even be the same ones who attacked Mitcha. I don't think it would be wise to ignore them. Or give them a chance to grow any stronger."

Daka let out a controlled breath, a minor display of her dwindling tolerance for matters beyond her control. "Very well. Then take some troops over to Nairn and deal with it. Just make sure you leave enough men here to ensure my safety up in the mountains. Now that Nÿat has arrived, we will be proceeding with the next phase of the plan. You can meet us at the entrance to the Old Homeland when you're done."

Özeransk nodded, and did his utmost to hide his sudden misgivings. Daka had outmanoeuvred him and he hadn't seen it coming. Tackling the Nairn issue was his idea, he'd pushed for it. He couldn't very well now object to leading the mission, not without raising suspicions.

But the consequence was that he wouldn't be present to keep an eye on the baroness as she made her discoveries in the Old Homeland. Whatever she was truly after, Nÿat and the mines were inextricably linked to her goals. That worried him. Despite all her explanations and assurances, he still didn't believe she was after anything so mundane as treasure.

8

Remember, they execute spies, Kirshtahll had mentioned in parting. Timerra really wished he hadn't.

An officer's uniform, a dubious Nmemian accent and a pretend cold had been enough to bluff his way through three brief encounters with the Nmemian military. Each time he'd been certain the game was up. How he'd managed to keep his nerve, only the gods knew.

When he'd reached his first objective, the town of Zèet-ársh, some seventy miles behind the Great West Wall, his luck had run out. Finding a whole town was one thing; finding a particular person within it was another. Requesting directions had become harder, resulting in the failure of a snivel and blocked nose to provide adequate camouflage.

Hence the locked cell in which he found himself. The Nmemians didn't go in for doors within their houses, but that did not mean they didn't know how to make a gaol secure. Escape was a waste of thought. He was cold, tired, more than a little hungry, and for the last few hours had had only Kirshtahll's parting comment for company.

He'd *really* come to wish that the general had just said, 'Good luck'.

The sound of keys jangling sharpened his mind and quickened his heart. A guard appeared and fiddled with the lock.

"Come."

Timerra got up off the cell's only furnishing, a straw mattress, and drew his cloak around his shoulders. As he moved closer to the cell door he discovered several more guards waiting outside, dashing his chances of overpowering one man and making a run for it. Whatever this night held in store for him, his fate was in the hands of the gods now. He stepped out into the corridor with a renewed bout of religious fervour gripping him.

"Hands," the guard with the keys ordered.

Heavy iron manacles were placed over his wrists and secured. The two other guards took up station behind him and the one with the keys led him away from the cells. They passed through several open areas, one that appeared to be a mess hall, another an armoury, before stepping out into a courtyard. An open-topped carriage awaited.

Timerra felt a glimmer of hope spark into existence; it was not the sort of transport used to convey a spy to his place of execution – not unless they treated the condemned like gentlemen in their final moments. This particular conveyance belonged to a rich man, that much was evident.

Aside from the coachman up front, two more guards sat in the carriage on the rear bench, facing forwards. They were armed with crossbows, both cocked and quarrelled. One of them gestured that Timerra should seat himself on the front bench.

"Where am I being taken?"

Neither crossbow holder made any attempt to reply. He sat back with a sigh, resigned to suffering in suspense a while longer.

The carriage lurched forwards with a jolt. He was relieved to note that the weaponry his escort cradled was not pointed directly at him. Most modern crossbows had a fairly light trigger and he had no wish for an unexpected pothole to lead to his demise.

They cleared the courtyard of the gaol and rattled their way down the cobbled streets of Zèet-ársh. A few torches were lit here and there, but otherwise the town was rapidly disappearing into gloom as dusk descended. Despite that, the place looked remarkably familiar. If he didn't know better, it could have been the back streets of Lamàst for all the architectural differences there were.

To his surprise, they reached the outskirts of the town and continued on into the countryside. It was a lot quieter here, not least because cobbles had given way to a softer surface over which the rims of the carriage wheels didn't grind so loudly. It was colder, too. He drew his cloak tighter across his chest.

It was hard to judge the distance, but after perhaps a mile the carriage slowed and turned off the main track towards a gated wall that materialised out of the darkness. Not quite a castle, but a fortified house, Timerra figured. Beyond the gate, glimpses afforded by a hazy moon suggested a formal garden either side of a gravel pathway. The latter led up to the entrance of a large and rather grand building. It was well lit by torches outside and candles within.

When the carriage rolled to a stop, one of his escort stepped down while the other remained seated, making it clear that any attempt at a dash towards the cover of darkness would be a rash move. Timerra wasn't bothered – he was more curious now as to where he'd been brought and why. A few suspicions were growing.

Crossbows directed him towards the entrance. It was already open, manned either side by two footmen. Framed by the door's surround was the silhouette of a man who could only have been the head of the house staff. They seemed to dress the same the world over.

Without a word, the head servant motioned for Timerra to stand in the middle of the hallway. The armed guards remained just inside the entrance, exuding the immutable purposefulness they had worn since he'd been placed in their charge.

While he waited, his attention was drawn to the furnishings. True to the Nmemian tradition, most of the carpets were on the walls rather than the floor. Though the word carpet didn't do these works of art justice; they were nearly tapestries, and of exquisite quality. None but the gods would have dared set foot on them. Nor was the floor modest. A mosaic made up of tens of thousands of tiny little hexagonal beads, polished smooth so as to resemble marble, depicted a great sea creature battling to subdue a mighty warship. So detailed was the scene that even the ship's rigging could be traced. From a few yards away it looked as fine as an oil painting.

Timerra straightened up suddenly from his half stooped position. He was being observed.

"I am Supreme Gal Ibissam," announced the tall apparition that had silently appeared behind him. The man had a thin, almost bony face, with an aquiline nose. "I'm told this was found in your possession," he said, holding out a small wooden box with brass corners and catches, and finely traced marquetry on its lid. It depicted the distinctive heraldry of the Gal's coat of arms. Timerra was relieved that the case containing the ornamental dagger Kirshtahll had entrusted to him a few days beforehand hadn't disappeared by sleight of hand during his capture.

He bowed formally, failing to hide a smile that relief had brought to his lips. "It is an honour, sir. My name is Timerra of Lamàst. I am the son of Rakmar, the Governor of Colòtt, and a lieutenant in the Alondrian army."

"Indeed," the Gal acknowledged. "Dressed as a Nmemian officer. Rather dangerous, wouldn't you say?"

"We live in dangerous times, sir."

"And dangerous times call for dangerous measures, is that it?"

"My commanding officer certainly seems to think so, sir."

Ibissam's eyebrow rose slightly. "And how is Padráig Kirshtahll these days?"

Timerra smiled again. The Gal had not forgotten the man to whom he'd given the ceremonial dagger some thirty years ago.

"He is well, sir. Though a little worried."

Ibissam snorted, but not derisively. "He has much to be worried about." He beckoned for one of the guards to step forwards. "The manacles won't be needed any further."

With his hand free again, Timerra removed his cloak. A footman took it from him.

"Come," the Gal said, "we can discuss matters further through here. You look as if you could use a drink."

There was no dispute from Timerra on that score.

Ibissam led the way through into a lavishly furnished room that lacked for nothing in the realms of comfort. To Timerra, the most endearing feature was the roaring log fire at its centre. Built on a raised stone hearth, it was covered by a large polished-copper funnel that became the chimney. Having spent the last few days travelling through decidedly frosty countryside, then hours languishing in an unheated cell, and finally a ride in an open carriage, warmth of any sort was bliss.

"This is my wife, Yissianna," Ibissam said, indicating an attractive woman clearly much younger than he. Timerra managed to get in a bow before the Gal dismissed her. "Yissianna, my dear, this young gentleman is from Alondria, despite his appearance. Would you mind giving us a few moments alone?"

Without a word, Yissianna nodded graciously and gathered up various bits of embroidery before heading out of the room.

Ibissam furnished Timerra with a healthy shot of some kind of orange-smelling liqueur before lowering himself on to one of the long chairs that formed a semicircle in front of the fire. He indicated for Timerra to be seated.

Opening the dagger case, he took out the letter that Kirshtahll had drafted and regarded it for a moment. It had clearly already received his attention, as the Gal didn't re-read all of it.

"So, Kirshtahll intends to invade Nmemia, does he?"

Timerra swallowed some of the liqueur, glad of its fortification. "Not by choice, sir. It is critical that the situation facing us near the border is resolved quickly. The Tsnathsarré have invaded the Northern Territories of Alondria, and unless he can get back there with his forces, they have free reign to do as they please. But while a large portion of the Nmemian army sits encamped just a few miles this side of the border, Alondris has tied his hands. He cannot afford to allow this situation to drag on indefinitely."

"But invade?" Ibissam challenged, his incredulity becoming more apparent. "He could start a war."

"Believe me, sir, that's the last thing he wants. He wouldn't have sent me to bring you this message otherwise."

"Young man, I appreciate the faith Kirshtahll is putting in me. But there is something you must understand. I am an advisor to the royal family on matters of culture. I may be considered a politician, but I am that only in the broadest sense of the word. I don't know that there's much I can do about this."

"I'm told you have the ear of your king, sir. Surely you could speak to him on our behalf? Our fight is with the Tsnathsarré Empire, not with Nmemia."

The Gal gave his head a brief shake. "What of this conspiracy he speaks of? Members of your own government are in league with my countrymen to cause a diversion?"

Timerra nodded. "That's what has brought our army down from the north and allowed the Tsnathsarré to invade virtually unchecked. All Kirshtahll seeks is the freedom to get back up there as soon as possible."

Ibissam sighed deeply, clearly worried by the enormity of what he was being asked to achieve. "You know, I presume, that I owe Kirshtahll my life? Thirty years ago he showed me mercy. Without that, I would not be here today. For the sake of my family's honour, I will do what I can. But I cannot promise anything."

"Thank you, sir," Timerra replied. "I know Kirshtahll does not expect guarantees. All he can do is place his hope in you."

Ibissam chuckled and rolled his eyes towards the ceiling. "He likes skating on thin ice, does he not?"

Timerra smiled back. The whole situation was a gamble.

"There is one thing, though," Ibissam went on. "You will have to return to Alondria with all haste and persuade Kirshtahll to give me more time. His letter indicates he will make his move in what is now only four days' time. I shall need at least a week. There are questions to be asked, facts to be ascertained, before I can approach the king. You must get Kirshtahll to agree to that."

"I can't guarantee the general will listen, but I will certainly try," Timerra said. "I'm sure he will understand the situation."

Ibissam sighed again. He got up and walked over to a desk that was furnished with writing parchment and quills and began to draught a note. He blotted it and attached a wax seal to it before handing it to Timerra.

"A passport through Nmemia under my authority. Diplomatic status, insomuch as I can grant it. As your return to Kirshtahll is now rather important, it would be unfortunate if any of my countrymen should delay you again unnecessarily."

Timerra placed the passport inside his tunic. "I am much obliged, sir," he said, with no small amount of genuine gratitude.

"May I also suggest a change of clothes. That uniform will only make you look like a spy. You know what we do to those, I presume?"

"General Kirshtahll was kind enough to make that clear to me before I left, sir."

The Gal smiled. "You are lucky the guards in Zèet-ársh recognised the crest on the dagger box, otherwise you'd not have come to my attention. Unchecked, their hospitality would not have been as warm as mine."

For the first time in days Timerra began to feel a little more optimistic about his chances of surviving this sojourn into foreign climes.

All he needed now was an offer of a warm bed for the night.

9

"Err, Jorra, how exactly did Yazcöp manage to see anything when he was watching the battle?"

Kirin's reverent and slightly apprehensive voice was little more than a whisper by Jorra-hin's ear.

By dint of reason, argument and no small amount of inspired guesswork, Jorra-hin had somehow managed to navigate them through the Old Homeland to the edge of the long abandoned city of Üzsspeck.

It was hard to tell that they'd actually arrived at anywhere, Kirin mused, staring forwards at nothing. The tunnel leading to the great cavern had been getting wider for some time, each step taken rendering their torches ever more impotent. For what seemed like an eternity, nothing but an unknowable void had lured them on, a strange kind of vertigo giving rise to a feel of constant falling.

Seth, practical as ever, had come up with a solution to coping with such a stygian world. He'd suggested that two of the group act as outriggers, tracing the walls on either side of the tunnel. When the distance between them took a dramatic turn, they knew they'd emerged into something larger.

"Stay here," Jorra-hin murmured, extracting his arm from Kirin's. He left her side and headed towards Pomaltheus. "And pray that centuries of neglect haven't ruined Dwarvish ingenuity," he added over his shoulder.

With Jorra-hin gone, Kirin felt bereft of support. She linked arms with Elona instead. The princess seemed only too glad of comfort. She'd been strangely quiet of late, perhaps succumbing to the oppressive darkness. Being in the Old Homeland wasn't like it had been in the tunnels under Alondris, whose familiar streets could be envisioned not far above their heads. Here, vast mountains, rugged and untamed, were heaped unimaginably high above them. The very thought of such might was troubling, weighing with ominous threat, as though little but some fragile agreement prevented the rocks from tumbling down. Here, they truly were in the very bowels of the world.

Kirin let out a quiet sigh. She was perfectly certain she'd never get used to being underground. There was a longing within her to see the sun again, even the cold, watery glow of the winter one they'd left behind. A glimpse of the moon would do. Anything – so long as it allowed her to see more than a few yards.

Jorra-hin reached Pomaltheus, relieved him of his torch, and traced his way round the edge of the tunnel wall where it emerged into the cavern. He came to a flight of steps cut into the rock that appeared to lead straight up the side of the cavern wall.

Kirin watched as he climbed, still mystified as to his intent. The steps levelled off at the height of the tunnel roof and Jorra-hin began to make his way along a narrow ledge. There was no balustrade, so he hugged the wall, probably fighting the lure of the abyss. That made her smile. He didn't much like heights, which was odd, considering he'd lived most of his life at the top of a mountain.

A little way along, something that looked like a stone drinking fountain came into view. Perched on a chiselled outcrop of rock, it projected from the cavern wall rather like the bow of a ship.

"I hope you're ready for this," Jorra-hin called back. His voice sounded rather hollow. Wherever they were, it was too vast even for echoes.

Raising his torch, he touched its tip to the top of the stonework. It made a quenching hiss, rather like hot iron touching water. Kirin held her breath in anticipation. There was a moment of nothing, then fire leapt out from the brand. Bluish flames took hold, spreading down several channels cut into the rock that supported the basin. They raced along gullies in opposite directions, fanning out around the perimeter of the cavern faster than any man could run. As they became more established, they turned first to orange, then to yellow, shedding ever more light.

Jorra-hin made his way back down to rejoin the group, collecting Pomaltheus on the way.

"Behold, the Dwarvish equivalent of daylight," he announced.

Seth closed in from the far side of the tunnel. Standing side by side, the group watched in awe as yard after yard of the great cavern became illuminated, revealing the true scale of its extent.

"Oil in the rocks," Jorra-hin explained. "The Dwarves built a system to channel it in order to illuminate their world."

"It's amazing," Kirin breathed, shaking her head with an incredulous air. The flames just kept spreading further and further away, each moment expanding the cavern like the unhurried birth of a new universe.

"How long will it last?" Elona asked.

"About eight hours. As I understand it, the oil is used up faster than it's replenished, so the flames die out naturally. Once the oil level has reached equilibrium again, it's ready for the next lighting. The Dwarves governed their days down here by this system."

"Can it be put out?"

Jorra-hin gave a casual shrug. "Water could be poured along the fire channels in an emergency, though I've not read of that ever having been necessary."

"Well, I'm impressed," Pomaltheus murmured.

High praise indeed, Kirin mused. Pomaltheus rarely expressed enthusiasm for anything that wasn't edible.

They remained at the tunnel mouth watching the fire progress. It took a long time for the flames to eventually meet up on the far side, having branched many times along the way to produce a lattice of illuminating fingers that covered the whole of Üzsspeck. Great polished-metal mirrors reflected the light, making it seem as though the roof of the cavern was held at bay by huge arms of flame. Kirin had never seen anything close to its like before. Beholding its splendour left her speechless.

The city was an odd mixture of buildings sitting in a great bowl. At the periphery, dwellings more akin to caves lined the cavern walls, whereas further in the structures seemed more conventional, albeit built for a place in which rain was something of a rarity. Their roofs, mostly flat, were clearly more for providing privacy from prying eyes than protection from the elements.

In the centre of the city lay the open space that had been known as the Great Gathering. Though she couldn't see them from her current vantage point, she knew its boundary was defined by the canals that had been designed to take water throughout the city. The very same that had been used to such deadly effect against the doomed Dendricá warriors.

"It's just as I pictured it, Jorra," she whispered.

Jorra-hin caught her eye and nodded. "I know. And you know what else will be just as we saw it…"

A shiver went down Kirin's spine. Visions of the Dendricá writhing in agony and dying in droves flashed before her eyes. For those who had escaped the first swift terror of the advancing

Dànis~Lutárn, or the rain of fire hurled at them by Lornadus and his mages, there had been only the inexorable horror of starvation and the eventual sweep of death's scythe. There was no telling how many had died, but whatever their number, their remains still lay in the Great Gathering.

"Well, if we're going, we'd better get to it," Seth declared.

Kirin let out a scoff. It was alright for him; he'd not heard Jorra-hin read Yazcöp's scroll. He hadn't seen fate deal so terrible a hand, and had little inkling of what lay ahead. Nevertheless, she followed his lead. Finding Jorra-hin's hand for comfort, she attempted to steel herself for what was to come, hoping that, just as she had down in the crypt beneath the Cymàtagé, she might eventually get accustomed to being surrounded by the dead.

They set off down the gentle incline and joined a path that wound its way through one of the city's outermost districts. It was eerie to walk amongst the strange buildings, so utterly deserted, so still and undisturbed for centuries. It gave the impression that the inhabitants had just stepped away, but could return at any moment. There was no place like it in what she now thought of as the 'land of the living', the normal world above, where sky was sky, not rock. Up there, abandoned buildings decayed, reduced to nothing by wind, rain, weeds and beetles. Down here, they were perfectly preserved. It made her feel as though she was intruding. Unseen eyes peered at her from within long forgotten homes, radiating a begrudging sufferance; how dare anyone disrupt the steadfast rule of peace.

"Ooh, look, more breadrooms!" Pomaltheus suddenly exclaimed, shattering the mood completely.

So much for reverence, Kirin mused. With the kind of childish enthusiasm that shows little regard for subtleties, Pomaltheus trotted over to the wall of one of the buildings and began breaking off the flattish platelets of fungus that Jorra-hin had introduced them to a couple of days ago.

Their proper name was *Torvàstos*, and they resembled mushrooms, though they had an almost bread-like taste if allowed to dry out a little. The Dwarves had cultivated them as a vital part of their diet, being one of the few things that would grow underground without much light. Over the years they'd sprung up in all manner of places they'd clearly never meant to be. When he'd first tried them, Pomaltheus had immediately renamed them, and no amount of correction or argument was ever going to change that now.

Knapsacks replenished, they moved on, at least some in the group mindful of their being the first to walk the streets of Üzsspeck in a millennium. At their relatively slow pace, it took nearly half an hour to reach the canal that separated the sprawl of dwellings from the Great Gathering. The surrounding buildings of the thoroughfare gave way rather abruptly to a humpbacked bridge spanning the waterway. Its rise and balustrades mostly obscured the view of what lay on the other side.

By an unspoken word the group drew to a halt. Jorra-hin gave Kirin's arm a reassuring rub. He had probably noticed she was still having trouble preparing for what they were about to encounter. She returned a weak smile.

"The *Dànis~Lutárn* is still in place, right?" Seth queried. Jorra-hin nodded. "Then in that case, one person should go ahead first. Just in case."

"You really know how to inspire confidence," Pomaltheus muttered, volunteering himself by stepping forwards.

He ventured on to the bridge with bold, seemingly unconcerned strides, only to stumble to a halt when the view of the Great Gathering hit him.

"Something wrong?" Seth called out.

Pomaltheus glanced over his shoulder and gave Jorra-hin a slow, knowing nod. He said nothing.

He continued on towards the crest of the bridge. As he reached it, something else brought him to a halt. "Gerroff," he protested. He waved his torch above his head, as though battling a particularly vexatious cobweb. Ducking away from the unseen attack, he jogged down the far side of the bridge and disappeared. "I'm alright," his disembodied voice proclaimed.

Seth raised a bemused eyebrow at Elona and offered her his arm. "Shall we?"

They approached the bridge with more caution than Pomaltheus. When the Great Gathering revealed itself, they both sucked in their breaths as the sight assailed them. They didn't linger. At the crest, as Kirin anticipated, Seth experienced an odd sensation, but made less fuss than Pomaltheus had done. Elona appeared to feel nothing. She stopped, disengaged herself from Seth and turned full circle with her arms splayed wide to see if anything would happen. When nothing did, she shrugged and continued on.

Jorra-hin took Kirin by the arm. "Ready?"

Kirin found her steps rather wooden, as though her legs were reluctant to carry her forwards. She felt like closing her eyes so as not to see what had stopped the others in their tracks.

As a distraction she glanced sideways. Through the bridge's stone balustrade she could see that the water in the canal was at a low ebb, now little more than a trickle. Its uninterrupted stream over the centuries had worn away the rock, creating a kind of gulley that confined what was left of the flow to just the centre of the channel.

As they reached the middle, Jorra-hin stopped to peer over the side. "You go on," he prompted.

Kirin stepped forwards. The moment she crossed the water's boundary, a wave of something diaphanous seemed to descend upon her. It was like being picked at by a thousand tiny hands – not an unpleasant experience, though it did make her feel a little giddy.

But terror struck her heart an instant later. Her restraint cast turned to ice. The air froze in her lungs, as though an immense weight sat upon her chest, preventing her from drawing breath. Immediately awash with panic, her hands flew towards the necklace, her fingers clawing but unable to get purchase. "Jorra!" she screeched, her plea wide-eyed and desperate.

Jorra-hin dived forwards. He cannoned into her, shouldering her in the midriff. She was thrown clear of the crest. Staggering backwards half way down the other side of the bridge, she tripped and landed heavily, sending a streak of pain shooting up her spine. The icy touch of the restraint cast receded. Air flooded back into her lungs.

The relief that came with it was quickly replaced by a cold dread. Jorra-hin was mired at the crest of the bridge. He sank to his knees and reached out for her. He looked like a man drowning. Then he collapsed face-first on to the cobbles.

Seth scrambled back up the bridge and hauled him clear, dragging him by his cassock collar. Dazed, confused, and wincing with pain, Kirin clambered to her feet and limped after them.

"What in the name of the gods is going on?" Pomaltheus blustered.

Seth lowered Jorra-hin down and rolled him over. His eyes were closed. He was unresponsive. Kirin dropped to her knees beside him and touched his cheek with the backs of her fingers.

"Jorra," she called softly. There was nothing. She shook his shoulders and tried again, more forcefully. "Jorra?"

First, an eyelid fluttered, then half opened. The other joined it moments later, sending a wave of relief flooding through Kirin.

"Duhk," he heaved with great effort.

Jorra-hin's woozy attempt at an uncharacteristic profanity matched Kirin's own sentiments exactly.

"Here, give him some of this."

Elona handed Kirin an unstoppered flask, which she pressed against Jorra-hin's lips. More water went down his neck than his throat, but it seemed to revive him. His hand found hers and his eyes closed again for a moment.

Kirin's relief was short-lived, eroded by anxious thoughts she could keep at bay no longer. The *Dànis~Lutárn* was still a potent force. It had clearly retained the ability to draw the Taümatha from nearby mages, just as it had from those who had constructed and transported it here. The ancient magic had sucked at the Taümatha in each of them. Elona hadn't been affected as she wasn't gifted. If Nikrá was right, then Jorra-hin was the most gifted of them all. That probably explained why his reaction to its touch had been more extreme. Whether he would come to the same conclusion remained to be seen. She wondered whether this incident might push his thoughts towards his being more than just an Adak-rann monk. She suspected it more likely he'd bury the experience in a shroud of denial.

She leaned in close. "What happened?"

There was a telltale pause before he answered, his eyes remaining shut. "I don't know."

He was lying. He wasn't very good at it; the tone of his voice gave him away. Deep down, Kirin knew. Jorra-hin's mind was the most astute she'd ever encountered. If she'd been able to figure out what had just happened, he certainly had.

So denial persisted. A lifetime in the Adak-rann blocked his mind. It was ironic, considering that his order strived for objectivity above all else in their pursuit of the truth.

She let the matter drop for now, mindful of Nikrá's urgings that he be allowed to come to terms with his nature at his own pace. She turned her questioning inwards instead.

"Jorra, my restraint cast turned to ice. Why did it do that? I didn't use the Taümatha, I swear." A sudden realisation of just how close her brush with death had been gripped her. She began to tremble. "It could have killed me."

Jorra-hin sat up and drew her close.

"Am I trapped here?" she whispered, the unbidden trembling getting worse by the second.

"No, no, no, of course not," Jorra-hin soothed. There was absolute conviction in his voice now.

"But the *Dànis~Lutárn* triggered something! What about getting out of here again? We're in the Great Gathering, surrounded by water, just like the Dendricá were. We have to cross the canals again to get out."

Kirin knew she was beginning to sound a little hysterical. She couldn't help it. Just trying to cope with the way her life had changed over the past few weeks was a struggle. She was barely keeping stride with it. She'd been the daughter of an ambassador, used to a life of pampering and respect. Now she was on the run, cold and hungry, buried in the depths of the underworld and surrounded by the dead. *And* wearing jewellery that could kill her. It was all too much. She burst into tears.

Jorra-hin rocked her back and forth, whispering comforts in her ear until she managed to regain some small measure of control. Her trembling eventually subsided, though she didn't let go of him, needing something to cling to for a little while longer.

"You didn't answer my question," she murmured. "How are we going to get out? I don't think I can face another scare like that." She kept her voice low enough that the others couldn't hear.

"I'll think of something," he whispered back, "don't you worry. Now, perhaps you'll let me up?"

Kirin pulled away and climbed to her feet. Her lower back gave a sharp twinge of pain.

Elona gave her a reassuring hug. "What a strange place this is," she mumbled.

Kirin smiled at Elona's kindness. Without effort, the princess could make sackcloth and ashes seem regal. She displayed such strength, even if she didn't feel it. Kirin drew herself up and resolved to try to do the same. She glanced round, catching Pomaltheus's eye. He partially suppressed a grin and gave her a wink.

Seth looked a little flummoxed by all the fuss. "Right, well..." he stammered, lifting his arms and letting them flop back to his sides, "I guess we should have a look around, then."

Kirin stared out across the stone expanse of the Great Gathering. Not far away began row upon row of the Dendricá warriors. It wasn't the disordered carnage she had been expecting, the aftermath of a chaotic battle against an unseen enemy. The fallen were all neatly marshalled, like troops awaiting inspection. Lain side by side, fully dressed in armour, shield on forearm, sword in hand, they seemed ready for battle in the eternity to which they'd passed. Their number was legion, stretching right across the Great Gathering.

"My gods," Elona whispered in subdued awe, "so many."

"The Custodians," Jorra-hin managed as he drew alongside, his voice something of a rasp, "brave men, gravely betrayed."

Kirin overcame her apprehension and walked across to the foot of the nearest warrior. She closed her eyes and pictured again the scenes of their battle, even more vivid now that she was standing in their midst. She remembered how she had felt listening to the account in Yazcöp's scroll; how a kind of kinship with these courageous soldiers had grown inside her as they'd fought an epic struggle against powers they couldn't even begin to comprehend. They had been valiant, so many sacrificing themselves for the good of their kin. Suddenly she felt ashamed that she had feared to tread amongst them. These men were to be honoured. They deserved her respect, not her abhorrence.

She opened her eyes and wandered a little way along the line, gazing down at the corpses arrayed in their forlorn battalion. Their sunken faces, little more than skulls after the ravages of time, stared back. Yet even now they seemed resolute. Though at peace, in their sightless eyes a hint of hunger for restitution still lingered. They seemed marshalled to exact it, too. Not in this life, perhaps, but certainly in the next. She couldn't help wondering whether the Dendricá had found a way to deliver retribution to Lornadus and his fellows.

The others joined her. Together they made their way across the Great Gathering, respectfully gazing down as though commanding officers inspecting a macabre parade.

"The ones to die last must have arranged the rest like this," Seth surmised.

"Gruesome task," Pomaltheus muttered. "I wouldn't like to have been the last one. That must have been a lonely way to go. I wonder which one it was."

"Márcucious," Jorra-hin asserted with some conviction.

"Who?"

"He was their leader."

"And why would he be the last to die?"

"I don't know," Jorra-hin shrugged. "Just a gut feeling."

Kirin chuckled and shook her head. Jorra-hin's gut feelings were usually more reliable than most other people's facts. She had no trouble believing he was right.

They continued their sombre inspection in silence until they came to the middle of the Great Gathering. Here the lines of soldiers were broken. Here, it seemed, the very last of them had died. The area was lit by a stone feature that in any other town square would have been a fountain. Yet this one was filled with burning oil instead of flowing water. Kirin wondered how it had become lit, since it seemed completely isolated from any other part of Üzsspeck's marvellous daylight. A chandelier, growing like a mythical tree, rose from the centre of the pool. All carved from a single rock, it was a masterpiece of craftsmanship, exquisite in its intricate detail. The stonemasons of Alondria were masters of their trade, but the level of sophistication to which the Dwarves had elevated the art was unsurpassed. Stone was, after all, the very essence of their chosen world.

Nearby, seeming altogether roughshod by comparison, stood a throne of sorts that had been constructed from various bits of equipment the Dendricá army had brought with them. On it sat the remains of their leader. His head was slumped. Both his hands were resting in his lap, one still clutching a parchment between ossified fingers. He had clearly died writing – his quill had fallen to the floor beside his foot. To all intent and purpose he looked like an old man who had simply nodded off. Were it not for the fact that his face was as threadbare as his garments, it seemed he might wake up at any moment, realising he had visitors.

Fifty yards or so behind the throne was a large area of baggage, the rest of the army's equipment. Seth and Pomaltheus went to have a root through it to see if there was anything useful. After a moment's indecision, Elona joined them.

Jorra-hin extracted his Record from one of his satchels and approached the Dendricá leader. Persisting in his reverence for the departed, he carefully teased the parchment from the dead man's grasp and replaced it with his own, just as he had with Yazcöp's scroll back in the crypt beneath the Cymàtagé.

He began to read Márcucious's last words, scanning through them quickly, but reading various bits aloud for Kirin's benefit.

'All our attempts at escape have met with failure. The curse that holds us here is unfathomable – it defies all our efforts to overcome it. Mage Holôidees, who came to collect Mage Yazcöp after his brave attempt to help us, said that it is the water that sets our boundary. Understanding this, we have tried repeatedly to stem the water's flow, but it has beaten us.'

"Holôidees," Kirin repeated. "That must the fifth mage, the one who finished writing Yazcöp's scroll."

"Indeed," Jorra-hin agreed with a nod. He returned his attention to the scroll.

'We wasted much equipment trying to build a dam to divert the canal water down just a single side of the Gathering. But without clay to seal the cracks, the water just trickled through.

Our attempt to catapult one of our men over the canal met with catastrophe. Never before have I heard a man scream so. Mercifully, his fate was swift; death came even before his body landed on the other side. I am aggrieved that we cannot retrieve him to be amongst his brethren.'

Jorra-hin scanned the document, his lips moving rapidly but in silence as he skipped several passages before continuing to read aloud.

'Before this day, we have not known defeat. Yet this enemy we cannot even see. The few of us that remain are too weak to continue, so now we wait for the inevitable. We have accepted our fate – the troubles of our earlier days, when the men still had fight left in them, have all gone now. Will and strength have deserted us. A man can only remain afraid for so long before even death becomes his welcome friend.'

Kirin closed in on Jorra-hin and laid her head on his shoulder, seeking strength to listen to such sorrowful words. He put his arm around her and skipped forwards a little more.

'There are only three of us left now, and I barely have the strength to write. When I think on the travesty that has befallen us, I am moved to anger. But gone are my days for vengeance.'

'The One who has stalked us will come for me soon, as he has all the rest. My only hope is that after we are no more, the Sentinels of the River will be placed to guard our lands. Perhaps in time our curse will become a blessing. In time, perhaps, we '

Márcucious's final words rolled off Jorra-hin's tongue and left a mournful, unfinished sentiment in their wake. "That was the last he wrote," he croaked in a hoarse voice.

Staring at the ancient warrior, noble in his bearing and full of dignity in his death, Kirin wondered what his dreams had been. "The curse becoming a blessing...?"

"Hmm." Jorra-hin pulled away from her and gently replaced the Dendricá leader's parchment back in his hand. "If you remember, Yazcöp's scroll ended with something similar. The writer, Mage Holôidees we may now presume, expressed his regret over the fact that the *Dànis~Lutárn* would never have the opportunity to fulfil its true purpose. It obviously wasn't meant to be just for trapping the

Dendricá here in Üzsspeck. Márcucious might have been told what that other purpose was. Perhaps he was under the impression that once the *Dànis~Lutárn* was no longer needed here, it would be taken to fulfil this other role."

"No longer needed – you mean, once all the Dendricá were dead," Kirin said, unable to hide her indignation. She felt a wave of revulsion wash over her at the treachery of Lornadus and his feeble-minded followers. "They could have come back to move the *Dànis~Lutárn*. Why didn't they? Why leave it here?"

Jorra-hin shrugged. "Shame, I suspect. Returning must have been their original plan," he went on, shaking his head. "Mage Holôidees probably had no way of knowing that Lornadus was about to fabricate a falsehood the likes of which would confound history for the next millennium. If Holôidees told the Dendricá about the *Dànis~Lutárn* being bound by water, it isn't too great an assumption to suppose that he also revealed its true purpose. He probably believed the mages would come back and sort this whole mess out. He wouldn't have known what Lornadus was planning to do until it was too late. And I doubt any of them could have anticipated that it would be twelve hundred years before anyone would set foot in this place again."

"Or that it would be us," Kirin added, giving him a wry smile.

Jorra-hin nodded pensively. "Strange how things work out, isn't it? I mean, what were the odds that we would find Yazcöp and the others, or read his scroll, or even find our way into these mines after all these years? It does seem as if the hand of fate is in this."

"And you're comfortable with that?" Kirin probed, staring into Jorra-hin's eyes.

"Not really." He lowered his gaze and sighed deeply. "It doesn't sit well with my Adak-rann sensibilities. I worry about what effect my involvement in all this may have on the history that will be written. I'm only supposed to record what happens, not help bring it about."

"We don't always get to choose our path, Jorra."

She saw the pain that comment caused in Jorra-hin's eyes. She was glad of Elona's return at that moment.

"Find anything?"

Elona pursed her lips. "No food, obviously. Weapons and armour aplenty, and some clothes – but you can imagine what they're like after all these years."

"Disintegrating on sight, I shouldn't wonder," Kirin chuckled.

Elona nodded. "We did find this, though." She handed Jorra-hin a strange-looking object. It was metal, possibly copper, and flat, as though a folded sheet. Although not the right shape, it reminded Kirin of a lady's fan.

Jorra-hin regarded the artefact for a moment, turning it over a few times. He tried teasing it open. There was some resistance, a little corrosion thwarting his efforts, but it gave way with a snap and opened out.

"Ah-h," he exclaimed. "It's a map."

"A map? Of where?" Elona demanded.

"The Old Homeland, I think."

The princess peered over his shoulder. "It doesn't look like any map I've ever seen before."

"Well, no, perhaps not. But then you've never been down a Dwarvish mine before, have you?"

Elona grunted in a somewhat unladylike fashion. "So…"

Jorra-hin smiled. He stooped to lay the map on the ground and then pointed to a circle on it that was marked with undecipherable symbols. It was no surprise that Jorra-hin seemed familiar with them. He'd been able to read every other Dwarvish sign they'd come across on their way here. They would not have made it as far as Üzsspeck without that particular ability.

"This is the city," he explained, his finger resting on the circle. "But instead of trying to depict landscape, the position of mountains, forests, towns and so forth, this map is intended to show which tunnels lead where. After all, it hardly matters what twists and turns a tunnel takes to get where it goes. The only important bits of information are the junctions and intersections where there is a choice of route to be had. Hence this map is diagrammatic, constructed with straight lines and simple corners, with only a logical depiction of crossroads, rather than any attempt at representing the true lie of the land."

Elona's scepticism was quickly replaced by a keen interest. She peered at the map more closely. "You know what this means?"

"Apart from the fact that we can now work out where we need to go?"

"It means others could follow this map."

"Indeed…" Jorra-hin said hesitantly, clearly unsure where the princess was going with this. "Who did you have in mind?"

"Well, don't you see? General Kirshtahll could use it to bring his troops north – in the middle of winter!"

Elona was excited. There was a sparkle in her eyes, which glinted a fiery red from the nearby flames.

"If he had possession of it," Jorra-hin noted.

"Well, yes, obviously." Elona lowered her voice slightly. "Listen, I think the time has come for us to consider splitting up. Some of us need to carry on to warn the army about what Daka is up to. But we also need to get a message south to Kirshtahll. Now that we know the mines can be accessed, he has a way of returning to the Northern Territories that doesn't involve crossing the Mathians. That's a vital piece of information. We must try to tell him."

"You realise, of course, that we still don't know for certain what Daka *is* actually up to," Kirin said.

"I know. But whatever she has planned, it won't be good for us. No matter what, the north is going to need Kirshtahll's help. Some of us are going to have to turn round and head for Kirsh."

"Kirsh?"

"If anyone knows how to get a message to the general, it will be Lady Kirshtahll," Elona explained. "And Kirsh is less than half the distance than it is to Colòtt. It will be the quickest way of contacting him."

10

Elona called Seth and Pomaltheus away from their scavenging and took the lead in the discussion that followed. She outlined her proposal. It did not go down well with the two mages.

"Why us?" Pomaltheus blustered.

Elona bit her lip as she tried to decide how best to sway them. She was a princess, by birthright at least, but that bestowed no authority here; in this endeavour, they were all equals.

"You know it wouldn't be safe for me to return to the south," she said, "every noble in Alondria will be looking for me. I'd be arrested within a day. And even if I made it to Kirsh, my presence there would put the House of Kirshtahll in direct conflict with the Crown. We can't afford that. The general will have enough trouble of his own if he has to defy Midana and leave Colòtt without her permission."

Seth acknowledged the arguments with a thoughtful 'hmm'. Pomaltheus's stony expression had not been dented.

"The same goes for Jorra-hin," Elona pressed on. "Nowhere south of the mountains is safe for him. If he falls into Dinac-Mentà hands – well, we all know what that means. Besides, we're going to need him to figure out what Daka is up to, which would be nigh on impossible if he's hidden away at Kirsh. As for Kirin…"

"She's going with Jorra-hin," Kirin cut in on her own behalf, in a tone that made it clear no truck would be had with argument.

Elona returned her gaze to the two mages. "So unless one of you wants to go alone, it's up to the both of you." Of the pair, Pomaltheus remained the most reluctant. She eyed him directly. "You do understand how important this is, don't you? The fate of the Northern Territories could be in the balance here. General Kirshtahll *must* be told about what we've discovered."

"Why couldn't we all continue north and send a messenger back from Mitcha?"

"Oh, come on, Pom," Seth muttered with a resigned sigh, "you know we can't risk entrusting this to anyone else. Besides, we may not have time. The Tsnath have already been to Jàb-áldis. They could be ready to launch whatever they've been planning. Face it, it's up to us."

Pomaltheus huffed and sat himself down, leaning back against the wall of the fire fountain. He closed his eyes, leaving Elona unsure whether he was still resisting the idea, or whether a begrudged concession had just been won.

At least Seth seemed to be on-board. "So how do we get there?" he asked.

"I'll make you a copy of this," Jorra-hin offered, waving the copper folding map. "I've already identified a suitable route for you to take back through the Old Homeland."

Elona let out a quiet sigh. She didn't like the idea of splitting up the group any more than Pomaltheus did; they'd come through a lot together these past few weeks. They'd learnt to depend on each other. Yet there was no other way. Someone had to go; Kirshtahll simply had to be told of the route through the Old Homeland by which he could bring his troops north. She'd go herself, if all else failed. But Pomaltheus and Seth were a better option.

Avoiding arrest wasn't the only thing on her mind. She had other reasons for wanting to continue on. Yet however much her motivation may have been influenced by a desire to see Torrin-Ashur again, she couldn't mention that. She had started out on this venture to help Jorra-hin. That had quickly become a mission to save the Adak-rann from Daka's nefarious plans, along with quite possibly the entire Northern Territories. Throwing personal considerations into that heady mix would level the high ground all her sacrifices had garnered.

While the rest of the group ate a meagre lunch of *Torvàstos*, Jorra-hin made a hasty copy of the Dendricá's map. When he was done, he went and wedged himself between the two mages.

"Your best route is to take these tunnels here," he explained, tracing his finger along several newly drawn lines, "to this entrance, which the Dwarves called *Hàttàmoréy*. If I've judged it correctly, you should emerge from the Mathians somewhere a little to the east of Am-còt, near the headwaters of the Alam-goùrd. From there you can follow the river south for a while, though you'll need to head west towards Kirsh before too long."

"How far is it?" Seth asked.

Jorra-hin cocked his head to one side. "I'm afraid there's no direct road you can take. Once you're out of the mountains, you'll hit the trade road to Am-còt. But following that will either take you too far south, or all the way up to Toutleth. Then again, there is a route from Toutleth to Kirsh. Torrin-Ashur and I used it back in the summer. That stretch would take you a couple of days by horse in good conditions. The only trouble is, going that way would double your overall journey."

"So you're suggesting we go cross-country?"

Jorra-hin nodded.

"Cross-country? In the snow?" Pomaltheus challenged, sounding positively aghast.

Jorra-hin tried to look apologetic.

"That'll be one hell of a trek," said Seth. He sucked in a breath as he estimated the task. "It'll probably take a week at least."

"A week!" Pomaltheus's head lolled back against the fountain wall with a thump.

"Followed by a relaxing stay as honoured guests of the Kirshtahll household," Elona chipped in.

Her attempt to give encouragement was water off a duck's back. The prospect of impending luxury did nothing to lift Pomaltheus's spirits. His eyes remained shut, as if the whole sorry mess might go away if he ignored it long enough.

Seth took the new map and made to roll it up. "The ink's still wet," Jorra-hin intervened, staying his hand, "best to leave it open for a while."

It was decided that they should rest for a few hours before going their separate ways. The break provided a chance to restock oil supplies from the fountain, a tricky endeavour given that it was burning, and press some of the still serviceable Dendricá lanterns into use. As was often his way, Jorra-hin took himself aside and updated his Record with recent events and discoveries. His scroll was getting ever longer; he'd already glued several extensions on to the original sheet. His ever-present satchel must have been stuffed with spare parchment. Only the gods knew how it had survived their journey so far intact.

Elona drew Kirin away and led her to the edge of the Great Gathering for a little privacy. A decent wash had become a priority. As they approached the canal, she noticed Kirin displaying a degree of hesitancy at going near the water.

"Don't worry, I'll fetch it. You stay here."

Elona cast around the discarded Dendricá equipment and found a bucket. It leaked like a sieve until it was only a third full, but it sufficed to dip hands into.

Partially undressed amidst so many dead, Elona felt oddly exposed, as though all those hollow eyes were anything but sightless. It made her wonder whether Althar was somehow with the warriors in the great beyond, maybe watching over her.

"Ye gods," she muttered, "if my father could see me now…"

Kirin smirked. "Mine, too. He'd be horrified."

Despite the quip, Elona detected the note of concern in Kirin's voice. "You'll see him again soon. We'll get back. Of course, I've a lifetime of incarceration to look forward to when we do. Or maybe even the delights of having my head cut off."

Kirin's eyes widened in shock. Elona just giggled. "Gods, what a mess we're in."

"I'm sorry I got you involved in all this. If I hadn't come to enlist your help, you'd still be back in the palace."

"Yes," Elona nodded, "where I'd have been bored stiff, to say nothing of Jorra-hin probably dead. I'd do it all again in a heartbeat."

Kirin smiled. She poured water over her feet and sucked in her breath at its icy touch. "Speaking of Jorra-hin," she said, "I'm wondering how he's coping with what happened when we entered the Great Gathering."

"What exactly did happen?" No one had seemed keen to discuss it earlier, so Elona hadn't asked.

"Well," Kirin shrugged, pausing to marshal her thoughts, "I think it was the *Dànis~Lutárn.* You know it was created with an ability to draw the Taümatha from its surroundings, including any mages nearby? When we crossed the water, I'm fairly sure it tried to draw power from those of us that are gifted."

"And Jorra-hin was affected the most."

"Precisely. The conclusions are not difficult to draw. Jorra must have realised this by now. He's not an idiot."

Elona scoffed at the understatement. "No, he's certainly not that. Stubborn as an ass, maybe, but not an idiot."

Kirin smiled, though her expression quickly became more serious again. "However much he wishes to be just an Adak-rann monk, he must suspect he's more than that now."

"Yet he still won't countenance the notion of it."

"Not yet, at least." Kirin's face became downcast. "It's made worse by the fact that he knows every step he takes now is writing history."

"Which must be the last thing he wants."

"It's tearing him apart," Kirin mumbled.

Elona slid her arms back inside her kirtle, allowing the material to soak up the excess water she'd not managed to rub off. Towels were a luxury firmly in the realms of dreams. She reached out and placed a hand on Kirin's shoulder. "You really love him, don't you?"

"Would I be wearing this if I didn't?" Kirin picked at the necklace, its specious form defying her touch. "I can't help wishing Mage Nikrá has it all wrong. If only I was the Natural mage, and not Jorra."

"You don't really believe that possible, though, do you?"

Kirin gave her head a forlorn shake. "I can't explain it, but somehow there's a bond between us. I know what he is, even if he won't admit it."

"Why does life have to be so damnably complicated?" Elona moaned. "My father used to say we are nothing but playthings of the gods, here to endure their contrivances for no loftier purpose than their entertainment."

"In that case," Kirin harrumphed, "I shall have words for them when we meet."

Elona laughed. She'd have rather more than just words.

They finished washing and picked their way back across the Great Gathering to rejoin the others.

"We should probably get going," Seth greeted without preamble. "I don't know how much longer the cavern fires will burn, but we should get out of Üzsspeck while it's still light."

Elona nodded. The map Jorra-hin was guarding, somewhat jealously she noticed, didn't go down to street-level in its detail, making the prospect of getting lost amongst the sprawling suburbs very real. On the way in, all they'd had to do was head for the middle of the city. Leaving required a much more targeted approach to pick up the right tunnel.

Jorra-hin stalled the group's departure. "There's one thing we should do first," he said. In answer of several questioning stares, he went on, "Whilst trying to escape their entrapment, the Dendricá catapulted a man over the canal. Needless to say, he died in the attempt. Their leader, Márcucious, was most grieved that they could not retrieve his body. I think the least we should do is restore this man to his kin."

"Have we got time?" Seth asked, sounding dubious. He took in the perimeter of the Great Gathering with a sweeping glance. "I mean, this place is vast. How are we even going to find him?"

It surprised no one that Jorra-hin had already thought of that.

"I've an idea of roughly where to look. Yazcöp recounted that the Dendricá were forced to access the Old Homeland via the *Trombéi* entrance," he paused to make brief reference to the map before pointing towards one of the canal bridges, "which means they would have entered the Great Gathering from over there. I suspect that's also the way they would have tried to retreat. Do you see that pile?"

Elona squinted to make out what Jorra-hin was pointing at. There was a heap of something just to the left of the bridge, though it was too dim to see what it was made of.

"Márcucious recorded that his men tried to stem the flow of the canal with some of their supplies," Jorra-hin explained. "I'll wager that's also where they attempted to cross, since I imagine they would have concentrated their escape efforts in one place."

"This morning I was a mage," Pomaltheus muttered, climbing to his feet with a series of huffs. "By lunchtime I'd been demoted to messenger, and now I'm a bloody undertaker. I wish this wretched day would hurry up and end."

Seth sniggered and clapped a hand on his friend's back.

They gathered their belongings and the few useful items they'd managed to scavenge and headed towards the bridge with Jorra-hin leading the way.

Treading a careful path through the ranks of warriors, Elona couldn't help but wonder at how quickly so much death became normal. As her eyes roved over the Dendricá host, she found it hard to associate their musty corpses with anything that could ever have been living. Her head knew it had been so, but her heart just couldn't make the connection. It was easier to think of them as macabre sculptures than forgotten soldiers.

The pile of equipment Jorra-hin had pointed out was a similar collection of military supplies to the one they'd already rooted through. There was no point wasting time examining it. Anything of real use had been consumed long ago by the Dendricá.

Elona wandered over to the bridge and leaned over the balustrade. A misshapen pile of packs, shields, parts of several handcarts, and even what had once been clothes and blankets, spanned the canal, all now calcified into a strange rock-like embankment. Jorra-hin's conclusion was correct, Márcucious's men had indeed tried to stem the water's flow just here. Upstream of the makeshift dam the water was deeper and wider; downstream, just a slow-moving trickle, though still an uninterrupted flow. Had it been a natural river, and not a Dwarve-hewn channel deep inside a mountain, silt might eventually have completed the Dendricá's endeavour, though probably not in time to have saved them. They'd been surely doomed, just as Lornadus had intended.

That cruel, heartless betrayal suddenly struck Elona. It made her feel unconscionably angry; the warriors had been responding to a plea for help when they'd been trapped. If there was any such thing as justice in the hereafter, she really hoped the Dendricá had managed to get their hands on those responsible.

"There," she exclaimed, first to spot the probable remains of the poor wretch who'd been flung out across the canal. She directed Jorra-hin's gaze to a point on the other side of the channel.

Out of place in an otherwise tidy street was a clump of what could easily have been mistaken as leaves swept into a pile at the base of a wall. With no bushes or trees in Üzsspeck whence such debris might come, she knew it couldn't be that.

"So how do you want to play this – me and Pom go across first?" Seth asked.

"I'll come with you."

Jorra-hin's volunteering took Kirin by surprise. She shot Elona a curious frown.

Pomaltheus responded with an indifferent shrug and set out across the bridge first. Seth drew alongside Jorra-hin, perhaps more wary of what might happen as they approached the crest.

Elona watched the two mages wriggle at the touch of the Dànis~Lutárn. She frowned when Jorra-hin didn't react at all.

Kirin moved closer, looking equally confused. "I don't understand," she whispered. "It doesn't seem to have affected him this time."

"So I see. Could he have shielded himself?"

Kirin made a moue. "I don't see how. Not consciously, at least."

Elona returned her attention to the far side. Jorra-hin led the way along the edge of the nearest buildings to the spot where the remains lay.

"We've found him," he called back, confirming what Elona had never really doubted. "Is there anything over there we could use as a stretcher?"

A quick rummage amongst the abandoned equipment uncovered a handcart that hadn't even been unloaded by the Dendricá. Elona shoved the packs off the side and grunted in dismay when its left wheel disintegrated, giving up in a puff of dust.

"So much for that idea," Kirin muttered.

Elona kicked at the remaining wheel, letting out a giggle; a burst of wanton destruction was curiously liberating. "And there we have it — one stretcher," she announced as the rest of the cart collapsed.

Seth collected the flatbed and returned to where Pomaltheus and Jorra-hin were waiting. The three of them lifted the warrior on to the board, attempting to do as little damage as possible to the delicate remains. Once the man was loaded on, Seth took one end and Pomaltheus the other. Jorra-hin, carrying all the torches, led them back across the bridge to the Great Gathering.

"We haven't got a clue who his friends were," Pomaltheus noted.

"Let's just place him at the end of that line over there," Jorra-hin suggested, gesturing with a torch.

The mages laid the stretcher down next to one of the other marshalled warriors. Jorra-hin advised against lifting the remains again; they'd already caused enough disintegration.

The group stood in silence for a few moments, paying their respects. Elona could think of little to say. The soldier, no doubt a volunteer, had died heroically in an attempt to free his fellow warriors. He deserved recognition. But his name was as lost now as his cause had been then. While that brought a certain sadness, the injustice of it stabbing at her heart, still no words came.

In a sombre mood they left the warriors in peace. Their own farewells were bayed with a degree of reluctance, as though each was still hoping to avert the parting of company. Yet moments later it happened. With none of his usual gusto, Seth set off across the Great Gathering, Pomaltheus woodenly following a few paces behind. The pair retraced their steps to the far side, to the point where they'd first entered the city's centre. Once over the bridge they were soon out of sight. The only sign of their presence became the telltale glow of their torches, at odds with the shadowy world of Üzsspeck's deserted streets.

Elona tried to dismiss the disquiet that had befallen her as she'd watched them go. There was no doubting the logic of their decision — all her earlier arguments still held true — but that did little to assuage her sense of loss.

Kirin was looking concerned, too, though probably for different reasons, Elona realised. She had turned towards the bridge they now needed to cross.

"Don't worry," Jorra-hin comforted. He took Kirin by the shoulders and turned her to face him. "You know what's likely to happen now, so you can be ready for it. Best take it at a run – lessens the time spent over the water."

"What about you?" Kirin murmured softly, touching his cheek with the backs of her fingers.

"I'll be fine." His reply was a little too hasty. He turned towards the bridge as though anxious to avoid discussing the matter further. Elona caught Kirin's eye and raised an eyebrow. She was certain Jorra-hin knew exactly what Kirin was really asking.

Kirin ventured towards the canal, approaching the rise of the bridge with timid steps. She veritably flew across the remaining span. She wasn't there long enough to suffer any discomfort over the water.

Jorra-hin joined her, for the third time crossing without any outwards sign of his being affected.

As she followed, Elona pondered how that might be. She was hardly an expert in Taümathalogical matters, but nonetheless found herself wondering whether the strength of Jorra-hin's denial of his true nature might somehow have managed to bury his abilities so deep that they'd been put out of reach of the ancient magic. From what little she knew of the art, she understood that the control of magic was all about exercising willpower. In every other aspect of his life Jorra-hin demonstrated great strength of will, so maybe that was enough to thwart the *Dànis~Lutárn*.

Trotting down the far side of the bridge and joining the others, she resolved to mention her theory to Kirin when they were next alone. Quite when then might be, she had no idea; the three of them wouldn't be out of each other's company any time soon.

It occurred to her that they could just confront Jorra-hin with the whole matter and be done with it. Get it out in the open. She'd never really understood the logic of Mage Nikrá's advice against such direct interference. Yet just as quickly as those thoughts occurred, Nikrá's pleading face and the passion of his argument surfaced and quashed the notion.

"Well, we'd best get to it, then," Jorra-hin said, taking the lead just as Seth would have done. He headed off along a street that inclined gently up towards the edge of the city.

They made faster progress now than when they'd entered Üzsspeck. Some of their reverence for the abandoned dwellings had worn off, dulling their curiosity. Fear of losing the Dwarvish daylight also nipped at their heels, spurring them on. Without so much as a wrong turn, Jorra-hin led them to the mouth of a tunnel that he declared would lead them to the *Trombéi* entrance.

"Why that way?" Elona queried.

"It's the route the Dendricá host used through the Old Homeland, which I take to mean it's an easy path, since there were so many of them," Jorra-hin explained. "Also, I think the *Trombéi* entrance emerges near the Vale of Caspárr. That should offer us a fairly quick way out of the Mathians. If we pick up one of the tributaries to the Sam-Hédi, we can follow the river down the mountains, which should lead us to the road between Halam-Gräth and Mitcha. All we have to do then is turn west. On the assumption that Mitcha is where we're heading?"

Elona nodded. Mitcha was the only logical destination to plump for. She motioned for Jorra-hin to lead on, smiling to herself. For a young man who had lived most of his life isolated in a monastery perched atop a mountain, he certainly knew his geography. By contrast, she, a well-travelled princess, found herself in no position to argue.

As they headed down the tunnel, the yellowish light of Üzsspeck receded behind them. It was an unpleasant return to debilitating darkness, a claustrophobic feeling after the welcome expanse of the city. They also faced a wind that moaned rather mournfully as it rushed past them, drawn by the fires behind. It played havoc with their torches, making them burn furiously and turning the flames a bluish hue, reducing their effectiveness still further.

They spent what felt like night in a grotto next to a veritable field of *Torvàstos*. Moisture from a small stream trickling through the rock had encouraged their growth. It made as good a spot as any in which to rest. Whether it was actually night or not, they had no idea; since being in the mines, without daylight to govern them, judging the passage of time was next to impossible.

They groped their way along the undulating tunnels for at least another day, passing junction after junction. Armed with the Dendricá map, Jorra-hin guided them through each one with none of the discussion and reasoned argument that had been necessary when navigating blindly on their way to Üzsspeck.

Very little else of interest came or went. The mine tunnels had become, for the most part, somewhat boring affairs, the Dwarves

111

having taken a rather utilitarian approach to this part of the Old Homeland. Not even the occasional carving on the walls provided much of a distraction from the monotony. Only Jorra-hin could read the things anyway, and even he didn't seem that bothered. Elona thought that decidedly out of character, considering his usual propensity for all things ancient. She wondered if it was a sign he was changing, perhaps becoming more focused on his future. It was hard to tell.

When they finally reached the *Trombéi* entrance, it was none too soon as far as she was concerned. Save for the fact that the tunnel appeared blocked by a rock-fall. She couldn't help fearing the worst.

"It's just an illusion, the glean Lornadus's mages left in place," Jorra-hin assured her. "Besides, we're trying to get out this time, so it should be easier to pass through."

In the same manner as when they'd encountered the seal under Jàb-áldis, Jorra-hin used his mastery of A'lyavine to help prepare their minds to 'see the truth', thereby enabling them to pass through the glean without hindrance.

"I hope Seth and Pomaltheus don't have trouble getting out," Elona said as she stepped through the rock wall before her.

"I have every faith in Pomaltheus," she heard Jorra-hin reply. "I've given him everything he needs to get through." His voice suddenly sounded terribly distant and muffled.

The gleans that had kept the mine entrances blocked for centuries were easily overcome with the right understanding, but it took faith. Hers, Elona knew, was augmented by Jorra-hin's abilities with the Tongue of the Ancients. She'd not have managed it otherwise. Every sense screamed at her that what she was doing was utterly impossible. It worried her that Kirshtahll had to do the same under Pomaltheus and Seth's guidance. He would need every ounce of their magely expertise if he was to succeed in bringing the army north via the mines. She just hoped the acolytes were up to the task.

She stepped through the seal into a blindingly bright glare. Its intensity made her gasp and immediately screw her eyes shut. After days underground, even the weak winter sun glinting off the snow outside the cave entrance hurt. She buried her face in her hands and spent a few minutes gradually acclimatising. Only after the shock of the light had worn off did she notice that the cold had also returned with a vengeance. Being in the mines had, if anything, been a comparatively warm experience. Now they were back in the world, high up in the Mathians in the middle of winter.

"It's nice to breathe fresh air again," Kirin declared, to the accompaniment of a stretch of feline proportions, her dulled senses reawakening.

"And to be able to see more than two yards," Elona added.

"Oh, look, Jorra..."

Jorra-hin, just emerged from the glean, turned to see what Kirin was pointing at.

"Ah, of course, another of the Vicar stones."

The menhir stood in an alcove a few feet away from the seal. The covering that had hidden it for centuries had been chipped away, but while a crude attempt had been made to replace the plaster, it had not stayed put, leaving parts exposed.

Jorra-hin approached the relic with his usual reverence and ran his hands over its surface, teasing a few of the looser bits of covering away. His fingers explored the carvings, tracing the indentations where the controlling spells of the *Dànis~Lutárn* had been chiselled into it by Papanos Meiter's hand. His lips moved as he silently mouthed the words. He froze when his fingers pressed into a crack that appeared to have split the rock in two a foot or so above its base.

"Just as I thought. The Tsnath have been here."

Elona tensed and spun round to face the cave entrance.

"No, no, not recently. Months ago. This is the menhir Daka's men found, before Kassandra fled to us."

"How can you tell?"

"Because it's broken. No doubt they wanted to take it with them, but damaged it trying to lever it free. And thus began my Record."

Now that he'd mentioned it, Elona did recall Jorra-hin explaining his supposition to Brother Heckart back at Jàb-áldis. When the stone broke, all the power stored within it had been released. The resultant wave of Taümathic energy had affected the Vessel, or Taümathakiya as his brothers had known it back then, and he'd been sent to investigate the cause.

"Should we try to hide it again?" Kirin wondered aloud.

"To what purpose?" Jorra-hin flicked a glance at her and shrugged. "It's just a stone, now, and the Tsnath already know it's here. Besides, it must weigh half a ton. I doubt we could shift it very far." He sighed. "No, we'll have to concede this menhir to the Tsnath and concentrate our efforts on trying to prevent them from getting their hands on the rest."

"We should head for Mitcha without delay, then," Elona prompted.

The three of them turned towards the cave entrance. Elona took a fortifying breath against the cold.

The harsh and unforgiving conditions of the Mathians rapidly made themselves felt. The gradient might have been in their favour, but everything else was arrayed against them. Elona felt the wind slice its frigid daggers through her clothing as though she wore little but a silk shift. The snow was waist deep everywhere except under the canopies of the densest trees, whose lower branches whipped like slave-drivers, scratching and clawing and deluging them with great clods of dislodged snow.

When they stopped to rest, producing fire proved impossible, making the absence of Seth and Pomaltheus and their incandescent abilities keenly felt.

Elona began to realise how overwhelmingly underprepared they were for this endeavour. They had neither hunting weapons nor skills to use them. Scavenging produced nothing; what the hibernating wildlife hadn't harvested for themselves, the snow had thoroughly buried. Even the prospect of some dry and relatively tasteless *Torvàstos* became a luxurious dream, utterly at odds with the reality that the last of that had been consumed more than a day ago. Now, hunger sapped their energy. When the sun set, just a few hours after they'd left the mines, it imposed a bitter night they survived only by burying themselves in a scooped-out snow hole and huddling together for warmth.

The second day they fared a little better. The ground levelled off a degree or two, the wind fell to almost nothing, and the snowdrifts weren't quite as treacherous. Offsetting these gains, their hunger and its debilitating effects only grew worse. A shepherd's hut, abandoned for the winter, proved a godssend for their second night. They achieved fire, the warmth of which almost made up for the lack of food. But only almost.

By the middle of the third day they were largely down out of the Mathians, somewhere along the southern edge of the Vale of Caspárr. They came across a small track and began to follow it. Elona saw the red and blotchy faces of her friends and knew hers looked the same. Battling aching joints that felt as though they had frozen solid, they could easily have been mistaken for bent and elderly peasants.

Eerily, there was no sign of any actual peasants, old or otherwise.

The Vale was fertile land, the best the Northern Territories had to offer, so there should have been some evidence of the populace. Even in winter, farms needed tending. Yet the place was deserted.

"I don't like the look of this", Elona murmured, almost in a whisper.

The glance Jorra-hin returned confirmed that she wasn't alone in her concern.

The chances of warmth, shelter and hot food were dashed at the first small hamlet they came across. Disaster had befallen the place. Blackened ruins lined the track running though the forlorn settlement, soot-covered stones and charred beams contrasting vividly with the purity of the snow that had fallen.

"Recent?" Elona wondered.

"I don't know how to tell." Jorra-hin glanced round and shrugged.

Kirin placed a hand against the fire-ravaged stonework of a collapsed wall. "Cold. Whatever calamity has visited this place, it wasn't in the last day or so."

Elona wasn't about to argue with that assessment. They poked about a little, found nothing and moved on. In a grave mood, their conversation was non-existent, leaving them alone with their thoughts. Uppermost on her mind, aside from dreams of food and warmth, was what could have caused the hamlet's destruction. Could it have been some natural disaster, she wondered, leading the villagers to abandon the place for the winter?

The alternative was rather more worrying. The Tsnath had made it as far south as the Jàb-áldis monastery, that much was known. They'd have passed through this region on the way. She rejected the idea that the same party would have wreaked such havoc, though; theirs had been a specific mission. Retrieving the Vessel from the monastery would have been far too important to risk jeopardising success for the sake of destroying a pathetic place of no consequence.

That didn't mean to say there weren't other Tsnath forces in the region.

"We must proceed with caution," she advised. "Until we know otherwise, we should assume the worst. There could be Tsnath about."

The track that had led them to the hamlet took them on to the main road between Halam-Gräth and Mitcha. Despite the snow having transformed the landscape, Elona thought she recognised the lie of the land from her journey earlier in the year. If she was correct,

Mitcha was another two days' journey, on horseback. On foot, wading through snow, much longer. Her worries began to deepen. Unless they found food and shelter soon, there was a very real possibility they might not survive. Every step drained their reserves, slowing their progress and making their destination ever more distant.

Her spiralling pessimism was cut short with a jolt.

"Someone's coming," Jorra-hin hissed, throwing his hands out and accidentally delivering Elona a blow to the stomach.

Fatigue instantly forgotten, they fled the track like startled deer. They found a holly thicket dense enough to hide behind and crouched down. Looking back, only then did Elona realise they'd left a trail of footprints in the snow, a perfect signpost to their location.

For several moments all was still. Then fleeting glimpses of two riders approaching from the east were snatched through the trees. Obscured by the forest, it was difficult to make out whether they were soldier or civilian.

The riders stopped at the exact spot where the trio's footprints made it obvious someone had departed the track. Elona held her breath.

After a brief consultation, one of the riders dismounted. "It's alright, you can come out."

Elona exchanged worried glances with the others.

"Stay here," Jorra-hin whispered, "I'll go. If I shout *run*, do so. Don't wait for me."

Before anyone could argue, Jorra-hin had slithered out from behind their cover and was striding towards the track. He stopped about ten yards short of the riders.

"My name is Jorra-hin. I'm an Adak-rann monk."

"Lost, are you?"

The rider's accent didn't sound as if it originated north of the border, Elona realised with some relief. In fact, it sounded distinctly southern, perhaps even from the Alondris region.

"As it happens, yes," Jorra-hin replied. "I'm trying to get to Mitcha."

"Mitcha?" the man on the ground retorted in surprise, glancing at his companion. "I wouldn't advise it. It's in Tsnath hands."

"What? H-how?"

Jorra-hin ventured a little closer.

"The bastards have taken over the whole region. Din't you know?"

Elona's heart nearly stopped. Worse news she could barely

conceive of hearing.

"What about the army?" Jorra-hin stammered.

"Gone. Well, most of it anyway."

"Most of it?"

The dismounted rider shrugged. "There's reports of some resistance over Nairnkirsh way. Our commander's trying to make contact with 'em."

"You're not alone?"

"No. There's Tsnath all over the place right now. We've been sent on to scout ahead, like."

"So how did you know I wasn't Tsnath, then?" Jorra-hin asked.

"Them bastards don't run off and hide at the first sign of trouble," the soldier still sitting on his horse snorted. He pointed to the tracks in the snow. "Who else you got with you?"

"Might as well show ourselves," Elona murmured to Kirin.

Together they rose from behind the holly bush and waded back towards the track, attempting to reuse some of their previous footprints in the snow to lessen the effort required.

As they drew closer, the mounted scout let out a low whistle. "Now, they ain't no monks!"

The other scout arrived at the same conclusion with a grunt.

Elona smiled, but otherwise ignored the curiosity displayed on the men's faces. "Your main party is coming this way?"

"Aye."

"How far back are they?"

"A mile, maybe."

Looking to Jorra-hin and Kirin for confirmation, Elona responded, "Good. Then we'll wait here for them."

The scout on the ground grasped the pommel of this saddle and swung himself up. "Can't stay with you, I'm afraid. Got to keep ahead of the others."

With a nod, the pair resumed their reconnoitre of the track. Elona looked longingly at their horses. Sadly, her aching, frozen feet didn't take priority in these circumstances.

A quarter hour passed before the main party came into view. There was no scurrying off into cover this time. Instead, the trio stood at the side of the track, plainly visible, in the hope of appearing as unthreatening as possible.

From first sight, it was clear the approaching group was not entirely of military origin. It was a rag-tag mixture of harried peasant refugees and dishevelled soldiers, every one of them haunted by a look of exhaustion. The man leading them had surrendered his horse to four youngsters, his shoulders to a fifth. Recognition of who he was brought a wide-eyed stare to Elona.

"Lord Borádin," she stammered, completely unable to reconcile her memories of the finely dressed pompous arse she'd met at Mitcha with the haggard, unkempt vision that came to a halt before her now.

"Your Highness?" Borádin lowered the young girl he was carrying to the ground. She ran off and clung to the skirt of another girl, perhaps an older sister. "Forgive me, but you're just about the last person I expected to meet."

"I – I could say the same, my lord."

Borádin gave her a wistful smirk. "I'm not sure whether I should salute you or arrest you," he said. He answered his own conundrum with a slight bow. The gesture was lacking the overt formality it would certainly have had a few months back.

"You've heard about my circumstances, then?" Elona asked.

"Indeed. It was probably the last message we received before our communications with the south were severed."

Elona frowned. "We are not able to send messages beyond the Mathians?"

Borádin hesitated before replying. "I can't speak for the whole of the Territories, but the Message Corps at Halam-Gräth was certainly destroyed. Given what has happened, I think it safe to assume that it was by Tsnath hands. I suspect they'll have used the same tactic elsewhere. How successfully, I can't say."

Elona nodded. The news just kept getting worse and worse. "I see. So what is your intention towards me?"

"Fear not," Borádin snorted. He gestured at the bedraggled crowd to his rear. "I've enough on my plate without prisoners. Let's just pretend the queen's edict never made it through."

Elona smiled, displaying her relief. She took a moment to introduce Kirin and Jorra-hin, then asked, "So, how is it you're up here? I thought you'd gone home."

"I did," Borádin replied with disdain, "and received a cold shoulder from my father when I got there. As you can imagine, he was none too impressed that General Kirshtahll had seen fit to dismiss me. It's something of an eye-opener, ma'am, when your own father tells you to go away and learn to be a man. So I ended up stationed over in Halam-Gräth…"

"Tanaséy Vickrà's home town?"

"That's right. Lord Vickrà was kind enough to furnish me with a letter of introduction. I'd not long been there when the garrison was ordered north towards the border. It turns out this was just before the invasion. And it was exactly what the Tsnath wanted." Borádin's voice took on a bitter edge. "As we were heading north, unbeknownst to us, the enemy had come round by sea and were landing in the Bay of Shallow Graves and the Sound of Goàtt. They overran most of Vickrà-dòthmore, including Halam-Gräth, from the south, coming up right behind us before we even knew what was happening."

Elona nodded gravely. "This is a lot to take in. You must understand, the first we heard of this Tsnath attack was from your scouts a short while ago."

At the mention of his scouts, Borádin indicated that they should get going again.

As the group began to shuffle onwards, Elona continued, "We knew the Tsnath were up to something, but we had no idea there'd been a full-scale invasion. How bad is it?"

Borádin sighed heavily. He flicked a hand at the young girl he'd been carrying earlier. She smiled timidly and came to his side. He lifted her back into her lofty seat.

"The situation is rather confused, Your Highness. Most of what we know is just rumour. But it's bad, that much I can tell you. As far as we can make out, our main army moved up from Mitcha to Taib-hédi when news of the invasion reached them. They marched straight into an ambush. The reports are that few survived."

"Ye gods," Elona groaned, shaking her head in disbelief, even though a small part of her wasn't that surprised. Kirshtahll's damming assessment of the army's effectiveness had prepared her for that. "And what of this pocket of resistance you're trying to meet up with?"

"Again, just rumours. A number of locals have told us that after its capture, the town of Mitcha was briefly snatched back from the Tsnath. The people all fled while they could, some to the surrounding villages. There were too many for them all to do that, though, and it seems the rest have accompanied their liberators into hiding up in the mountains. We think somewhere southeast of Tail-ébeth."

The mention of Torrin-Ashur's home town make Elona perk up. She suppressed the urge to ask if there was any news of Torrin-Ashur himself, allowing Borádin to continue.

"We can't get south at the moment, so short of just moving around trying to stay out of Tsnath hands, I figured we might as well try to link up with them."

"You couldn't get south – even from Vickrà-döthmore?"

"No. The Tsnath have forces guarding the Dumássay Gorge, though I suspect that's more to prevent southern reinforcements coming north than stopping refugees fleeing south."

Elona's mind was reeling from all the catastrophic news she'd heard in the past few minutes. What made it all the more devastating was that they'd been too late to prevent it. If Jorra-hin had made his discoveries a few weeks earlier, they'd have been able to warn Kirshtahll and stop him from leaving Mitcha. With the army at full strength, he'd have put a stop to the Tsnath's plans. He always had in the past.

What they were going to do now, she really didn't know. Mitcha was lost, the army was lost, the warning they carried with them was too late, and all the sacrifices they'd made had just become futile. She felt like bursting into tears. It took every ounce of her strength not to do so.

"It looks as if we'll have to join you for now," she said, avoiding Borádin's sight lest her emotions be too visible.

Borádin shrugged. "You'll have to take the rough with the smooth, I'm afraid. I have no comfort to offer you."

"I didn't come here to be pampered," Elona bristled, then immediately regretted it.

"If you'll forgive my curiosity, what *did* you come for?"

"We had some information that we were intending to give to Brigadier Jàcos. That's why we were heading for Mitcha. But it doesn't seem to matter now."

"It must have been damned important to warrant you coming in person, even if you didn't know about the invasion. The dangers of crossing the mountains alone – the passes must be nearly impossible to get through by now."

"They were," Elona confirmed. "We stopped at Jàb-áldis on the way, but even so, it was tough going."

Borádin didn't see Jorra-hin's curious frown. Elona caught it out of the corner of her eye and glanced a silent warning at him not to say anything.

A few moments later Borádin's scouts reappeared and he took his leave to hear their report.

Answering Jorra-hin's questioning stare, Elona explained, "I want to keep the existence of the mines just between the three of us for now."

"Why?" Jorra-hin whispered back.

"Because I don't want to give Borádin the option of heading south through the mountains just yet. We need him here. He's heading towards whoever liberated Mitcha, and I want to find out who that is, as well as more of what's happening up here."

"And what if they turn out to be nothing more than a bunch of refugees like these people?" Kirin asked, flicking her eyes over her shoulder.

"Well, then we'll have to tell him. But let's wait and find out before taking that decision."

11

"This is taking too long," Torrin-Ashur whispered to himself, getting more and more agitated as the minutes slipped by.

His cramped dugout was lined with faggots to insulate against the cold, but that didn't stop what little warmth he had from leaching away with alarming speed. His limbs were already going numb. A square canopy, made of birch-lath and camouflaged with snow, lay just inches above him, restricting his movement to little more than a wriggle. It was like being buried alive in an icebox.

He was more worried for the state of his archers than himself, though. They needed to be able to spring into action at the right moment. Crucially, their bowstrings needed to remain taut. They couldn't afford the attack's primary weapon to lose its bite.

Letting out a quiet huff, he tried to settle himself. It was always this way before an ambush. The waiting was a kind of torture all of its own. An overactive imagination fed him a constant stream of things that could go wrong, and it really wasn't helping that the Tsnath were taking so long to move on from their last reported position. Though he knew he could only blame himself for their lack of cooperation; his men's successes in earlier raids had put the enemy on edge.

He strained forwards to peer up through a small slit just in front of his nose. The sky was heavy with the expectation of snow. That, at least, was a comfort. When they'd first started raiding the Tsnath for supplies, to cover their tracks afterwards they had only attacked when snow was falling. The Tsnath had been quick to adjust tactics, ceasing all movement in such conditions. So now he could only risk engagements when it was likely to snow soon after. That made planning the attacks more difficult, increased the risks, and brought the need for two extra precautions. The first was that no Alondrian was to return to their main camp unless the anticipated snow materialised and covered their tracks. The last thing they could afford to do was to lead the Tsnath back to the women and children.

The second was a shade more gruesome; no Tsnath soldier could be left alive.

He wasn't comfortable being the harbinger of merciless slaughter. But there was no choice. His men simply weren't in a position to take prisoners. Nor could they afford to let so much as a single Tsnath escape to summon reinforcements.

He'd begun to realise why, in years gone by, the Tsnath had always stopped their raids over the winter months. Warfare was so much harder with snow on the ground. It was ironic how, in this age-old game of cat and mouse, the tables had so utterly turned; they warred when they should have rested, and now Alondrians were the mouse struggling under a heavy Tsnath paw.

The prize he'd been waiting for finally rolled into view. He breathed a sigh of relief. It wasn't the largest convoy they'd taken, only three carts, but it was well guarded, which meant the Tsnath considered it valuable. A squad of eight riders rode in front and a similar one brought up the rear. Each cart had two drivers.

Torrin-Ashur began to ready himself, tensing and relaxing his muscles as much as he dared without disturbing the camouflage above him.

He watched through his tiny snow slit as the forward body of riders passed a prearranged point, a small, snow-burdened bush at the side of the track. Soon after, the first of the carts rolled past. He counted the seconds away under his breath until the middle cart drew alongside, then mentally shouted, *Now.*

As though they'd heard him, two groups of archers exploded from the ground, appearing like wraiths shrouded in a cloud of scattering snow. A hail of arrows flew at the convoy, hitting it from the front and the rear. Both escorts were decimated in a single volley. A few unfelled riders panicked and fled sideways into the forest, taking an unchallenged route from the killing ground.

There was no shelter within the trees.

Torrin-Ashur shot to his feet as though his legs were coiled springs, their only purpose to catapult him skywards. His sudden appearance spooked a Tsnath horse heading straight for him. The creature reared up, throwing its rider off balance. He darted forwards and slammed his blade home with vicious force, unseating the rider and pushing him backwards off his horse. He set upon the man in an instant. The tip of his sword took the dazed soldier through the throat, severing windpipe, cleaving bone and pinning the Tsnath's paralysed body to the trunk of a pine tree. Blood guttered from the man's mouth, draining him of life. Torrin-Ashur hesitated a second, then put boot to breastplate and yanked his blade free. The Tsnath's head lolled. The rest of him remained where it was, propped against the trunk, crimson stains scarring the pure white snow around him.

Torrin-Ashur became vaguely aware of his men darting about at the periphery of his vision, finishing off engagements of their own. As he cast about, he already knew all threats had been dealt with.

The strike against the convoy had taken but a minute from start to finish. More than twenty Tsnath soldiers had just died.

Sergeant Nash waded through the snow towards him.

"We lost one of ours, sir. A Mitcha man."

"What? How? They weren't supposed to be fighting."

Nash gave a little nod. "He wasn't. He was crushed up against a tree by a panicked horse. Got himself impaled by a broken branch."

Torrin-Ashur grimaced. A sudden vision of Emmy's plight came to mind, a little girl with a wooden stake through her chest, covered in blood. Only there was no Kirin to come to the rescue.

He pulled himself together. There was no time to dwell on the loss. "Detail some of the men to sweep the area in case we missed any Tsnath." He glanced round. The *Sèliccia~Castrà* was nearly silent within him; nothing remained that posed a danger. That did not mean a wounded soldier wasn't lying somewhere waiting for his moment to slink away. "Have the rest help unload the carts."

Nash snapped off an informal salute and strode away, barking orders. Everyone moved with a purpose. None needed reminding that time became their greatest enemy immediately after an attack.

The Tsnath dead were left where they'd fallen. The dead Mitcha man was buried beneath the snow – there wasn't time to dig a real grave. Any horses that hadn't already run off were rounded up and set free; they were of little use deep in the mountains at this time of year. Someone had suggested earlier that they'd make good food, but the Mitcha people had not been keen. Clearly they didn't consider their circumstances that desperate yet.

The spoils of the raid were spirited away by a train of porters. Emptied carts were smashed to deny the enemy their use. With the last of the Mitcha men on his way, a few of the Ashurmen remained to cover their tracks, smoothing over any footprints with brushwood brooms.

Leaving the scene, Torrin-Ashur cast a backwards glance and allowed himself a satisfied nod. A light dusting of snow would be all that was needed to obliterate any trace of the route they had taken.

*

Two hundred yards away, three Tsnath trackers, under the cover of thick white cloaks, lay watching as the Alondrians made their departure. With orders not to intervene, they remained in position until the last enemy soldier was out of sight. Only then did they make their move.

Two began to track the retreating Alondrians.

The third took off in the opposite direction, expertly gliding through the trees on running skis. It took him a mere half hour to reach his destination.

He glided up to his commander scarcely out of breath.

"Sir, it's over."

Özeransk smiled at the news. The bait had been swallowed. He spared a thought for the loss of Tsnathsarré life, but didn't let that ruin the welcome feeling of anticipation the news had brought. The sacrifice would be worth it if it led to the whereabouts of the Alondrians responsible for all the raids they'd suffered recently. Having arrived from Mitcha with his reinforcements, he'd been shocked to hear of the scale of the attacks. It had become imperative to deal with this pocket of resistance, whatever the cost.

He rubbed his hands together in satisfaction and glanced at the man standing beside him. "Commander Streàck, ready the men. And get a message sent over to Minnàk – let him know we're moving out."

"Aye, sir."

The camp was galvanised into action. Özeransk was well aware that his presence kept the men on their toes. He was known as a strict commander, who expected the best from his men. Yet he was also a soldier's soldier, experienced in battle and not above enduring the same privations as those he led. For that the men respected him, and in the Tsnathsarré way of things, that had an authority all of its own.

Streàck returned to Özeransk's side. He looked up at the uniformly grey sky, pregnant with snow. "It'll be coming down in sheets soon, sir, mark my words."

Özeransk shrugged. "Doesn't matter. Our trackers will leave a trail a blind man could follow. Two days, Commander, three at the most, and we'll be rid of these pilfering Alondrians."

"Aye, sir." Streàck let out a chuckle. "Then maybe we can get the hell out of this wretched stuff." He kicked his boot at the powdery blanket surrounding his feet. "I hope this Ranadar was a rich son of a bitch. Something's got to make this trip worthwhile."

Özeransk regarded the mercenary thoughtfully for a moment, then clapped a hand on the man's back. "Beyond your wildest dreams, Commander."

He was careful not to allow his own doubts to show. As each day passed, he was becoming convinced that Daka was after something else entirely. The lure of treasure just didn't add up anymore.

However flawed the man's avaricious dreams may have been, Streàck was right about one thing; before the men had even finished breaking camp, visibility closed to a hundred yards. It was as though the gods had started throwing snowballs.

Özeransk smiled. The miserable weather played right into his hands. It would give the Alondrians a false sense of security.

*

It snowed for the remainder of the day and much of the night. Torrin-Ashur awoke from a fitful couple of hours sleep to find that the trees overhead hadn't shielded him much and another foot of powder had buried his bivouac, creating a burrow from which he didn't particularly want to emerge.

But emerge he did, albeit stiffly. He grunted at the sight of Nash making his way over, hauling himself through the drifts. No matter how early he rose, he hadn't yet managed to beat the sergeant into action first thing in the morning. A steaming mug of goat broth exchanged hands. Torrin-Ashur knew it was as near to breakfast as he would get.

"How are the rest of the men?"

"Like death warmed up, sir."

Torrin-Ashur let out a mirthless chuckle. To all intent and purpose he'd forgotten what it felt like to be warm.

As he thawed his fingers round the mug, his thoughts drifted back to his first jaunts into these very mountains. They had been great adventures full of fun and discovery.

Gods, how things had changed.

He wondered whether it would ever be possible to return to those days of innocence, to be able to look upon this majestic landscape and see it once more as a thing of awe-inspiring beauty. Presently, the

Mathians were nothing but frigid, vast and inhospitable; a place that could provide sanctuary or sudden death, with little but a god's whim between them.

After a groggy start, the men broke camp quickly. Those carrying the Tsnath supplies moved out and Torrin-Ashur had the remainder set about erasing the evidence of their stay, though he did wonder whether there was any point now. A break in the clouds served as a welcome reminder that blue sky still existed, but it also meant no more snow for a while. From here on in, they'd leave a trail, no matter how careful they were. He checked the route they'd arrived by late the night before and noted that not so much as a dimple remained in the snow to evince their footprints. They'd already put a considerable distance between themselves and the ambush site, making it nigh on impossible for the Tsnath to pick up their scent. That would just have to be enough.

It was after midday by the time they reached the vicinity of their main camp, the caves at the foot of Mount Àthái. Lying southeast of Tail-ébeth, not far from the headwaters of the River Ébeth, to Torrin-Ashur they had been an obvious place of refuge, though hopefully not so to the Tsnath, who didn't know the area like he did.

The raiding party were acknowledged by the first of the lookouts stationed some two miles short of the caves. They passed other manned positions every bowshot length all the way back to the camp. After days of practice, using arrows as carriers, a message could now be sent up the mountain in under a minute; far less time than it would take any enemy forces to cover the same distance. Short of having their own messaging crystals, it was the best early warning system they could devise.

On approach, several horses at the perimeter of the camp caught Torrin-Ashur's attention. They were bedecked in blankets and tied up under some trees. A frown creased his brow; as far as he was aware, their inventory of livestock didn't include such creatures.

Most of the Mitcha porters exchanged their burdens for food and hot drinks from waiting relatives. Torrin-Ashur watched as two of the men downed their packs and went over to a young woman anxiously searching amongst the returned party. There was a stifled cry. He cringed, desperately wanting to avoid getting involved. He was too drained to offer much comfort for the loss of a loved one.

He was saved by a shout.

"Sir," Botfiár came running over, "we've got new arrivals. And you will *not* believe who."

Torrin-Ashur was too tired to respond enthusiastically. "So tell me."

"Princess Elona, sir."

"*What!*" Fatigue vanished.

"I know, sir."

"Where is she?"

"Over with the wounded..."

Botfiár wasn't given a chance to finish his sentence. Torrin-Ashur tore off across the snow like a greyhound, leaving the corporal with a *But* poised on his lips.

He pelted up the slope towards the mouth of the cave they were using as a hospital, slipping on the compacted snow that had become something of an ice slide. He made a mental note to have someone cut steps into it. Scrambling over the rocks that lay across the cave entrance, he practically exploded into view, taking the nearest casualties by surprise.

Relief flooded through him when he saw Elona. She was facing away from him, clad in layers of furs that completely masked her lithe figure. It was her ash blond hair cascading down her back that gave her identity away. She was kneeling, comforting a wounded soldier undergoing surgery at the hands of old Cosmin. Preoccupied, she didn't turn round, so he quietly stole up behind her and waited.

When she did finally realise someone was watching her, she glanced over her shoulder. Her eyes widened. She turned back to her patient and gave his brow a quick wipe, then nodded once at Cosmin and stood up.

As she turned, Torrin-Ashur noticed the sling supporting her left arm. Something in him thumped, leaving an unsettled feeling in his stomach.

For a moment the pair of them just stood there, two feet apart, staring at each other. Her face bore the touch of the Mathian winter, her flawless skin now reddened and blotchy, her lips cracked and flaking. Yet she was still a thing of beauty.

Elona was the first to abandon her reserve. She threw Torrin-Ashur a one-armed hug, burying her face against his shoulder. A thrill coursed its way through him. It was the first time in weeks that he'd felt a glimmer of warmth.

"Dammit, you gave me a fright," he whispered in her ear.

"A fright?" She pulled away slightly and looked up into his eyes.

"Botfiár told me you were with the wounded. I feared the worst."

Elona smiled. "I'm alright." She saw him glance at the sling. "Just a cut. We ran into a small group of Tsnath the other day. I didn't get out of the way in time, that's all." There was a pause as her eyes took on a saddened look. "Torrin, I heard about Tail-ébeth. I'm truly, truly sorry."

Pain crossed Torrin-Ashur's face. He nodded solemnly and quickly changed the subject. "What in the name of the gods are you doing here?"

Elona sighed. "That's a long story. To tell it, we'll need Jorra-hin."

"You dragged Jorra up here, too?"

"It was more the other way around. I've also bumped into another of your old acquaintances."

"Oh?"

"Lord Borádin."

"Borádin!" Torrin-Ashur's reaction was loud and drew attention from all quarters of the cave. "What's *he* doing here?"

"Trust me, a lot has changed. You'll barely recognise him. He saved my life when we ran into the Tsnath, so you might consider giving him a second chance."

Torrin-Ashur's mouth opened and closed a couple of times as his brain fought for something to say. The idea of Borádin being anything other than a foppish dandy wasn't one his mind could cope with at short notice.

Elona hastily arranged for one of the Mitcha women to take over assisting Cosmin, then led Torrin-Ashur out of the cave. She slid her way down the icy path outside, emitting a gleeful squeal. Clearly it wasn't the first time she'd taken flight. Maybe having someone cut steps wasn't such a good idea after all, Torrin-Ashur mused.

He spotted Botfiár waiting at the bottom of the slope.

"Corporal, I'm told Brother Jorra-hin is here. Please find him and bring him to the War Chamber."

The corporal saluted and hurried away, leaving Elona with a bemused smile on her lips. "War Chamber?"

Torrin-Ashur shrugged. "Well – we had to call the caves something. It got very tiresome referring to them as, 'the one at the end', 'the second from the right', 'the big one in the middle'."

The big one in the middle had become the main accommodation area. Early on, someone had facetiously called it Little Mitcha. The name had stuck. The War Chamber was beside it, on the left. It was a rather grandiose title for what was little more than a fifty-foot deep crevice with an entrance that let all the heat out, despite attempts to build a snow wall to limit the relative size of its opening. But it was the smallest and least useful of the caves, so it served as a place for administration and planning.

The fighting men had laid claim to the leftmost cave, which had summarily become the Barracks. The Hospital was to the right of Little Mitcha, which just left the stores, affectionately known as Ranadar's Treasure, since right now the food it contained was worth more than gold.

They found Borádin in the War Chamber. Torrin-Ashur was shocked to see the state the man was in. He looked haggard. His beard, so fashionably trimmed before, was now ragged. His hair was unkempt. As for his attire, it was a mishmash of furs and dented armour that had been gleaned from many different sources. The contrast between this vision and the immaculately presented one Torrin-Ashur had faced on the Forum at Mitcha was hard to comprehend. Elona was right; he was barely recognisable. Except for the shield he was holding before him.

"You've put a few more dents in this thing since I last saw it," Borádin observed, placing the shield back where he'd found it.

"It has served me well," Torrin-Ashur replied, regarding Borádin cautiously, not quite knowing how to deal with the man.

After an awkward interlude, Borádin cleared his throat. "I appreciate, my lord, that this is a rather difficult situation, given our last encounter. But I trust you'll accept that being thrust into war can change a man." He stepped over and reached forwards. "Perhaps we can let bygones be bygones?"

Torrin-Ashur hesitated a moment before taking Borádin's hand. It had not escape his notice that the nobleman had just acknowledged his title. There was genuine firmness in his shake, too, not the limp insincerity of someone just going through the motions.

"So tell me, how did you manage to find us?" Torrin-Ashur asked.

"You seem to have left a mark on the people of these parts." Borádin took a seat on a rock. Torrin-Ashur and Elona found similar perches. "As I explained to Her Highness…"

"Just Elona."

The nobleman acquiesced to Elona with a nod. Torrin-Ashur raised an eyebrow at her but said nothing to interrupt.

"After Mitcha, I ended up stationed at Halam-Gräth. At the

outbreak of hostilities I was sent north towards the border. We had no idea we were facing a full-scale invasion at the time, but it wasn't long before we started to hear about our army's defeat at Taib-hédi. In light of that, I decided there was no point trying to meet the Tsnath head on, so I proceeded south. I'm no coward, but nor do I relish the idea of throwing my life away. Besides, I'd managed to collect an assortment of refugees and survivors, and I had them to think about."

"So how is it you're still up here in the Territories?"

"The Tsnath have occupied the Dumássay Gorge." Borádin's reply was blunt.

Torrin-Ashur's eyes widened in shock. Though, with hindsight, Borádin's news probably shouldn't have been that surprising, he realised. Little information about how the invasion had affected the other parts of the Northern Territories had reached him, but judging from the total whitewash the Tsnath had inflicted on Mitcha and the March of Ashur, it stood to reason the rest of the region had suffered similarly. "So there was no way south?"

"No, and I have to confess, after discovering that, I was at something of a loss," Borádin said. "Then I began to hear rumours of the liberation of Mitcha. That offered a glimmer of hope that some of our forces were still intact."

"You seem to be becoming something of a legend, Torrin," Elona teased, elbowing him in the ribs.

"Not intentionally."

"Well," Borádin continued, relieving Torrin-Ashur of his moment of embarrassment, "be that as it may, I kept coming across people who had heard of what you'd done. At first I thought it was your father they were talking about – they were attributing the action to *Lord* Ashur. At the time I knew nothing of Tail-ébeth's fate."

Borádin didn't voice sorrow, but there was sympathy in his eyes. Once more the reminder of the horrors of his home town's fate stabbed at Torrin-Ashur's heart. He attempted to remain impassive, but doubted he could entirely hide his emotions. In some ways he wished he could wash the name of Tail-ébeth from everyone's memory, most especially his own, so that it would never again be mentioned.

"So you decided to head this way," he concluded, attempting to deflect the conversation away from so painful a subject. "I assume, then, that somewhere between the Dumássay Gorge and the March of Ashur you ran into the princess?" He switched his focus to Elona and raised an eyebrow. "Perhaps now would be a good time for you to explain what you're doing this side of the Mathians."

As if he'd been waiting for his cue, Botfiár delivered Jorra-hin at that moment. Kirin and Nash followed him in. Torrin-Ashur rose and greeted his friend with a shoulder to shoulder bump. He bestowed on Kirin a warm smile, touching his chest and extending his hand forwards in the customary Nicián greeting. She reciprocated.

Nash couldn't help frowning as he delivered a salute to Borádin. "Well, this day's getting stranger and stranger," he muttered under his breath. He moved to stand behind Torrin-Ashur.

"Found anything yet?" Elona enquired of Jorra-hin when the greetings were over and the newcomers had found a place to sit.

Jorra-hin shook his head. "I've left young Paulus in charge of his friends doing the searching. He'll come and tell us if they find anything."

Torrin-Ashur flashed a confused glance at Elona.

Ignoring his unspoken question, she took a deep breath and launched into an account of everything that had happened since Torrin-Ashur had left Alondris several months earlier.

He was thunderstruck when she related what she'd done to rescue Jorra-hin. "So you're an outlaw now?"

Elona made a moue.

"And you," he eyed Jorra-hin, "a Natural mage?"

The young monk huffed. "I was framed for Nÿat's murder. That does not make me a mage."

Elona exchanged glances with Kirin before continuing with her account. As the details of the flight from Alondris, the journey up to Jàb-áldis and the attack on the monastery by Daka's men came pouring out, Torrin-Ashur's jaw sagged lower and lower. Borádin seemed equally stunned. Elona had obviously withheld many details from the nobleman until now.

Jorra-hin took over the story at the point where they'd escaped Jàb-áldis, explaining the significance of the Vessel, the Vicar stones, and what the *Dànis~Lutárn* really was, recounting how it had been used to trap the Dendricá and how the mages of the day had tried to cover up their iniquitous deeds by sealing the Old Homeland. For Torrin-Ashur, it was a lot to take in all at once.

The ramifications of being able to access the passages through the Mathians did not escape him, though. Aside from explaining how Elona had managed to accomplish the journey up from the south at this time of year, the long-term strategic advantage was immense. "So much for Ranadar and the Dwarves," he muttered. "So much for the treasure, too."

Jorra-hin grunted in agreement. "Daka was never in this for the treasure. It's the power of the *Dànis~Lutárn* she's after." His tone ensured that that gravity of his conclusion was understood by all present.

"But for what?" Torrin-Ashur asked. "I understand the *Dànis~Lutárn* is controlled by the Vicar stones, and its purpose can be altered by changing the spells inscribed on them. And I accept that Daka is probably aiming to bend the *Dànis~Lutárn* to her will. But what can she actually achieve with it?"

"It's the most powerful Taümathic entity ever created, Torrin. She could do almost anything with it. She could turn it into a weapon to use against us."

"Us?"

"Well, whatever forces Alondria musters against her," Jorra-hin clarified. "She could use it to repel any army sent up to dislodge her from the Territories. The name *Dànis~Lutárn* more or less means *Great Divide*. It conveys the idea of a barrier, a great fence, if you will. Though it was initially configured to stop the *Sèliccia~Castrà* from passing through it, that wasn't its ultimate purpose. Its creators simply tried to use it to remove the *Sèliccia~Castrà* from the Dendricá first, after which the *Dànis~Lutárn* was going to be deployed somehow to protect the Dendricá's lands. The Dendricá leader, Márcucious, wrote of a hope that the *Sentinels of River* would protect them forever after his death. I am presuming that the *Dànis~Lutárn* was intended to defend the Dendricá so that they wouldn't need the *Sèliccia~Castrà* anymore."

A frown crossed Nash's face. "Sir, do you remember the day we first met Kassandra?"

"How could I forget?" Torrin-Ashur scoffed, patting his arm and wincing at the memory of wading out into the Ablath and the arrow wound he'd received for his troubles.

"Well, sir, just before that, remember we made our way along the river looking for evidence of Tsnath activity? We came across that strange tower in the middle of the river..."

Torrin-Ashur's eyebrows rose. He snapped his fingers as the memory popped into mind. "The Sentinel."

Jorra-hin's concentration narrowed. "You know what these

sentinels are?"

"Possibly," Torrin-Ashur replied slowly, making it clear he wasn't certain. "There are six stone towers sitting in the middle of the River Ablath, at various points along it. These days no one seems to know what they're for, or who built them. But people have always called them Sentinels."

"Interesting," Jorra-hin murmured, looking as though he was reading some invisible text at his feet. "Six towers, six Vicar stones. A coincidence? Too much so, methinks. Perhaps each tower was meant to house one of the stones, maybe as a way of controlling the *Dànis~Lutárn.*"

"It was to be set up as a defence along the Ablath?" Torrin-Ashur challenged, his eyes bulging at the enormity of such an undertaking.

Jorra-hin nodded.

"It's powerful enough to do that? The border is six hundred miles long!"

"Now you begin to understand the terrifying nature of what the mages had created. Mage Yazcöp was fearful of it with good reason."

Torrin-Ashur whistled softly. It was hard to conceive of anything *that* powerful, outside of calling on the gods.

Nash tentatively cleared his throat. "Another question..." he proffered, this time directing his gaze at Jorra-hin. "Why were the mages so intent on depriving the Dendricá of the *Sèliccia~Castrà* that they'd risk making something even more dangerous?"

Torrin-Ashur nodded. It was a good question. Not least because he and a fair number of his men were now empowered by the ancient magic. If there was something so terrible about it, now would be the time to know it.

Jorra-hin shrugged. "The mages felt it had simply become too powerful. They didn't like the idea that something their predecessors had created had gone beyond their control."

"Out of the frying pan, into the fire," Kirin murmured.

Jorra-hin nodded.

After a pause to let matters sink in, Borádin asked, "Clearly this is a grave matter. But without wishing to sound the harbinger of doom, what are we supposed to do about it? Even with my men and yours combined," he glanced at Torrin-Ashur, "and all the rest we've picked up between us, we'd still be lucky to push two hundred soldiers fit to fight. The Tsnath have already wiped out twenty times that number."

"Kirshtahll will come," Elona insisted.

"Assuming he gets the message we've sent," Jorra-hin said.

"He'll get it. Pomaltheus may moan a lot, but he's not one for giving up." Kirin sounded quite convinced. "As for Seth, he's the most determined person I've ever met – besides you." She flashed Jorra-hin a smile.

"But even if Kirshtahll realises he can come north through the mines, he still has to be free to do so. What if he's engaged with the Nmemians? For all we know he could be in the middle of a war of his own right now." Torrin-Ashur didn't mask his exasperation at the mounting odds against Kirshtahll being able to help. "How long do we have? How much time does Daka need to change what the *Dànis~Lutárn* does?"

"I don't know." Jorra-hin gave a helpless shrug and shoved his hands up the sleeves of his cassock to keep them warm. He shivered. "A few days maybe. It depends who's helping her and how much preparation has already been carried out. They could have new controlling spells ready, in which case all they really have to do is apply them to the menhir."

Torrin-Ashur shook his head. It was getting worse. "We don't even know if Daka has managed to gather the remaining menhir yet. If she has, it may already be too late. Even if he could set off immediately, it will still take Kirshtahll time to get his troops up here."

Borádin sighed in dismay. "Then whatever is going to be done, it's down to us to do it. I don't know about you, but this isn't painting me a rosy picture. I mean, gods, we don't even know where the baroness is."

"Maybe not," Jorra-hin countered, "but there might be a way of pinning her down." All eyes held him with stares that demanded an explanation. "We do know of one place she has to go for her plan to succeed."

"Üzsspeck," Kirin supplied, answering frowns from the others. "That's where the *Dànis~Lutárn* is now. She must go there to retrieve it."

"That's where she's most vulnerable, too."

"How so?" Torrin-Ashur could not see the strategic connection in Jorra-hin's logic.

"It's the one place that having us heavily outnumbered won't give her such a massive advantage."

Torrin-Ashur gave the idea of tackling Daka in Üzsspeck some thought, but just kept hitting obstacles.

Borádin was clearly thinking along the same lines. "We've still only got two hundred men. In a pitched battle, we would be annihilated. Amongst city streets, maybe things would be different. But from your descriptions, Üzsspeck is a large place. Daka could still have us significantly outnumbered."

"But would she?" Jorra-hin challenged. "Think about it, my lord. She has no idea we know what her plan is. She has no idea we know anything about Üzsspeck, or that she must go there. She's probably marching towards the Trombéi entrance as we speak. But why would she feel the need to take a large fighting force with her into the mines themselves? She's not aware she has anything to fear *inside* the Old Homeland, other than her own men."

"Huh?" Elona murmured, her forehead wrinkling.

Jorra-hin chuckled. "From what Kassandra told us, clearly the baroness is not a trusting soul. She had those three scribes murdered, just for knowing a little about her plan. What she's after is a secret to be shared only with her most loyal men. Until she can wield the power of the *Dànis~Lutárn*, she is still vulnerable to betrayal. Trust me, she will take as few troops into the Old Homeland as she thinks she can get away with."

A pensive look began to cross Torrin-Ashur's face. But, unless he'd missed something along the way, even if the field had been levelled somewhat in terms of troop numbers, there was still one very large obstacle standing in the way of any plan they might conjure up.

"Just one problem. The only entrance that we know of is this one in the Pass of Trombéi, the one you and Elona emerged from. Which not only happens to be nearly a week's hard march away, but will also have Tsnath crawling all over it by now. So just how are we supposed to even get to Üzsspeck?"

"We're sitting under Mount Àthái, are we not?" Jorra-hin replied. He added an impish smirk and proceeded to rummage in his satchel. He pulled out several copper sheets bound together at the edges and unfurled them with great reverence. "This map shows every tunnel in the Old Homeland. We used it to navigate our way from Üzsspeck to the Trombéi entrance. Now, if you look here," he pointed, "you'll see there's an entrance called *Niliàthái*. In Old Dwarvish, *nili* means beneath or under."

"Beneath Àthái." The light dawned on Torrin-Ashur. "You mean there's an actual mine entrance right here?" His rising excitement was tempered with doubt as he glanced at the rocks surrounding them.

"Somewhere in one of these caves, yes."

Torrin-Ashur clicked his fingers. "That's what you've got young Paulus and his friends looking for, isn't it?"

Jorra-hin nodded. His smirk widened into a grin.

12

Dawn's first light was still hours away from lifting the horizon out of obscurity when the huge gates in the Great West Wall were cracked open. Two men poured oil over the hinges in an attempt to prevent them from squealing. Even so, given their size, some noise was inevitable.

Kirshtahll held his breath. The bulk of the Nmemian army was known to be a fair distance away and unlikely to hear or see any activity at the wall itself, but there was no telling what forward units might be patrolling closer to hand, perhaps within earshot.

The last thing he could afford was for the Nmemians to get wind of what was happening while his forces were divided. Being caught with half his army still on the wrong side of the wall might tempt them to take advantage of the situation. The only way for his plan to succeed was for the Nmemians to be caught in total surprise by a fully assembled Alondrian army standing on their turf. Until then, stealth was paramount.

"Gentlemen, mount up," he ordered quietly.

His commanders saluted and disappeared into the darkness to join their men, leaving him to mount his destrier. He glanced down at the Governor of Colòtt.

"Are you a praying man, Rakmar?"

"I was thinking of becoming one, General."

Kirshtahll gave him a thin smile, though it was probably invisible in the pre-dawn murk. "Now would be a good time. The odd god on our side wouldn't go amiss."

"I'll mention it. May fate smile upon you."

Kirshtahll reached down and clasped the governor, forearm to forearm. "Upon us all. If this goes wrong, we're going to be in the biggest battle since the Kilópeé War."

Rakmar retreated out of the way, heading up the nearest flight of steps to the parapet of the wall.

The army began to move out. Row after row of cavalrymen led the way through the gate first. As each phalanx cleared the wall they peeled off left and right in alternate succession, spreading out into a long line, the full extent of which wouldn't be evident until the sun graced the day.

Since Kirshtahll's arrival from the Northern Territories with a shade less than eight hundred cavalry, every horse in the March of Colòtt had been pressed into service, boosting their numbers to nearly twelve hundred. That would look impressive from a distance, but only with the destriers and coursers at the front, masking the rounceys and sumpters that made up the rest. He knew that if the latter were called into action, a very different picture would emerge. Many of the extra riders were not even trained horsemen; most were farmhands. If they had to charge, a good portion of them would be unseated before they even reached enemy lines. The rest would likely meet the unfriendly end of a pike within yards of the forward Nmemian ranks.

As his infantry began marching past, Kirshtahll was acutely aware that even their number was misleading. Despite entering enemy territory, half of them weren't armed. Fewer still had any armour to speak of. And yet he was asking them to face a foe that not only bristled with weaponry, but was well trained, well disciplined, and outnumbered them more than two to one. If battle was joined, they would be slaughtered in their hundreds.

"Gods, smile upon us," he let loose in a whisper. He'd become something of a religious man himself in the last day or so. His faith, usually not much more than tepid, was the only thing still holding him together at this point. The gambit of his life was about to be played out, a stratagem that would either be the greatest military bluff or worst military blunder in Alondrian history. His one consolation was that if it all went south, he wouldn't be around to suffer the consequences. His men had a right to expect him to be at the front, leading the charge. And that's exactly where he intended to be. The chances of survival were non-existent.

It was a course born of desperation, the wisdom of which he couldn't help but question. Yet now was not the time for doubts, he chided himself. Courage and conviction were the order of the day.

The last of the infantry, the Colòtt militia, filed past in the twilight. Rakmar's son, Timerra, led them through the wall. It was fitting that he should be the one to guard the gate to his father's lands.

With his entire straw army finally in Nmemia, albeit only by a matter of yards, Kirshtahll spurred his mount into a trot and passed through the wall to join them. The gates were closed behind him, with little regard for stealth. There was a certain finality to the clunk of bolts and crossbars being rammed home. Up to that point it had seemed possible to call off the whole ludicrous operation. Now the gates were shut, it somehow felt too late.

The wait for dawn was the longest hour of Kirshtahll's life. When the sun's first rays gradually chased the stars from the sky, they revealed a cold mist lingering across a frost-encrusted landscape. He wondered whether to take advantage of the ethereal cover to move his troops forwards a little, away from the wall. In the end he decided against it; there was a risk that a lack of crisp control might afford the Nmemians a hint of inexperience on the part of their adversaries.

Movement suddenly caught his attention. A Nmemian cavalry unit came cantering over the brow of the hill on the left flank. It was just a patrol. Their surprise was absolute. The speed with which they reined in their mounts and skidded to a halt was almost comical.

"Well, that's wiped the grin off their faces," Kirshtahll muttered.

Another long hour followed, this one filled with frenetic activity on the Nmemians' part as they mobilised their army. A ridge shielded them from view, but Kirshtahll knew the sound of a bugler marshalling troops when he heard one. Things only really started to get interesting when they began bringing their men forwards.

Nmemian tactics seemed to have changed little in the thirty years since he had last faced them, he noted. There was still much strutting about and posturing, demonstrations of their commander's ability to manoeuvre his forces back and forth across the battlefield. Sometimes a regiment would advance to taunt their enemy, only to fall back again when it became clear the bait wasn't being taken. Kirshtahll had impressed upon his commanders several times that under no circumstances were they to react to the Nmemians. The only chance of his plan succeeding was for the enemy to believe that iron discipline was responsible for holding them in check, not the terror that doubtless rooted many of them to the spot.

As time dragged on, Kirshtahll realised he was feeling calmer now than had been the case earlier. It was born of there being no more decisions to take. All the debates about whether to proceed or not were past. He was fully committed, for better or for worse. And while the outcome of the day was still very much shrouded in the minds of the gods, he took comfort from the fact that he knew his duty, and would pursue it to his last breath. There was peace in knowing he had done all he could.

The fly in the ointment of his mood was his growing impatience. That, and the pins and needles in his backside. He'd been in the saddle for hours. It was possible his horse had gone to sleep, too. He dismounted and stomped around, getting blood to flow back where it was needed. A droll thought crossed his mind; he *and* his mount were getting too old for this sort of nonsense.

The nonsense took a turn while he was momentarily facing away from the Nmemians.

"Sir," one of his commanders uttered, gesturing forwards.

Kirshtahll turned. Two Nmemian soldiers were venturing out from their lines. Between them they carried a wooden table. Another soldier emerged carrying a chair. Two more followed, drapes of cloth hanging between them from poles that they supported over their shoulders.

"Finally," Kirshtahll declared. He didn't remount, but stood holding his horse's reins in one hand, his other stroking its nose as he watched this turn of events.

The table was placed exactly half way between the two opposing armies. The lay of the land was such that this meant it was in a slight dip, in full view of all the men assembled on both sides of the shallow valley lying between them. The chair was placed on the Nmemian side of the table, and a cloth pavilion with no front or rear walls was erected above it.

The soldiers withdrew to their lines, from which four other figures then emerged. These, Kirshtahll was sure, would be the Nmemians' overall commander and his three chosen lieutenants. They began making their way down to the pavilion.

"Lord Huron, Lord Ruther, Lord Saldir, with me," Kirshtahll ordered.

The three commanders immediately dismounted. They were about to advance when Kirshtahll stalled. He turned and caught sight of Timerra.

"Lieutenant, I might need a runner. Join us."

Timerra's eyes widened, but he dismounted without hesitation.

It was only a few hundred yards to where the Nmemians had pitched their invitation to parley, yet it seemed a very long walk indeed. So much depended on the next few minutes that Kirshtahll felt his mouth going dry.

The Nmemian commander was ensconced behind the table by the time Kirshtahll's party reached the pavilion. His immediate subordinates stood behind him. He made no attempt to stand as the Alondrians entered.

"I am Commissar Rolarn," he announced without preamble.

"And I suspect you already know who I am," Kirshtahll responded bluntly.

Rolarn's eyes squinted for a second. "Yes, General, I do." He paused for a moment, then declared, "You have an act of war committed by bringing into my country your army."

Kirshtahll raised his eyebrows, feigning surprise. "Have I?"

"I insist immediately that you withdraw. One hour will I give you."

"That's very generous of you. And then what?"

Rolarn's eyes bulged. The taunt was not lost on him. "I shall unleash my army. Any of you that remain on our soils will be crushed."

Kirshtahll nodded. "Then we have nothing more to discuss. I shall see you in one hour." He turned to his flanking officers. "My lords, shall we..."

They made to leave. At the last second Rolarn called out, "Wait."

Kirshtahll turned to face the commissar again, deliberately staring into his eyes. It clearly made the man feel uncomfortable.

"Why have you come?" the Nmemian demanded.

"To settle matters."

"And what possibly can you hope to achieve?" Rolarn snorted derisively. "You are outnumbered greatly."

Kirshtahll allowed a sardonic smile to touch his lips. "Commissar, you are forgetting your history. I fought in the Kilópeé War. We were told a similar thing back then, too. You might want to consider how that conflict turned out."

While Kirshtahll somehow managed to maintain his composure, the Nmemian commander began to look less confident of his position. His discomfort turned to indignation.

"Always you Alondrians are so arrogant," he spat. "You think you can be here and order me around on my own soils?"

"Commissar, I have been ordered here to resolve the threat you pose to Alondria's western border. Resolve it I shall. Quickly. I have no more time to waste. The Tsnathsarré have invaded the north of my country and I'm urgently needed elsewhere. But as long as your forces pose a threat, I must be here. So let's get it over with and then those of us left standing can go home and get on with more important things."

Shock registered on Rolarn's face. Events were obviously not transpiring in the way he'd been led to believe they would. But the Nmemians were known for nothing if not for their pride. That he was deliberately being left with little room in which to manoeuvre was probably baffling the man.

Kirshtahll turned to go, gathering his officers with him. He paused briefly at the pavilion entrance. "Until one hour, then..."

The Nmemian leaders wasted no time returning to their lines. Nor did they dally removing the pavilion and its erstwhile furniture. Before Kirshtahll had made it back to his horse, it was as though the meeting had never taken place.

"Excuse me, sir," Timerra spoke up nervously as they arrived back at their lines, "but does this mean we're actually going to have to fight them now?"

"Does that worry you, Lieutenant?"

The young lad answered with a dry swallow. Kirshtahll glanced back over his shoulder at the Nmemians. "You're not alone. It's all down to you now."

"Me?"

Timerra went as white as a sheet, no doubt beset by sudden visions of leading the forlorn hope, the first to sally forth and take on the Nmemians. Kirshtahll hadn't meant it like that and quickly divested the young man of any such illusions. "I meant, it's down to the fruits of your recent foray into enemy territory."

A little colour returned to Timerra's cheeks.

The Nmemians began preparations in earnest, dispensing with their posturing. Their display of prowess had not deterred their enemy, as they'd no doubt hoped it would.

Kirshtahll walked up and down his line, speaking with his commanders and encouraging the men. His mere presence and confident air inspired them, that much could be seen in their responses. Yet all he could think of was how different it would be if they were privy to his thoughts.

The hour Rolarn had prescribed was the fastest of the day so far. Its end came and went. Still the Nmemians remained in their formations. The tense standoff started to drag on interminably, each passing minute lasting an age. Kirshtahll began to wonder what they were up to. A failure to attack now would be a terrible loss of face for Rolarn, something for which his Nmemian pride would never stand.

After a further half hour the Nmemians finally brought their archers to the fore. The prelude to action. Kirshtahll ordered the braziers lit for his own archers to flame their arrows.

With a sinking heart, he realised his bluff had been called.

He beckoned for his horse to be brought forwards and he mounted up. He adjusted his shield on his forearm and drew his sword. It had been a long time since he'd had to do this, but a warrior never really forgets how to go into battle. Experience took over, his actions driven more by instinct than conscious thought. That left room for other things. Regrets, mostly. He thought of his wife, his lovely Karina. Her silvered hair, braided into a crown in her favourite style, filled his vision, as did the familiar lines on her face, etched there by her humour. Never again would he make her smile. The last thing he would give her would be tears.

The Nmemian archers readied their bows. Arrows were nocked. Stances were taken. Breaths gulped. And then held.

A small troop of horsemen suddenly burst into view on the right hand side of the field. They galloped down the line in front of the foremost Nmemian ranks. Though only eight riders, moving very fast, they caused a faltering in what had appeared to be the inevitable slide towards engagement.

Four of the horsemen held standards aloft, the colours of high nobility streaming out behind them in the wind. It was too far distant for Kirshtahll to make out the detail from across the battlefield, though even if he been able to distinguish them, his knowledge of Nmemian heraldry was too rusty for that to have enlightened him as to who had just arrived.

The troop rode straight up to the senior Nmemian officers, almost running them down as they brought their horses to a very abrupt halt. They dismounted immediately. There ensued a confrontation, evident to Kirshtahll only through much animated gesticulation. Moments later an order visibly rippled along the Nmemian lines and their archers stood down.

Kirshtahll decided he might risk breathing again.

After what seemed like a lot of dithering, the table and pavilion sallied forth to the same spot as before. This time, however, two chairs were brought out, one placed either side of the table. When the preparations for parley were complete, only one man, one of the recent arrivals, walked forwards.

Kirshtahll decided to reciprocate and dismounted, handing his shield to a waiting footman. He unbuckled his sword belt and handed that over too.

It felt odd holding the attention of some fifteen thousand soldiers spread across both sides of the field, every one of them no doubt wondering what in the name of the gods was going on. Were they taking part in a war, or a parade?

It was a question Kirshtahll had been asking himself ever since this Nmemian fiasco had flared up.

When he entered the pavilion he discovered that the Nmemian who had come to parley with him had not seated himself, but stood waiting. In front of him, on the table, was a small rectangular box covered with a cloth.

"General Kirshtahll, I presume?"

"Indeed."

The Nmemian nodded in acknowledgement. "I am Prince Kassem."

Kirshtahll had no need to hide his surprise. The manner of the man's dress had already suggested he was going to be dealing with someone of the highest status. Kassem wore robes very much traditional of his people's nomadic past, in his case of a cloth almost white in colour. There was a splash of indigo defining the edges where the garment overlapped, itself stitched with gold thread. Despite the manner of his arrival on horseback, he was immaculate. His beard was neatly trimmed, partially masking thin lips which seemed to wear a smile with ease.

Kirshtahll bowed in respect. "Your Highness."

"Shall we..." Kassem waved a hand to the seats that had been provided and the two of them took their places.

"No Rolarn?"

"Commissar Rolarn is no longer in command."

"I see." Kirshtahll made no attempt to hide his curiosity.

"General, if I may say so, you have played a most dangerous gambit here today. Had I been delayed even just a few minutes more, I suspect my intervention would have come to naught."

"It was a most timely arrival, Your Highness, I must admit. But I have had little choice in these matters."

"Be that as it may, I must now ask you to withdraw your men from my country."

"I can only do that if I can be sure there is no longer a threat to Alondria."

Kassem nodded gently. "I understand your position, General. But in turn you must understand mine. We are Nmemians, and even if I say it myself, the greatest thorn in our side is our pride. A prince I may be, but even I cannot order our forces to disperse while a foreign army occupies our land. Surely you can see that?"

"And if I do withdraw, what then? What guarantees do I have?"

"Guarantees, General?" Kassem harrumphed good-naturedly. "Do you honestly believe either of us are in a position to demand guarantees?"

Kirshtahll smiled. "No, perhaps not."

"Please understand, I know why you are here. You must believe me when I tell you that it came as a shock to us to hear what was happening. I am truly sorry that any of my countrymen have caused you to be diverted from your duty in your Northern Territories. I give you my word that if you withdraw, then I will see to it that our forces do the same in a day or so. It cannot be sooner. The appearance of us running away with our tail between our legs must be avoided, no?"

Kirshtahll didn't respond immediately, but contented himself with looking Kassem squarely in the eye. What he saw there was enough.

"Your word suffices, Your Highness. We will withdraw."

Kassem sighed with great relief and sat back in his chair. "Thank you, General."

Kirshtahll smiled, his own relief just as evident. "May I ask you a question?"

"Please do."

"This whole business has been a mystery to me from the start. What have your people been offered in order to create this diversion?"

"Once Gal Ibissam informed us of what was going on, I had enquiries made on the matter. As you may know, the Tsnathsarré cause us problems with our trade across the Great Inland Mäss. Our navy is not yet sufficient to protect all our merchant shipping. In return for distracting you from the north, the Tsnathsarré offered us unrestricted access."

"A lucrative deal to some, no doubt."

"To my whole country, in fact."

"A deal that you are prepared to forgo?"

Kassem grunted. "The Tsnathsarré do not border us – you do. I have argued that it will be to our greater advantage for us to foster better relations with Alondria than with the Tsnathsarré Empire. We will just have to build a bigger navy."

Kirshtahll smiled again. "Thank you, Your Highness."

"You are welcome. Oh, by the way, Gal Ibissam requested me to return this to you." Kassem slipped the cloth off the box on the table in front of him. It came as no surprise to Kirshtahll to see a wooden case sporting brass corners and catches, with intricate marquetry inlaid on the lid. "He said that a gift is a gift, even if it has to be given twice."

Kirshtahll chuckled. "I sincerely hope there will be no need for a third time."

Kassem rose from his seat. "It has been a pleasure meeting you, General. I trust that if we meet again, it will be under less trying circumstances."

"Let us hope so."

Kirshtahll picked up the dagger case, tucked it under his arm and then saluted Kassem. He made to leave, but he faltered and turned back to face the Nmemian prince.

"Your Highness, if I may say so, when the day of your accession comes, Nmemia will truly have herself a worthy king."

Kassem bowed at the compliment. Both men knew Nmemia and Alondria were parting on what was possibly firmer footing than had existed for years.

Sheer relief lent Kirshtahll a lightness of step that made him nearly run back up the rise to his awaiting army. He had to make a very conscious effort not to look like he was fleeing back to his own lines like a coward. But to his own troops he couldn't hide his smile.

When he came within earshot of the Great West Wall, he called up to an anxiously waiting governor.

"Rakmar, be so kind as to have someone open the gate."

Rakmar slapped his hand on top of the parapet. "No," he shot back, and then laughed. "I'll damned well do it myself!"

Kirshtahll remained in front of the gate as each and every man in his army marched or rode his way back into Alondria. The relief on their faces was a sight to behold. They'd not had to fight, and there would be no tales of great heroism regaled to grandchildren, but every one of them had earned their general's respect this day. In the face of overwhelming odds, many ill equipped and untrained, they'd done everything he'd asked of them. And by so doing, they'd won. Admittedly, a strange victory, but a victory nonetheless.

Kirshtahll was the very last man to return through the wall. As some of the men moved to shut the gates, he intervened. "No. Leave them open."

Rakmar came over and pumped his hand. "Well done, sir. Very

well done indeed."

"Must have been all those prayers you offered."

"Oh yes, there were a few, I can assure you." Rakmar paused and frowned at the gates. "We are leaving them open?"

Kirshtahll glanced back across the battlefield that so nearly was. Just as his army had dispersed, so too had most of the Nmemians. Though there was still some activity where Prince Kassem sat, surrounded by various other figures. "I hope you don't mind, Rakmar. It's a show of good faith."

He spotted Timerra not far away, directing his militia back to Lamàst. "Lieutenant."

Timerra trotted over.

"I'd like you to have this." Kirshtahll handed him the dagger case that he'd had tucked under his arm all this time.

"Sir?"

"You've earned it. Your bravery last week in contacting Gal Ibissam for me was instrumental in averting a war." He turned to the governor. "You should be proud of your son, Rakmar."

The governor clapped a hand on Timerra's shoulder. "I am, Padráig, I am."

*

Kirshtahll decided to allow the men to enjoy some festivities that evening, though he didn't join in himself. His mind had already turned to the next problem at hand; how to get his troops back to the Northern Territories where they were urgently needed. He was sat in the governor's private chambers discussing the matter when there was a knock at the door.

"Come," Rakmar ordered.

A rather flustered-looking lad from the Message Corps stepped into the chamber. He glanced from general to governor and back again, possibly wondering to whom he was supposed to deliver his message. He went for the military option.

Kirshtahll scanned the transcript, registering abject disbelief as he did so. Such was his surprise that he choked on his drink.

"What is it, Padráig?" Rakmar demanded in alarm.

"See for yourself." Kirshtahll held out the slip of paper.

Rakmar's jaw fell open. "You've been relieved of command?" He shook his head, flabbergasted. He reread the message. "Because of your recklessness? Ye gods, are they mad? What are they thinking back in Alondris?"

"Thinking? Now you're making assumptions, my friend."

"But Padráig, this is madness."

"Indeed it is."

Rakmar's brow became deeply furrowed. "But you don't seem to be that bothered by the order?"

"That's because I'm going to ignore it." Kirshtahll turned his attention to the corpsman. "What's your name, son?"

"Tork, sir."

"Well, Corpsman Tork, I need you to do your country a very great service."

Tork swallowed nervously.

"Besides yourself, who else knows about this message?"

"Just me, sir. I'm the only one on duty. Everyone else is celebrating, sir."

"You took the message down yourself?"

Tork nodded.

"Good. That makes things easier. So first, let me ask you a question. Do you think I deserve to be relieved of command?"

Kirshtahll knew it was a particularly unfair question. The poor lad didn't know where to look.

"He doesn't," Rakmar prompted, as though to help the lad out.

"Listen, Tork, I'm going to confide in you something that very few people know," Kirshtahll went on. "There is a conspiracy rife amongst some of our nobles. They believe that Alondria would be better off without the burden of the Northern Territories. Do you believe Alondria would be better off without that burden, Tork?"

Tork's glance bounced between the floor, the general, the governor, and the floor again. "N-no, sir."

Whether the lad had spoken from the heart or had just given the answer he thought he was expected to give didn't really matter. "Neither do I," Kirshtahll said. "In fact, I've spent the greater part of my military career dedicated to the protection of the Territories. But do you know what's happening up there right now?"

The corpsman gave a tentative nod. Rumours had been circulating for days. As part of the Message Corps, Tork had probably seen more than his fair share of messages passing back and forth concerning the matter.

"What you probably don't know, son, is that the Tsnath were the ones that conspired with the Nmemians to pull me down here. This brouhaha we've just gone through today was all a pretence to get me out of the way so that the Tsnath could run amok in the north. Now I need to get back up there with my men to help put a stop to them. You understand that, don't you, Tork?"

A firmer nod this time. The lad was beginning to be won over. Hardly surprising, given the pressure he was being put under.

"Good. So here's the thing, Tork. I know this message has been orchestrated by the conspirators, even if it purports to have come with the queen's authority. But if word gets out that I've been relieved of command, my men won't follow me back to the Territories. So I need this message to be suppressed for a few days. Will you help me do that, Tork?"

The lad looked downcast. Now he was conflicted. "How, sir? Alondris knows the message was received. It will have been logged at their end."

"But they don't know it has been delivered, do they?"

"No, sir, I suppose not."

"Then here's what we'll do. There's a lot of revelry going on this evening, plenty of opportunity for accidents. We'll say that you were about your business, but got caught up in some scuffle. You were hit on the head, and when you came to, you couldn't remember things for a while." Kirshtahll turned to Rakmar. "You have somewhere quiet to look after an injured man, don't you?"

"Of course."

"There we are, then. We'll get your head bandaged and find you a bed. All you have to do is feign a loss of memory for a few days. No one will blame you for not delivering the message. It won't be your fault. And you'll have done Alondria and the people of the Northern Territories a great service."

"Though, of course, you'll have to keep that a secret," Rakmar added.

Tork tottered on the edge of his decision for a moment, then fell squarely in league with the plan. "Alright, sir. So long as it's not seen as my fault. You know the punishment for interfering with Message Corps business."

Kirshtahll smiled. "Don't worry, son, you have my word. You keep your end of the bargain and no one else will ever know. I'll also see to it you are handsomely rewarded when this whole business is over."

Rakmar summoned Timerra, briefed him on the plan and what was needed. Tork was led away to recover from his injuries.

With the chamber to themselves once more, Rakmar said, "This is a bad business, Padráig. How far up does this conspiracy go?"

"I don't know. But they clearly have the ear of our esteemed queen. They've probably fed her some cock-and-bull story of today's events, having realised that I've circumvented their diversion. They're desperate, clutching at straws trying to stop me from taking the army back north."

"But to what end? What do they have to gain by assisting the Tsnath?"

"Money. Many in the south have been bleating on for years about how much it costs us to maintain our position in the Northern Territories. By letting the Tsnath take over, they think they'll be relieved of that burden."

"But..." Rakmar stammered.

"I will not let it happen," Kirshtahll cut in. "I shall get my army north if I have to level the Mathians to do so."

"Then gods help the mountains," Rakmar replied with a grim smile. "Will you go by the Am-gött?"

"That was my thinking. The western end of the mountains is the nearest route from here in Lamàst. But I suspect I shall meet heavy resistance up there. The Tsnath aren't fools; they'll have the Am-gött covered. Though my greater worry is how much more resistance I may encounter as I traverse Léddürland, Nairn and Ashur to get to Mitcha. I have no intelligence reports giving me any idea of what sort of strength the Tsnath have up there."

"From what you told me of that earlier message you received, we've already lost a lot of men. You could end up going the same way, you know."

"You can keep that kind of cheery thought to yourself," Kirshtahll muttered back.

13

Of the several thousand men remaining with the baroness after Özeransk had departed for Nairnkirsh, most had been left at the base of the mountains, guarding the mouth of the valley which went on to become the Pass of Trombéi. Only four hundred trusted men, all of them Daka's own, were allowed to accompany her to the location of the Trombéi entrance to the Old Homeland. Gömalt had advised that such a number was more than sufficient – he'd actually advised fewer still, but Daka had insisted on the greater force. The mountains themselves provided protection in a way that no army could, and their only concern was an attack from the rear. Those remaining below could deal with that, in the unlikely event that the Alondrians managed to muster a force large enough to pose a threat. Gömalt was confident they would not.

It was good to have reduced the overall size of the force that had had to climb the valley. Moving a large army up such terrain in the conditions of winter was a slow business. Even so, down to four hundred, they still hadn't made good time, mainly because Daka had insisted on accompanying the operation. She didn't suffer deprivation, make do with basic amenities, or eat cured rations. Her presence alone had added days to the journey.

And now that they'd arrived at the caves, the damned Alondrian mage was taking forever to perform his task.

Roumin-Lenka drew alongside and placed a hand on his forearm. "Patience, Gömalt, patience," she murmured by his ear.

Gömalt scowled. "It'll be the middle of bloody summer if he doesn't get a move on."

"The seals have kept the Old Homeland closed for centuries," she said, as if he needed reminding. "Removing them was never going to be easy. Mage Nÿat has no reason to take longer than is necessary."

Gömalt grunted in disdain. Vital though the mage was, he didn't like the man. Didn't trust him. There was an aloofness about the Alondrian that seemed designed to grate on his nerves. Yet it was the man's motive that bothered him more. Without doubt Nÿat was a powerful mage, and they did need him. But he was a mystery, an unpredictable quantity that could not be fully controlled. *That* was what bothered Gömalt most of all. Anyone else could, if it came to it, be threatened and coerced into submission. Not so Nÿat. His powers made him unassailable. The only leverage they had over him was pandering to his lust for power. He would help Daka become Empress of all Tsnathsarré, and she in turn would grant him a place at her side, to rule over all matters of a Taümathalogical nature within her realm. That's what the man wanted. Or so he said. That's why Gömalt didn't trust him. Once the mage got what he wanted, what was to stop him wanting more?

Gömalt had been with the baroness long enough to know that she wasn't naïve. Nor was wishful thinking her way. She was cold, calculating and ruthless. That's why he served her; they were like-minded. So perhaps she had a long-term plan for controlling the mage – one she just hadn't confided to him yet. He hoped that, just because her goal was so nearly in her grasp, she hadn't allowed this crucial detail to slip through her fingers.

He turned his attention back to the mage. Nÿat looked as if he was practicing meditation, facing what he had determined to be the entrance to the mines. He had his eyes closed. It had been this way for an hour.

It remained that way for another.

Then, rather suddenly, the mage announced, "Ah-ha, I have it!"

Nÿat made a show of raising his hands in magely fashion and uttering something unintelligible, probably in the Tongue of the Ancients. At first nothing happened, but Nÿat turned to his audience, showman that he was, and gave them a reassuring nod, suggesting that, contrary to any visible evidence, everything was proceeding according to plan.

The changes were initially so subtle that they might almost have been mistaken for figments of the imagination. As minutes passed by, very gradually the rock of the cave wall took on an insubstantial quality. The surface began to shimmer, before eventually melting away.

"And there you have it. The Old Homeland."

Though he hated to admit it, even Gömalt was finally impressed. He'd tested the wall earlier and it had seemed very solid indeed. Even to the extent that he'd doubted Nÿat had correctly identified the location of the entrance.

Nÿat turned to Roumin-Lenka. "Time to put that Dwarvish knowledge of yours to work."

"Mage Nÿat," Daka cut in, "the seal, can it be restored?"

"No." He wafted a hand towards the carved stone in its alcove beside the tunnel entrance. "Perhaps if the menhir had been intact, I might have been able to draw on its power. But that is lost to us. Why?"

"For the sake of the rest of the men. I don't want them getting ideas about entering the mines themselves. Especially not the ones we left further down the mountain. Remember, a large proportion of them are mercenaries, expecting a share of what they believe lies within. Which, as you and I both know, doesn't exist."

"They'll find out sooner or later," Nÿat pointed out.

"So long as that's after we have secured the *Dànis~Lutárn* and it has been reconfigured, then it won't matter. But until that time, I need them to believe they're going to get paid."

Nÿat held up his hands, as though in submission. "I can set in place a simple illusion. It will have no substance, but it will ward against a casual glance."

Daka nodded. "Gömalt, bring in the retrieval teams."

Gömalt made his way to the mouth of the cave, shielding his eyes from the glare outside. Five groups of ten hand-picked men were waiting. They'd set up camp fires and were busy trying to stay warm. All stood as he approached. "Come."

The men collected their equipment and hurried inside the cave. As they gathered round the baroness and the mage, a lit torch was passed between them so that they could ignite their own brands.

Daka turned to face Roumin-Lenka. "Each leader knows how to use your maps?"

"They could redraw them in their sleep," Roumin-Lenka replied, with her usual lack of deference.

"Good." Addressing Nÿat, the baroness said, "And they know how to overcome the seals to reach the menhir?"

Nÿat nodded. "It is much easier from the inside. I trust you have suitably impressed upon them the absolute necessity that none of the remaining stones are damaged?"

Gömalt grunted. "They know." He glared at the gathering. "They know that if they fail, it would be better to slit their own throats than return."

The baroness addressed the men. "Assemble the stones in

Üzsspeck. We will join you there." To Nÿat and Gömalt she added quietly, though not without some excitement in her voice, "Once we have all the menhir assembled, we can gather the *Dànis~Lutárn* into the Vessel. Then victory shall be ours."

*

Döshan pulled his blanket tighter around his shoulders and shivered some more. Why in the name of Bël-aírnon the emperor had had to insist that he travel down to the border with the rest of the reinforcements, he couldn't fathom. He could have followed on behind *after* all the waiting around had been done.

But advisors didn't argue with emperors.

Omnitas, for his part, seemed to be enjoying his time away from the palace. The comforts of Jèdda-galbráith were a world away from this infernally damp, frozen landscape, but the emperor didn't seem affected by the cold. He had insulation, both natural and worn. Furs jammed beneath armour bulged where not constrained, giving him a rather barrel-like appearance. His stature, a little diminutive on foot, was enhanced by his being perched atop a great war horse. One might even have called it an inspiring sight. If one was in a generous mood, Döshan mused sourly.

He let out a sigh. The truth was, he felt more bored than cold. Cut off from his usual network of contacts and the inner workings of the capital, there was nothing to do out here in the wilds but wait. And he didn't do that well.

He'd tried meditation. Unfortunately, devotions to Bël-aírnon could only fill part of his day. Which left eating or wandering aimlessly round the camp trying to pick up what little intelligence he could. The latter wasn't easy, though. The men tended to become more guarded when he passed by. Unlike his spies, he wasn't faceless. He was Advisor Döshan, closely associated with the emperor. Not a person around whom loose tongues wagged freely. Pity. It wasn't that they feared him as such, he was just on a different stratum of the hierarchy to most of them. He felt impotent.

Wondering whether Kremlish was up for another game of cards, he glanced round the camp. His fellow advisor was nowhere to be seen. Instead, he spotted the runner assigned to him heading in his direction. Interest piqued, he climbed down from the wagon he and Kremlish shared as quarters and waited patiently for the man to draw closer. The runner jogged round camp fires and tents and stopped a yard short, giving a curt bow with his head.

"Advisor, this was just received at the falconry."

The runner dropped a tiny metal cylinder into Döshan's hand before being dismissed. Döshan climbed into the back of the wagon and dug out his reading glass. Messages from Özeransk were so small that without optical assistance it was too much of a strain to decipher the words.

He read Özeransk's missive twice, then sank back against the side of the wagon and pondered the matter for several minutes. Eventually, he shrugged off his blanket and descended from the wagon again and threaded his way over to the emperor.

Omnitas didn't dismount. Döshan was used to looking up at him, but not usually to such an extent. A destrier was considerably more daunting than a dais step.

Due deference done, he opened, "Sire, word from Lord Özeransk."

"Ah. Proceed."

The emperor gently spurred his mount and the creature began to walk. Döshan scuttled alongside, with four hulking guards not far behind. Fortunately, the snow throughout most of the camp had been trampled already and was relatively compact, otherwise he'd have had to wade to keep up. That would have been exhausting.

"Sire, I'm not quite sure what to make of it. Özeransk has been separated from Daka."

"Separated?"

"He has had to leave her to deal with some unexpected resistance. But he says that by the time this message is received, the baroness will have left for the mountains. She is making her move."

Omnitas scowled. "I had expected by now to know what she's up to. Still no word on that?"

"None, Sire. But Özeransk recommends crossing the border with your troops and holding them in a state of readiness. He will send word as soon as Daka shows her hand."

That news seemed to inflate the emperor. It wiped the scowl off his face. "Good. I have become bored just sitting here."

Döshan hid his grunt. That made two of them.

14

Torrin-Ashur struggled to surface from a failed attempt to grab some desperately needed sleep. Someone was shouting his name; these days that was never good. Sitting up, he discovered his head throbbed with an unpleasant, fuzzy ache, its courtship with oblivion having been thwarted soon after the first kiss.

Mac, the source of the shouting, came scrambling over the lip of the cave entrance. "Lieutenant, we've got trouble!" The barrel-chested mercenary peered into the gloom, unable to see where his quarry had hidden himself.

"What kind of trouble?"

"The Tsnath kind."

Torrin-Ashur's heart began to race. "How many?"

"Lots."

Torrin-Ashur groped for his boots and wrestled his feet into cold, damp leather. They were stiff from being nearly frozen. Too late came the realisation that he shouldn't have taken them off in the first place. "How the hell did they find us?" he muttered. He didn't wait for a reply. "The signal came up from the lower lookouts?"

"Aye."

As soon as he was booted, Torrin-Ashur grabbed his sword belt. He was still fumbling with the buckle when he jostled past Mac and stumbled out into the daylight. The brightness hurt his eyes and exacerbated his headache. There was no time to pander to that now.

"Alright, listen up. Get the women and children into Little Mitcha. Silfast," he cast about for the corporal, "grab the mayor, take charge of the Mitcha men and start shifting our supplies and equipment into the main cave. Food first. Nash, get the rest of our men up on to the barricade."

The sergeant launched straight into action without his customary salute. To Torrin-Ashur's knowledge, Nash was the only soldier in the camp with any real experience of the carnage they could expect if it was a significant force marching towards them. Clearly he needed no second bidding to be about preparing to repel them. As for the rest of the men, with the exception of Mitcha's liberation, which had been rather unplanned, their contact with the enemy had been carefully orchestrated, pitching them against limited numbers. What they faced now was probably going to be their first taste of full-scale battle.

Borádin emerged from the mouth of the Barracks looking very much as if his awakening had also been a rude one. "What's going on?"

"Tsnath coming up the valley," Torrin-Ashur called back. "We're going to need your men."

"Where?"

"Up there." Torrin-Ashur pointed to the barricade. The horseshoe shaped mound of compacted snow, some nine or ten feet high on the outer side, extended around the entrances to all five caves. With its crenellated upper parapet providing some protection, it resembled a giant ice sculpture. Having had water repeatedly poured over it, which had frozen almost instantly, it was as hard as rock. Torrin-Ashur prayed it would prove as sturdy.

Borádin didn't look convinced. He gave the fortifications a quick assessment and returned a worried frown. "We won't be able to hold that for long."

"I know."

Once the nobleman had reached him, Torrin-Ashur explained the rest of his plan, born of desperation a few weeks previously in the sincere hope that it would never be needed. Having heard the details, Borádin gave his head a woeful shake. "If this fails, we're going to be supping with the gods tonight."

"It's not like we have a choice." Torrin-Ashur shrugged helplessly. "If we fled up the valley now, we'd be lucky to stay ahead of the Tsnath. To stand any chance at all, we'd have to abandon our supplies – and probably the elderly and the wounded. That I won't do. Anyway, without supplies, even if we made it over the ridge, how long would we last? The Tsnath wouldn't need to follow us – they could just leave us to freeze to death."

Borádin let out a resigned sigh. "You know, my lord, you have a penchant for painting rosy pictures. I'd have been better off staying put in Vickrà-döthmore." He smiled thinly and left, muttering to himself as he went to organise his troops.

"Where's Princess Elona?" Torrin-Ashur called out.

"Here."

He spun round. She had stolen up behind him without him noticing. "I want you in Little Mitcha with the others."

"Giving me orders now?" she challenged, arching an eyebrow. "I can take care of myself, you know."

"So says the cut on your arm." He stepped a little closer. "People are going to die out here today. You're a princess. I can't be responsible for you being one of them."

"I'm not asking you to be responsible for me," she bristled.

Torrin-Ashur shut his eyes, letting out something between a sigh and a groan. This wasn't going how he wanted. The last thing he needed was people arguing with him just now, even if they were princesses. "Look, Elona, I've already lost my family, my home, my lands. I may even have lost my country. I don't want you added to that list. So, please, just do as I ask."

Elona softened. "Alright. At least that's a reason I can respect."

A lock of ash blonde hair fell down the side of her face. He tucked it back behind her ear. "And while you're at it, try to keep Jorra-hin and Kirin out of trouble."

Elona clasped his hand to her cheek. "I will. But in return, there's to be no 'supping with the gods' for you." She flicked a glance at Borádin, having picked up on his phrase. "That's an order from *me*."

Torrin-Ashur smiled. "Yes, Your Highness." A mock salute undercut the seriousness of his tone.

He watched for a moment as Elona hurried towards the hospital. Since arriving in the camp, she'd spent most of her time there. Some of the wounded still clung to life solely because of her encouragement. There was no denying that her presence had bolstered morale, and for that he was grateful. It didn't matter that she had fallen from grace in the eyes of the queen. As far as the people here were concerned, her presence showed them they were still important. A princess of the realm was in their midst, prepared to face the same hardships and risks as they. But for all that, he couldn't help feeling a wave of nausea course through him at the thought of her being here at all; in danger, with nothing he could do to guarantee her safety other than vow to defend her to his last breath.

All around him the camp became a hive of activity. People and supplies were transferred to the central cave. Baskets of arrows were hauled up to the barricade and distributed amongst the assembling archers. On the face of it, they weren't short of munitions, but then he had no previous experience to draw on to know whether what they had was enough. It was difficult to tell how long the fighting might last. They didn't even know how many Tsnath they were facing. Either way, it didn't take a magister to know their supplies might vanish all too quickly in the thick of battle.

The time the early warning from the lower lookouts had bought them seemed to vanish in the blink of an eye. In the midst of the preparations, a shout went up from the barricade. "Sir, lookouts returning."

Millardis had spotted the movement. Torrin-Ashur climbed up to the parapet and followed to where the man was pointing. Elam was just emerging from the trees on the far side of the open ground that lay downhill of the barricade. The mercenary led a small group of men. They looked exhausted. Little wonder, when some of them had just skied two miles up the valley like foxes before hounds, certain death chasing their tails.

Elam glided to a stop just inside the compound. "The Tsnath won't be far behind," he heaved, struggling to catch his breath.

As soon as the last of the lookouts was through the barricade, six men shouldered a huge ball of snow into the opening. Somehow that made Torrin-Ashur feel a little safer. It wouldn't stand up to a sustained attack, but he took comfort from the fact that the enemy was unlikely to have any heavy support. This wasn't going to be a long siege, with catapults and trebuchets pounding his walls. They were facing a frontal attack by mobile troops armed only with hand weapons. Whatever the outcome, the duration of the battle wouldn't be measured in days or weeks, it would be measured in hours, perhaps even only in minutes.

"Any idea of their strength?"

"Hard to say." The mercenary paused, still gulping in lungfuls of air. In a lowered voice he managed to add, "Thousands, I would guess."

"Gods be merciful." Torrin-Ashur swallowed hard. He turned to Botfiár, standing just a few yards away awaiting orders. "Light the beacon, Corporal, then join the others on the barricade."

"Aye, sir."

Botfiár ran over to a pile of brushwood and tore off an outer layer of snow-covered branches. He poured on a horn of oil and thrust a torch into the heart of the wood. There was a whoosh as the oil caught. Flames took hold quickly, driving out moisture and producing a thick cloud of grey smoke that rose like a dirty smudge against a pristine white background. It would be visible for miles. He lingered a moment to make sure the beacon wasn't going to die out, then left and took up position on the defences.

Tense minutes passed before Torrin-Ashur caught the first signs of the Tsnath approaching. They displayed no sense of urgency. Instead, they took their time to assemble, remaining deep within the trees where they were safe from Alondrian arrows. Trying to hit them now would just be a waste of vital munitions. It came as no surprise that these Tsnath were well disciplined. They were here with grim intent.

While the enemy made their final preparations, Torrin-Ashur went round making his. "Remember, lads, the archers must do the initial damage. The rest of you keep them supplied and shielded. Stick to the drill we've been practising."

Borádin left his position and made his way over, keeping a wary eye on the swelling Tsnath ranks.

"What in the name of the gods are they waiting for?" he murmured. "They've already assembled enough men to wipe us out several times over."

"Every moment they delay works in our favour."

"This plan of yours had better work, Torrin." Borádin rolled his eyes skywards and hurried back to his men.

Watching him go, Torrin-Ashur shook his head; he still found it hard to comprehend how much the nobleman had changed since all the bravado and posturing at Mitcha just a few months ago.

Movement beyond the barricade quickly drew his attention back to the Tsnath. Their archers were taking up positions just inside the tree line, close enough to the edge to make their shots whilst retaining some degree of cover. With the open ground that lay between them spanning less than a hundred yards, they didn't need to aim that high. The overhead branches would not be a hindrance.

Torrin-Ashur stole a glance up the mountain. Nothing stirred. He sought out Tomàss and was unsurprised to find the man standing nearby with an expectant gleam in his eye. "Ready?"

"Aye, sir!"

"Then begin."

The former slave had two other men with him. Makeshift kettle drums were slung across their midriffs, fabricated from metal sheeting off some old shields tied over wicker baskets. Tomàss began hammering out a beat which his troop attempted to follow. A cacophony ensued. Torrin-Ashur nodded; for now, the discordant din was good enough.

It acted as a catalyst. A flight of Tsnath arrows soared into the air, indiscriminately peppering the compound. The missiles arrived in silence, seemingly just materialising in the snow.

In that instant the beat from the drummers transformed; danger had bared its teeth, bringing the *Sèliccia~Castrà* surging to the fore. The ancient magic began stamping out its own rhythm, strengthening the sense of power Torrin-Ashur could feel rising within him. He knew the same would be true for most of his men. Even those who had arrived with Borádin seemed bolstered, despite knowing little of the War Song.

"Steady, men," he called out. "Don't waste your arrows while the enemy is still within the trees."

The Tsnath maintained their barrage, flight after flight of arrows arching overhead. Their archers seemed to have worked their way round much of the camp's perimeter, delivering peril from all sides except the rear. A number of defenders succumbed to the deadly hail.

Only when the Tsnath realised arrows alone were not going to win the day did the assault lessen. The lull provided a welcome respite for the defenders, though what formed up to replace the barrage boded nothing good. The forward Tsnath ranks solidified into rows of shielded infantry. The archers repositioned themselves at the rear, where they weren't quite as effective.

"This is it!" Torrin-Ashur shouted, rather needlessly. "Archers, ready your bows."

For a moment it seemed as though the valley itself held its breath, a strangely calm prelude to a mighty cry that cut loose from the Tsnath lines. Their charge began. They poured forwards in their hundreds.

Deep powdered snow awaited them. Immediately in trouble, their attack slowed to a mired crawl just yards beyond the trees.

"Now!" Torrin-Ashur cried.

A volley spat out from the barricade. The advancing troops used their shields as much to balance themselves as to cover their vulnerabilities. Clear of the protection afforded them by the forest, they became easy targets for defenders who'd had weeks to practice judging the range and honing their aim. The Alondrian numbers were few, but their bite was vicious.

Just short of half way across the clearing, the forward Tsnath ranks faltered. Soldiers began to stumble. Gaps opened up in their line.

"Surprise, surprise," Nash muttered to no one.

Torrin-Ashur overheard and nodded grimly. The Tsnath had run into defensive measures the sergeant had overseen; sharpened stakes rammed into frozen ground. Hidden beneath the snow, the stealthy barbs assaulted foot and shin without warning.

The Tsnath advance disintegrated into a confused mêlée. A minute later, the first wave of attackers gave up and retreated. Torrin-Ashur's archers harried them all the way back to the trees.

Their arrows only stopped when more hit bark than bodies.

*

Özeransk's jaw tightened. He'd made the classic mistake of underestimating his opponent. The weeks of easy success early in the campaign, against an enemy that seemed to have little idea how to conduct itself, had lulled him into an air of complacency. He should have known better – now he was up against the few Alondrians who had shown any mettle to speak of since the invasion had begun.

He let out a curse towards Bël-aírnon that would have made Adviser Döshan cringe.

"My lord?" Commander Streàck queried.

Özeransk snapped out of his self-recrimination. "We need a change of tactic. Summon the officers."

Streàck scurried away, shouting orders.

An idea was forming in Özeransk's mind. He'd heard of a manoeuvre used against defensible positions such as the one he faced now. It was not one that he'd ever had need to use before, or even see in action. His battles were usually pitched, though recently ambush had been his tactic of choice. Now that he was effectively laying siege, he needed to rethink.

What he could not do was simply wait the enemy out. He had no idea what supplies the Alondrians had, but it would be more than his own men had brought with them. And the Alondrians had one vital thing he didn't – shelter. Whatever action he took, it had to deliver results quickly. He had numbers on his side, but little other advantage.

He toyed with the idea of negotiation, then dismissed it. He doubted his ability to bluff the Alondrians into believing their situation was hopeless. Moreover, he didn't think they'd trust him to honour any agreement they might reach; Daka's treatment of those she'd taken captive would not have endeared these Alondrians to life under

Tsnathsarré rule. Besides, he wondered if he was even in a position to guarantee the terms of their surrender. One thing was certain; he'd not be party to an agreement that others might later rescind. It was better for his enemy to die in battle than in betrayal. At least there was honour in that. Not like the shameful demise Daka had inflicted on those that had surrendered at the battle of Mitcha. Visions of that barbarity still made him shiver with revulsion.

So attack it was.

And if that silenced the drumming, so much the better. The wretched beat, whatever it was, had really started to grate on his nerves. It may have been intended to bolster the Alondrian defenders, but somehow it got under his skin, almost as if it was designed to taunt.

*

Torrin-Ashur took advantage of the respite to take stock. His men had suffered some losses, four of his archers were dead, two others were wounded, and some of his shieldsmen had been hit. Bad though that was, he knew it could have been much, much worse. Tsnath arrows had arrived from such random angles and in such quantities that sometimes they'd been impossible to dodge. Yet the number of shields that now bristled like porcupine bore testament to just how many injuries had been avoided by quick reactions. The War Song had made all the difference, lending his men extraordinary anticipation the likes of which he'd have found hard to believe had he not seen it with his own eyes.

Borádin's troops had not fared so well. Torrin-Ashur counted some fifteen that had been hit, though more seemed to be wounded than dead.

"Round one to us," the nobleman greeted as he drew near.

Despite their losses, Borádin's men appeared buoyed by their unexpected victory. Relief, tinged perhaps with the beginnings of a hope that they might actually survive, was evident in their looks.

Torrin-Ashur gazed downhill towards the trees. The open ground was littered with dozens of dead Tsnath. His defenders had certainly inflicted more damage than they'd been dealt. It gave him little comfort; the enemy had soldiers aplenty and could bear such losses, while he was under no illusions about how much longer his defenders' luck could hold out. "How are your men for arrows?" he asked Borádin.

"Less than half what we started with." The nobleman heaved a sigh and looked round the compound. "But the Tsnath seem to have been generous with theirs. We should gather up all these strays." He kicked at one near his boot. "The ones that have landed in snow should still be fit for use."

"Yes!" Torrin-Ashur chided himself for not having thought of that. If they had time, they could almost replenish their stocks from those peppering the area. Even those that had hit shields might still be serviceable, if they could be prised free without losing their heads. At close range, they didn't have to be particularly accurate. He issued Nash with orders to see to a collection, then turned back to Borádin. "We still need to make what we've got left count. I suggest we have the archers conserve if we can – wait for good targets."

As advice went, Torrin-Ashur knew it was forlorn. The Tsnath's first wave had only been driven back by the constant volleys his men had kept up. He figured they might be able to repulse one more attack of a similar nature, though even that was an optimistic assessment; next time, the enemy would know what to expect and their resolve would undoubtedly have hardened. Ultimately, whether it was the next attack, or the one after, it was still inevitable that the Tsnath would eventually reach the barricade, at which point the battle would descend into the chaos of hand to hand combat. The outcome of that was bleak to contemplate.

He stole another glance up the valley. Still nothing stirred.

Borádin noticed and raised his eyebrows, but said nothing. There was nothing *to* say. Both of them knew how precariously their fate hung in the balance.

"Uh-oh, look..." Borádin gestured forwards.

The Tsnath were assembling again.

Torrin-Ashur nodded. "Gods be with us," he offered, already turning.

"Yes. Rather that, than us with them!"

Torrin-Ashur ran back to his position grinning. He felt strangely comforted by Borádin's presence, despite how odd that would have seemed just a short while ago. They were brothers in arms now. They'd fought together. It was a sobering thought that they might even die together.

"What the hell are they doing?" Nash demanded just as Torrin-Ashur got back to his men. The sergeant suddenly snapped his shield sideways to deflect an arrow that would otherwise have hit his shoulder. He might as well have been swatting flies for all the concern he showed.

Torrin-Ashur looked across towards the Tsnath to see what Nash had noticed.

In three separate places, lines of shielded Tsnath infantry edged out of the trees. About twenty men apiece, some fifty yards separated one line from the next, the gaps quickly filling with archers who hung back, hugging the trees for cover. Each line of infantry waited while another row of men assembled behind them, then they shuffled forwards a few steps. Rank by rank, the formations grew into squares. They bristled with interlocking shields, not only at the fronts, but at the sides and tops as well.

Despite his advice to Borádin, Torrin-Ashur ordered his archers to resume their defence. The effect was minimal. Arrows either ricocheted harmlessly off the enemy's tortoiseshell cover, or embedded themselves in their shields. Either way, they inflicted no injuries. It quickly became clear to him that unless a weakness opened up, shooting at them was largely a waste of munitions. *That*, he was painfully aware, was the one thing he could least afford.

The Tsnath didn't charge. Their progress was methodical, if rather cumbersome. It worried Torrin-Ashur that it was being conducted without serious loss. When they reached the extent of their previous attack, they slowly began to trample virgin snow.

"What the..." Nash blurted out.

"Oh, gods!" Torrin-Ashur exclaimed. His heart sank as he realised the Tsnath had devised a means of circumventing Nash's hidden barbs.

The front rank of each formation began laying down their shields, effectively creating their own road over the snow. Soldiers behind them passed their shields forwards, dropping replacements into position to maintain a wall of protection at the front. The phalanxes moved forwards a few paces, and the procedure was repeated. Shields continuously rippled over the heads of the advancing soldiers, and when the first to be laid had served their purpose, they were retrieved from the back and recycled. Torrin-Ashur watched, both fascinated and horrified.

"Target the front ranks only," he ordered his archers. "Aim low." The enemy's only vulnerable spot seemed to be their feet just after they'd laid their shields.

Arrows darted forwards. One or two found gaps and inflicted

injury, though nowhere near enough to bring the enemy to a halt. They didn't even falter.

A momentary hiatus in the drumming caught Torrin-Ashur's attention. Tearing his gaze from the Tsnath's menacing advance, he glanced back into the compound. Tomàss quickly resumed his beat, an arrow conspicuously protruding from the lower part of his drum. But he only had one other companion now; the third man had taken a hit and was slumped in a heap right where he'd been standing. Torrin-Ashur prayed that the two remaining men could still make enough noise. They'd have to. He couldn't spare anyone off the barricade to provide a replacement.

The enemy formations marched on, relentlessly closing the gap to the barricade, shield length by shield length. They suffered to a greater extent the closer they got – bloody trails in the snow marked the paths the phalanxes took – but their advance was still inexorable. The Alondrian archers simply weren't having any real impact. All their efforts achieved was a rapid depletion of supplies.

Torrin-Ashur realised with increasing dread that he was utterly powerless to stop this second wave from reaching his defences.

"Archers, hold," he ordered. Looks of consternation and outright disbelief flew at him like daggers. "Wait until they reach the foot of the barricade," he added, "*then* let them have it! *Everything* you've got left!"

With the exception of its entrance, the barricade presented an ice wall the Tsnath would somehow have to climb. It was vital that the defenders still had something left to make that task costly and time-consuming. It was all about delaying the enemy as long as possible now. If the Tsnath breached the defences, with the numbers they had on their side, the fighting would be over in minutes, War Song or not.

As the enemy came within ten yards, their archers shifted aim away from the wall and further into the compound, bringing relief to the defenders on the ramparts. Though it was merely the calm before the full fury of the storm; none of the defenders could be in any doubt about that.

The Tsnath advance reached the base of the barricade and came to a halt. There was nothing to give them purchase up the wall; no handholds, no contours, just smooth, steeply-inclined ice. To even attempt any kind of scaling of the obstacle, they had no choice but to partially dispense with their shields.

"Archers!" Torrin-Ashur cried.

A withering volley lashed out. Tens of floundering Tsnath were hit in an instant. Screams of agony, shouts of rage and the roar of battle cries all clamoured together to assault ears unfamiliar with the horrors of full combat. The Alondrians continued to unleash flight after flight of arrows down the barricade; soldier fell upon soldier. Yet the Tsnath pressed with ever greater force, sheer weight of numbers driving them on.

Torrin-Ashur watched the chaotic scene below him, appalled at the scale of the carnage. Each of the three phalanxes had to be at least four hundred men strong; over a thousand enemy all baying for Alondrian blood. He'd be lucky if his archers had half that number of arrows left. Even if every one of them was made to count, which was impossible, the Tsnath would still pour three times the number of men over the parapet than he had to withstand them.

As more and more Tsnath were felled, their bodies became the very ground their comrades climbed over. They inched up the barricade corpse by bloody corpse. It wasn't hard to imagine them as a swarm of ants intent on overwhelming captured prey, their horde incapable now of comprehending failure.

The distance between arrow and target reduced to mere feet. Torrin-Ashur cried out, "Archers, fall back to the cave entrance." At first, only some men responded, barely able to hear the order above all the clamour. As the bowmen gradually got the message and withdrew, taking their nearly empty quivers with them, swordsmen took their place.

For the last time, Torrin-Ashur stole a glance up the mountain. *Still* nothing stirred. His hopes of salvation faded. Desperate as it had been, it seemed his plan was destined to fail.

Sword drawn, with Borádin's trophy shield slung on his forearm, he stepped up to the parapet. Strategy, planning, outcome and consequence all slipped from his mind as he gave himself utterly to the all-consuming beat of the War Song thundering in his ears.

His entire field of view was awash with Tsnath, mired in a mixture of bloodied snow and bodies. Filled with sudden anger at the hand fate had dealt him, he lunged at the first enemy soldier to successfully crest the barricade, decapitating the man in a single blow. His cry was one of fury and his sword a blur as he slashed and stabbed at anything that moved within his reach, ancient magic all that stood between felling friend instead of foe.

Dreadful minutes passed as his men put up a valiant resistance, holding the Tsnath at bay far longer than any could have expected. The odds they faced were horrendous, the outcome inevitable. Even with the War Song inflicting death with terrible efficiency, the enemy numbers simply overwhelmed them.

One by one Torrin-Ashur saw his men forced back. They dropped off the wall into the compound and tried to regroup. In the face of pressure from four Tsnath attackers, he lost his own footing and toppled backwards. Somehow he managed a somersault, surprising even himself as he landed upright six feet below.

Tomàss abandoned his drum, snatched up his weapons, a sword and a dagger, and flew into a group of Tsnath that had breached the compound just behind the entrance. His roar was feral, his blades flailing scythes. He danced his way through the attackers as though water swirling around rocks, his weapons exploiting weaknesses with every thrust. He was death incarnate.

Drum beat silenced, the clash and clamour of battle remained, the roars of violence, the ring of steel on steel, and the screams of the wounded and the dying. Above it all, only now, a low, ominous rumble came from higher up the valley. The drumming had done its task, masking the sound, the battle doing the rest to distract the Tsnath.

Torrin-Ashur's heart soared as his hope was flung a lifeline. "Fall back!" he screamed.

To a man the Alondrians disengaged and turned tail towards the mouth of the main cave.

Torrin-Ashur found himself one of the furthest away, bringing up the rear with a small handful of men. Tomàss suddenly appeared at his side.

A squad of enemy soldiers scrambled down off the barricade at its lower, northern end, close to where it abutted the rocky wall of Mount Àthái. They spilled into the compound in front of the entrance to Little Mitcha, threatening to cut off the retreat.

The sound of the rumbling from above the ridge grew louder with each passing second. The Tsnath became more and more distracted by it. Those chasing the Alondrians towards the caves wavered, glancing at each other in confusion.

Torrin-Ashur barrelled into the soldiers blocking his path, nothing on his mind but getting through them. Killing was not his objective, yet they mired his efforts to bypass them and gave him no choice but to engage. He was vaguely aware of Tomàss having to do the same.

Even with the War Song coursing through his veins, fear stabbed at his heart. He was on borrowed time. The protective magic could not shield him from the juggernaut that was coming.

With a gods-spawned scream of fury, a hurtling maelstrom exploded across the skyline. The deafening, thunderous roar ripped the valley apart as churning snow and forest debris tore over the ridge. At such speed, its leading edge soared clear across the compound, momentarily blotting out the sky. In an instant, thousands of tonnes of unmitigated devastation obliterated the defensive barricade. It simply ceased to exist.

The inescapable fist of the mountain's wrath didn't falter, punching down on the Tsnath still beyond the compound without mercy. It was as though the Mathians themselves had risen up to be rid of the invaders sullying their slopes. Low and mighty were swept away like twigs in a raging, storm-riven sea.

Pure instinct prompted Torrin-Ashur to make one final, desperate lunge for the safety of the cave. He was an instant too late. His legs were hammered sideways by a force intent on his annihilation. His world turned into a tumbling, whirling chaos, smothering him completely. His body slammed up against something bone-crushingly solid.

Oblivion took him.

*

Özeransk found himself in a dimly lit world. The maelstrom that had swept down the mountainside would have carried him away to certain death had he not been thrown into the branches of a pine. How the tree had remained rooted, he could not fathom, but clinging to it for dear life had been the only thing that had saved him. He knew he was extremely lucky that none of the debris the avalanche had carried with it had piled into him. He could have been crushed to pulp with ridiculous ease.

His mind reeled at the calamity that had suddenly turned near victory into total defeat. The change in circumstance, so rapid and unexpected in its advent, was disorientating enough, but he'd also been mauled by the raging torrent, flipped over and over before fetching up where he had. He thought he was more or less upright, but it was hard to tell. The snow held him in suspense. Without being able to move, or see anything other than a grey blur, it almost felt as if he was flying.

It occurred to him that since he could discern some light, he couldn't be that far beneath the surface of the snow. By working his hands back and forth, up and down, he was eventually able to move his arms upwards by pulling on the tree that had saved him. It was a supreme struggle. The snow mired him as though someone had set him in clay. He forced down a moment of panic that he might not be able to free himself and tried again.

His persistence was rewarded. He felt the resistance give and found his right hand was free to move. Little by little he excavated a small hole by grabbing handfuls of snow and compressing it into balls and tossing them away. He managed to free his other hand, and from there on progress was much faster. With his arms clear to the elbow, his head finally emerged into sunlight and he let out a great sigh of relief. It was almost a laugh.

The rest of the excavation proceeded methodically. It was still a struggle, but one he knew would result in freedom, no matter how long it took. He worked with a will, ignoring the throbbing pain of frozen fingers.

Once he was clear to the waist, the matter of his legs arose. His right leg felt as though it was set at an awkward angle. He couldn't tell how bad it was until he could move it, but the shooting pains he suffered as he tried flexing his muscles didn't bode well.

A few minutes later, he was free. He lay exhausted from the effort for several minutes, simply staring up at the sky. The clear, untroubled serenity of its expanse seemed absurd against the mammoth catastrophe that had overtaken him.

His knee ached terribly. If it wasn't broken, it was certainly sprained. He gritted his teeth, hoisted himself up and put his weight on it.

He glanced around, disorientated by the change in the scenery. So many of the trees in which his men had taken shelter from the Alondrian archers had been stripped away. Gone were the bodies of the men that had fallen before the avalanche hit. It was as though nature had decided to wipe the bloodied slate of battle clean.

His mind still struggled to take in the holocaust. He was horrified to discover just how few men were left. He waded through the newly deposited powder, wincing with each step, to a group of equally stunned survivors. They were dazed and shocked into milling apathy. He knew he needed to rekindle their sense of purpose, otherwise despair might take over. In this environment, that was an enemy just as deadly as any other.

It took over an hour to gather up those still alive, or at least, those they could find. When all was said and done, out of the force that had come up the mountain with him, only a fraction remained. Özeransk could hardly bring himself to believe the scale of his defeat. He didn't consider himself a boastful man, but it was true to say that he'd had many successes against far greater foe than the few Alondrians he'd engaged today. Yet it was his army that was now in tatters, not theirs.

Then it hit him, the full realisation of just what had happened. Yes, his army had been decimated by a force of nature, but the avalanche had been a weapon the Alondrians had used against him. They'd *known* it was coming. It all began to make sense now. It was all about the beacon they'd lit. Earlier, while still approaching their camp, he'd not been able to fathom why in the name of the gods they'd deliberately signalled their exact position. The grey column of smoke had unerringly guided him to his target.

Now he knew. They'd sent up a signal, not to him, but to men they must have stationed further up the valley. Those men had initiated the devastating slide, probably with little more effort than pushing a few snowballs down the mountain.

"Aírnon's bloody beard!" he exclaimed aloud, to the surprise of the men surrounding him. He didn't explain his outburst.

The strangest thing was that he didn't feel angry, or full of hatred. Aggrieved by his losses, yes, and perhaps a little ashamed that he hadn't foreseen what was coming. But more than that, he felt relieved. He'd not been defeated by an indiscriminate act of nature, or even the gods. He'd been defeated by his enemy. And that, oddly enough, engendered in him a begrudging admiration for the small Alondrian force that had put up such incredible resistance.

The question was, had they survived? They'd retreated into some caves at the back of their compound. The entrances to those were now utterly buried and he simply didn't have the men and resources to dig them out. His primary concern now had to be getting back down to the bottom of the valley so that he could regroup.

15

Torrin-Ashur had always imagined the afterlife would be free of pain. He was slightly disappointed.

"I think he's coming round."

"About time."

The first voice had sounded soft, concerned, nice. The second, none of those things. Cosmin. Torrin-Ashur ran his tongue round a very parched mouth and prepared to announce his return from the dead. He managed an incoherent gasp.

"Here, shove this down him," Cosmin muttered, airing his brusque bedside manner.

A flask was held to Torrin-Ashur's lips. It was only water, but it felt good enough to be the gods' own nectar. "Where am I?" he croaked.

"Don't worry, you're safe."

Cracking open an eye, he discovered his surroundings to be very subdued. Wherever here was, it was obviously underground. He focused a little harder and discovered Elona ministering to him. Gods, it must have been some knock that he'd recognised Cosmin's voice before hers. He tried sitting up – an ill-advised move, instantly regretted. A really quite wretched groan escaped him.

"Stupid boy," Cosmin admonished.

"What in the gods' names happened to me?"

Elona leaned forwards and mopped his brow. "The avalanche. Just as you dived into the cave, the entrance was flooded with snow."

"Ah." That explained why all he could remember was a white blur. "And the prognosis?"

"You'll live," Cosmin muttered. His tone suggested this outcome was entirely undeserved. "You had a few broken bones, which I've mended, but the bruises you'll have to live with."

Torrin-Ashur sighed and flashed a wink at Elona. "Half the job done is better than none, I suppose."

"You can have a *whole* thick ear, if you like," Cosmin growled back. "Now, if you don't mind, I've wasted quite enough time here. I've got real patients to attend to."

The uncaring demeanour didn't fool Torrin-Ashur for an instant. He regarded Cosmin's ancient face, furrowed with concern and fatigue. It was clear he was tottering on the edge of exhaustion. As the old man rose stiffly from his knees, Torrin-Ashur caught his hand. "Cosmin – thank you."

The mage nodded bashfully and shuffled off.

"We thought we'd lost you for a while," Elona murmured as soon as Cosmin was out of earshot. "You had me very worried."

Torrin-Ashur let out a dismissive grunt. There were parts of him that he wished were still supping with the gods, despite earlier instructions to avoid such pursuits. His breathing was laboured, every intake delivered with daggers. Some of the bones Cosmin had mended must have been ribs.

"What's the situation with the Tsnath?" he asked, trying to divert his mind from the pain. "Have they tried digging us out yet?"

"Probably."

An inconclusive answer, if ever there was. Torrin-Ashur's eyebrows knit together.

"We're not in Little Mitcha anymore," Elona explained, as if that would help clarify matters.

It didn't.

"No?"

"We're inside the Mathian Mines."

Torrin-Ashur sat up straighter. "The mines? Jorra found the entrance?"

"Cosmin did. Magic being able to sense magic, or some such. Not that he's taken any credit for it."

"That's Cosmin through and through," Torrin-Ashur nodded. "Well, this is good news, however it came about. But still, the Tsnath – can they follow us?"

"Jorra-hin doesn't think so."

Torrin-Ashur sighed in relief. If Jorra-hin was happy, then so was he. With fears of imminent threat assuaged for the moment, his mind turned to other things. "So, how long have I been unconscious?"

"Two days."

"What! Ye gods, how far into the mines *are* we?"

"Just short of the city of Üzsspeck."

Galvanised by shock, Torrin-Ashur struggled to his feet, gritting his teeth against a bedlam of aches and pains that warned him it was a bad idea. He felt about ninety. "Where's Borádin?"

"Surveying a bridge."

Elona chuckled at the look of confusion flashed her way. She tucked herself under Torrin-Ashur's arm and attempted to guide his woozy steps. "We've come to a gorge that Jorra-hin says was part of the city's defences. There's a suspension bridge across it, but Mac is dubious about trusting it, what with it being so ancient."

"Do we have a choice?"

"Not really."

A line of flame burnt in a ledge high up along the wall, lifting the passage out of what would otherwise have been total darkness. Its dim orange glow illuminated scores of Mitcha folk squatted in two opposing lines, looking every bit the train of refugees they were, a ragtag mix of families and lost souls, interspersed with meagre piles of belongings. Some nodded as Elona and Torrin-Ashur stumbled by. Most just watched with a subdued glaze in their eyes. They'd been through a lot in recent weeks and it was taking its toll.

The passage opened out into a large cavern that appeared to have been naturally formed. Its walls were rough and irregular, unlike the tunnel, where the ordered craftsmanship of those who had hewn it was plain to see. There were signs that the cavern had been worked to suit the Dwarves' purposes, though; a shelf about three yards wide ran along the wall either side of where the passage emerged. Beyond its edge there was nothing but a black void. The far side of the gorge was indiscernible, save for the tiny glow of a burning arrow someone had shot across, presumably in an attempt to determine the chasm's extent.

Two bastions of Dwarvish engineering, carved stone buttresses to which suspension ropes were attached, proclaimed the bridge head. Standing some twelve feet high, they towered over a group of men inspecting some very large knots. Torrin-Ashur recognised Jorra-hin, Borádin, Nash, Elam and Mac, and the mayor of Mitcha, but not several other townsfolk who were with them.

Elona cleared her throat to garner their attention.

"Torrin!" Jorra-hin exclaimed, leading the charge to swamp the newly resurrected.

Torrin-Ashur felt quite the celebrity; it was certainly nice to have been missed. Light banter abounded, fuelled mostly by relief that he was alright. He let it run for a minute before cutting it short. "So, how do we stand after the Tsnath attack?"

"Could be worse," Borádin answered with a shrug. "We lost about fifty men."

"Fifty? Gods – that's a quarter of our fighters."

"I know. But we held our own."

"Yes, we did," Torrin-Ashur nodded solemnly. Memories of the battle outside the caves swamped him. They had certainly beaten the odds, even if luck had played its part in that outcome. "But we've still got a job to do. Losing so many is going to make that even harder."

Borádin sighed. "There's no pleasing him." He rolled his eyes at the mayor. "We could just as easily have been massacred to a man."

"Aye, we still have that delight to come," Mac supplied with a mirthless grin. He received a thump on the shoulder from Elam. "Well, it's true," the burly mercenary protested.

Torrin-Ashur raised an eyebrow. "What's he on about?"

"A couple of Tsnath were swept into the cave along with you," Elam explained. "After we'd encouraged them to surrender, we – err – had a little chat."

"I see." Torrin-Ashur decided not to pursue what Elam's idea of chatting entailed. "And…?"

"Well, the good news is that the Tsnath only have between three and four thousand troops in the area. There are other forces in the Territories, but one lot's guarding the Am-gött, and the rest are blocking the Dumássay Gorge, so we don't have to worry about them for now."

"We knew some of that from what Lord Borádin was able to tell us," Torrin-Ashur acknowledged. "I'm not sure how this constitutes good news, though?"

"Well," Elam shrugged, "at least we know what we're up against."

Torrin-Ashur shook his head in dismay. They were outnumbered ten to one and then some. "I don't think I want to hear the *bad* news."

"You're not going to like it," Mac agreed.

"Why don't you shut up," Elam snapped. As a rebuke, it was water off a duck's back to Mac. Elam's attention returned to Torrin-Ashur. "The Tsnath emperor has agreed to supply Daka with reinforcements, to help control the Northern Territories in the long term. It seems they mean to stay."

Torrin-Ashur nodded again. He wasn't surprised. From the intelligence they'd managed to gather since the beginning of the invasion, they already knew the Tsnath were undermanned. If the enemy had any long-term ambitions in the Territories, they had to have additional troops coming in from somewhere. "Well, there's not much we can do about that. So let's take things one step at a time. What about this here bridge?"

"This way, sir," Nash indicated, stepping back over to the pillars. "Mac says he knows ropes and he's none too happy about the state of these." The sergeant patted a knotted junction that formed the end of a handrail, producing a small cloud of dust that lingered in the listless air. "He says we'll be lucky to get anybody across without it falling apart."

"I think it will be fine," Jorra-hin countered from behind.

Torrin-Ashur glanced back at his friend. "Based on what?"

"Tsnath have already been across it."

"The Tsnath – you mean Daka's men?"

"Yes."

"And how have you come to that conclusion?"

Jorra-hin shrugged and ran a hand through his unruly hair. "We couldn't find the menhir that should have been at the *Niliàthái* entrance, where we came in. It wasn't in the outer cave like the one at the *Trombéi* entrance, nor was it inside the mine tunnel. What we *did* find, though, was an alcove that it could have been sitting in."

"So you're suggesting the Tsnath have already retrieved it?"

"Yes," the monk nodded. "From the inside. And according to the map of the mine tunnels, this is the only route they could have taken to get back to Üzsspeck."

"We did pass a junction with a tunnel that leads to the *Dikàthi* entrance a little way back," Borádin mentioned, raising an eyebrow to proffer his alternative.

"Could the Tsnath have gone that way?"

"Why would they?" Jorra-hin came back, meeting Torrin-Ashur's gaze. "You have to remember why they're here. In order to gather the *Dànis~Lutárn* back into the Vessel, they have to assemble all the remaining Vicar stones in Üzsspeck. It would be madness to take the *Niliàthái* menhir out of the mines, lug it and the *Dikàthi* menhir miles and miles through the Mathians – in deep winter – only to bring both back inside again. Trust me, they came this way."

"Across this bridge."

"Exactly. A group of men carrying heavy slabs of rock."

Torrin-Ashur heaved a sigh. He hid the wince of pain it caused. "Well, in that case, care to join me in testing your theory?"

Jorra-hin didn't bat an eyelid.

Nash did. "Sir, perhaps you should let someone else try?"

"I trust Jorra-hin's judgement," Torrin-Ashur countered.

Borádin tossed a small rock into the darkness of the chasm. An abrupt silence followed as those gathered held their breath, gazing into the void whilst resisting its vertiginous lure. It seemed a long time before the distant sound of rock skittering off rock returned.

"Alright then, let's not be falling off," Torrin-Ashur muttered under his breath.

His first steps out on to the suspended timbers of the bridge's walkway were gingerly taken. They precipitated neither creak nor sway. Whether that was a good thing or not, he wasn't sure. Ropes that had lost much of their natural give, having sat dormant for centuries, probably would appear rock solid – right up to the point they disintegrated without warning. Not a comforting thought.

With Jorra-hin beside him, he descended the initial gradient, holding the dusty rope that formed one of the handrails tightly in his left hand. In the other he held a torch aloft. Its light didn't project further than a few yards, illuminating the slats beneath his feet, along with the ropes holding everything together, but little else. The cavern's roof, floor and walls might as well have been on some mythical plane for all the evidence of their existence.

"The walkway is beginning to rise again," Jorra-hin noted after about forty yards.

That was a relief. They may have reached the middle, as near as they could figure it, but when Torrin-Ashur squinted forwards, he still couldn't see anything of the far side. Either the burning arrow that had been shot across had gone out, or the dip in the bridge had lowered his line of sight below the ledge, blocking his view of its guttering flame.

Jorra-hin let out a sigh of trepidation. "Well, here goes." Handing his torch to Torrin-Ashur, he gripped one of the handrails with both hands and proceeded to conduct the time-honoured assessment of structural worthiness used the world over – the jump-up-and-down test. Cautious at first, he became increasingly confident when his initial efforts didn't end in catastrophe.

"There you are, you see. I told you so."

"Seems solid enough," Torrin-Ashur called back to the others. "I think it's safe to begin sending people across, a few at a time. Nash, start with some of our lads. We don't know what's up ahead, so let's be prepared." He turned to Jorra-hin and suggested they carry on to the far side. "If the Tsnath have already been along here, that means they've beaten us to the *Dànis~Lutárn*, doesn't it?"

"It looks that way."

"Damn. There goes our chance of ambushing them at Üzsspeck. Will you be able to tell if they've taken the magic with them?"

"*You* will be able to answer that, Torrin. As a custodian of the War Song, if the *Dànis~Lutárn* is still present, the moment you encounter it, you'll drop to your knees in agony."

"Oh. Nice."

Jorra-hin chuckled.

Corporal Botfiár was the first to follow them across the gorge, leading a squad of Ashurmen in an extended line, prudently spreading the load on the bridge.

Torrin-Ashur let them assemble around him before beginning his briefing. "Alright lads, listen up. Jorra-hin believes the city isn't too far ahead now. The Tsnath might be there, so our approach must be quiet." He noticed that the men had lanterns rather than torches. Nash had probably seen to that. He doused his own torch and had Jorra-hin do the same with his.

Tick handed him a napkin containing some bread and a chunk of venison. "From the Princess, sir. She thought you might be hungry."

"She'd be right." Famished was more the word.

They set off in single file. Munching on his provisions, Torrin-Ashur lapsed into thought. He was in two minds about wanting to find the Tsnath in Üzsspeck. His primary goal was to disrupt their plans for using the *Dànis~Lutárn*, to which end catching them within the confines of the underground city was a necessity. Offsetting that, his recent altercation with the forces of nature had left him feeling like an old man. The prospect of another fight did not fill him with glee.

It took the squad almost half an hour to cover the remaining distance to the city, the need for caution slowing them down. The gradual encroachment of an orange glow defining the shape of the tunnel ahead was what eventually brought Torrin-Ashur to a halt. He raised a clenched fist. The men dropped into a crouch at the edges of passage, closing the shutters of their lanterns. Contrasting with the relative darkness, the glow ahead became more pronounced.

Jorra-hin tiptoed over and whispered, "Clearly someone has set the city's light ablaze. It wouldn't still be burning from when we came through it a while ago."

"So the Tsnath are there, then."

"They've been there. They may not be there now. Üzsspeck daytime, if you want to call it that, lasts about eight hours, if left unattended. I don't imagine it takes very long to gather the *Dànis~Lutárn* back into the Vessel, so there is a possibility that the Tsnath have been and gone already."

"Well, there's only one way to find out." Torrin-Ashur turned to Millardis. "M'Lud, get back to the others and warn them not to come any further forwards until we send word. The rest of you, leave your lanterns here and follow me."

Leading the way, Torrin-Ashur crept along the tunnel, placing his feet like a predatory cat. The last few yards to the cavern opening he took on his belly. His ribcage screamed at him to stop the torture.

Thoughts of pain were dismissed by his first glimpse of Üzsspeck. For a moment he couldn't quite believe his eyes. Listening to Jorra-hin and Elona recounting their experiences of coming through the city had given him an impression, but it was like encountering the centre of Alondris for the first time – no matter how vivid the telling, somehow other people's descriptions just fell short. He certainly hadn't been prepared for anything on such a vast scale. Whole mountains sat above the enormous cavern. Bathed in an orange hue from the sheets of flame that ran up the walls, the view reminded him of stories his father had told of giant lava pits beyond the Mäss of Súmari, far to the south of Alondria, great furnaces that made the very ground smoke and tremble.

Jorra-hin settled beside him. "Quite a sight, isn't it?"

"Oh, so-so," Torrin-Ashur scoffed quietly, making a middling gesture with his hand. He pointed to what could be seen of the open space in the centre of the city. "That's the Great Gathering?"

"Yes. If the Tsnath are still here, that's where I'd expect them to be."

"Alright, we need to take a closer look." Torrin-Ashur turned to face the lads behind him. "Botfiár, Tomàss, you two come with Jorra-hin and me. We're going to slip down into the city and have a poke around. Silfast, you and the rest of the men stay here and keep watch. Don't break cover unless you see us get into trouble."

Torrin-Ashur gave Jorra-hin a nudge, prompting him to his feet. The once black cassock the young monk habitually wore was looking decidedly grubby. Threadbare in places, and now basted in a layer of dust off the tunnel floor, he blended in well with the stone surroundings.

Keeping low, they scurried across the stretch of open ground to the nearest buildings and took cover amongst the strange architecture. Torrin-Ashur had to take a moment to catch his breath before setting off deeper into the city.

Flitting quietly through the deserted streets was an eerie experience. Torrin-Ashur couldn't quite picture the place as a flourishing neighbourhood, which it had obviously once been. Only his wheezing broke the silence now.

Nearing the city centre, he aimed Jorra-hin at a tall building whose door had parted company with its hinges, leaving its remains leaning crookedly across the opening. "Botfiár, Tomàss, find some cover and keep watch out here. Jorra-hin and I are going to see if we can get a better view of the Great Gathering. We won't be long."

Torrin-Ashur gently pushed the debris aside and ducked under the stone lintel. As he straightened up, the low ceiling delivered him a painful reminder of the traditionally limited stature of those who had built Üzsspeck. The angle he had to stoop at to avoid further collisions was back-breaking.

"Look for steps," he whispered to Jorra-hin. "There must be some way of getting to the roof."

Very little light penetrated the room, so their search was mostly conducted by fingertip.

"Over here," Jorra-hin murmured a minute later.

Torrin-Ashur groped his way towards the sound of Jorra-hin's voice. The steps his friend had discovered were made of stone, which meant there was no danger of them creaking or collapsing. He mounted them one at a time, holding his hand high to ward against any more bruised foreheads. The flight rose up one floor to a landing that backtracked to the start of the next flight. Two more ascents found him at the top of the building and facing a doorway leading out to a flat roof. The exit had probably been covered with a hanging of some sort, all traces of which were long gone.

"Excellent," he whispered as he emerged. The building had a commanding view of the Great Gathering, just as he'd hoped. A parapet wall a little over a foot high enclosed the roof area, providing ideal cover. Resorting once more to crawling, he slithered his way to the edge. His chest didn't scream at him so much this time. He only felt about sixty now.

"Not a lot happening," he noted after a few minutes of observation. It was clear that the only people in the Great Gathering were the

Dendricá, and they weren't moving. The stillness gave him pause for a moment of reflection. "Hard to imagine so many perished here; it seems so peaceful."

"Not when I close my eyes, it doesn't," Jorra-hin grunted. "There are times when I wish I'd never read Yazcöp's scroll. So what do we do now?"

Torrin-Ashur shrugged. "No idea. But tell me something – Daka needs time to work on the menhir, doesn't she?"

"To reconfigure the *Dànis~Lutárn*, yes. The old spells have to be removed from the Vicar stones and new ones applied."

"So, given that she's not still here, she's must be taking the menhir some place safe to have the work done. Back to Mitcha, I would image."

"Mitcha?"

"Why not? It's central to the Territories, it's fortified, and it's already in her hands. *Again.* It's got everything she needs."

Jorra-hin let out a thoughtful 'hmm'. "That's not good for us. You couldn't possibly take the town again, Torrin. From the stories I've heard, you were lucky the first time, but Daka won't make the same mistakes twice. She'll have the place buttoned up so tight, even the rats are probably finding it hard to come and go as they please."

Torrin-Ashur nodded. Jorra-hin was right about that. When he thought back to how they'd managed to snatch the townsfolk out from under the Tsnath's noses, it seemed incredible that they had succeeded. That mission had been foolhardy, and he'd vowed never to be so reckless again.

He was just about to stand up and make his way back down to ground level when something caught his eye. Squinting harder to make out the details, he started to grin. "No – it can't be…"

"What?"

"There," Torrin-Ashur pointed across the Great Gathering, "aren't those your Vicar stones?"

On the far side of the Gathering, partially obscured by a pile of the Dendricá's abandoned equipment, stood five stones in a rough circle. They reminded Torrin-Ashur of giant elongated eggs, split down the middle from top to bottom such that a flat surface had been created on one side. Because nothing was moving in their vicinity, he'd missed them earlier.

Jorra-hin's reaction was not one of surprise, but of confusion. "I don't understand, the Tsnath wouldn't just have left them here.

They're too important."

"I don't see anything that looks like the Vessel."

Jorra-hin scanned the area again. "Neither do I. It's about the same size as the Vicars, but shaped like a teardrop and looks as though it's made out of dark glass."

Torrin-Ashur smiled with relief. "Then we're *not* too late. Daka must have sent men into the mines in advance. She's still on her way here."

"Then the *Dànis~Lutárn* is still in place, too," Jorra-hin cautioned, placing a restraining hand on Torrin-Ashur's forearm. "Just remember, that means you can't go near the Gathering."

That was a sobering thought. It seemed so strange to Torrin-Ashur that he couldn't simply cross the nearest canal bridge without some ancient force tearing him down. Still, it was a limitation he'd have to deal with later. Right now, something else was bothering him. "You're right about the Tsnath, though. Where are the men who brought the stones? Given how important they are, why aren't the Vicars being guarded?"

"Against whom?" Jorra-hin raked through his mop of unruly curls with his fingers, combing out the carcass of a dead beetle that had probably arrived by cobweb. "They've no reason to suspect anyone else is here." He shrugged, then smiled. "They've probably gone exploring, hoping to find some of Ranadar's treasure."

Torrin-Ashur nodded. He had to admit, if he'd been in the Tsnath's shoes, he'd probably have done the same. He made to withdraw from the parapet.

"No, wait..." Jorra-hin grabbed his arm and held him down, pointing to the left of the ring of stones, "that long, low-looking building just the other side of the canal, see it? There's light coming from inside."

Torrin-Ashur stared intently. "Well spotted." He studied the building for a minute, wondering what to do. "How many men do you suppose there are? You've seen one of these menhir up close — how many would it take to carry one?"

"Six, perhaps eight. Five menhir — that gives you between thirty and forty men."

"Assuming all of them were porters. Still, even if they brought a few more, we've got enough fighters to deal with that sort of number." Torrin-Ashur's mind raced away as he started plotting. "If we approached from around the side of the Gathering, we could take them by surprise. Borádin's men can retrieve the stones afterwards, once we've secured the area."

"And then what?"

"Well, without the Vicar stones, Daka won't be able to gather the *Dànis~Lutárn* back into the Vessel. That means she can't move it. Down here, it's useless to her. All we have to do is get out of the mines, go into hiding and stay out of her hands long enough for Kirshtahll to return with the rest of the army."

"What about the Tsnath reinforcements the emperor is sending?"

Torrin-Ashur sagged a little. The odds were long, he knew. But they had to try. To fail to do that would be to admit defeat. "Look, like I said before, there's nothing we can do about them right now. It's Kirshtahll's job to keep the rest of the Tsnathsarré Empire out."

"Not just his job," Jorra-hin countered gently. "It's the job of the *Dànis~Lutárn*, too."

Torrin-Ashur frowned.

"Remember the Sentinels, those stone towers along the Ablath?" Jorra-hin reminded him. "If we could get the *Dànis~Lutárn* to the river, we could try to complete the task Mage Yazcöp set out to achieve all those years ago. We might be able to stop the Tsnath reinforcements at the border."

Torrin-Ashur bit his lip as doubts flood in. "It's too dangerous. To get our hands on the *Dànis~Lutárn* we'd have to wait for Daka to arrive with the Vessel. If we fail to defeat her, she'll have what she came for – and the gods only know what the consequences of that will be."

"*If* you fail. But think of the gains if you succeed," Jorra-hin urged. "If the Tsnath reinforcements can be held at bay, it would make the task of reclaiming the Territories from Daka much easier. If they are allowed to consolidate their position, even Kirshtahll might not be victorious."

Torrin-Ashur blew out a breath. What Jorra-hin was suggesting was a far riskier strategy than just making off with the stones now. Taking on forty odd soldiers was one thing, but there was no telling what size force Daka might be bringing with her. If they attacked now, success was reasonably within their grasp. Delaying and facing greater odds dramatically reduced their chances.

Yet he couldn't deny there was merit in trying.

It was a big decision to take, and a burden he was unwilling to shoulder on his own. Too many lives depended on it, to say nothing of the fate of the Territories.

"Come on, let's get back. We need to discuss this with Borádin and the others."

*

Roumin-Lenka maintained her calm exterior, but on the inside she brimmed with the excitement of a child. She was the first of her people to set eyes on the heart of the Old Homeland in eighteen hundred years.

Üzsspeck was fabled and revered within her culture, even though the stories of the riches therein were nothing but myths and legends, originating from the lies of men. Yet that hadn't stopped the idea of Ranadar's treasure being wholeheartedly adopted. There was something quintessentially Dwarvish about the notion of fabulous wealth buried in the mountains that couldn't fail to kindle their primal emotions. There wasn't a man or woman of her kin that hadn't fallen asleep to dream of one day standing where she stood now.

Movement below caught her eye. She watched as Gömalt proceeded apace back up the slope towards the mouth of the *Trombéi* tunnel. He'd taken a platoon down into the city to reconnoitre. He returned alone.

"The menhir?" the baroness demanded with typical impatience.

"They are assembled in the Great Gathering, my lady."

"All five?"

Gömalt nodded. Daka's lips trembled slightly in anticipation. She untied the belt around her fur coat and allowed the garment to fall open. It was much warmer here on the edge of the city than it had been back in the tunnels.

"There's just one thing that worries me, my lady," Gömalt cautioned. "There's no sign of our advance party – the place seems completely deserted."

Daka responded with a dismissive air. "They're soldiers, they're probably asleep somewhere." She turned to Nÿat. "Shall we..."

"After you, Baroness." The mage gestured forwards with a slight bow.

Daka led the way out of the tunnel with Nÿat beside her. Gömalt fell in close on her heels. Roumin-Lenka took her place next to him. Behind them, men dragged the Vessel using a harness that allowed it to be pulled along as though it were a cart hitched to a team of horses.

"You are concerned?" Roumin-Lenka murmured.

Gömalt glanced across at her. "Men don't just disappear without good reason." He gripped the hilt of his sword a little tighter and glared round at the strange city. "Be on your guard," he muttered, catching the eye of the captain in charge of the detachment of men bringing up the rear.

Gömalt advanced down through the city streets as though he expected the worst at every turn, yet they reached the Great Gathering without incident. They crossed the nearest canal bridge and met up with the platoon he had left there. Even then he didn't look comfortable.

"Peace, Gömalt," Roumin-Lenka soothed quietly, placing a hand on his forearm. "What is there to fear?"

"I don't like being in such an alien place," he grumbled. "It dulls my edge."

Roumin-Lenka shrugged and wandered away. There was nothing she could do about that; he'd just have to deal with it. To her, Üzsspeck felt like home.

Gömalt ordered some of the detachment to guard the canal bridge. The rest he stationed round the area of the stones.

Roumin-Lenka found herself close to one of the Dendricá. She stooped to examine the dusty corpse, ensuring that the handle of her battle axe didn't disturb any of the delicate remains. "These are the soldiers against whom the *Dànis~Lutárn* was deployed?"

Nÿat came alongside her and peered down, stroking his beard to a point. "Why yes indeed, my dear. The fabled Dancing Warriors."

"There are so many," she said, straightening up to gaze across the rest of the Great Gathering, littered with the forlorn shapes of the dead.

Nÿat clasped his hands together across his midriff. The diamond in the medallion at his chest swayed, catching some of the torchlight and glinting orange hues. "Just over five thousand, so I'm led to believe."

Roumin-Lenka gave her head a single shake, registering displeasure. "They turn the city into a grave. My people would not have left them here like this. The dead, even of our enemies, are always taken to a proper place of burial so that they may be at peace."

Nÿat snorted. "The city has been silent for centuries. I doubt these souls have been disturbed."

The mage's tone was too casual for Roumin-Lenka's liking. "That matters not."

"We should get on with what we came here for," Daka's impatient voice cut in.

"No reverence," Roumin-Lenka whispered under her breath, turning away. Daka's only concern was her ambition. Roumin-Lenka had a natural admiration for the baroness's vision, but no liking for the woman.

The feeling was probably mutual.

Nÿat turned and hurried over to the circle of stones. He allocated two men to each one and instructed them to swivel the menhir so that the text upon them was facing outwards. When that was done, he ordered the Vessel to be placed in the centre.

Satisfied that everything was positioned as it should be, he glanced round, catching the eye of each man near the stones.

"When I give you the word, *slowly* turn the Vicars to face the Vessel. Keep an eye on each other. The stones exert a controlling force, which must be kept in balance on all sides of the Vessel as I gather in the *Dànis~Lutárn*. So they must all be turned together. Understand?"

Ten men nodded back at him, their anxiety palpable.

*

Jorra-hin's anxiety had transcended worldly bounds. He tried to lie as still as the Dendricá surrounding him, hardly daring even to breathe. His mind was reeling; the man helping the baroness was none other than the Deputy Chancellor, the very man he'd supposedly murdered back at the Cymàtagé. When the mage's familiar voice had drifted over him, he'd nearly jumped out of his skin. It took all his willpower to remain motionless now, masquerading as one of the long dead soldiers in whose armour he was so incongruously clad.

He wasn't alone. Borádin and about thirty other men were secreted within the lines of the Dendricá beside him. But such knowledge did little to soothe ragged nerves. How he'd let Torrin-Ashur talk him into doing this, he couldn't fathom. It was partly his own fault, he had to admit; he was the one who had suggested they try to snatch the Vessel as well as the Vicar stones. Lesson learnt. Next time, he'd keep his damned mouth shut.

If there was a next time. Painfully aware that he'd almost entirely abandoned the Adak-rann tenet of not getting involved, he knew he'd need a degree of luck just to survive the next few minutes. All he could think was, if these were to be his last moments, who would record what was about to take place? If he wasn't around to do it, would all that was about to happen disappear into the mists of time, like the fate of the Dendricá before him?

Possible failure as a Recorder wasn't his only discomfort. Frustration was building that he couldn't see what was going on over by the stones. He desperately wanted to sneak a glance, but dared not move, not even slightly. All he could do was listen.

Nÿat had issued instructions to Daka's men about turning the stones. There'd been some scraping sounds, so presumably they'd done that. Now all he could hear was Nÿat mumbling in A'lyavine, some incantation too low and too distant for the details to be discerned. Whatever the mage was doing, nothing obvious was happening.

Jorra-hin began to have grave doubts about whether he'd even know when the deed was done.

But then a tingling sensation brushed over him, as though he'd been enveloped by a wave rolling up a beach. He knew the retreating touch of the *Dànis~Lutárn*. Once again it had drained him of all his strength.

He felt an immense sense of relief rise up from the Great Gathering. It was as though the very souls of the Dendricá had collectively sighed at their release from captivity.

"*Is that it?*"

"*I believe so,*" Nÿat answered the man who had spoken. "*Remember, Gömalt, it is important now that no one touches the Vessel directly.*"

Jorra-hin's blood ran cold. Of all the names that could have been mentioned, *that* one filled him with dread. It was hardly surprising that Baroness Daka's right-hand man was here. But what would his reaction be to the discovery that not all the bodies surrounding him were long dead Dendricá?

If he had had the strength, Jorra-hin would have fled.

But he didn't. He had no strength at all.

He fought the debilitating loss from the depths of his soul. He tried to scream, to issue the crucial signal upon which Torrin-Ashur's plan of attack depended.

A pathetically weak gasp was all that emerged.

No one heard it.

*

"Is that it?"

"I believe so," Nÿat answered.

Gömalt let out a quiet snort. He'd expected more. The world's most deadly weapon had just been stuffed back in its box without any commotion whatsoever. At the very least he'd expected a little histrionics from Nÿat, who mostly only seemed to do things for show. It was all a little underwhelming.

"Remember, Gömalt, it is important now that no one touches the Vessel directly."

Gömalt glanced at the baroness. It was she who needed to heed the mage's warning. Of all people, she was the one who thought herself above such mundane things as rules. None of the rest of the men had wanted to go anywhere near the Vessel, even before Nÿat had empowered it.

He turned to a group of soldiers loitering nearby. "Get the stones on to the stretchers and take them back across the bridge. Mage Nÿat, if the Vessel is covered, presumably we can manoeuvre it without danger?"

"Certainly."

Gömalt nodded. He turned to Alber. "Find some blankets or something to cover this thing with," he said, flicking a hand at the Vessel. "Then see to the men getting it hitched back into its harness." He lowered his voice. "And make it quick. The sooner I'm out of this place, the better."

"I know what you mean," Alber muttered. "I won't be sorry to see the sun again."

Nÿat went over to converse with the baroness, leaving Roumin-Lenka to wander over to Gömalt's side. She looked strident and alluring in the fiery tint of the city's light. It was as though her stature had grown since being in Üzsspeck.

"We are departing immediately?"

She sounded disappointed. Gömalt gave her a sly smirk. "We've got what we came for."

"Speak for yourself."

"You want to go prospecting?" he taunted. "I didn't think you believed in the treasure."

Roumin-Lenka pulled a face. On a little girl, it would have been a moue. On her, it was an altogether more fearsome expression, somehow bringing the scar on her cheek into prominence, as if to say, 'remember what I did to the man who gave me this'.

"I am the first Dwarve to set foot in this city in eighteen hundred years. I see no reason why I should not look around."

Gömalt shrugged. "Be my guest. I doubt the baroness would mind if you stayed behind. But don't expect her to wait for you."

"I expect nothing of Daka except to be paid," Roumin-Lenka murmured coldly. "It would be advisable that she remembers that, whether I stay here a while or not."

Always suspicious. Earning the trust of a Dwarve was next to impossible. Even after having slept in the same bed. Gömalt sighed and turned his attention to how the preparations were going for their departure.

Something caught his eye.

"What the…" he exclaimed in shock, seeing a long dead soldier attempt to rise. A rare moment of panic made a bid for dominance. It was cornered and crushed.

Thirty more dusty warriors rose to their feet. With a cry that sounded altogether too hollow and ghostly they charged towards the Vessel. Many of Daka's men had already returned to the bridge with the menhir. Those that remained fell back in confusion. Only Gömalt remained rooted to the spot, his mind in turmoil as he tried to make sense of what his eyes and ears were telling him. But it quickly dawned on him that, whatever these wraith-like warriors were, he alone was facing a platoon of them. Those odds sent him scurrying backwards.

"My lady, run," he shouted as he dashed towards Daka. "You men, get the baroness out of here – now!"

He tried to regain control of the rest of his troops, but it was no use. They were in full flight, to a man convinced that the Dendricá army was coming back from the grave. Scores more of the ancient warriors poured over three of the canal bridges on the far side of the Gathering. Superstitious fear routed his men completely, driving them to desert the Gathering. The Vessel was left undefended.

Gömalt screamed at them all the way back to the canal bridge. There he manage to regain their attention, though that fell woefully short of control. With some of the apparent Dendricá close on his heels, he was forced to retreat across the bridge. Lethal though he was, he was no match for the numbers hounding him.

Reaching the far side, he laid into his men with manic fury. Dagger in hand, one quivering wretch he impaled through the stomach. The savage attack shocked the rest. *He* was the one they should fear the most. They recoiled from him.

"Get back over there!" he roared, grabbing the next nearest soldier by his tunic collar and shoving him towards the bridge. He kicked another up the backside, propelling him after the first. "They're not dead men, you imbeciles. Just Alondrians dressed in old armour. Now get back over there!"

It was too late. One of the enemy hurled a barrel at the centre of the bridge. Its slats burst on impact. A torch sailed through the air and landed in its midst. Flames erupted across the cobbles. At the same instant a surge of fire rushed along the canal, engulfing the bridge completely. The one and only man Gömalt had managed to force back towards the enemy was devoured. The wretch screamed in agony, arms flailing. He was reduced to a writhing heap in seconds.

No sooner had his cries died down than a sizzling sound began to steam down from the edges of the cavern.

"The light!" Roumin-Lenka screamed above the confusion. She dashed to Gömalt's side and pointed at the cavern walls. "They are dousing the flames. We will be in darkness in minutes."

Gömalt's eyes darted to the stones. They were safe on his side of the canal. The Vessel was a different story. Already Alondrians swarmed round it. Their intention was clear; they were going to steal the *Dànis~Lutárn*.

"Torches, now!" he ordered.

"They intend to use the *Niliàthái* and *Dikàthi* tunnel," Roumin-Lenka panted, pointing across the gathering at the sporadic torches that lit the route the Alondrians were going to take back through the city. "If we move fast, we might be able to cut them off by going round the Great Gathering."

Gömalt nodded and turned to Daka. "My lady, you must withdraw. Get back to the *Trombéi* tunnel. I will pursue the Alondrians, but you must make haste to alert our troops outside. Tell them their treasure has been stolen – that should motivate them. Have them head back towards Mitcha. If the Alondrians manage to stay ahead of us and emerge at the *Dikàthi* entrance, then you should be well placed to intercept them."

"And if it is the *Niliàthái* entrance?" Roumin-Lenka prompted.

"Then they will meet Özeransk," Gömalt answered.

"Do not fail me," Daka snarled. "Get my weapon back. And kill these wretched Alondrians. Not one of them is to live!"

Never before had Gömalt seen the baroness so seething with

anger. The gods help anyone who fell afoul of her now. He was just glad he'd not be in her path for a while; even his position offered little protection from that kind of wrath.

*

Torrin-Ashur raced across the Great Gathering leading most of the Ashurmen and about fifty volunteers from the men of Mitcha. He headed straight for Borádin. The nobleman was overseeing the loading of the Vessel into the harness the Tsnath had fashioned for it.

"They have the Vicar Stones. What happened?" he shouted as soon as he was near enough to be heard. "Why didn't you move sooner?"

Borádin grimaced and flicked a glance towards Jorra-hin. "Ask him. I was waiting for his signal."

Torrin-Ashur vented his disappointment with a string of expletives. Things had not gone as well as he'd hoped. But he knew it wasn't Borádin's fault. "Well, at least we got the main prize." He gestured across the canal towards the Tsnath. "We don't have much time. We were lucky they panicked, but they've realised their mistake now. They're trying to cut us off."

Borádin nodded. "We're nearly done here."

Torrin-Ashur left Borádin to finish securing the Vessel and hurried over to where Jorra-hin was still on the ground. The monk had managed to sit up, though his head was resting on drawn-up knees.

"Are you alright?"

"Sorry I let you down," Jorra-hin murmured, not looking up. "I did warn you this might happen."

"Never mind that. We've got to go."

Jorra-hin let out a mirthless chuckle. "Fate's a strange creature. We started out hoping to get the Vicars and not the Vessel. Now we have the Vessel and not the Vicars."

"Fate will see us lose that, too, if we don't get moving. The Tsnath are already trying to cut us off!"

Jorra-hin extended his arm for assistance. Torrin-Ashur hauled him to his feet. The young monk wobbled and sagged. He would have hit the floor again had Torrin-Ashur not been quick to catch him under the arms and hold him up.

"That bad?"

"If the *Dànis~Lutárn* and I never cross paths again, I shall be supremely happy."

Torrin-Ashur half carried, half dragged Jorra-hin towards the edge of the Gathering. By the time they reached the canal bridge the cavern was appreciably dimmer. Over his shoulder, Torrin-Ashur could clearly make out the bobbing path of torches as their carriers raced through the city streets. The oil his men had managed to divert from the Gathering's central fountain to the far canal was still burning fiercely, otherwise the Tsnath would already have been pouring over the bridges. The last Alondrian had to be off the Gathering before that happened. Clashing in the confines of the city's streets was one thing, but a battle out in the open was an eventuality they could not afford.

"Come on lads, move it," he shouted back to those bringing up the rear.

The enemy had already made it a quarter of the way round the Gathering. "This is going to be a close run thing," he gasped to Jorra-hin between breaths. Hauling the nearly dead weight of the young monk was agony on his barely recovered ribs.

Borádin chivvied the tail enders on as they struggled with the Vessel. It fought them every step of the way. Floating as it did on some ethereal carriage, it effectively weighed nothing. Hauling it at speed should have been easy. It was not. It was almost impossible. Jorra-hin had warned everyone involved in the attack that it must not be touched once the *Dànis~Lutárn* had been returned to it. That made controlling its unnatural inertia almost impossible. Like a petulant colt refusing to submit to the rein, it wanted to drift everywhere except where they wanted it to go. Those harnessed to it quickly tired and had to be relieved at frequent intervals. Every change of man cost time.

The retreat hadn't got much more than half way back to the *Dikàthi* tunnel by the time the light from the cavern walls finally died out, leaving them with only a sparse string of torch bearers stationed along the route to guide them through the streets.

"Damn these buildings," Torrin-Ashur cursed aloud. In the thick of Üzsspeck's urban sprawl, he couldn't get any kind of a fix on the progress of the Tsnath. Unencumbered, they had to be gaining rapidly. Anxiety suggested they'd be around the very next corner.

He grabbed the nearest torch bearer, one of the Mitcha men. "Run on ahead and alert Sergeant Nash that we'll have Tsnath on our tail by the time we get to the tunnel. Tell him to be ready, but to check his targets before letting loose with his arrows."

Without a word, the Mitcha man sped off up the hill.

Torrin-Ashur knew they wouldn't be out of the woods even when they did make it to the relative safety of the tunnel. The Tsnath would pour down it after them, snapping at their heels every step of the way. He didn't like the idea of leaving men to engage in a rear-guard action, but the cumbersome nature of the Vessel was going to make it necessary.

The men were shattered by the time they reached the edge of the city. With no sign of the enemy, Torrin-Ashur's hopes rose slightly.

"Alright lads, this is the last stretch," he panted, trying to catch his breath, "we're nearly there."

The men launched themselves out across the open ground leading up to the tunnel mouth. No sooner were they clear of the buildings than torches began appearing off to their right. Tsnath poured out from between ancient dwellings like hornets from a disturbed nest.

The remaining distance the Alondrians still had to cover suddenly went from yards to miles. Torrin-Ashur screamed at his men to keep going no matter what. They put everything they had into a final burst of speed.

Ahead, Nash emerged from the mouth of the tunnel with a squad of archers. They dropped to one knee and began laying down cover. The Tsnath faltered, but did not stop. They replied in kind, some arrows aimed at the tunnel, the rest at those trying to reach it.

Coming under attack, Torrin-Ashur felt a surge of power from the War Song. Jorra-hin became light on his arm. The pain in his chest vanished. It was as though youth had returned to an old man.

Out of the darkness, he sensed more than saw an arrow sailing towards one of the men straining at the Vessel's harness. He dived forwards to barge the unsuspecting target aside.

Jorra-hin, momentarily bereft of support, stumbled into the Vessel's path. His bare hand brushed the teardrop's side. As though hit by a bolt of lightning, he was instantly lifted off his feet. His body sailed through the air and landed in a crumpled heap yards away.

Torrin-Ashur struggled to comprehend what had just happened. A giant invisible hand had just swiped his friend away, like a rag doll flung down by a child in a tantrum.

Overcoming his confusion, he dashed over and hauled Jorra-hin up off the floor. There wasn't a shred of response in him; his body was inert. He could do nothing but sling him over his shoulder and stagger on towards the tunnel.

*

"Give them another salvo," Gömalt ordered.

The twang of bowstrings and swish of arrows sounded, seeming louder within the cavern than he was used to. There was still no retaliatory response from the tunnel, nor had there been to the last few salvos. The clatter of arrows hitting nothing but rocky walls suggested the softer targets that had been there earlier had withdrawn.

"Reconnoitre forwards," he ordered.

He had the bulk of the fighting contingent Daka had brought to Üzsspeck with him. The baroness had only needed enough of an escort to ensure her personal safety back to the *Trombéi* entrance, plus some men to carry the menhir. That left a force of about eighty to chase after the Alondrians. What he didn't know was the enemy's strength. Yet inside the tunnels neither side could fully bring their forces to bear, so it didn't matter who outnumbered who. Outside, it would be a different story. The odds there were stacked in his favour.

A minute of disorganised confusion in nearly pitch dark conditions ensued before a squad of nervous men began edging their way towards the tunnel entrance. Their caution tried Gömalt's patience.

"It's clear, sir," the detachment captain called back.

Gömalt scrambled up and advanced. Roumin-Lenka fell in beside him.

"Why didn't the Alondrians light the fire channel?" she wondered as she reached the tunnel entrance.

"It would have silhouetted them as targets," Gömalt muttered, giving the matter little thought.

"Shall I light it now?"

Gömalt nodded. "We might as well be able to see what we're walking into."

The flame from Roumin-Lenka's torch singed into the tunnel's oil-bearing channel and took hold. A blueish stream of light rapidly flowed its way along the wall, disappearing round the first bend in a matter of seconds. The flames settled down into the familiar yellow and orange flickers of ordinary torches.

Gömalt demanded rapid progress along the tunnel. It was perhaps imprudent, but then he made sure to hang back behind the front runners so that he would not bear the brunt of any nasty surprises the

Alondrians may have left behind.

He did not expect his men to stall less than a mile further on.

He barrelled his way through the troops and dropped to his knees at the edge of a stygian chasm. The severed remnants of a suspension bridge tapered off below him into the darkness.

The tunnel on the far side was illuminated, allowing him to judge the distance across the nothingness. It was an impossible obstacle. He picked up a blunt axe that had been discarded. With a roar of fury, he hurled it out into the void. Those around him shrank back, trying not to become the object of his fuming glare.

Roumin-Lenka pushed her way forwards and joined him. "*Dörgànk*."

"What?" he demanded.

"The chasm – it is called *Dörgànk*."

"You knew this was here?"

"Yes."

"And you didn't think to tell me?" Gömalt rounded, more viciously than was wise.

Roumin-Lenka's hand darted out and gripped his chin, pulling him close to. "Remember who it is you are talking to, Gömalt," she growled near his ear. For a moment her eyes glowered with the reflection of the flames that lit the tunnel. In them was an infernal glint.

Gömalt relaxed and mumbled an apology between scrunched lips. His face was relinquished. He allowed a suitable pause for tempers to subside before asking, "Is there a way round?"

"No. But there is another way to cross."

"A bridge?"

"Of sorts. But it will take time."

"Explain…"

"The *Dörgànk* was a secret part of the city's defences," the Dwarve explained. She stepped over to the side of the tunnel and probed the darkness, looking for something. "Fortunately, we are on the city side. It was intended that if Üzsspeck ever came under attack, the bridge could be severed. This never happened. But the city's defenders had the foresight to devise a way of re-establishing the bridge if ever it did."

"How?"

"By flooding the gorge with water. There is a large reservoir that can be released into it from this side. All we have to do is find the sluice gate and open it."

"And then we swim across?"

"That shouldn't be necessary. A pontoon bridge should rise up with the water level, provided that it hasn't rotted away over the years."

Gömalt peered back over the edge of the gorge. Only his imagination pictured a floating bridge at the bottom. "How long will it take?"

Roumin-Lenka shrugged. "I don't know. It wasn't designed as a quick way to repair the bridge, just a way to get across without one."

Finding the sluice gate took only a matter of minutes. There was really only one place it could be – a little further along the narrow ledge that lined the side of the gorge. It took far longer to open it. Scale deposits formed from minor leaks that had long since sealed themselves had effectively welded it shut, rendering its opening mechanism inoperable. After wasting half an hour with various men attempting to make it work, Gömalt lost patience and ordered the use of brute force.

An axe was brought to bear. The poor unfortunate wielding it did not fare well; four blows, and the gate gave way with a loud crack. A torrent of water erupted from the hole, punching the man out into the middle of the gorge. His scream was completely drowned out by the roaring cascade. All trace of him was gone in an instant.

More out of curiosity than concern, Gömalt stared at the man's brief trajectory before collecting himself together and turning away with a shrug.

Since it was probably going to take hours to fill the gorge, and the noise of the waterfall was uncomfortably loud, he decided to return to the city. He posted a detail of five men to monitor the progress. "Send word as soon as the surface of the water comes into view," he ordered.

On the way back down the tunnel the detachment captain came alongside. "This delay is going to make it difficult to catch up with the Alondrians, sir".

"Yes. But now we may have surprise on our side."

"Surprise?"

Gömalt turned to Roumin-Lenka. "With your knowledge of this *Dörgànk*, how likely is it that the Alondrians know about the reservoir?"

"It is not likely. It was not common knowledge, even in Ranadar's day. The *Dörgànk* was meant to be a secret."

Gömalt nodded. A wolfish grin appeared on his face. "Good." He turned to the captain. "The Alondrians think they have prevented us from pursuing them. Our eventual advance will not be expected at all. That gives us an advantage."

16

For what seemed the thousandth time, Kirin wiped a damp cloth over Jorra-hin's sweat-beaded brow. There was still no sign of him returning whence the glancing blow with the Vessel had sent him. There was no indication that he would *ever* return. Mage Yazcöp's account of what had happened to poor Silas when he'd accidentally come into contact with the Dànis~Lutárn told only that the man had lost his mind, not that he had recovered. That thought, unbidden yet again, merely reinforced the lines of worry etched on Kirin's face.

Outwardly Jorra-hin appeared to be suffering a fever, but she knew it was not from any normal kind of sickness. Although the accursed restraint cast prevented her from practicing the Taümathic arts, she could still sense the touch of magic. She was certain the Taümatha was doing something to Jorra-hin now, something he was resisting. It seemed as if he was engaged in an epic struggle, a war in which his very soul might be both battlefield and prize. The only comfort his restless, tortured condition gave her was that it showed the struggle was not over. Jorra-hin was still fighting. She prayed again for his strength.

A gentle hand settled on her shoulder. She looked up to find Elona standing behind her.

"You must be tired. Someone else could watch him for a while. You should get some rest."

Kirin rose to her feet. "I cannot sleep. But thank you."

Elona leaned forwards and touched her forehead to Kirin's. "He'll be alright, you know. He's too stubborn to give up." Her words were full of conviction. "You know what he's like; he'll probably wake up any moment now and launch into a long and boring explanation of what just happened."

Kirin smiled for a moment before a tear betrayed her bravery. "Has Cosmin had any luck with bypassing the seal?" she asked, trying to change the subject before the solitary escapee was joined by others.

Elona shook her head. "This seal is much stronger than the one at the *Niliàthái* entrance."

"It would be," Kirin nodded. "Yazcöp's account told us the *Dikàthi* entrance was the first glean the mages constructed. It was part of their original plan to force the Dendricá into using the *Trombéi* entrance so that they had no choice but to pass through Üzsspeck. The mages were fresh when they created this one. It stands to reason it is the strongest, even without the menhir to bolster it."

Elona chuckled. "Now you're even sounding like him," she teased, nodding down at Jorra-hin.

A curious look came over Kirin. "Sounding like him…" she repeated, trying to wrangle a thought from the illusive to the definitive. "Of course, it's not about trying to overcome the glean, it's about understanding what it is."

"Cosmin is well aware of its nature."

"Yes, but perhaps I can help. Jorra has been teaching me how to pronounce A'lyavine. You know how it is when he speaks it – his pronunciation is so pure that everybody simply understands. Perhaps if I try saying that phrase he used…"

"But what about your restraint cast? Will it be safe for you to try?"

Kirin nodded. "I think so. Speaking in A'lyavine isn't actually using magic – it's just making use of the language to lend clarity to the mind."

"Semantics. As far as I'm concerned, it's all magic."

Kirin pouted. "Jorra wouldn't see it that way."

"Well," Elona sighed, "if you're confident it won't put you in danger, it's certainly worth a try. I know Cosmin would appreciate the help."

Kirin bent down and mopped Jorra-hin's brow one last time, then gestured towards one of the Mitcha women who had been helping her. The townswoman took over the ministrations without a word.

Elona led the way through the tunnel towards the entrance. They had to pick their way through the Mitcha folk lining the passageway, some asleep, weary from days of walking, but most restless this close to being back in the real world again. Only a Dwarve could be comfortable stuck underground for so long, Kirin mused.

The tunnel ended at the foot of what appeared to be a cave-in. Before it milled a throng of people, none of whom were doing very much other than looking perplexed and prostrating their impotence before the gods.

Elona found Cosmin and wasted no time in explaining what Kirin had suggested.

"By all means, give it a try, m'dear," the old mage consented to

Kirin, his thick beard bouncing as his head bobbed. "Can't do any worse than me."

Elona went to stand next to Torrin-Ashur. The look on his face suggested he didn't like the feeling of helplessness their current circumstances imposed.

Kirin walked up to the rocky downfall and reached out to touch it, as if to reassure herself that it was actually there. Which, she realised too late, was precisely the opposite of what she ought to have done. She stepped back several paces and closed her eyes.

She tried to picture in her mind the words Jorra-hin had used on the previous occasions when they'd passed through other seals. Since all her lessons with him had been based around reading books of one sort or another, it was easier to say the words if she was reading them, as though they were written on her eyelids. She was silent for several minutes, then took a deep breath and tried to utter the words that had formed in her mind.

"*Aya döma...*" she began aloud.

"NO!"

Kirin's eyes snapped open. She spun round. Jorra-hin was standing a few yards behind her, listing to one side as though drunk. His eyes were screwed shut. He was in pain.

Kirin rushed over and flung her arms around him. "You're alright!" she blathered into his cassock. Relief made her sound almost accusatory.

"I don't feel alright. I need to sit down. And I *really* need something to drink," Jorra-hin rasped, "my throat feels like it's full of sand."

Kirin steadied him while he lowered himself to the ground. One of the Mitcha folk provided a canteen from which Jorra-hin gratefully took several long draws. Handing the canteen back, he leaned his head against the rock wall and let out an enormous sigh.

"Why did you stop Kirin from trying to open the seal?" Cosmin asked, shuffling over to his side and squatting down.

"She was about to use the Taümatha." Jorra-hin's reply sounded as though he was angry. "The restraint would have killed her."

Kirin paled. "I don't understand. I was only trying to speak in A'lyavine."

"No – you weren't." Jorra-hin groped around for her hand. "You wanted to overcome the seal. I could feel it. *Desire*, Kirin. Remember Emmy? How you tapped into your feelings, your desire, in order to heal her?"

"How could I ever forget?"

Jorra-hin nodded, still with his eyes shut. "So tell me, what does *Aya dömasti* mean? That was what you were going to say, isn't it?"

A look of confusion came over Kirin, her forehead screwing up in concentration. It was as if the words were foreign to her. "*I command*," she answered hesitantly.

"Exactly. You were about to order the seal to disappear."

"But – I don't understand. That's not what I wanted to say. I was trying to remember what *you* said when you got us into the mines at *Niliàthái*."

"I know. But the A'lyavine that came to mind was trying to interpret what was in your heart."

Kirin trembled at the realisation of just how close she had come to making a fatal mistake. Jorra-hin's grip on her hand tightened.

"How did you know?" she asked.

"I'm not sure. I don't have any recollection beyond a few minutes ago. I just remember surfacing like I'd come up from the bottom of the sea. I had this overwhelming feeling that you were in danger."

Kirin leaned forwards and kissed him long and hard. "Thank you," she whispered.

Cosmin suddenly clapped his hands together and rubbed them briskly, snapping everybody out of their reverie. "Right, well, now that we've cleared that up, perhaps we can get out of here."

No one disagreed with that.

*

Gömalt watched his spy push through the rest of the men to deliver his report. As soon as it had been possible to get someone across the *Dörgànk*, he had dispatched the man forwards to find out whatever he could about the enemy without alerting them to the possibility of Tsnathsarré pursuit. Gömalt was rather hoping that that would come as a swift and deadly surprise when the time was ripe.

The spy arrived in front of him.

"What of the Alondrians?" Gömalt demanded, giving the man little time to compose himself.

"I managed to get in with them, sir. They did not suspect me; I was just another unknown face in the crowd."

A frown crossed Gömalt's brow. "Is that so…"

"They're not one single regiment, sir. Some of them are soldiers, remnants from various units, but most of them are civilians – the ones that escaped from Mitcha. I could have been anyone, sir."

Gömalt's eye's widened. He shot Roumin-Lenka a quick glance. "So who is commanding them?"

"They call him Lord Ashur, sir."

"Ashur? Impossible. He was killed when we dealt with Tail-ébeth." Gömalt paused as a thought struck him. "Unless – how old would you say he was?"

"Young, sir, early twenties, I should think."

"Ah, Torrin-Ashur, then," Gömalt concluded. He gave Roumin-Lenka a longer glance and drew a finger along his jaw, tracing the scar Kassandra had inflicted. "The son who thwarted me at the River Ablath. The son with whom I have a score to settle."

Roumin-Lenka didn't react.

Gömalt returned his attention to the spy. "So, did you manage to learn anything of their plans?"

The man smiled in anticipation of the credit he was about to earn.

"Yes, sir. I was able to loiter nearby while their leaders met to discuss their options. Sir, they understand what the *Dànis~Lutárn* is and what it can do. They are going to try to keep it out of the baroness's hands as long as possible."

"Are they indeed?" Gömalt rubbed his chin thoughtfully. That could cause a problem. With the emperor on his way down, the baroness needed a speedy resolution to this situation, or her plan would fall apart. "Did they discuss where they are going?"

"To the River Ablath, sir."

Gömalt's frown returned. "The border?" That made little sense. "Why up there?"

"Their plan when they attacked us at the city, sir, was to steal the Vessel and the stones. With them both, they hoped to deploy the *Dànis~Lutárn* along the river, to keep the emperor out of the Tep-Mödiss."

"The original plan of the mages who made the *Dànis~Lutárn*," Roumin-Lenka said. "The Alondrians can't do that now – we have the stones. So why would they still want to go to the border?"

"Probably because it's the last place we'd look for them," Gömalt concluded. "They are desperate."

The captain of the detachment leaned towards him. "Sir, if most of the Alondrians are civilians, we shouldn't have too much trouble dealing with them. We could do it ourselves." He shifted his attention to the spy. "How far behind them are we?"

"About half a day, sir. But there's more you should know. The Alondrians think they have some sort of magic protecting them now."

"Magic?" Gömalt frowned back.

"Yes, sir. The same as all those dead soldiers lying in Üzsspeck had. I didn't really understand all they were saying, but that's the gist of it."

Gömalt caught the captain's eye. "That puts a different slant on things. According to what Mage Nÿat told us, this magic, the War Song, they called it, transformed the Dendricá into a formidable fighting force. If the Alondrians we are chasing are indeed in possession of this magic, and it protects them as it did their ancestors, we have a different kind of problem on our hands."

"We need to inform Daka and her mage of this development," Roumin-Lenka advised.

"Yes, and quickly." Gömalt returned his attention to the spy. "What of the route they were planning to take?"

The spy shook his head. "Sorry, sir. It wasn't discussed."

Gömalt considered that for a moment. He tried to put himself in his quarry's shoes.

"First, Ashur will probably head north, to pick up the road that goes from Mitcha to Tail-ébeth," he surmised. "Then he will turn west, away from where he may reasonably assume there to be Tsnathsarré forces."

"You mean at Mitcha?" Roumin-Lenka asked.

Gömalt nodded. "West also takes him into the March of Ashur."

"His own lands."

"Indeed." Gömalt smiled. "Where he will no doubt feel safer. If I were him, I'd then follow the Ébeth up to the border, where it flows into Loch Shëdd, a little to the east of the Stroth Ford."

The captain of the detachment let out a derisive snort. "If we know where's he's going, we can trap him."

Gömalt's smile became a grin.

"Captain, the last remnant of the Ashur household will die within sight of the ruins of his own home. As will all those with him."

Roumin-Lenka did not share such confidence. She wore a frown rather more sceptical. "And what of this War Song?"

"We have Nÿat," Gömalt replied, his grin undiminished, "and we have the menhir. We have the means of controlling the *Dànis~Lutárn*, even if the Alondrians have the Vessel. We must get back to the baroness as quickly as possible. There is much to do."

*

Omnitas looked perplexed, Döshan noted, and well he might. For his presence in the Tep-Mödiss was not only known, anticipated even, but now actually sought.

"What do you make of this?" the emperor demanded.

Döshan had no need to familiarise himself again with the message the emperor wafted at him. It had been received, not from Lord Özeransk, but from Baroness Daka herself, and he'd read it in disbelief several times before allowing it to reach its intended recipient.

"Perplexing, Sire, truly."

"She wants me to join her at Tail-ébeth? *Wants* me there?"

In truth, the message had been worded such that it read like a summons. But Döshan knew the emperor would never acknowledge that, so it had been interpreted as an invitation. Either way, it made little sense.

It may have annoyed the emperor that his entry into the Tep-Mödiss had not gone unnoticed, robbing him of any element of surprise, but as far as Döshan was concerned, it was to be expected. Daka had her spies, just as they had theirs.

The baffling element of the baroness's latest move was that she had invited Omnitas to join her for the final victory. The last remnant of Alondrian resistance was to be crushed at the place where the campaign had begun. Near a town whose presence in the land had been wiped clean off the map. Döshan shuddered at the thought of the fate awaiting the wretches being herded into her trap. His mind didn't dwell there long, however. It couldn't afford to. His skills needed to focus on teasing Daka's intent out of the fog.

"Sire, I see only one logical explanation for this: Daka knows you are here, and wishes to seem like she is currying favour with you."

"Damn the woman!" Omnitas exploded, drawing dangerous attention towards Döshan from the elite guards mere yards away. They remained in their places, much to his relief. "I do not trust her. She would not curry favour with the gods, except as a last resort. And I do not see her seeking last resorts. She has all but achieved her goals." Omnitas rounded on Döshan and pinned him with an uncomfortable glare. "So *what* is she up to?"

Döshan bowed low, doing everything possible to avoid angering the emperor. He wished, nay prayed hard, that he could answer the emperor's question. But Daka's intentions eluded him.

17

The future looked bleak from Torrin-Ashur's perspective. It had taken days and days just to get the people down from the mountains and across to the bridge over the River Ébeth. He had no idea what they were going to do when they eventually reached the Ablath. It was no longer a destination, just a lack of alternatives. With both the Vessel and the Vicar stones in their possession, there had at least been some point in trying to reach the border. All the Ablath offered now was a place to hide a little longer, and pray that help came up from the south before it was too late.

He wished it had been possible to leave the bulk of the people in the Mathian Mines. At least they would have had shelter there. But the enemy wouldn't give up trying to track them down – possession of the Vessel ensured that. If the Tsnath had skirted round the mountains and re-entered the mines from either the *Dikàthi* or *Niliàthái* entrances, his people would have been trapped.

So here they were, out in the open, with death stalking their every move. If the Tsnath didn't get them, winter probably would. He let out a sigh. The people followed him almost blindly in their belief that he would somehow deliver them. That he'd managed to do so thus far, against some unfavourable odds, only bolstered their faith.

Brooding thus, he leaned against the stone bridge spanning the Ébeth, elbows propped up on the sidewall, watching soldiers mingled with townsfolk trudge past.

"You look worried," Borádin observed, peeling off from his troops as they marched by.

"Aye." Torrin-Ashur snapped back to the present and drew himself up.

"Well, we made it this far, and still no sign of the Tsnath," Borádin offered. "That's got to be good, surely?"

"The lack of enemy lurking behind every bush isn't what's bothering me."

"Oh? So what is?"

"All these people."

"What about them?"

Borádin's reply sounded almost callous, but after the sacrifices he'd made recently, Torrin-Ashur knew it wasn't that. "Suppose we do make it to Loch Shëdd, what then? Can these people survive the rest of winter without shelter? We won't be able to build a proper camp – all we can do is keep moving around in the hope that Kirshtahll arrives before the Tsnath find us."

Borádin acknowledged with a gloomy nod.

"It would have been better if I'd never liberated Mitcha. I've probably sentenced most of these people to freeze to death." Torrin-Ashur shut eyes, fighting off a rather unexpected tremble in his lips. Gods, he was at a low ebb.

"When was the last time you spoke to any of the people of Mitcha, my lord?"

A look of surprise passed between Torrin-Ashur and Borádin. Neither had realised their conversation could be overheard.

The mayor of Mitcha's daughter approached, snow lending her steps stealth.

"Katla."

"Lord Ashur, have you asked anyone from Mitcha how they feel about having been liberated?"

The question struck a chord. Abashed, Torrin-Ashur realised that he hadn't had a meaningful conversation with anyone from Mitcha besides Katla, her father and a few members of the town council. His blank look was all the answer she needed.

"Then I'll tell you – they feel free. And they're glad of it. We may be freezing out here, but that's better than being held prisoner at Mitcha." The force of Katla's words was a shock; she was angry. Her tone barely softened as she continued. "No one blames you for the situation we're in. You're a lieutenant being asked to perform the duties of a general. You've done what you thought was best."

Torrin-Ashur didn't want to object to someone being complimentary, but he needed to set the record straight before anyone else started expecting miracles.

"I've been running round like a headless chicken for the most part, Katla. Until now I've been lucky, that's all. That could change. I may yet end up getting you all killed."

Katla shrugged. "None of us are under any illusions about what might happen. But we'll still follow wherever you take us, and we'll put up with whatever hardship that entails."

"Why?" Torrin-Ashur challenged, at a loss to see justification for such allegiance.

"Because you're the only one left up here still trying to do something about the Tsnath. If we have to face them, we'll face them. And if we die, we die."

"Dying is easy to speak of, Katla," Borádin interrupted, his voice conciliatory. "Not so easy to do."

Katla was undeterred. "Freedom is worth fighting for, my lord. This is our home, our land. I would rather die a free Alondrian than live here under a Tsnath boot."

Torrin-Ashur gave his head a single, saddened shake. "I respect anyone prepared to give their life for what they believe in – whether they be enemy or friend." He turned to face the direction the people were travelling in and pointed to the crest of the small hill that lay in front of them. "Even so, when you get to the top of that, you may change your mind. You'll be able to see Tail-ébeth on the other side. When you do, you will know what the Tsnath do to their enemies."

He turned away, too proud to let a woman see tears welling in his eyes.

*

Elona sucked in her breath at the sight of Tail-ébeth. She'd expected significant damage, but not the utter devastation that lay before her. Reduced to rubble, and now blanketed with snow, it was a forlorn and deserted scene, jarring painfully with her memories of its vibrancy. The week she'd spent within its walls, embraced by the simplicity and warmth of its welcome, had been idyllic; an uncluttered hospitality that had contrasted so pleasantly with the complexities of life in Alondris. All that was so utterly gone now that it left a hollowness within her. She felt violated; something had been stolen from her that she'd never get back.

Something else stirred within her, a feeling of anger, a cry for justice. She felt a strange surge of power flow though her, a determination of sorts, as though she wanted to deliver retribution. She knew it was the effect of the *Sèliccia~Castrà*, that in its own subtle way it was bolstering her, giving her strength. From what she'd heard, she also knew that with the War Song usually came a warning.

Beside her, Torrin-Ashur stood still, beholding the awful fate of his home. She could only imagine the pain he was feeling. His eyes glistened, which had little to do with the chilled wind that blew gently towards them, save only that it heralded a sickening reminder of the desolation below.

It took a whistle and a shout from behind to shake him out of his reverie. He tensed and caught her eye. Something was amiss.

Mac was running towards them. About a hundred yards off, his hand waving in the air and pointing back along the road towards the Ébeth was clear enough sign of the urgency.

"Tsnath!" Torrin-Ashur hissed.

Elona flashed a glance at Borádin. He looked confused. Both of them scanned the area, frowning.

"Where?" Borádin demanded.

"Everywhere. We are nearly surrounded."

Elona's eyes widened in fear. "I don't see them."

"You will. Borádin, we need to get everybody up here now."

The nobleman needed no further prompting; the first day at the Academy taught the value of high ground. He ran down the slope issuing orders in rapid succession, chivvying townsfolk and soldier alike up on to the brow of the hill before it was too late.

Torrin-Ashur scanned the remains of the town and surroundings again. He seemed to settle into a curious sort of calm.

"Poetic," he murmured.

"What?"

"For me, this war started here. And now it will end here."

"I'm not sure I follow."

"Elona, I know you can't see them yet, but there are thousands of Tsnath out there. This is going to be our last stand."

The mayor of Mitcha came charging up the hill. He wasn't the youngest of men and Elona wondered if he might collapse when he reached the top. He proved more resilient.

"Are we going to have to fight?" he heaved, drawing in lungfuls of air.

"Yes," Torrin-Ashur answered bluntly. "And it's going to take everyone."

The mayor gave a grave nod. "Katla told me about what she said to you earlier. She was right about one thing – we'll do our part."

Torrin-Ashur smiled. It was tinged with sadness, Elona could tell. "It will be an honour to fight alongside you once more."

A deep sense of admiration for the mayor washed over Elona. Here was a man who, with no training and very little experience, was prepared to take up arms and face an overwhelming enemy. She could see the fear in his eyes – it mirrored her own – but she knew with certainty that it would not deter him from his duty.

Her thoughts jumped to Midana and the way her sister exercised her power. It drove her to a sudden realisation; ruling these people was not a right – it was a privilege.

*

Özeransk saw the urgent way in which the Alondrians crowned the nearby hill and turned to Daka, "They know we're here, Baroness."

"Then we might as well show ourselves, hmm?"

Özeransk found Daka's gleeful anticipation distasteful.

"Allow them to surrender, I urge you."

Daka's eyes froze. Her hair, controlled to the last strand, made her look as immutable as a marble statue.

"No."

"But they are mostly civilians. What threat are they to you?"

"I don't care what they are. They have defied me. Now they will pay the price. As did they."

Özeransk followed the baroness's nod towards the ruined town. In that moment he knew all was lost for those he had come, in no small measure, to admire for their bravery and resourcefulness.

He came to a decision he'd been mulling over for a while now and let out a sigh. He knew he might regret what he was about to say.

"Then their fate is in your hands. I will take no part in it."

Daka said nothing. Though she was as hard to read as ever, he thought he saw in her eyes a hint of some private victory just won.

*

"Well, shiver me timbers," Mac muttered, letting out a long breath as if venting steam. He'd seen to the tail enders, herding them up the hill, and now that he'd joined them at the top he could scan the horizon and see the true extent of the pickle they were in. "At least at sea you can usually make a run for it."

"Your sails will have to remain furled this time, old friend," Elam said, giving him a slap on the back.

"Aye." Mac shook his head at the way the odds were stacking up against them. The Tsnath, having realised that neither their presence nor their trap were any longer a secret, had broken cover to reveal their strength. It was no surprise to see them in their thousands. The bulk had massed in a great semicircle just to the north of the hill. They had further regiments, led by a phalanx of heraldry, pouring across the Ébeth. The latter took up station just a short distance beyond the bridge, cutting off any possibility of an Alondrian retreat in that direction. "They ain't payin' us enough for this," he muttered.

"They ain't payin' us at all," Elam chuckled, "in case you'd forgotten."

"Ah, my point exactly!" Mac waggled his finger skywards, "A fine carry on for a mercenary."

"Or even a pirate."

"Arrgh! And all I ever wanted was a palm tree to call me own."

Elam knocked shoulders with him. "You'd best go and see to Ida and your young ones."

"Aye. Save me a nice spot near the front. If the world's going to end, I don't want some blithering landlubber blocking me view."

With that, Mac trotted off to find his wife.

*

Torrin-Ashur passed behind a line of men preparing themselves as he searched for Jorra-hin. One soldier caught his attention more than the rest. The man seemed rather short, almost Dwarve-like. Fully dressed in armour liberated from the Dendricá in the Great Gathering, he was facing the enemy, sword already drawn. It wasn't that which brought Torrin-Ashur to a halt, though. It was that the man had plunged his scabbard into the ground beside his foot. "Why have you done that?" he asked, gesturing towards the empty sheath.

"Brother Jorra-hin told me the Dendricá used to do it," piped a young voice. "We are the Dancing Warriors now, my lord."

Torrin-Ashur reeled. "Paulus? What in the name of the gods are you doing here?"

Paulus's eyes squinted in confusion, as if he'd been asked a completely nonsensical question. "My lord?"

"You're…" Torrin-Ashur stopped. He had been about to remind the young lad that he was only twelve; that he should have been with the other children; that the front line was no place for him. But those words wouldn't come. The lad was calm. There wasn't a trace of fear in him. The realisation Torrin-Ashur came to was as much a shock as the lad's identity. "You hear it, don't you?"

"The War Song? Yes, sir."

"Since when?"

"Since the day you ambushed that Tsnath party chasing Elam and Mac."

"But that was months ago!"

Paulus responded with a shrug, as if to say that was hardly his fault.

Any justification Torrin-Ashur felt he had for forbidding Paulus to fight was reluctantly pushed aside. The way the ancient magic spread was still a mystery, but if it had chosen Paulus, so be it. Besides, with a heavy heart he realised that it would make little difference whether the lad was in the front line or at the back of it. They were all going to meet Tsnath steel this day.

"Alright. Remember, the War Song will help you, but it doesn't make you invincible. You still have to be careful."

The lad nodded.

Torrin-Ashur patted him on the shoulder, then turned to seek out his original quarry. He found Jorra-hin over by the Vessel, hefting a large war axe.

"Careful with that thing. You're liable to do more damage to yourself than the enemy."

"I'm not planning on using it against the enemy," Jorra-hin growled, "I'm planning on using it against that..." He nodded towards the relic.

Torrin-Ashur's eyebrow rose.

"I'll not let the *Dànis~Lutárn* fall into the hands of the Tsnath," Jorra-hin explained. "If it looks like it might, I'll smash the Vessel myself. I'd rather see that bastard Nÿat in hell before I let him get his hands on it."

Torrin-Ashur's eyebrow rose even further at the vehemence with which Jorra-hin spat out the former Deputy Chancellor's name. It was unusual in the extreme for him to be discourteous. Then again, in this instance, there was some justification. "I thought you said you couldn't destroy the Vessel?"

"I probably can't. Mage Holôidees tried to do so when the Dendricá were trapped in Üzsspeck. His attempt turned out to be a futile gesture. But I'll still try. It's what he would have done."

Torrin-Ashur accepted Jorra-hin's resolve without further challenge. "Well, just make sure they don't end up using it against *us*." He caught Kirin's eye. "Look after him. If he goes, there'll be no one to write of our heroic exploits."

Kirin laughed at his wink, though it failed to mask her apprehension.

Torrin-Ashur turned to see if he could find Nash, but instead spotted Borádin doing the rounds, speaking with the defenders, both army and civilian, giving out encouragement and words of advice. The nobleman even stopped and spoke to Tomàss. Torrin-Ashur paused to watch. Their conversation lasted at least a minute and ended with Borádin extending his hand. Torrin-Ashur shook his head; it was a wonder how much the nobleman had changed since the war had begun.

Resuming his search for Nash, he found the sergeant organising those around him with a skilled and experienced hand.

"Sergeant, a quick word..."

Nash trotted over. "Sir?"

"I'd like you to do me a favour – watch Elona's back for me. When the action begins, I probably won't even be aware of where she is. But I'd like to know she's safe."

"Safe?"

"Well, as much as she can be, given the mess we're in."

"Where will she be?"

"Fighting."

Nash grimaced.

Torrin-Ashur gave a helpless shrug. "There isn't a hope I could convince her not to. You saw how she nearly bit my head off when I asked her why she was wearing armour."

A flicker of a smile crossed Nash's lips.

The incident, from just the previous day, had proved how Elona hadn't quite succeeded in doffing her position as a princess of the realm. She was used to commanding authority and slipped easily into old ways.

"I'll stay close, sir."

Torrin-Ashur nodded and glanced round the hilltop. "So, are we ready?"

"Well, we've got every able-bodied man and quite a few of the women armoured up and ready to fight. My main concern is that the centre of our defensive ring is very exposed. We haven't enough shields for everyone. Those in the front line need them most, so those left in the middle won't have much protection when the arrows start to fly. Speaking of which, we're really low on supplies. Our archers will be out within a few minutes of this whole brouhaha kicking off."

Torrin-Ashur couldn't help smiling at Nash's choice of words. "Aye, it's going to be a day for swords, that's for sure." He reached out and shook Nash's hand. "May the gods be with you, Sergeant."

"With you too, sir."

Torrin-Ashur finally made his way back to Elona. He grabbed hold of her breastplate and swung her round to face him, giving the armour a good tug. It was on securely.

"You be careful," he said gently.

Elona put her head against his shoulder, holding herself close; it was not entirely an intimate moment — two sets of ancient armour touching at the chest was never going to be that.

"Gods, if Midana could see me now," she murmured. "The whole world has gone completely mad."

"I keep thinking I might wake up soon," he whispered back, holding his cheek against her soft hair, feeling her warmth. He felt her grip on him tighten.

"If you do, come and find me."

"Count on it."

Borádin came over and joined them.

"Well, my lord, I suppose this is it."

"Indeed." Torrin-Ashur nodded back at Borádin and clasped the nobleman's forearm. "I can never thank you enough for remaining with us these past weeks."

Borádin smiled. "There is no thanks necessary, Torrin. If anything, I should thank you. You've helped me discover my duty." He glanced at the gathered enemy in the distance. "And if the worst befalls us today, my father will remember me with honour."

They both turned to face the massed ranks of the Tsnath, as ready as they'd ever be for what the enemy was about to throw at them.

*

It was something of a snap decision. Özeransk raised his hand to shoulder height, bringing his troop of cavalry to a halt. Commander Streàck drew alongside him, still wincing from the broken leg he'd suffered in the avalanche.

"Sir?"

Özeransk didn't answer for a moment. He was still wondering about the wisdom of what he was considering doing. Daka would be furious. That tipped it; he was past caring what she thought.

"Commander, lead the men on and join the emperor as planned. Tell Omnitas I will follow shortly. I hope."

"Sir?" Streàck asked again, displaying a growing concern.

"I'm going to speak to the Alondrians."

Streàck looked aghast. "On your own? They'll kill you!"

"Maybe." Özeransk let a wistful smile thin his lips. Strangely, Streàck's bleak prediction didn't worry him. It only confirmed in his mind what had to be done.

With a look of consternation, Streàck saluted, then waved his arm forwards. The troop continued on round the base of the hill towards the bridge over the Ébeth, where the emperor had stationed his troops.

Alone, Özeransk heaved a sigh and dismounted. The snow wasn't as deep as he'd expected, which was good, as it would make the trudge up the hill less of a struggle. For a man of his standing, it would have been more seemly to ride, but he didn't want to appear threatening. Approaching the Alondrians on foot demonstrated a degree of humility. He wasn't the conqueror come to demand their surrender.

The wall of people ringing the hilltop was ragtag to say the least. There was no commonality to their dress, save for the distinctive and somewhat outdated armour many of them wore. The only thing they did all share was a haggard expression, now tinged with curiosity.

He stopped thirty yards short of their line when a group of archers raised their bows towards him.

"*My name is Özeransk,*" he called out in Alondrian. "*If he is willing, I would speak with your commander.*"

Several of the Alondrians conferred for a moment, then a small group stepped forwards. Two of those who approached him were soldiers, one appeared to be a monk, and the last a very attractive young woman, despite the grime that hid most of her complexion. She looked a little incongruous, clad in armour that was far too big for her.

The four came to a halt in front of him but said nothing.

Özeransk wondered how best to begin.

"*Firstly, you must understand, I am not in a position to give you guarantees. However, if you lay down your weapons and accompany me, I give you my word that I will do everything in my power to ensure your safety.*"

"*Accompany you where?*" This came from the taller of the two soldiers, a young man, perhaps just into his twenties, with an unshaven face that looked tired and older than its years.

Özeransk pointed across the hilltop towards the bridge over the Ébeth. "*Down there. Those are the Emperor Omnitas' forces. They are not under the command of Baroness Daka. I am in good standing with the emperor. I am prepared to speak with him on your behalf.*"

"*But you just came from Daka's lines?*"

Özeransk's attention flicked to the other Alondrian soldier who'd just spoken. This one had a noble bearing and had made more effort to maintain his appearance, though his clothes were an even greater mishmash than those of his fellows. "*True, I was with Daka. But we have parted company. I do not agree with her intentions. You should know, she means to destroy you. Not for any military objective, but simply to make an example of you for having defied her. You will find no mercy in that direction.*"

"*So why do you offer us the chance of salvation, Lord Özeransk?*" the young woman asked. "*I've heard of you. You are a powerful warlord in Tsnathsarré.*"

"*And who might you be, that my renown has made it past your pretty ears?*"

"*My name is not important.*"

Özeransk was not surprised by the rebuff. He smiled and bowed slightly. "*Of course not, Your Highness. But your beauty betrays you. That and the rumours we have heard that you were in the region. Much to your sister's displeasure, as I understand it.*"

The princess looked annoyed that she'd been recognised. "*My question still stands...*"

Özeransk shrugged. "*I am a soldier. I fight my enemies when I have to. But I do not visit wanton destruction upon civilians without good reason. Unlike some.*" He wafted his hand towards the ruins of Tail-ébeth. "*What happened here was a shameful thing. I had nothing to do with it.*"

"*Then who did?*" the tall soldier demanded.

The young man sounded more than just bitter, prompting a thought to occur to Özeransk. "*Would you be Lord Ashur, Torrin son of Naman?*"

The Alondrian nodded.

Özeransk allowed his expression to soften. "*I have heard Tail-ébeth was your home. I am truly sorry for your loss. It was on Daka's orders that it was sacked. Her right-hand man, Gömalt, led the attack. He is nothing but a vicious thug who revels in death.*"

"*I've heard of Gömalt,*" Lord Ashur said. "*From the baroness's daughter.*"

"*Kassandra? She is here?*"

"*No. She is far away. Safe.*"

Özeransk nodded. "*That is good. Her fate, should she fall into her mother's hands, I shudder to contemplate."*

"*And what of our fate, should we decide to accompany you?*" This came from the one in the cassock.

"*I cannot guarantee your freedom. The truth is, you would probably be held hostage. Especially the princess. Such is the way of diplomacy in war, I'm afraid. But you and your people would at least be alive.*"

"*Lord Ashur,*" a girl from the ranks behind them called out, "*remember what I said to you earlier. I meant every word of it.*"

Özeransk cocked a curious frown, but he was not rewarded with an explanation.

The monk laid a hand on Lord Ashur's shoulder and spoke in low tones, though Özeransk was still able to hear what was said.

"*Torrin, consider this: if we accept, the Vessel will end up in Tsnathsarré hands. That's as good as us handing it to Daka ourselves.*"

"*But are we in a position to prevent it? I mean, Jorra, look at them all down there. We're outnumbered ten to one. We may fight to keep it from her, but she'll probably still end up with it anyway – after we're all dead.*"

"*Maybe. But, and I say this as a brother of the Adak-rann, as someone who considers history important, I don't want to be recorded as one who handed victory to Daka without a fight.*"

Özeransk could contain his curiosity no longer. "*This artefact you stole from the baroness, what is it? Why does she want it so badly?*"

He was met with four faces stunned into silence.

Half a minute passed before the monk found his voice.

"*You don't know? But you were with the baroness. How is it you are ignorant of her goal?*"

"*Daka trusts no one, least of all me. She has always suspected my loyalties lie with the emperor. Today I have proven her correct.*"

The monk shared a look of surprise with his friends. "*Emperor Omnitas is also not aware of Daka's intentions?*" he asked.

"*No. He placed me with the baroness as a means of spying on her.*"

There was another moment of silence while the monk marshalled his thoughts. He glanced back towards the Ébeth bridge, then returned his concentration to Özeransk.

"*Then, my lord, you and your emperor have walked into a trap just as surely as have we.*"

Özeransk found it was his turn to be silenced. And to frown.

"*Lord Özeransk,*" Princess Elona said, "*the artefact, which the ancients called the Vessel, contains the most powerful magic ever created, the Dànis~Lutárn. Daka means to control it and turn it into a weapon. If she*" *succeeds, the known world will be at her mercy."*

"She will use it against Tsnathsarré and Alondrian alike in the pursuit of her ambitions," Lord Ashur added. *"I'm afraid your offer of sanctuary, honourable as it was, is of little help to us. We have no choice but to stand and fight."*

*

"Yon Tsnath seems to be in a bit of a hurry," Mac called from his position further along the line.

Torrin-Ashur nodded. Özeransk was at as close to a gallop as the terrain allowed, heading towards the emperor's forces at the bridge. He was carrying a rather urgent warning.

"I wonder what they're waiting for?" Borádin said, drawing attention to Daka's lines to the north.

Torrin-Ashur shrugged. "I'm amazed they even let us get established up here." He unbuckled his sword belt and plunged the scabbard into the frozen ground. Withdrawing the blade, he ran his fingers over the engraved lettering along the fuller.

siad-ida Sèliccia~Castrà

He'd read those words a thousand times and not truly grasped their meaning. Yet now, within sight of his ruined home, he not only understood them, but knew they were about to be heeded. He could feel the War Song's anticipation coursing through him, like a hound at the leash yearning for the hunt. The ancient magic was going to come storming to the fore at any moment like never before. He was almost afraid of what that would feel like.

His thoughts switched to those who stood on the hilltop with him. Possessed of swords like his, each one similarly engraved, he realised Paulus was right. His sword was no longer a unique family heirloom – but the general weapon of the Dendricá, in whose armour many of his people now stood. They truly were becoming the Dancing Warriors.

Borádin pointed at the scabbard standing free. "You did that when we had our call-out. Is there a significance?"

"A Dendricá tradition. It marks the ground on which you begin a battle. You don't let the enemy take it from you. If you are victorious, the field is yours and you can reclaim it later."

Borádin immediately unbuckled his belt and marked his spot.

One by one, the rest of the defenders followed suit, plunging their scabbards into the ground. Within a minute, the whole hill had been declared as theirs.

Torrin-Ashur glanced over at Tomàss, standing nearby with his sword resting in the crook of his arm. He seemed so relaxed he might even have been asleep.

"What, no drum?"

The former slave hefted his shield and slapped the flat of his sword against it. Its sound-worthiness passed muster. He grinned like a madman and started to beat out a rhythm.

"*siad-ida Sèliccia~Castrà*," he cried out, prompted by some inner inspiration.

Jorra-hin, not far away, nodded in agreement, as though the words had been directed solely at him. He drew a deep breath and bellowed out the words at the top of his voice.

His perfect pronunciation carried the A'lyavinical exhortation to the ears of every man, woman and child on the summit. There was no need for translation; the meaning was clear.

It was felt.

hear ye the War Song inundated their minds. It resounded in their hearts and hardened their resolve. Fear was banished.

The beat Tomàss had begun was taken up by others as the power of the War Song awakened within them. The clamour spread solidly all around the hilltop until every defender hammered out the rhythm in perfect unison. It became a wave of percussion that rolled down the slope towards the Tsnath.

When it broke upon them, the Tsnath answered with their opening salvo. A dark and angry cloud of arrows arched skywards.

The Alondrian response was instant. As one their guard went up, percussion becoming protection in the blink of an eye. That the physical beat had ceased mattered not; the War Song thundered in their ears. The defenders flowed with a precision and timing the likes of which not even the most disciplined military ranks could equal. Not a single arrow of the opening volley struck a soft target.

The Tsnath didn't stop with just one volley. Their bombardment continued to rain in, swarm after swarm, thousands of deadly strikes apiece. Given the staggering volume of missiles, it was inevitable that some defenders were eventually hit. A shield could only be in one place at a time, no matter how fast it was moved.

As Nash had predicted, Alondrian quivers emptied within a matter of minutes. The twang of their bows fell silent having inflicted only minor casualties on Daka's forces. It made no odds, such was their overall strength.

With the last Alondrian arrow spent, a horn sounded across the field. The Tsnath began their main advance up the hill. No longer targeted by archers, they didn't bother to run. The gap between opposing forces closed inexorably, every step of the Tsnath's malevolent march threatening their intent to sweep the Alondrians from the hill.

At fifty yards out, they finally broke into a charge. They slammed into the front ranks of the awaiting Alondrians with terrible force. No snow rampart protected the defenders now, no fist of the mountains would level this field. Torrin-Ashur knew the War Song alone stood between his people and the annihilation the Tsnath were here to deliver.

True to its purpose, the ancient magic surged to ever greater heights, transforming the defenders into an iron wall, impenetrable, immutable. The first wave of Tsnath were stopped in their tracks; their front ranks withered and died as Dendricá blades darted around them with near invisible speed, lethal in their precision, one in their intent.

Only the sheer weight of the Tsnath's numbers made any impact. The constant pressure of soldier upon soldier pouring towards the defenders gradually shrank the Alondrian circle, herding them into a tighter and tighter group. Knocking shoulders with one another, it became harder to respond to the fluid grace of the *Sèliccia~Castrà*.

The battle raged on in full fury for what seemed an eternity, the relentless savagery of the Tsnath undiminished right up to the moment a recall sounded. They gave up the first wave of their attack and withdrew, leaving hundreds of their fallen comrades littering the field. Hundreds more of their injured were dragged back with them as they re-grouped at the foot of the hill. Arrows took flight once more.

Torrin-Ashur took advantage of the relative lull to take stock of their position. They'd suffered a lot of casualties of their own. Even with their protector, a measure of death was unavoidable in the face of such onslaught.

"We seem to have survived the first wave," Borádin declared in relief, panting as he surveyed the scene of devastation that surrounded them.

"Aye, but how many more will there be? Look at them all down there. They've got enough troops to keep throwing at us until they eventually succeed, War Song or not."

"The question is, will they?"

Torrin-Ashur snorted. "It's Daka down there – of course they will."

But despite his conviction, he noted the Tsnath weren't acting as he'd have expected. They were neither taunting the Alondrians in a futile attempt to get them to break ranks, nor did they seem to be making any further moves to press home another attack. Even the intensity of their volleys diminished. Yet he could see no reason why they didn't just surge forwards and get it all over with. Another attack like the last would probably be the last.

He began to feel uneasy, even though the War Song's power still flooded through him with staggering force.

His disquiet was shared. Confused looks passed between the defenders as each felt a shift within them.

*

A dark fury roiled across Daka's face. She stabbed at Nÿat with an accusatory finger. "*This* is what the War Song can do? Why did you not warn me?"

Gömalt held his breath. Daka in a rage was a fearsome thing.

"This magic – it is the same as the warriors in the mountain had, yes?"

Nÿat appeared anxious, a change from his usual smug look of self-confidence, Gömalt noted.

"I believe so, Baroness."

"Then deal with this rabble. They have made me look weak. Annihilate them!"

Nÿat wrung his hands together, hard enough that the whites of his knuckles showed. "Baroness, we have not finished reconfiguring the menhir. The controlling spells are in transition. If we release the *Dànis~Lutárn* now, I cannot guarantee being able to regain control of it."

"The weapon will attack those protected by the War Song, will it not?" Daka demanded.

"It will." Nÿat's manner became subservient. He didn't even meet the baroness's gaze. "We have not yet changed the nature of what the *Dànis~Lutárn* will do. But we have already started to change the spells on the menhir. It may not respond to them when we wish to return it to the Vessel. I must caution you, Baroness, this could jeopardise its future use."

"Release it."

"But your other conquests – surely they are more important?"

"Release it NOW!" Daka screamed.

Nÿat scurried away, gathering the scribes that had been assigned to him as he went.

Gömalt kept his distance, well out of the way of the baroness. Fury had seriously clouded her judgement; disastrously so. But he wasn't going to risk telling her that. With the mood she was in, she'd be liable to send him against the Alondrians next – on his own.

*

Torrin-Ashur's unease grew with each passing moment. Something was wrong. Terribly wrong. A fear, virtually a dread, was rising within him. He'd not felt like this before – ever.

Suddenly he spun round, convinced that danger was creeping up behind him. All he could see was his own people, standing around the Vessel. Beyond them, down the other side of the hill, the only Tsnath to pose a threat were half a mile away, content simply to continue blocking the path to the bridge. They were making no moves to advance. Whatever Özeransk had said to the emperor, it had kept him out of the engagement thus far.

He caught Elona's eye. She looked scared. Her sword was crimson and her breastplate splattered; she had been in the thick of the fighting. But now she was trembling. When he looked down at his own hands, he noticed that he too was shaking. Something was dreadfully wrong.

"Jorra…"

As the monk's name passed his lips he crumpled into the snow, gritting his teeth against a fiery pain that enveloped him from his head to his toes.

"*Help…me!*"

Elona dropped to her knees, gasping for breath as though drowning. Borádin went down beside her. Nash reeled sideways clutching both hands to the sides of his head, as if trying to crush his own skull. A few yards away Tomàss landed in a heap, writhing in agony. Beyond him, Mac and Elam staggered about, fighting off a feverish scourge, barely still standing. Both collapsed at the same moment.

One by one, all those touched by the War Song succumbed to the hand of an unseen terror.

*

Jorra-hin looked round in startled confusion. "Oh gods, no, no, no…" He sprinted towards the front line and gazed down the hill towards the Tsnath formations. They were still not advancing. Instead, one solitary man stood in front of them, his hands held high, as if exulting the gods.

"No!" Jorra-hin cried out. He ran back to Kirin. Like him, she was unaffected by what was going on. "It's Nÿat. He's doing something with the *Dànis~Lutárn.*"

"How? We have the Vessel right here."

"I don't know, I don't know," Jorra-hin wailed, clenching and unclenched his fists in desperation. He stomped back and forth, urgently searching for answers. His ears were filled with cries of agony, preventing him from thinking clearly. There was no time to waste. His friends were helpless before a merciless foe.

A sudden vision flooded to mind of how it must have been for Yazcöp when the ancient mage had desperately tried to save the Dendricá in Üzsspeck.

"Nÿat hasn't reconfigured the *Dànis~Lutárn* – he's just found a way to release it again."

Kirin glanced at the Vessel, then back at Jorra-hin. "But it needs water, doesn't it? At Üzsspeck, the *Dànis~Lutárn* was bound by the water of the canals."

"Snow *is* water!"

Jorra-hin hadn't meant to round on Kirin like that. He just wasn't used to facing such desperate circumstances. He *had* to do something.

He grasped the war axe he'd purloined earlier and took a step towards the Vessel. He got no further. He was pummelled to the ground, not by the power of any magic, but by the force of a Tsnath arrow hammering into his chest. It missed his heart by no more than an inch.

He heard Kirin scream his name. She seemed strangely distant, as far away as a solitary cloud on the horizon. The sky became hazy and seemed to be disappearing. Shock thwarted comprehension of his plight; his normally so logical mind couldn't grasp what had befallen him. With mild curiosity, he wondered why he felt so cold as the world began to slip away.

He barely felt Kirin frantically pull the Tsnath arrow from him before its venom-laced tip could poison him further.

He had but a dim perception of her gently lifting his head to cradle it in her lap.

He only had the vaguest sense of her crying, the drops of her tears as they touched his face.

He didn't see her place her hands around his head and close her eyes, preparing to summon every ounce of desire that existed within her.

*

Kirin knew that to heal Emmy back in Alondris she had summoned a power she had not known she possessed. She had done it for a complete stranger. Her simple compassion for a young child unfairly struck down had been enough then to bring Emmy back from death's clutches.

That was incomparable to the depths of desire she now plumbed. Unparalleled love drove her, and nothing in all of creation could stop its primordial force. She reached deep inside and drew forth the wellspring of Taümathic power that had been amassing within her ever since she had been a child; since the day a visiting mage had healed her, and in so doing set within her the ambition of a lifetime.

She knew that through this moment she would die.

Fate had decreed that it was *for* this very moment that she had lived at all.

The instant the icy grip of the restraint cast around her neck touched her skin, she knew that she had succeeded.

*

Jorra-hin's eyes flickered open. For a moment he was confused, unable to recall where he was, or what he was doing lying in the snow. But he knew the face, streaked with tears, that smiled down at him, beckoning him back to into the world.

He sat up. Only then did he notice the restraint cast, no longer a set of fluid rings, beautiful jewellery to those ignorant of its vile purpose, but now a melding mass creeping over Kirin's skin.

"Kirin, what have you done?"

Kirin's lips blossomed into the most beautiful smile he'd ever beheld.

"I have fulfilled my destiny."

"But Kirin, you are dying!"

"Yes. My life for yours."

"No, Kirin, no," Jorra-hin wailed. Tears of anguish flooded down his face at the realisation she had sacrificed herself for his sake. The screams of those around him continued unabated, growing ever more terrible, but he slammed the door of his mind shut against them, against all else but Kirin. "You shouldn't have done this," he choked, sobs threatening to engulf him.

"Fate decreed it so. Do not deny me my fulfilment, Jorra."

Kirin smiled again. It quickly became an expression of pain. She shivered violently, her strength wilting as the restraint cast advanced, turning more and more of her skin to silver. Jorra-hin reached out to support her.

"I'm so cold, Jorra."

He pulled her close, holding her head next to his.

"Listen to me. You are the key to what happens here today."

"Not now, Kirin."

Kirin gripped his arm. The imperative nature of what she wanted to say pushed through to the surface. "Nikrá's prophecy – *when Those of Grace hear again, the Unwilled One comes.* The Dancing Warriors have heard again..." she said, struggling to get the words out.

"It's not important now, Kirin."

A spark of defiance gave Kirin strength. "It is of *utmost* importance. *You* are the Unwilled One."

Jorra-hin's first thought was that she had become delirious in her last moments.

"Don't you see?" she continued, desperation in her voice. "Nikrá said you had to discover the truth on your own. But there's no time now. You must believe."

"Kirin, I'm not the Unwilled One. I'm no harbinger of *times of great strife.*"

"*times of great strife* are your path, not your doing. You *are* the Unwilled One, Jorra, the one without will. You have resisted your calling your whole life. You've never had any desire to follow the Mages' Path. But the Taümatha is a part of you. I know you know that."

Kirin's eyes slipped closed for a moment. She was fighting a desperate battle Jorra-hin knew she could not win. It took supreme determination for her to force them open again.

"It's up to you now, Jorra. Fulfil the prophecy. Fulfil your destiny. Become who you really are."

"Oh, Kirin, don't ask me that," he moaned in torment.

"Jorra," she whispered, clinging to his arm with the very last vestiges of her strength, "for me – do it for me. Promise me..."

Jorra-hin laid Kirin down on the snow. He kissed her lips, the only part of her that was not covered by the advance of the silvery shroud.

"I promise," he whispered.

Kirin sighed her final breath. A faint smile was etched upon her lips, an expression she would wear for eternity.

She looked so beautiful, so serene. A silver lady now at peace.

Jorra-hin remained motionless for several moments. Every which way his mind went, he could not see a path to undoing what had happened. The finality of fate's hand was upon him. There was no way back.

He gripped the handle of the war axe he'd dropped, simply for something to hold as the rest of his body was wracked with great convulsions. His anguish poured forth as never before.

Yet the world he'd shut out for Kirin forced its way back in, the cries of agony denying him time to grieve, their brutality wrenching him to the present. Something in him changed. Irrevocably.

He rose to his feet with great deliberation. There was a seething fury about him. A fire raged in his eyes. With a force hitherto unknown to him, he flung the axe away, sending it whirling over the heads of those lying around him in the snow. It landed hundreds of yards down the hill, nearly at the Tsnath lines.

He looked up into the sky, issuing a challenge to the gods, a scream of ferocious rage. The very earth trembled. The snow around his feet melted away, as if fleeing in terror.

Kirin believed him to be the Unwilled One. It had taken the death of love to tear away the veil behind which he'd hidden the truth all his life. A raging stampede of Taümatha coursed through his body.

He knew who and what he was now.

Amatt's whole prophecy slammed into his mind with savage force.

'when Those of Grace hear again,
the Unwilled One comes.
times of great strife are His path.

under the heel of a new Master the Land will reel.
as water divides, so shall the Peoples be,
then by their own hearts will They be betrayed.'

Nÿat had unleashed the *Dànis~Lutárn* once more.

Kirin had unleashed an infinitely greater power – destiny. A true prophecy could not be stopped, no matter what was arrayed against it. It was simply history in reverse.

Jorra-hin knew this now with a certainty that was absolute.

He *was* the prophecy.

He strode towards the front line and gazed down at the massed Tsnath ranks and the man in front of them. Lifting his arms to the sky, just as Nÿat was doing, he released every restraint all his years in the Adak-rann had taught him to set in place.

The sky ceased to be a clear blue. A tumult of dark and foreboding clouds materialised as if summoned from the depths of the underworld. Great brooding continents collided together, issuing thunder that roared with horrendous force, shaking the very ground with its clamour. The percussion pounded Jorra-hin's chest. It stunned all who heard it.

The Tsnath at the bottom of the hill looked up in sudden terror. Lightning laced the maddened rebellion above their heads, raging across the sky time and time again, arcing from one horizon to the other as though two great celestial armies sought each other's annihilation. The firmament was rent in two, the very elements writhing with Jorra-hin's agony, seething with his anger, eager to give vent to the terrible extent of his wrath.

With a venomous glare at the stunned Tsnath troops, Jorra-hin reached out and grasped a handful of sky with his right hand. He flung it towards one of the menhir Nÿat was using to control the *Dànis~Lutárn*. An immense bolt of lightning streaked down from the clouds. The stone disintegrated in an explosion of granite shards, leaving nothing of the ancient relic but a hole in the ground. The bodies of men unfortunate enough to have been close by littered the area like trees blown over in a hurricane.

The destruction of the menhir released the Taümathic energy that had been stored within it. Like a wind, it surged outwards seeking a new vessel. Jorra-hin's robes thrashed about him as though caught in a sudden and violent storm. He leaned into the force of the oncoming power, managing to stand his ground only for a few moments.

Inundated by such a vast store of magic, he was reduced to his knees. He cried out in pain as his body absorbed the savage assault.

With iron determination he brought the destructive power of the storm to bear again, one by one annihilating what remained of the Vicar stones, removing their control over the *Dànis~Lutárn*. Each explosion released yet more power. It tore into him, sating its primal need to be bound.

Yet no body of flesh and blood could remain filled with the kind of power that now raged and convulsed within him. It felt like a thousand tormented bulls rampaged through his veins, threatening to tear him apart. The imbalance inside him was anathema to the natural order of things. He was a living rift in the Taümatha, and it sought redress. He couldn't last long in such a state.

He crawled towards the Vessel on his hands and knees, his eyes shut against an indescribable agony. The frenzied madness of the Taümatha set his blood on fire. The freezing touch of the snow was barely a balm against his skin.

Reaching the Vessel, he hesitated, wondering just for a moment what would happen when he touched it.

But now was not the time to doubt destiny.

With both hands he grasped the Vessel and hauled himself to his feet. He hurled all his will at the obsidian relic, challenging it to overcome him. It did not suck at his mind, as it had done with all those who had beheld it in the past. He felt the *Dànis~Lutárn* recoil from him.

The accumulation of knowledge and magic from all those who had created the ancient power, more than two hundred great mages, was now within him. The controlling forces the stones had once exerted upon the *Dànis~Lutárn* were his to command. With a power it was incapable of resisting, he bent the scourge of the Dancing Warriors to his will. It retreated back into the Vessel like a terrified child fleeing the path of a ravenous beast.

The instant the task had been achieved, Jorra-hin sank to his knees, overwhelmed by a desire for death and blessed release.

But he could not let himself go. His promise was not yet complete. He had only rescued the Dancing Warriors from their tormentor.

There was still a prophecy to be fulfilled.

*

If Kirshtahll had harboured any doubts he was heading in the right direction, they were dismissed by the shocking display of celestial firepower witnessed in the distance. Such a disturbance had to be of unnatural cause; a great store of the Taümatha had been unleashed. With something akin to dread, he wondered if he was already too late.

Since leaving Colòtt he'd spared neither horse nor rider to bring his army north. The advent of two half-frozen mages and their hard-to-swallow tale of passages beneath the Mathians had radically altered his plans, diverting him from a route north that would have taken him via the Am-gött. It had shaved weeks off the journey.

The only question was, had that been enough?

He handed back the looking glass to Agarma. "Your eyes are younger than mine, Captain. Tell me what you see."

Agarma squinted through the leather-bound tube, scanning the horizon ahead. He shook his head. "Sorry, sir, but I can't make it out clearly. There's something going on atop that hill, but I couldn't tell you what. Is there anything over there?"

"Tail-ébeth, or what's left of it."

The looking glass tracked left, following the Ébeth south. "I see movement, sir. Cavalry, I think, by the bridge."

Another deep sense of foreboding washed over Kirshtahll. "They must be Tsnath." *He* was leading the only cavalry in the north that the Alondrians could field.

He spurred his mount and ploughed on towards the river.

*

Torrin-Ashur felt the agonising attack of the *Dànis~Lutárn* retreat, leaving him utterly drained. He lay gasping in the snow, unable to muster the strength to stand. A full minute passed before he was even able to draw his legs up to his chest and roll on to his knees. From there he slowly climbed to his feet, propping himself up hand on knee. Still bent double, he swayed for a moment and had to wait for his head to clear. Yet with each beat of his hammering heart, he grew stronger.

So did the War Song. The unfathomable ancient magic seemed to have a memory of sorts. It knew the violation of the *Dànis~Lutárn*. He felt its sense of outrage flood through him.

Though still dazed, he looked round, trying to make sense of the situation. He possessed sufficient wit to realise something significant had happened while he'd been oblivious of all else but agony. Things had changed. For a start, the sky seemed in full riot. It had been a clear blue before the *Dànis~Lutárn's* attack. The force that had called its rage into existence appeared to be subsiding, but even so, ominous dark clouds still roiled with supernatural velocity.

He spotted Elona sitting in the snow hugging her knees and staggered over to her. He held out a hand to pull her up. "Are you alright?"

She nodded, clearly still shaken. "What happened?"

"We were attacked by the *Dànis~Lutárn*. The question is, why did it stop? I need to find Jorra."

Glancing round, he was surprised to find Jorra-hin seated with his back up against the Vessel. His friend had gone to such great lengths to berate others never to touch the thing for fear of the consequences.

He started making his way over. He'd only taken a few paces when the sun managed to find a gap in the dissipating clouds, allowing light to glint off something shiny. At first he couldn't figure out what it was. The realisation, when it hit him, was like a punch to the stomach. Kirin. He stumbled to a halt and could do nothing but stare. He knew what had happened, but wished it had not.

Managing to tear his gaze away, he forced himself on towards Jorra-hin. The monk looked dreadful. A huge amount of blood soaked the font of his cassock. "Jorra, what happened? Are you hurt?" he asked, dropping to one knee.

Jorra-hin's eyes remained screwed shut, his face a contorted mask of pain. His hand blindly scrabbled about before latching on to Torrin-Ashur's forearm. "Torrin," he gasped, wrenching the name out with great effort, "you must get me to the river. I don't have much time."

"Jorra, there's an entire Tsnath army between us and the Ablath."

"The Ébeth will do. We must get the Vessel to the river."

Torrin-Ashur frowned. He didn't know what good it would do to transport the relic to the river, but the desperation in Jorra-hin's voice could not be ignored.

He glanced over his shoulder to assess the distance from the summit of the hill to the nearest part of the Ébeth. Just over half a mile of open ground to cross, albeit with the first stretch downhill. The route was clear at the moment, but that wouldn't remain the case.

To the south stood the Emperor's troops. They'd taken no part in the battle thus far, and might, if Özeransk had had his say, remain bystanders. Then again, now that they knew what the Vessel was, they might make a bid for its possession when they saw the Alondrians charge down the hill.

Regardless of that, the bigger and more definite threat lay to the north. One end of Daka's troops was positioned perilously close to their path. As soon as they saw the Alondrians head for the river, they would charge.

The only certainty on offer was carnage.

"I don't know if we can make it, Jorra. It's an awful long way."

Jorra-hin's grip tightened. "If I don't get to the river, I'll die. Then these lands will never be protected by the *Dànis~Lutárn*."

Torrin-Ashur just felt confused. Jorra-hin wasn't making any sense. "But without the stones, what's the point? The *Dànis~Lutárn* is useless to us without them."

"It is not useless. The Vicar stones are no more. I destroyed them. Their controlling power is within me now. But I can't hold it in much longer; it's far too powerful. We must deploy the *Dànis~Lutárn* — that's the only way to keep it out of Daka's hands. You *have* to get me to the river."

Question upon question flooded to Torrin-Ashur's mind, each one dismissed of necessity. It was obvious Jorra-hin's time was running out fast. "Alright, hold tight. It will take a few minutes to get things organised."

Jorra-hin nodded, still with his eyes tightly shut.

Torrin-Ashur heaved himself up and ran over to Borádin and Elona, beckoning Nash as he went. The mayor of Mitcha was nearby and joined them.

"We need to get Jorra-hin down to the river. He says he can deploy the *Dànis~Lutárn*."

"What? How?" Elona demanded.

"Only the gods and Jorra-hin know that. It doesn't matter. What does is that we have a chance, a small chance, to thwart Daka. We have to try."

Borádin assessed the odds against them with little more than a glance. "The Tsnath outflank us."

"I know. It isn't going to be easy. I have to confess, I'm not sure what our best course of action is. I don't think a small force would make it."

"Then we stick together," the mayor asserted without hesitation.

Nash nodded. "Everyone in one defensive formation."

"Giving up the high ground?" Borádin challenged. "We'll not

regain it if we move."

"With what the Tsnath threw at us earlier, sir, the advantage this hill gives us is minimal," Nash said. "Even if we all stayed put, how many more attacks like the last one do you think we can withstand?"

Nash's inference, essentially their unavoidable defeat, fell heavily. It was clear to Torrin-Ashur that everyone understood their end was coming. Where they met it mattered little. The only victory within their grasp was to deny Daka her prize. That wouldn't alter their fate this day; it would only determine how they'd be remembered.

"At least with the river behind us we'll have some protection – the Tsnath won't be able to attack from that direction," Nash added. "We may even get some of our people across."

The Ébeth was an unfriendly torrent at this time of year. It would offer no safe passage. Torrin-Ashur gave his head a forlorn shake but held his tongue; denying the others a glimmer of hope at this moment served no purpose.

"Alright, we all go. Get everybody ready – and hurry, Jorra-hin doesn't have much time."

Word of the new objective spread quickly throughout the remaining Alondrians. They abandoned everything except their weapons and formed up into a tightly knit defensive circle, the non-combatants in the middle, along with Jorra-hin and the Vessel. Being in no fit state to stand, Jorra-hin was loaded on to a handcart. Cosmin was beside him, though such was the power that raged within the monk that there was nothing the old mage could do to ease his pain.

The Ashurmen took the lead. Borádin's men lined the left flank to bear the brunt of Daka's closest troops. They poured down the hill towards the river as fast as they could. It quickly became impossible to keep the formation together and it morphed into an elongated oval, weak at the sides where the defenders were thinnest spread.

Their unexpected charge caused confusion amongst Daka's forces. A dash to the river made little tactical sense, the Ébeth being an obstacle to thwart a well-prepared army, let alone a ragtag band of townsfolk. It bought them a few precious minutes while the Tsnath adjusted their thinking.

But that was never going to be enough. A horn sounded from the main Tsnath ranks, a series of hoots that could be heard clearly even on the far side of the hill. Immediate activity within the force by the bridge suggested they were about to come to bear. Torrin-Ashur's heart sank; they were going to be caught in a pincer movement, just as he'd feared.

With legs fit to crumple and lungs ready to explode, they made it to within two hundred yards of the river's bank before the first of Daka's men slammed into their left flank. Borádin's men didn't break, but the defensive bubble was pushed sideways, slowing them down and elongating their route. More Tsnath amassed in front of them, blocking the path to the Ébeth.

Torrin-Ashur hunkered down with grim determination and summoned every ounce of speed he could muster, flinging himself into the enemy. His world became a storm, little more than a blur as the *Sèliccia~Castrà* replaced thought with pure instinct, a raging power that seemed hell-bent on the destruction of everything within his path. The executive arm of the War Song vented its fury unfettered by any other concern.

The Ashurmen swept in behind him and tore their way through the Tsnath lines. No enemy soldier within sword-length escaped the deadly reach of Dendricá steel. Scores fell before them. None were left wounded. The War Song took no prisoners.

Only when the Ébeth's shockingly frigid water swirled about his feet did anything other than the ancient magic's thunderous beat pierce Torrin-Ashur's consciousness. He came to a halt, panting for breath, amazed that he'd actually reached the river. Not that it was sanctuary. Its fast-flowing torrent was dangerous and forbidding. It offered only a swift and brutally cold death to anyone who might try to cross. Here was the mission's end. Fate would have it out with them now, one way or the other.

He turned back to help bolster the tail enders. Just as he did, the defensive circle caved in on the north flank. A wave of Tsnath soldiers poured through the breach, hacking at those less well armed in the middle. Two of the men transporting Jorra-hin were cut down, ejecting him out of the cart. He sprawled face first on blood-tainted snow.

One of the enemy tried to get in for the kill.

Jorra-hin opened his eyes. As though some fearsome beast had reared up in front of him, the attacker turned and fled. Borádin was there in an instant to silence the man's terrified screams.

*

Jorra-hin fought against the raging fire within him and staggered on unaided. All the while the carnage of battle thrashed itself out around him, though he was mostly unconscious of it; his mind held but one thought – get to the Ébeth.

He stumbled the last few yards to the water's edge and slid down the bank on his backside. The numbing shock of freezing water swamping his boots brought a degree of clarity to his thoughts. It struck him how the river's powerful torrent flowed past without heed of the history being written along its banks. He wondered if that was how it was for fate, too; decreeing events and stamping out its will, regardless of the ruin in its wake. He was its puppet now, more than ever.

Struggling to regain his feet, he climbed on to a small rock, little more than a stepping stone, and put his hand down into the water. The swirling rush stilled into a flat calm as though a blanket had been thrown over it. The surface solidified into a frozen jetty that extended to the middle of the river. Beckoning to those hauling the Vessel through its invisible quagmire, he slowly shuffled away from the bank. Barely able to stand on solid ground, let alone on ice, his steps were ungainly. He slipped and fell every few paces, but doggedly clambered up and carried on each time.

When he reached the furthest extent of the jetty, he turned.

"Unharness the Vessel." His voice came as a rasping hiss, words forced out between clenched teeth as he fought excruciating pain on every level of his being.

The men were quick to do as instructed. He shooed them away with a flick of his fingers.

For more than a millennium, the Vessel, the focal point for the most powerful entity ever created, had sat on its bulbous end with its teardrop tip pointing skywards. Only occasionally had it tipped sideways under Taümathic influence.

Now, with all the knowledge of the ancients flowing through him, Jorra-hin knew the ridiculous simplicity of the *Dànis~Lutárn's* deployment. No complex spells or long forgotten incantations were needed to release it to carry out the purpose for which it had truly been created. It required only that the Vessel be upended, as though a bottle.

Following the gesture of his hand, the obsidian relic rose above the ice. Slowly it rotated in mid-air, resisting his command, but powerless to deny him. When it was finally upside-down, he clapped his hands together and thrust them towards the ice. The Vessel shot towards the river's surface, hammered from above by a manifestation of inexorable will. Its tip shattered the jetty and the rest of its sleek form vanished into the water. Cracks streaked across the ice, sending Jorra-hin scurrying back towards the bank, his temporary jetty disintegrating inches behind his fleeing heels.

Where the Vessel had disappeared the water began to shimmer. Something tremendously powerful vibrated beneath its surface, creating tiny waves that danced about in every direction as if trying to escape what was coming. A growing tremble in the ground, felt even by those on the bank, portended something of cataclysmic proportions.

Suddenly, the sound of a mighty rushing wind erupted along the entire length of the Ébeth. All its water exploded into the air, as though a line had been ripped up hundreds of feet into the sky, sucking the contents of the river with it. The great plume hung at its apex for an impossible moment, the laws of creation suspended, before its untenable position collapsed and it cascaded back into the riverbed. The roar was tumultuous, the rival of an ocean storm, as water thundered down on to the rocks. Shockwaves barrelled through the ground, felling Alondrian and Tsnathsarré even as they fought.

The battle ceased. Astonishment reigned supreme on both sides of the conflict. Flabbergasted stares beheld the river, comprehension completely overwhelmed. Never in recorded history had such things been witnessed.

As the Ébeth sloshed and heaved, gradually settling back into itself, all eyes gravitated to the harbinger of the calamity. He stood near the edge of the river, drenched by a wave that had leapt up over the bank. He looked like a piece of flotsam washed up on the shore, his curly mop of dark hair plastered to his head, his cassock more rag than robe.

He seemed forlorn, alone, pitiful.

Until he spoke.

'as water divides lands, so shall the Peoples be,'

The A'lyavinical quotation carried across the battlefield, inundating every mind. It brought a dreadful sense of finality to all that had led up to this moment. The whole host of the celestial realms could not have heralded a clearer message.

It was finished.

Jorra-hin walked through the stilled chaos, every eye tracking him. Men, friend and foe, shrank out of his way as he approached.

"*There is one amongst you,*" he called out in Tsnathsarré to Daka's forces, "*the mage from Alondris. Bring him to me.*"

There was hesitation within the Tsnath ranks, which was probably the result of their confusion over what was going on. The only thing that seemed certain was that they were facing someone it would be unwise to resist.

A shuffling amongst the soldiers preceded a parting of their number to reveal a rather worried-looking man. He wore flowing robes, a fur coat and a huge medallion at his chest. He was thrust forwards as though the Tsnath were only too happy to eject him from their midst.

"Mage Nÿat, you will come with me to answer to the Cymàtagé and to Alondria for your treachery."

Nÿat paled. It was a death sentence. "I don't think so," he answered quietly.

No wasn't an option Jorra-hin was about to permit.

Nÿat made a quick flick of his wrist and summoned an intense ball of fire, a White Light. He tried to hurl it. The flames never left his fingertips.

"It is widely believed that I have already killed you, Nÿat. After what has happened here today, believe me when I say, *nothing* would please me more than to turn falsehood into fact."

Nÿat swallowed hard and shook his hand, trying to dissipate the flame he had summoned. It refused his command. Beads of sweat began to form on his brow.

"Tell me," Jorra-hin continued, his tone almost conversational, "what was it Baroness Daka offered you? What morsel enticed you to betray your own people? A place by her side? More power? The Chancellorship of the Cymàtagé, perhaps?"

Nÿat had begun to shake. He was trying to free himself of the Taümathic shackles by which he was bound. His effort was futile.

"You of all people should understand why I've done what I've done," he gasped, as though the words had been extracted from him by force.

"*I* of all people?"

"Clearly you are a Natural mage. The Dinac-Mentà will never let you be free. I sought to end their tyranny, to be rid of them. Through Daka, I could have achieved that."

Jorra-hin considered Nÿat's reasoning for a moment. He did not, for an instant, accept it.

"You used the Dinac-Mentà against me. You framed me for your murder and set them after me, like hounds to the fox. Because of you, Kirin also had to flee. Now she is dead. *Because of you!*" Jorra-hin's lip trembled. The ground beneath his feet reciprocated, causing a few more bystanders to step away. "True, I have no love for the Dinac-Mentà. But if you think that will sway me to accept your excuse for bringing war upon us, that doing away with the Dinac-Mentà would *ever* be justification for your self-serving, petty interests – you are gravely mistaken."

"Petty?" Nÿat managed to scoff, perhaps unwisely. "The unification of two great empires under one ruler, with mages free to be what they're supposed to be. Is that what you call *petty*?"

"And how many lives would that have cost? How many towns would Daka have destroyed to impose her rule? How many Tail-ébeths would there have been, annihilated just for being an irritation?"

"I had nothing to do with Tail-ébeth's fate," Nÿat objected. "That happened before I even arrived in the Territories."

"You gave Daka her reason for being here!" Jorra-hin thundered. He struggled to control his anger. It so wanted to slip his restraints and wreak havoc. The gap between him and those closest widened further still. "You supplied her with information about the *Dànis~Lutárn* and what it could give her. Every death that has occurred here," Jorra-hin drew himself up, "*I* lay at your feet."

With a look of disgust still clouding his features, he turned to address Daka's troops.

"*You have seen the terrible power of the Dànis~Lutárn. Lay down your weapons.*"

Few made any moves to comply. Jorra-hin wondered for a moment whether their minds were still a little too stunned by all that had happened to respond. Then again, they were Tsnath – nothing, if not stubborn.

"*What will be the terms if we do?*"

This question came from an unexpected quarter. Jorra-hin glanced over his shoulder. To his surprise, he discovered that it was Lord Özeransk who had spoken. The man appeared to have led the emperor's forces forwards from the bridge, but had stopped short of engagement with the Alondrians. Cavalry were arrayed in formation either side of him, giving the impression considerable damage could still be done if he gave the word. Emperor Omnitas, surrounded by guards and no small amount of heraldry, was positioned slightly to the rear, out of any immediate danger.

Torrin-Ashur and Elona joined Jorra-hin at his side. Borádin and Nash positioned themselves just behind.

Özeransk nodded to one of his fellow riders, not one clad in armour, but in robes and furs of a more courtly persuasion. Both dismounted, though only Özeransk came forwards.

Jorra-hin acknowledged him with a nod. "*The power Daka sought, the Dànis~Lutárn, has been released. It is out of her reach now. And yours, for that matter.*"

"*I suppose that is a good thing,*" Özeransk replied, not hiding the wistful smile that twisted his lips as he scanned the length of the Ébeth. "*Though to be sure, it would help if I knew what it had been released to do.*"

"*It has become a barrier through which those with hostile intent cannot pass. It follows the course of the Ébeth and the Ablath, and now divides our peoples, just as its creators originally intended. You saw what happened when the Dànis~Lutárn was used against the Dancing Warriors on the hill? That is what will happen to any who face it with malice in their hearts.*"

Özeransk beckoned forwards the other man who had dismounted with him a few moments ago.

"This is Advisor Döshan," he introduced, switching into Alondrian. "He is authorised to speak on behalf of His Supreme Majesty, Emperor Omnitas."

Döshan bowed politely. "Mage Hin."

Jorra-hin raised an eyebrow. Mage Hin? Before half an hour ago he'd never even wielded magic. Now somehow he was *Mage* Hin. How his name was even known by a complete stranger from a foreign land was a bafflement that would have to remain so for the moment. "I would bid you welcome, were the circumstances more favourable."

Döshan nodded. "While the Emperor's own forces have not engaged you directly, there is no avoiding the fact that we have invaded your country."

"So what is it you have to say, Advisor Döshan?"

Döshan considered his words carefully. Jorra-hin appreciated that. There was something that warmed him to the advisor. He sensed a devout man, politically astute, a man not above the manipulation of others when occasion demanded, but nonetheless an honest man who tried to serve his emperor well. Above all, he recognised a fellow scholar. So he waited patiently.

"Mage Hin, it pains me that there has been enmity between our countries. As you know, my people have desired the return of the Tep-Mödiss for centuries."

"You cannot have it."

The rather matter-of-fact statement stalled Döshan for a moment, but he recovered well and continued, albeit having lapsed into his native tongue, "*You must understand, therefore, that when the Emperor heard of a plan he believed could return these lands to us, he was unwilling to forbid it.*"

"*He has done more than merely watch from the side-lines, Advisor,*" Jorra-hin replied, loud enough to ensure the emperor heard for himself. "*He is sitting atop a war horse, ahead an army, well inside Alondria.*"

Döshan momentarily looked alarmed. He bowed to hide his discomfort, seeing as how there was little he could do to refute the observation. "*We were aware that Baroness Daka had ulterior motives for her actions, though we knew not what,*" he pressed on. He gestured to the Ébeth, "*It becomes apparent, now, what she was seeking to control. A great power has been unleashed here today. I warrant it was not all your doing?*"

Jorra-hin grimaced. "*No. I was merely the instrument of its deployment. Its creators have been dead for a thousand years. Their vision and my destiny, so it seems, have been a long time coming.*"

Döshan nodded. "*And this power, in Daka's hands…?*"

"*A catastrophe for both our peoples.*" Jorra-hin glanced behind him. "Mage Nÿat, for the benefit of Adviser Döshan, why don't you explain your part in Daka's plan. What was it you were going to do for her?"

Nÿat's shaking had become quite violent. He remained silent.

"There is nothing to be gained by holding out on us, Nÿat. We will have the truth, whether you surrender it willingly or not. So what was it Daka wanted of you?"

Nÿat sagged. The heat of the fire he could not dispel had burned him, as might a day under a bright sun. His lips were cracked and his eyes creased against the intensity of the light. "I was to reconfigure the *Dànis~Lutárn* into a weapon. A small change to its nature."

"A change?"

Nÿat licked his parched lips. "Just as it was able to incapacitate the Custodians of the War Song, so I was to make it incapacitate anyone who opposed the baroness's will. With that before her, she could have ruled any kingdom she wished."

"*Alondria and Tsnathsarré would only have been the first,*" Jorra-hin observed to Döshan. "*Such unbridled ambition rarely knows limits. The world would have trembled before her.*"

Döshan looked aghast. He shivered at the horror of such a thought. "*A calamity of unparalleled magnitude has been averted,*" he stammered. "*And now you control this power?*"

Jorra-hin said nothing. He merely allowed a thin smile to touch his lips.

"*So what is it you propose?*" Döshan asked.

"*Agree to withdraw in peace, and you will be given safe passage back to Tsnathsarré.*"

Özeransk's eyebrows rose. He gestured towards Torrin-Ashur. "He *has agreed to that?*"

Jorra-hin turned and drew Torrin-Ashur and Elona a little further away so as to be out of earshot.

"What's happening?" Torrin-Ashur demanded in low tones. "Kirshtahll is here. He is just the other side of the river. But I think he's waiting for a signal from us before he does anything."

Jorra-hin was slightly taken aback by the discovery of nearly a thousand cavalrymen marshalled on the far bank of the Ébeth. It took him a moment to digest the fact that Kirshtahll had somehow arrived. Fate was really wielding its authority this day. "He is a prudent man," he acknowledged. "He knows his presence here could tip the balance back to conflict. Now is a time for treading carefully."

Torrin-Ashur frowned. "But we have the *Dànis~Lutárn*, don't we? We have the upper hand now."

Jorra-hin lowered his voice to barely a murmur. "The *Dànis~Lutárn* is doing what it was made to do, protecting these lands from invasion by hostile forces. It needs no bidding, no control, no Vicar Stones. This is its natural state. Changing it now would take a thousand mages. Hereabouts, I know of only two who might be willing to try." He caught Cosmin's eye. The old mage hadn't heard what was said, but he nodded back in deference anyway.

Elona stared at Jorra-hin with wide eyes. Torrin-Ashur swallowed hard.

Jorra-hin gave them both a careful nod. "So let us not upset the delicate balance we have arrived at, otherwise none of us will leave this battlefield standing."

"But, you have power. You are a mage now?" Elona whispered, airing her confusion.

"Yes. But I am not as formidable as I may have appeared. I was only able to wield the power contained in the Vicar Stones long enough to deploy the *Dànis~Lutárn*. It has largely dissipated now, thank the gods. I could not have withstood it much longer."

"You are able to hold Nÿat, though."

Jorra-hin nodded, glancing back at his captive. "I am a Natural

241

mage. Nÿat is just a Follower of the Way."

"So what are you going to do with him?"

"I was intending to take him back to Alondris to face justice. But he will not go willingly, and without me to hold him, he could still be dangerous. Perhaps it would be better to let him decide his fate now."

Torrin-Ashur's expression became one of alarm.

Jorra-hin was not concerned. "Nÿat, shall you face justice here, or in Alondris?"

Nÿat's reply was as simple as it was expected. "Here."

Jorra-hin nodded. "So be it, then. It is your White Light..."

With something akin to relief, Nÿat smiled. The mage's fire flared briefly at his fingertips before leaping into a much larger ball of flame. It engulfed him in an instant. His scream was brief. As the residual orange cloud rolled skywards and dissipated, only melted snow was left to mark the place of his passing. Not even a trace of his jewellery remained.

Elona paled. "Gods, just like that?"

"By his own hand," Jorra-hin murmured. He felt oddly detached. Maybe he'd expected some sense of satisfaction, or perhaps revulsion. Neither of those feelings wracked him. After all the death and destruction that had come about, he was just too numb to care that much.

Prompted by the incandescent display, and possibly under the misunderstanding that Nÿat had been dispatched by force, Döshan hurried back over from having had a rapid consultation with the emperor.

"Mage Hin, I have been authorised to accept your terms."

"What terms?" Torrin-Ashur demanded.

"In return for laying down their arms and withdrawing in peace, I have offered the Tsnath forces safe passage back to their own country."

Jorra-hin saw a thousand mixed feelings overwhelm Torrin-Ashur in that moment. The injustice of Tail-ébeth alone cried out for retribution. He understood that. Kirin's loss pierced his own heart; a wound that would never heal. But vengeance, though sometimes sweet, was always short-lived. If there was to be a legacy from this day, it needed to be a lasting one. One worthy of the sacrifices that had been made.

"It is for the good of the people, Torrin. I know it is hard. We have all lost so much to the hand of injustice."

Elona placed a gentle hand on Torrin-Ashur's arm and turned him towards her. "Torrin," she urged quietly, "please. We are done. No more fighting."

Torrin-Ashur swallowed hard. He was tottering on the precipice of a decision that could alter the course of history. For a moment, Jorra-hin truly didn't know which way his friend might go. He sighed a great sigh of relief when he finally received a reluctant nod.

"But not Daka, Jorra. She must pay. And Gömalt. The rest can go."

Jorra-hin turned to the awaiting Tsnathsarré.

"*Then, with two exceptions, you are free to return to Tsnathsarré in peace.*"

"*Exceptions?*"

"*Baroness Daka and her man Gömalt are to be surrendered.*"

Döshan raised his eyebrows up at Özeransk.

"*Mage Hin, we have no concern over the fate of Gömalt – he is a commoner,*" the warrior said. "*However, Emperor Omnitas would need to be consulted on the matter of the Baroness.*"

Jorra-hin gestured approval with his hand. Özeransk nodded to Döshan and the advisor withdrew to speak with the emperor once more. Their conversation was brief and he returned without delay.

"Mage Hin, Emperor Omnitas makes a counter proposal that may be acceptable to you," he said, resuming his flawless Alondrian. "The Council of Barons is very powerful in Tsnathsarré. One of their number cannot be given up so easily. However, you have given us insight into the baroness's true intent here today. She has committed an act of treason against Emperor Omnitas. His Majesty offers, therefore, to deal with her according to Tsnathsarré law."

Jorra-hin raised an eyebrow at Torrin-Ashur. "Trust me, that fate is worse than anything you might wish to inflict, Torrin. I urge you to accept."

Torrin-Ashur's response was far from instant. His eventual agreement clearly came at great personal cost.

With the matter settled, Özeransk took a step forwards and reached for his sword. Several of the Alondrians standing nearby tensed.

Torrin-Ashur didn't flinch.

The Tsnathsarré nobleman lowered himself to one knee and presented the hilt of his weapon, the flat of the blade laid across his forearm.

Torrin-Ashur hefted the weapon and held it high. It was a striking stance. It seemed everyone present held their breath.

It was a long moment.

A sigh of relief moved through the onlookers as Torrin-Ashur lowered the blade and bid Özeransk stand. He flipped the sword over and presented it back.

"As one soldier to another, you may keep this, on the condition that you will never again draw it against Alondria."

With a flick of an eye towards Jorra-hin, Özeransk smiled. "After today, you can be assured of that." He turned to Daka's men. *"The Baroness, where is she?"*

There was a ripple of whispered enquiry amongst the soldiers. One of them shuffled forwards, reluctant to come too close.

"My lord, she has fled the field. I do not think we could catch up with her."

"Gömalt was with her?"

"Yes, my lord."

Özeransk sighed. "I'm afraid, Lord Ashur, Daka has run away. But do not worry, there is only one place she can go. Neither she nor Gömalt will escape their fate. You have my word on that." He turned his attention to the bedraggled assortment of Alondrians milling about nearby. "These people, they are from Mitcha?"

"For the most part, yes," Torrin-Ashur answered.

Özeransk regarded Jorra-hin. "Do your terms extend to all Tsnathsarré forces in the region?"

"If they withdraw peacefully."

"Good. Then allow me to accompany you. I will see to it that our forces withdraw from Mitcha without a fight."

*

It was the strangest feeling he had ever felt, an Alondrian general ahead a force of cavalry, allowing a Tsnathsarré emperor to march through Alondria without lifting a finger to stop him.

Kirshtahll leaned across to Temesh-ai. "I'll be damned," he murmured, "I... *will*... be... damned."

Temesh-ai answered with a quick nip from a bottle he was keeping warm under his cloak.

"I never thought I'd see such a day," Agarma intoned from just the other side of the doctor. "I cannot believe that's actually Omnitas. I mean, the bloody Tsnath emperor, right there, within bowshot. Gods!"

Kirshtahll growled in agreement under his beard. But he also shot a cautioning glance towards the captain, just to make sure nothing untoward was about to let slip.

An hour passed before the Tsnath had adequately left the field and Kirshtahll felt it was safe to lead his forces across the Ébeth bridge without the risk of clashing with the enemy and bringing further disaster upon the day. Whatever deal Torrin-Ashur and Jorra-hin had struck, until he knew the details, he was of a mind not to make matters worse.

He nearly choked when he came upon the battlefield proper and saw the scale of the carnage that had been wrought.

Torrin-Ashur was slumped back to back with Elona, who, gods be damned, was as much covered in blood and gore as the lieutenant. A certain anger rose within him that he found hard to quell. Agarma had clearly paled.

The sight of Borádin laid flat out nearby without a care for the coldness of the snow also took Kirshtahll by surprise. The nobleman was surrounded by his men, all of whom looked as though they'd been through the mill. The people of Mitcha, the mayor being the most recognisable amongst them, had fared little better. Exhausted all, they sat in clumps, tending wounds, divesting themselves of armour, hugging each other, clearly dazed by their ordeal and not a little amazed that they weren't dead.

Kirshtahll had seen many battlefields, trudged through the mud and bloody aftermath of more conflicts than he cared to remember, but none had been like this. It was beyond comprehension. So many dead. So many Tsnath dead. Bodies lay everywhere, several deep in places. How could such a force as this, a thousand maybe, fifteen hundred at the most, civilian more than soldier, have wreaked so much devastation on a superior enemy? He just couldn't grasp it.

He noticed a solitary figure up on the hill, head bowed, looking very forlorn. The black cassock and curly hair made him instantly recognisable. Jorra-hin for some reason had retreated away from the rest to be alone. Kirshtahll thought it best to leave him be.

But he wanted answers. He aimed his horse at Torrin-Ashur, drawing to a halt a few paces short.

The lieutenant wearily climbed to his feet. Elona followed, struggling under the weight of her armour, which was fit for a man and swamping her. He'd expected some warmth of welcome, but got none. He understood why.

"You've drunk in the halls of hell this day," he said, dismounting.

"It's no place for the living, that much I know myself."

With little emotion showing, Elona wandered up to him and simply tipped herself forwards into his chest. There was a clank of armour. "Padráig," was all she said.

He hugged her tightly until some of her trembling had subsided. What nightmare they had been through, he could only wonder. Horrors would haunt them for the rest of their days. Such ghosts filled his past, too. He resolved to go gently.

Without quite letting go of the princess, he moved her to one side and faced Torrin-Ashur. He nodded and waited for the lieutenant to speak.

"It is good to see you, sir," the lad finally managed.

"Aye. And you – alive. I feared we might not be in time."

"It was Jorra-hin who saved us. You saw what happened?"

"Saw it? My horse damned nearly threw me and bolted back to the mountains!"

"It was the *Dànis~Lutárn*, sir. Jorra managed to release it into the Ébeth. Now it protects our lands."

"Protects? How?"

"The Tsnath can never again invade with hostile intent, sir. The Great Divide would stop them before their feet met dry land this side of the Ablath. We are finally free, sir."

Kirshtahll couldn't begin to understand how that could be true. But the joy those words brought made it worth taking things a little on faith. The details could come later.

He turned to Agarma. "Captain, let's get these people back to Mitcha. They deserve to go home. Tell our men to free up the horses."

18

Özeransk made good his offer to facilitate the surrender of Mitcha. The occupying forces relinquished the town without resistance once the Tsnathsarré nobleman had explained the situation.

Kirshtahll did not stay long in the town; there was too much for him to do elsewhere. He rode out a few days later to oversee the retreat of the remaining invasion forces, and to help where he could with bringing some normality back to the Northern Territories.

For the remainder of those who had trudged back through Mitcha's gates, the town would never be the same again. It wasn't simply that the place had been looted and many a cherished heirloom lost, but more that the town seemed empty of the life it had once possessed. Katla had summed it up best with a remark that it was like trying to settle into a stranger's house; it felt cold and bereft of known comforts.

No household had escaped the ordeal of the last few months unscathed and nothing could assuage the sense of loss that seemed all-pervading. Being in familiar surroundings merely reminded people of those now missing. Many had fallen so recently, during the final battle, that memories and emotions were still raw wounds which had had no time yet to heal.

It was with brave faces hiding broken hearts that the townsfolk tackled the task of rebuilding their lives.

Torrin-Ashur saw it all when he walked the streets, giving encouragement where he could, painfully aware of how little he had to offer. Everywhere he went, he encountered wives without husbands, parents without children, young and old without the other to look after them.

Compounding the difficulty of adjusting back to life within walls was that so much change piled up around them. Even simple, everyday things were different now. Commerce had collapsed completely and, with winter upon them, everything was in short supply. To give them their due, what was left of the council worked feverishly to restore a semblance of order. The mayor, along with his daughter, became a cohesive force that fought to prevent Mitcha's soul from slipping away.

In stark contrast, Torrin-Ashur felt increasingly redundant. He wasn't in charge here, and didn't want to be. He found himself included in the council's deliberations, but he had no experience of running a town. That had been his father's job. Here, even Eldris's counsel would have been better than his own. What Mitcha didn't need right now was another soldier getting in the way. There wasn't even much the Ashurmen could help with. The fabric of the town wasn't where the Tsnath had wrought their devastation; hearts needed mending, not houses, and the former Pressed's skills were ill suited to that task.

He was brooding upon such matters, only half-heartedly listening to the council's discussions, when his thoughts were interrupted.

"Sir," Nash beckoned, poking his head round the door to the chamber. "We have some new arrivals."

The sergeant disappeared before Torrin-Ashur could ask who had turned up. He excused himself from the struggle against the chaos still reigning over the town's affairs and stepped outside.

"Kassandra?" he exclaimed, almost skidding to a stop in the square.

"Torrin."

The bedraggled young woman he had once hauled out of the Ablath was utterly gone. In her place, a subtle smile on her lips, was a lady of such presence that every man in the vicinity stopped to stare. She dismounted with graceful ease and handed her reins to a boy who, probably sensing opportunity for coin, had magically appeared from nowhere. The small group of her fellow travellers joined her on the cobbles. Torrin-Ashur paid them little heed for the moment. He was still reeling.

"Forgive me," he stammered, "but you are the last person I expected to see." He thought how that might have sounded and added quickly, "Though your arrival is a pleasant surprise." He kissed the hand she held out.

Kassandra lowered the hood of her cloak to reveal her auburn hair in all its glory. "I never thought I'd return north myself, Torrin. I have no choice, however."

"Oh?"

"I must face my mother."

Torrin-Ashur's eyes widened in shock. It was a moment before his fuddled mind managed to formulate a reply. "Whatever for?"

Kassandra didn't get a chance to answer.

Elona appeared at the edge of the town square, accompanied by Captain Agarma. Kassandra surged towards her, cloak trailing behind as though caught in a breeze. She tried to curtsy, but Elona threw her arms around the noblewoman.

"What are you doing here?" she demanded keenly.

Kassandra hesitated, glancing back over her shoulder at Torrin-Ashur. "Is there somewhere we can talk? There are things I must tell you."

Torrin-Ashur nodded. "Nash, would you find Lord Özeransk and ask him to join us in the council chambers."

At that moment, not least taking Agarma by surprise, Elona deserted Kassandra and dashed towards several other members of the party that had arrived. She careered into the arms of a tall young man, who lifted her off her feet and spun her around, his face a beaming smile. Another of the arrivals, with bushy dark hair gathered through a ring at the nape of his neck, received an equally enthusiastic greeting.

"Pomaltheus, Seth, you're here!" Elona jabbered, her elation abundantly clear to all. Agarma's look of concern receded.

"Of course we are," the taller of the pair replied. "You didn't think we'd abandon you to these frozen wastes, did you?"

"Seth's speaking for himself. He's the one who insisted we do battle with snow and ice once more to come and rescue you. Me – I'd have left you up here."

"Oh, Pomaltheus," Elona put a hand to his cheek, "such fibs don't become you." She gave him another hug, then linked arms with both of them and steered them towards Torrin-Ashur.

"Without these two, Jorra-hin and I would never have made it out of Alondris."

Torrin-Ashur recalled the stories Elona had told of their flight from the capital, and the subsequent journey north. They had seemed fabulous at the time, and not wholly believable. Only later had he realised she'd not been exaggerating. He gave each mage a heartfelt handshake.

"Speaking of Jorra-hin," Seth said, "is he here? And Kirin?"

Elona shared a pained glance with Torrin-Ashur. "Jorra-hin wishes to be alone at the moment. I'm afraid I have some bad news." She paused, struggling to find the words. "Kirin died during the battle with Daka's forces at Tail-ébeth."

"What!" Pomaltheus gasped, anguish instantly transforming his face from joy to sorrow. His whole body sagged.

"Jorra-hin has taken it badly. His grief is deep."

"Then he needs friends around him," Seth declared, his tone almost accusing others of failing in their duty of care.

Elona and Torrin-Ashur shared another look.

"Much has changed," Torrin-Ashur cautioned. "Jorra is not the same man you knew a month or two ago."

"Nonsense," Seth retorted. "Jorra is Jorra."

"Indeed," Torrin-Ashur bowed his head, though his manner suggested care needed to be taken in the next few moments, "and I more than any want him back as my friend. But he has been forced to assume his true nature in a cruel way. He is a mage like no other. His power rages within him, and while he seeks to master it, he wishes solitude. A wish we have granted him."

Pomaltheus let out a grunt. "Well I'm not happy about that."

"But we will honour his wish," Seth cut in, nipping any rash thoughts in the bud.

*

The meeting between Kassandra and Özeransk was, to Torrin-Ashur's mind, most revealing. Kassandra was much taken with her illustrious compatriot, despite him being older.

Less surprising perhaps, Özeransk seemed equally enamoured of her. Kassandra did have that effect on most of the men around her, though in truth few but the Tsnathsarré nobleman stood a chance of such captivation bearing fruit.

Özeransk for his part had turned out to be a man of impeccable bearing. Though they had been mortal enemies not many days earlier, somehow Torrin-Ashur had found it hard not to warm to the nobleman. Özeransk was the first Tsnathsarré man he'd ever spent time with, and his preconceptions had taken quite a battering.

The barriers had really come tumbling down after it became apparent that they'd faced each other outside the caves at *Niliàthái*. When Özeransk had realised that it was Torrin-Ashur who'd orchestrated the avalanche that had devastated his forces, instead of reacting with bitterness or anger, the nobleman had purloined a supply of something akin to Brock and invited him to get very drunk. He'd learnt a new Tsnathsarré phrase that evening, *Sai-raska*. Apparently, it was reserved as a toast of honour between those who'd shared the battlefield, though more usually between those on the same side.

Özeransk's explanations of Tsnathsarré culture had been somewhat slurred, to say nothing of their being received by a befuddled mind, so none of it had made much sense at the time.

Still, it had been hard to sustain enmity after that.

"So, now that introductions have been made, perhaps we should move on to other matters," Torrin-Ashur prompted. "Lord Özeransk, you should probably tell Kassandra of your news first."

"Indeed." Özeransk turned to Kassandra. "I have received orders from the emperor. I am to proceed to Castle Brath'daka with all haste."

"Brath'daka," Kassandra's eyes immediately narrowed, "why?"

"The emperor has ordered your mother's arrest. She has been stripped of her title. Her lands are forfeit."

Torrin-Ashur had expected at least some reaction from Kassandra, shock perhaps, or maybe satisfaction that her mother was going to get her comeuppance. But there was nothing. Kassandra didn't even flinch.

All she said was, "And what of Gömalt?"

Özeransk tilted his head aside. "The emperor does not care for the fate of such lowly instruments." The nobleman's gaze momentarily fell on Torrin-Ashur. "Others here *do*."

Kassandra looked confused.

"Lord Özeransk has informed me that, under your mother's orders, Gömalt was responsible for the destruction of my home town," Torrin-Ashur explained.

"Tail-ébeth? It is gone?"

"Utterly."

Kassandra looked stricken. "I am so sorry, Torrin. I did not know."

"There is nothing for which you need to be sorry. You had no hand in what befell Tail-ébeth."

"It was my family that brought ruin upon you. I know my mother. She is hard of heart, with no mercy in her. She will have acted against your town out of spite."

"Spite?"

"For helping me, for giving me sanctuary when I escaped her clutches. I'm afraid it is I who brought her wrath down on you."

Torrin-Ashur took a moment to digest this unexpected slant on Tail-ébeth's fate. But it changed nothing. He was determined that it wasn't Kassandra's fault. He would not allow what her mother had done to afflict her daughter any more. The baroness had caused enough pain there already.

He rose from the bench he was sharing with Elona and knelt on one knee before Kassandra. He took her hands in his. "Know this: I have nothing but admiration for the courage you showed when you fled Brath'daka. You are as much a victim in all this as anyone. So I forbid you to share any blame for what your mother has done, do you understand?" Kassandra's lip trembled. "In fact, I hail you as a hero of Alondria. Had you not come to us that day, your mother's plans might well have succeeded. You brought us the warning we needed, setting Jorra-hin on his quest to uncover the truth. Without that, we would have known nothing of the *Dànis~Lutárn*. The weapon your mother sought would have been hers for the taking. Alondria is free today because of you."

At that Kassandra lost the battle to maintain her composure. Torrin-Ashur remained kneeling for a moment, until Özeransk stepped in to lend comfort. Torrin-Ashur rejoined Elona on the bench.

"As for Gömalt," he added, "Özeransk has invited me to accompany him to Brath'daka."

"You will kill him?" Kassandra managed between sobs.

"If the gods allow it."

Kassandra closed her eyes. She looked relieved. Her faith in the gods' permission for justice was clear.

"I shall come with you, too," she said, regaining a measure of control over her emotions. "There is something I must do."

19

As the brooding edifice loomed in front of them, Castle Brath'daka didn't look quite so forbidding when it was surrounded by snow, Kassandra mused. Although its architecture would never allow it to sit peaceably within the landscape it had been built to subdue.

She smiled when Özeransk turned to Torrin-Ashur and said to him in Alondrian, "*Beautiful place, is it not?*" He had clearly mastered sarcasm in another man's language.

Torrin-Ashur glanced back over his shoulder. "*Are you sure you want to do this?*"

Kassandra hesitated for a moment, building up the courage to answer. "*I must.*"

Torrin-Ashur sighed. He'd made it clear several times that he didn't think it was a good idea she was here. "*Alright — just so long as you know, this is your last chance to turn back.*"

There was no turning back.

The portcullis was down when they reached the foot of the granite walls. That was not unusual. It was just fortunate that Özeransk was a well-known visitor, and that word of the emperor's orders had not reached the castle, otherwise the gates would have been shut too, with a loaded crossbow lurking behind every arrow loop and crenulation the castle had to offer.

Kassandra pulled the hood of her cloak a little tighter, ensuring none of her features could be seen. Her presence could very well lead to the raising of suspicions rather than the portcullis.

Özeransk held up a gauntleted hand and the two hundred strong detachment of Tsnathsarré horseman the emperor had sent to support him drew to a halt. Özeransk alone rode forwards to the gate. There was a brief exchange that Kassandra couldn't hear clearly, then with relief she saw the portcullis begin to rise.

She continued to hold her hood close as the troop rode through the gatehouse tunnel and on into the courtyard. It was a place she had never thought she would see again.

*

Alber scurried along the corridor towards Gömalt's chambers and hammered urgently on the door.

"Go away."

The irritated growl from within made Alber hesitate. Gömalt had been in a foul mood for days. Not only was he suffering from the baroness's temper, as were all in the castle, but he was also dealing with the sudden departure of Roumin-Lenka.

Alber knew his master had been labouring under the impression that there had been something between them. After all, he and the Dwarve had shared a bed for several months. What his master had failed to grasp was the mind of someone raised entirely within the Dwarve Nation, to say nothing of that someone being a woman.

Dangerous depths for any man to plumb.

What seemed to have escaped Gömalt was that Dwarvish relationships, even their carnal ones, were liaisons of mutual gain. Alber thought everyone knew that.

The baroness's plan had died, her ambitions along with it, and Roumin-Lenka had decided there was no benefit in remaining. She had been paid what was owed, after a certain amount of threatening behaviour, and that was that. It didn't help that the Dwarve had then upped and left without even saying goodbye.

Gömalt was hardly a love-struck youngster crying over his loss, but he had been sent spiralling into a vile and somewhat dangerous mood from which he had yet to surface.

Having hammered a second time, Alber swallowed nervously before speaking. "I'm sorry, sir, but we need you. We have visitors."

There was no sound of movement from inside the chamber. Just the sudden opening of the door, almost sucking Alber in with it as it was thrown aside. Gömalt stood there red-eyed and ragged. He looked like he'd not slept or shaved in days.

"Who?"

"Lord Özeransk."

"Where?"

"Courtyard."

"Who the hell let him in?" Alber didn't need to answer. "I'll flay the skin off the backs of every man on duty," Gömalt growled as he surged down the corridor. "So what does Özeransk want?"

"He's asking to speak with the baroness."

Gömalt stopped mid-stride. "Damn the gods!" he thundered. "She's been drinking for days. She's in no fit state to be seen by anyone."

*

Kassandra felt revulsion wash over her as Gömalt came through the keep door and started across the courtyard. She knew she was safe. Even the Daka assassin, with all his skills, could not reach her, not with Özeransk, Torrin-Ashur, and two hundred of the emperor's finest protecting her. But the feelings of dread that nearly overwhelmed her came unbidden, heeding not one jot the logic of her reasoning.

She leaned towards Torrin-Ashur and whispered, "*The one on the left is Gömalt. But be careful, the other is Alber – fiercely loyal.*"

"Lord Özeransk, it is good to see you," Gömalt greeted. Kassandra could tell he was feigning civility. What he was thinking was anything but friendly. She had never seen the man looking so scruffy before, though. That surprised her. Things had obviously gone downhill since the defeat in Alondria. "We were not told to expect you."

"It is not always possible to send word on ahead, Gömalt. Still, no matter. I'm sure the baroness's hospitality will be as warm as always."

Gömalt hesitated. That, too, was unusual. "I'm afraid the Baroness is – indisposed at the moment."

Özeransk raised an eyebrow. "Drowning her sorrows?"

The derogatory response immediately put Gömalt on guard. Özeransk was not here to play a friendly game.

Gömalt searched for a response. Özeransk saved him the bother. "Well, I have something that might cheer her up."

"My lord?"

"Her daughter."

Kassandra drew back the hood of her cloak and gave her head a quick shake to loosen locks that had been cramped too long. Auburn waves cascaded down her back.

"Quite a revelation, wouldn't you say?"

Gömalt's eyes bulged, narrowed, then widened again as a variety of thoughts seemed to make a dash though his mind. He turned to Özeransk with confusion creasing his brow.

"How? I mean, where did you find her? I thought she'd been taken south of the Mathians."

Torrin-Ashur dismounted, as did a number of those around him. Kassandra knew he understood very little of what was being said, yet that didn't really matter now. What he was here to do needed little guidance, only opportunity.

"Ah, to answer that question, Gömalt, I think you'd better ask this young man." Switching seamlessly into Alondrian, Özeransk continued, "*He's so very much been wanting to meet you. His name is Torrin-Ashur. I believe you made him a lord.*"

Kassandra saw Gömalt's eyes widen in alarm. He wasn't protected by any magic, but he did have keen senses. And he was no fool. He knew trouble the likes of which he'd never faced before was advancing towards him with more than a purposeful look in its eye.

He backed away. His hand went for his scabbard, but it wasn't there. Almost without faltering, his other hand flew to the smaller blade that was always in his waistband.

Sword against dagger. Expecting Torrin-Ashur to move in for a quick kill, Kassandra looked on with tense anticipation. She nearly choked in horror when he didn't proceed as she had anticipated.

"*Are you a gods-fearing man, Gömalt?*" Torrin-Ashur asked, coming to a standstill about ten paces short of his adversary.

He hadn't even drawn his sword. 'What are you playing at?' Kassandra wanted to scream. She only just managed to hold her tongue.

Gömalt swallowed and cast about for a better weapon with which to defend himself. Alber took a step forwards, only to find four crossbows suddenly aimed at him. He froze.

"*Lord Özeransk, could we find Gömalt a sword? He seems to have forgotten his.*"

"What?" Kassandra gasped. "*Torrin, no. He is not a man to toy with.*" Torrin-Ashur turned and stared back at her.

"*I have never killed a man in cold blood before. Gömalt will not be my first, no matter what he deserves. Our fates are in the hands of the gods now.*"

Özeransk unbuckled his own sword and tossed it over to Gömalt. Kassandra noted the nobleman's wary looks, warning his crossbowmen to be doubly on their guard now that Gömalt was armed more effectively. Whatever Torrin-Ashur was doing, Özeransk was taking no chances. The assassin's death was a certainty. Only the hand that would deliver it was still undecided in Kassandra's mind. She had doubts.

She had not been at Tail-ébeth.

Gömalt had.

By the way fear seemed to be gaining a foothold in him, it was clear he knew something of what was coming. He slipped Özeransk's sword from its scabbard and flung the empty sheath away. It skidded across the cobbles.

Its owner scowled. "I did not lend you my sword so that you could abuse it."

Gömalt didn't seem to hear. His eyes were fixed on his opponent.

Torrin-Ashur unbuckled his sword belt and lowered himself to one knee. Holding the tip of the scabbard against the cobbles, he slowly withdrew his blade, one by one revealing words engraved along its fuller. The scabbard he carefully laid sideways on the ground before his feet.

Kassandra heard him offer a short prayer. *"For you, father."* A certain knowing took hold of her.

Gömalt had never been one for procrastination. He flew forwards without warning, darting in to strike a quick blow.

To Kassandra, it appeared as though all Torrin-Ashur did was stand up and step sideways. There had been a blur of movement with his sword, but it had been too quick to really discern. Gömalt's lunge carried him past his target and he came to a standstill a yard or two further on.

Torrin-Ashur didn't turn. After a moment's pause, he stepped forwards, picked up his scabbard, wiped away a small smear of blood from the tip of his blade and slowly re-sheathed it. Only then did he walk round to face the assassin.

A crimson line across Gömalt's throat was the only evidence a deadly blow had been delivered. Not that there was much blood. The wound was surgical in its precision.

"A faster death than you deserve," Torrin-Ashur murmured, leaning in close to the assassin's ear.

Gömalt crumpled to his haunches. For a moment he tottered there, then slowly his torso collapsed backwards. His head made a sickening thud against the cobbles.

Torrin-Ashur reached down and retrieved Özeransk's sword from where it had fallen. He collected the discarded scabbard, sheathed the blade and made to present it back to its owner.

A feral scream erupted from Alber. The henchman lunged towards Torrin-Ashur with murder in his eyes. Four quarrels slammed into his chest. His body was stopped in mid-flight and thrown backwards, as though an invisible beast had snatched back a fleeing morsel.

Torrin-Ashur waited a moment. He eyed the twitching remains of the henchman, checking that there was no further threat. Satisfied, he handed Özeransk his sword.

"*I am indebted to you, my lord. Justice for my family and my town would not have been possible without your help in bringing me here.*"

'You're welcome' might have been Özeransk's reply. Kassandra noted that the words seemed to be stuck somewhere in the warlord's throat.

Torrin-Ashur came over to her. She tried to dry the tears that had come unbidden. He raised a questioning eyebrow. "*Not pity, surely?*"

"*Relief*, Eck em-hidda."

Torrin-Ashur may not have known much Tsnathsarré, but those words had been the very first she had spoken to him, and by his smile she knew he remembered what they meant. *Him me that saves.*

"*Well, it's up to you now.*"

Kassandra nodded and slipped off her horse, landing lightly.

Özeransk and Torrin-Ashur escorted her into the castle keep, where, almost immediately, they encountered Halfdanr, master of the serving staff. He stopped dead in his tracks when he saw who was approaching.

"Mistress Kassandra? But – it can't be."

"Oh yes it can. Where is Anna?"

A blank look briefly crossed the servant's face, before recognition came to the fore. He singularly failed to hide the fact. "Anna?"

With a forcefulness that surprised even her, Kassandra gripped Halfdanr's chin and shoved him hard up against the corridor wall. "Where is she?"

"D – d" Halfdanr stuttered.

"Dead?"

The man attempted to shake his head. "Du – dungeon," he managed between scrunched lips.

Kassandra stepped back. Abhorrence drained her fight momentarily.

Her grip had been so hard that nail marks had been left in Halfdanr's jaw. He massaged his face as he spoke again. "I'm sorry, my lady, but you know how it is here. There was nothing we could do. Your mother…" He stared at the floor, abashed, and didn't finish the sentence.

He didn't have to. Kassandra knew exactly how it was where her mother was concerned.

"And Michàss?"

Halfdanr shook his head once. "Gömalt. The morning you were found missing. I'm sorry."

Kassandra stepped back further and had to lean against the wall for support. She found herself trembling. Closing her eyes for a moment, she fought her emotions. It was a battle quickly won, rage surfacing to rid her of weakness. When she opened them again, a dangerous glint had replaced tears. Without a word, she stormed down the corridor, setting such a pace that Özeransk and Torrin-Ashur nearly had to run to keep up.

Kassandra threw back the large oak door leading down to the lower regions of the castle with such force that it slammed against the far wall and bent the catch. A chip of the stone hit her shoulder. Such was her resolution, she barely even noticed.

The dungeons were not a part of the castle she had ventured into much in all the years she'd lived at Brath'daka. But its layout was simple enough and her lack of familiarity made little odds.

Two keepers, neither employed for their intelligence, eyed the invasion with startled looks. Their fetid breath and unwashed bodies assailed Kassandra's nostrils and made her grimace. If this was how it was for the gaolers, only the gods knew what it was like for the wretches in their charge.

"You have a young woman down here. Her name is Anna. Where is she?"

Fear made itself evident on the keeper's faces. Kassandra had never met them before, but there must have been sufficient resemblance between her and her mother to make identification a simple matter. They knew who she was. They also knew it was not wise to argue with an angry Daka. The one before them now was more than just angry.

The keeper holding a firebrand wafted it towards an oaken door with massive wrought iron hinges. Subtlety had not been part of the design of this feature of the castle.

"Keys," Kassandra demanded.

"Just bolts, my madam," the man replied, ignorance supplying his etiquette.

Kassandra swept forwards.

"*Perhaps one of us ought to…*" Torrin-Ashur suggested, intercepting her before she had managed to loosen the first bolt.

Some of the whirlwind driving Kassandra on subsided. She gave way to Torrin-Ashur's advice.

Özeransk snatched the firebrand from the keeper and passed it over.

*

Torrin-Ashur withdrew the bolts and pushed the door against objecting hinges. It would only open half way. The stench that assaulted him was like a punch to the guts. Rats would have abandoned such a festering pit, a hole lifted straight from the lowest halls of hell. He gagged and clamped a hand over his nose before stepping through into what was utter darkness save for the spluttering flame of his torch.

Inside the cell, a short flight of steps led down into little more than a damp hole in the ground. With great reluctance he began to descend. No one could have accused him of being a coward, but the spirit of this place horrified him. The overwhelming desolation was enough to terrify the soul, the despair of the wretches left there to rot having soaked into the very walls. It was an atmosphere to devour all hope.

He sensed more than saw two prisoners chained to the wall just beyond the bottom step. Their eyes were really the only thing he could discern clearly, wide and fearful, reflecting the orange glow of the firebrand and giving them the look of demons. Very wretched demons.

Neither of them was a woman, he realised. Anna had to be elsewhere. Confusion gripped him for a moment as he cast around. Several pairs of manacles lay empty on the floor. There appeared to be no one else present. He almost called out to let the others know Anna wasn't there, but at the last moment, something caught his eye, more a shadow than a form, a slightly different kind of darkness to the rest of the appalling abyss.

He lowered the torch and directed its light into the farthest corner of the pit. There was an alcove, a natural fissure in the rock from which the dungeon had been hewn. Rags had been jammed into it. Rags that trembled.

Torrin-Ashur knelt down, bringing the torch closer. He reached out and gently pulled some of the fetid cloth out of the hole. The bundle whimpered and tried to shrink away.

"I've found her," he called back.

He propped the torch against the rock and reached into the fissure to extract Anna. He could feel her petrified shivers. It amazed him that she weighed almost nothing. He had no trouble lifting her. Yet she was so terrified that her whole body curled into a ball, making her awkward to carry.

Kassandra gasped in horror when she saw the wretchedness of her former maid. Her friend. Torrin-Ashur knew from what Kassandra had told him that she would not have escaped the castle all those months ago without Anna's help.

It stood to reason, then, that without Anna, the Northern Territories may well have become part of the Tsnathsarré Empire on a permanent basis. She could not have known it, but this pathetic bundle had helped save Alondria.

With great care Torrin-Ashur carried her over to a stool and tried to sit her down. She refused to uncurl, so instead he gently placed her on the floor near the wall. She immediately scampered off to a corner and tried to melt into the stonework.

"Where are the keepers?" Torrin-Ashur rasped. His voice had gone very dry.

"They've fled" Özeransk replied. "I didn't think them worth pursuit."

Torrin-Ashur grunted. "They're dead men if I ever see them again." He glanced at Kassandra. "There are two other prisoners down there. What of them?"

"We'll release them," Kassandra answered. "But later. I want my mother to face what she's done. That comes first."

Torrin-Ashur was somehow relieved he wasn't Baroness Alishe Daka. Her daughter was radiating a cold fury he would not have imagined her capable of a few hours ago.

*

Halfdanr was sent to fetch the baroness, with strict orders to tell her only that Özeransk was here to see her. The consequences of failure in this regard were made abundantly clear to him.

It was a while before the doors to the great hall were pushed open, by the baroness herself rather than a servant on her behalf. She applied herself to them a little too energetically, and relied on one of the handles for support a little too long. It pulled her off balance, causing her to stumble as she entered the hall. Sorrows as great as hers evidently needed a lot of drowning, Özeransk mused. He kept his face impassive.

She straightened and attempted to regain her composure, clearly annoyed that she had made such a spectacle of herself. She took a few unsupported steps into the hall.

Özeransk wasn't alone at the far end of the long banqueting table, but he was the only person upon whom the baroness's eyes deigned to alight.

"Lord Özeransk."

Özeransk would normally have risen to his feet at Daka's entrance. He would normally have greeted her with a bow. He did neither. That seemed to escape her attention for the moment. What did not was the smell; obviously one she found quite revolting. Her inebriated comprehension of the situation caused her forehead to crease as she cast around for the source of the insult to her nostrils.

She eventually spotted the dishevelled form of Anna perched on one of the chairs not far from Özeransk. The girl's legs were drawn up to her chest, her chin buried between her knees. She rocked gently back and forth, an occasional whimper escaping her.

"What," Daka exclaimed, "is *that* doing here?"

"That, Baroness? *That? That –* is a girl!" This wasn't meant to be his fight, Özeransk reminded himself. But he was angered by Daka's staggering capacity for indifference towards the wretchedness she had inflicted.

Strange how a befuddled mind is able to take things in its stride and apply a certain logic that only makes sense when considered from the bottom of a bottle. Daka simply adjusted her question to accommodate the objection to her choice of pronoun.

"What is *she* doing here?"

Özeransk only just managed to hold himself in check. "You'll have to ask your daughter that," he answered smoothly, belying his disgust.

Confusion reigned supreme on the baroness's brow. She stared back for several moments, before realising that he was looking at something behind her.

She spun round. Again, a little too energetically. With no handle to support her, she had to sidestep to remain on her feet. Only then did she see her daughter standing beside the door. Kassandra had chosen the spot knowing that her mother would not even think to look behind her when she entered the hall. The baroness glanced at Torrin-Ashur, standing on the opposite side of the doorway, but there was no recognition there. He was dismissed as inconsequential. Her gaze quickly returned to her daughter.

"You!" she roared.

"Yes, mother. Me."

Daka let out a scream and launched herself across the chequered flagstones.

Kassandra lashed out, backhanding her mother across the jaw before she collided with her. The force sent the baroness sprawling sideways.

For a moment Kassandra looked on in shock. Then she shook her hand and flexed it several times as the pain awoke her to the reality of what she had done.

Once, she would have fled in mortal terror. Özeransk knew of her life before her escape to Alondria, how she had lived in constant fear. But that had changed. Now she waited calmly for a response.

It wasn't the rage-filled tantrum Özeransk had expected. Quite the reverse. The blow must have been a sobering one.

Daka spluttered and spat something on to the floor. Blood.

Halfdanr was standing just outside the hall, looking in. Daka pinned him with a fierce stare. "Where is Gömalt?" she demanded.

"I know not, my lady."

"Find him!"

"Don't bother," Kassandra rescinded. "Gömalt is dead."

For all her fuddled thinking, Daka seemed to take this news quite easily. Or she just plain didn't believe it. She glanced back at Halfdanr. "Well don't just stand there. Do something!"

"Such as?"

The sheer incredulity on Halfdanr's face was a sight to see. Özeransk noted the man truly couldn't believe he'd just answered the baroness back like that. On any other day, it would have been a death sentence. On this day, Kassandra simply dismissed him by closing the hall doors, shutting him out.

The baroness staggered to her feet and wiped the edge of her mouth on her sleeve. A red smear stained her cream-white dress.

She snorted. "It's been a long time since I saw my own blood. It appears my daughter has finally found her spine."

"Yes, mother. More so than you could possibly know."

Daka nodded and headed for a chair. "Pity you had to wait so long."

"Pity that's all you ever cared about."

Daka let out a sigh as she sat. "So, Gömalt – is it true?"

"Yes."

"How?"

Kassandra pointed at Torrin-Ashur.

"And who is he?"

"Lord Ashur. Torrin, son of Naman. From the town you had Gömalt destroy because they gave me sanctuary."

Daka laughed; for some strange reason she actually laughed. Perhaps at the irony of it all; perhaps just stepping across the boundary of sanity for a moment.

"So why did you come back? There's nothing here for you now."

"There is one thing."

Kassandra approached her mother and grasped the necklace she wore, the one she always wore. She gave it a tug, not so much to rip it away, but enough to break the clasp rather than undo it properly. Özeransk assumed it was her way of saying she didn't want it as something to wear.

"Why?" Daka asked.

In reply, Kassandra walked over to Torrin-Ashur and handed him the jewelled piece.

"*Keep this safe. It is important.*"

He frowned at it, clearly understanding not one iota of its significance.

The significance was not lost on the baroness. "I see," she sighed, "the end of dreams for yet another. So what happens now?"

Kassandra went and stood behind the chair on which her maid was perched. "I've known Anna almost all my life." Reasonable though she may have sounded, she had clearly not forgotten her fury. She twisted the chair so that Anna was facing the baroness. "Yet she doesn't even recognise me now. All she did was help me escape your tyranny, and you did this to her?"

"That was Gömalt's doing."

"***Do not*** try to abdicate your responsibility for this!" Kassandra barked, only a whisper less than a scream.

Özeransk jumped at the sudden force of the retort. Daka blinked in shock.

"So what happens now?" Kassandra repeated the question coldly. "If it was up to me, you'd suffer the same fate you inflicted on Anna. I'd see you languish in your own dungeon until I decided to let you out. *If* that day ever came."

The baroness smirked, though it was a grim sort of distortion of lips, lacking humour. "But it is not up to you, is it." It was a statement, not a question. Her eyes moved to Özeransk.

"No, it is not," he replied evenly. "The emperor knows of your plans. He knows you would have used the *Dànis~Lutárn* against not only Alondria, but against him, against the Tsnathsarré Empire."

"You helped me."

"True," Özeransk dipped his head. "At the emperor's behest. As a means of watching you, to understand what you were up to. I failed in that respect, I must confess. I did not foresee the extent of your ambition, or the means by which you had hoped to achieve it. It pains me to admit, I would have been too late to stop you by the time I understood your plan. Fortunately, others were more vigilant." Özeransk caught Torrin-Ashur's eye and acknowledged him with a nod. As the Alondrian had no idea what was being said, his reply was a frown.

Daka shrugged. It was obviously no surprise to her to hear such things.

"So what does that odious cretin intend for me?"

An eyebrow rose on Özeransk's brow. Such a brazen insult against the emperor was decidedly unwise, considering it was in front of a man who had just declared his loyalty in that direction. Did the woman really wish to court death so wantonly? There was no need. To death she was already wed.

"You will be taken to Jèdda-galbráith. There, if you are lucky, you will be beheaded."

To give her due credit, Daka reacted with a certain calm to that stark revelation. "That is what you call luck?"

Özeransk compressed his lips. "Considering what other options the emperor has at his disposal, yes, I do." Omnitas wasn't the tyrant some of his predecessors had been, but he was not above ordering an execution when occasion demanded. What preceded it would depend on how angered he was. "So it would be wise to avoid trading further insults."

That message seemed to find a mark. Daka remained silent.

"Furthermore, your title and your lands are forfeit. You hereby possess nothing but the clothes you stand in."

Daka's eyes narrowed. "Not even the emperor has the power to do that," she challenged in a quiet voice. "The Daka line is older than his own."

Özeransk smiled. Calmly, with a deliberation designed to annoy the woman before him, he withdrew a scroll from within his robes and unfurled it on the table.

"I received this only yesterday," he said casually. "It is a reply from His Majesty to a suggestion I made a few days ago. It seems he likes my sense of irony, since he has agreed to my request."

Daka's eyes narrowed further still.

"Your title and lands have been granted to your daughter. So fear not, the Daka line continues."

The thinning boundary between sanity and what lay beyond in Daka's mind was irrevocably breached.

"No!" she screamed. With a mighty lunge, she dived for Kassandra with rage-driven fury.

In an instant, Torrin-Ashur darted forwards and smashed his fist into her face before Kassandra could bear the brunt of her wrath. Daka reeled backwards, unconscious before she hit the floor.

Kassandra stood staring down at the still form of her mother, or at least, the woman who had given birth to her.

"*I am Baroness Daka now?*" she stammered in Alondrian, for Torrin-Ashur's benefit.

"*Indeed you are, my dear. Baroness Kassandra, of House Daka, incumbent of this castle and entitled of its lands, as decreed by His Supreme Majesty Omnitas, Emperor of all Tsnathsarré.*"

There was the sound of sobbing.

It wasn't from Kassandra, though there were tears brimming in her eyes.

It was from Anna. She was staring, eyes wide, at the former baroness, sprawled on the floor. Her mouth formed the same word over and over again, like a mantra, though hardly any sound accompanied it.

Ayass.

Torrin-Ashur cocked a questioning glance at Özeransk.

The nobleman smiled. "*It means, 'Free'.*"

20

Mixed feelings coursed their way through Torrin-Ashur as he beheld the walls of Alondris, just a few miles ahead. Alongside the Great North Road the mighty Els-spear flowed untroubled towards the city, heeding nothing of the turmoil that had recently beset the land of its origin. So much had happened since the days of war, since the departure of the Tsnath and the reckoning with Daka, that it felt like another world had dawned in the Territories.

Here, little seemed to have changed at all.

Back in the north, Mitcha had begun to recover. Grief still surfaced occasionally, but smiles and laughter had returned, rejuvenating the town's nearly lost soul. It seemed to Torrin-Ashur that their community was closer knit now than it had been before. They'd shared hardships and borne each other's losses, shoulder to shoulder; that forged bonds like no other.

In the wider region, the March of Ashur was now little but a sparsely populated strip of land between the marches of Ràbinth and Nairn. Tail-ébeth could have been rebuilt, but he'd argued against it. There was no one to live there, so what was the point? The fact that he couldn't face living in a place that would forever remind him of what had been lost was something that he kept to himself. Besides, a better idea had eventually been proposed, resulting in the place being turned into a memorial, a great cemetery where the dead of three armies were buried; the Tsnathsarré, the Alondrians, and the Dendricá, who'd been retrieved from Üzsspeck and laid to rest alongside their descendants, their battle finally won.

That these arrangements left Torrin-Ashur without a home mattered not. It would have taken a small army to prise him from the people of Mitcha, who'd wholeheartedly adopted him as their own. They'd even started referring to him as Lord of the North – there was no such title as Lord Ràbinth, since giving the march a lord of its own would have caused friction with the military commanders who'd always used Ràbinth as a base of operations.

The title was unofficial, of course, and he had no idea how such things were going to be received within the upper echelons of power. With some trepidation, he realised it would not be long before he found out.

There was one thing that had changed this far south; every trader, every peasant, every noble they met, seemed to know who he was. Every conversation regaled the stories that had filtered down from the mountains, many significantly embellished, others fabrications from the start. Separating fact from fantasy was becoming a near-constant battle in its own right.

That made Torrin-Ashur realise the importance of people like Jorra-hin, whose brothers in the Adak-rann strove without respite to record the truth, keeping fictions firmly at bay. He'd not appreciated their true value before. Now, with first-hand experience of how the enthusiasm of the populace so easily exaggerated the facts, he had come to realise how vital it was that someone at least tried to record what actually happened with an objective eye.

Not that the Adak-rann's version of events would hold much sway for a while. As far as reality was concerned, the jubilant crowd that finally welcomed them into Alondris was having none of it. They wanted heroes, and the truth be damned.

The Toning was not sounded for Elona when she entered the city, as custom would normally have dictated. The word on the street was that Queen Midana had ordered it silent. Whatever her reasoning, if it had been to belittle Elona in the eyes of the people, then it was a plan that kicked back like an obstinate mule. Since the Toning couldn't be rung, every other bell in the city tolled instead, peals clamouring across Alondris in competition to sound loudest and longest.

Throngs of people poured out of every shop, house, street and alleyway to witness the procession to the People's Square. For many of those who had come down from Mitcha, it was the first time they had been to the capital, and it was proving an overwhelming experience. The townsfolk glanced round like excited children, gawping at awe-inspiring architecture the likes of which they'd never dreamt of seeing. Torrin-Ashur remembered that feeling, though there had been rather less attention paid to him when he'd first encountered it.

No such anonymity now. It was hard to tell exactly who the enthusiastic locals were cheering for or waving at the most. The natural progression of tale-telling had elevated all those marching through the streets into conquering heroes. To hear the cheers, it was almost possible to believe the entire Tsnathsarré Empire had been subjugated.

Mired in exultation and inundated with well-wishers thrusting flowers at any hand as would take them, it took hours to reach the city centre. When finally they arrived, the contrast between crammed streets and deserted square was jarring.

Only Jorra-hin was there to meet them. He cut a lonely figure. He had not adopted the garb of his magely brethren, Torrin-Ashur noted, but was dressed in a new black cassock with a touch of red piping at the collar and cuffs. It was clearly a statement, a sign of how he intended to conduct himself in future. He had always been a brother of the Adak-rann, and he was going to stay that way. Torrin-Ashur was glad; despite having witnessed first-hand what had happened at the Ebeth, it was still hard to think of the young monk as a mighty mage.

He climbed down off his horse and walked out to meet him.

Jorra-hin bowed, as he had the very first time they'd met.

Torrin-Ashur hugged, as befitted a friend.

Somewhere in the middle, they came to an understanding.

Ice broken, Elona, Pomaltheus and Seth wasted no time in joining them. Now it was embraces only, even for princesses.

"How have you been?" Torrin-Ashur asked when he got the chance. He'd not seen Jorra-hin for nearly two months.

There was no answer.

Jorra-hin's attention was fixed on the sight of the solemn charge the northern throng had conveyed to the city.

With the reverence of a holy relic, Kirin, the Silver Lady, had been carried by a host of volunteers, all eager to bear her bier. They'd travelled a thousand miles to bring her home. They'd have gladly gone a thousand more to honour her.

*

With no bidding necessary, a path opened up for Jorra-hin. He drew close to the platform on which Kirin lay. Her body was draped with two richly embroidered standards, one Alondrian, one Nicián, laid diagonally so that her feet and her head remained uncovered.

A great sadness descended as his grief momentarily slipped his control. He reined it in quickly, realising that it was not only he who had been affected. "I'm sorry," he muttered to Torrin-Ashur, glancing sideways. "My power sometimes escapes me, particularly when my emotions run away with themselves."

Torrin-Ashur placed a hand on his arm. "Kirin means a great deal to us all. We understand."

Jorra-hin nodded and tried to put a brave face on things. He only partially succeeded.

The procession resumed, with Jorra-hin now at its head. He led the way across the vast cobbled expanse of the People's Square towards the middle of the Cymàtagé steps. A small delegation awaited them. The Nicián ambassador and his wife stood before the others in their party. Between them, as though their own, was Emmy.

They waited with indescribable patience as Kirin was brought closer. Jorra-hin's heart went out to them.

When Kirin's mother saw her daughter's face, with its subtle silver smile eternally set, she could hold her composure no longer. The ambassador wrapped his arms around her and held her tight.

It was all Jorra-hin could do to constrain his power; it so wanted to explode forth and give vent to his emotions, a grief that besieged his defences, seeking to overwhelm them. Only with the same iron determination with which he had brought the *Dànis~Lutárn* to heel did he manage to subdue the Taümatha now.

"Ambassador, my lady," he opened, bowing to each in turn, "your daughter gave her life for mine – there is no greater love than that. Words cannot adequately speak of the debt I owe." He turned to address all the gathered throng, spread out right back across the People's Square. "Kirin saved our land. The people of this kingdom owe the freedom they enjoy today entirely to the love she demonstrated for us. For me."

He had to pause. He could not speak again for several moments as he desperately tried to regain command of his voice.

"The name of Soprina Kirin-orrà DelaMorjáy will be honoured for all time in Alondria."

He didn't immediately realise that he had slipped into A'lyavine. His words had meant to be personal, not a proclamation. Yet they proceeded forth with the power of a royal decree. They were sensed throughout the city, writing law absolute into the hearts of the people of Alondria.

Emmy had no need for such a law. She stepped forwards and placed a single white rose on Kirin's chest. But she did not withdraw her hand. Instead, she closed her eyes and allowed a smile to settle upon her lips.

Jorra-hin gasped. A sudden, searing pain stabbed at his lungs, as though the air had been sucked away. For a moment the world stopped, holding its breath as a little girl desired with all her heart to give back the gift she had once received.

Struggling to recover, Jorra-hin placed a shaky hand on Emmy's shoulder and gently drew her back. When his breath had returned, and his hammering heart had stopped trying to burst from his chest, he leaned down and whispered in her ear, "A gift is a gift, Emmy. Kirin would not want it returned."

Emmy stared up at him, bleary-eyed and utterly mystified. She clearly had no understanding of what had just happened. He knelt down and drew her to him. "We both loved her very much," he murmured. "Trust me, she knows that."

Taking Emmy's hand in his, he rose and nodded to those carrying Kirin, indicating that they should follow him towards the Cymàtagé. By an unspoken word, Torrin-Ashur held the rest of the crowd back. Only the bearers and Kirin's family ascended the great marble steps. They passed through the huge bronze doors at the top and crossed the obsidian floor towards the incongruously small door on the far side of the entrance hall. The magnificent chandelier and the stately mages peering down from their lofty perches were hardly noticed. Martiss, manning his usual position as gatekeeper to the hallowed halls within, watched intently as the party approached. When they drew near, he rose, rounded his desk and bowed most solemnly. He remained with his head lowered until the party had passed.

Jorra-hin conducted them through the myriad corridors of the Cymàtagé interior, the route lined with silent mages and sombre acolytes, as still as statues, until they arrived at the doors to the stairwell that led down to the crypt.

As they wound their way deep into the bowels of the earth, a seemingly never-ending descent, Jorra-hin remembered the last time he'd come down here, the day his life had changed forever. When he had run from the Dinac-Mentà, that life or death chase through pitch black tunnels, he had been running towards Kirin. As though only yesterday, he remembered his shock, then euphoric relief when he'd so unexpectedly encountered her. How full of life she had been. How wonderful to hear her greeting. How much he wanted that again.

At the bottom, as he'd requested, the tunnel that led towards the burial cavern was lined with torches, all lit and burning steadily. The crypt hadn't seen this much light in centuries, if ever. It made the place far less disconcerting than it had been when he and Kirin had first ventured this way searching for Mage Yazcöp's resting place. He was glad of that. Though burials were normal practice for the nobility of Niciá, it had not been easy to persuade Kirin's parents to allow her to be interred beneath the Cymàtagé. Had the tunnel been left dark and forbidding, they might have changed their minds before reaching the hidden sanctuary he intended as Kirin's resting place.

At the end of the passage, where the tunnel opened out into the main burial cavern, he bid the rest wait while he went forwards to prepare the way. Emmy's grasp was there to stay, so he allowed her to accompany him. Actually, he was glad to have her by his side. Her little hand tightly griping his somehow gave him strength. Kirin would have smiled at that.

As torches had also been set around the perimeter of the cavern, it wasn't necessary to grope through a stygian void to find the entrance to the lower crypt. Though the torchlight didn't extend quite as far as the pillar, Jorra-hin found that he had only to walk in a straight line. So long as the pillar obscured the light from at least one of the torches on the far side of the cavern, he knew he was on course.

When they reached the glyph-covered column, he drew Emmy round to the side where the door was concealed.

"Why don't you do this bit?" he suggested. "All you have to do is paint the wall with the fire." He handed her the torch. "*Think dragons!*" he added in A'lyavine, giving her a wink.

Emmy smiled and did as instructed, wafting the yellow flames over the surface of the pillar. As she did so, fiery symbols appeared. She sucked in her breath as the A'lyavinical glyphs began to glow, revealing the hidden archway. She stepped back involuntarily at the sound of a click, gawping wide-eyed at an opening where there hadn't been one before.

She glanced up, her face agog. Jorra-hin ruffled her hair. "Well, well, you clever thing. You must have the knack."

With her hand once more firmly back in his, they pushed their way inside.

Having descended the spiral staircase to the lower level of the crypt, it only took a moment to light the lamps in the iron chandelier. Then the rest of the party were summoned to join them.

With some difficulty, Kirin was carried down the spiral steps and finally laid to rest on a newly created plinth directly beneath the chandelier, right in the centre of the chamber.

Jorra-hin ushered the bearers out so that only he, Emmy, the ambassador and his wife remained.

"As I explained to you, Ambassador, my lady, this is a special place. It is a place of the highest honour that I can think to accord Kirin. I know that in your country it is the practice of your families to prepare a Scroll of Life for your loved ones..."

"We have not yet done so, Mage Hin," the ambassador interrupted, as though he'd been remiss.

"I am a brother of the Adak-rann, Ambassador, nothing more. And if you will permit, as such, I would like to contribute to Kirin's Scroll of Life."

Kirin's mother smiled. "We would be honoured. In the olden days, it was usual for a scholar to prepare the scrolls. It is only in recent times that family members have assumed that responsibility."

Jorra-hin nodded. "Thank you. The honour would be mine. I have others to complete, too." He waved his hand around the crypt. "Those who lie here have largely been forgotten by history. But if their Scrolls of Life were known, theirs would *be* our history. Over here is Yazcöp – the bravest mage who ever lived. There, Nickölaus, and over there, Joseph." Jorra-hin put his hands on Emmy's shoulders and gently twisted her round, using her to point the others at another plinth to their left. "That is Mage Holôidees, a great historian – *a bit like me*," he whispered in Emmy's ear, "to whom we are much indebted for his efforts to tell us the truth."

Finally, he stepped over to the remaining grave in the crypt, ushering Emmy just in front of him, his hands still reassuringly on her shoulders.

"And this..." he murmured in hushed tones, "this is Amatt the Blind, our most revered prophet." After a moment to gather himself, he turned to face Kirin's parents. "You may not understand how this is possible, but Kirin knew these men well. They were the greatest mages of their day, the bravest, the most honourable. Kirin could not be in better company. And for what she has done, Kirin's Scroll of Life will lie with theirs, for she has written herself into the history of Alondria."

Kirin's parents remained for a while longer, shedding their tears, saying their goodbyes. When the time came for them to ascend the stairs to return to the others who were waiting above, Jorra-hin rubbed

Emmy's arm fondly. "You go with them. I'll be along in a minute."

Kirin's mother held out her hand and warmly clasped the little girl to her as she went up the steps.

Once alone, Jorra-hin stepped back over to Amatt's plinth.

"You have finally been fulfilled, my friend; only one thing remains, and that will be complete before this day is out." He turned to address the other mages. *"Honoured brethren, the travesty you fought so bravely to prevent has at last been set right. So be at peace. Your deeds will be known. The history Lornadus adulterated will be purified; this I pledge in the name of the Adak-rann."* He moved over to the new plinth and placed a reverent hand on the still, serene and ever beautiful Silver Lady, clothed in the emblems of her peoples, both native and adopted. *"My brothers, this is Kirin. Her compassion knows no bounds. She is a great healer, even of nations. Welcome her into your hallowed halls."*

A gust of wind blew through the crypt, coming from nowhere, with nowhere to go. It extinguished all but one of the lamps in the chandelier above where Kirin lay.

"Eternal Light, be ye never overcome by darkness."

As Jorra-hin ascended the spiral staircase, the remaining tiny flame flared for a second before settling into a steady glow, bathing its charge in a gentle hue.

Emerging from the crypt's entrance into the larger chamber, Jorra-hin did not discover the burial party waiting for him. They were nowhere to be seen. Instead, hooded figures in darkened robes lurked in the shadows at the edge of the chamber. Some bore torches, though not in such a way as to reveal any of their features.

He was not surprised by this turn of events.

"I wondered when you would show yourselves," he opened. He sounded almost conversational. Those who knew him better might have noticed a dangerous edge to his voice.

"You know why we are here. We cannot allow your kind to roam free."

Jorra-hin smiled a mirthless smile. Did the Dinac-Mentà really not know an army of Dancing Warriors awaited him in the People's Square? That the whole of Alondris expected him to reappear at any moment? That they'd storm the Cymàtagé if they thought anything had happened to him?

"You *cannot* allow?"

The figure doing the talking, as far as Jorra-hin could make out, shuffled nervously. "*Will* not allow. Through our intervention, we have kept the balance for centuries."

"The Dinac-Mentà have committed murder for centuries, I'll grant you that. How many lives have you taken, just because they had power, because you feared what they might become? Never giving them the chance to prove you wrong, to prove they were good at heart – that they were innocent."

"We have done what we must. Balance must be maintained."

"By overloading the scales with injustice? You've not kept anything in balance. Your efforts to place obstacles in the path of fate have brought nothing but suffering."

The Dinac-Mentà spokesman shuffled again, clearly a worried man.

Jorra-hin glanced round. Four separate septagem, groups of seven mages, huddled together, ready to summon the power of the Septis Dömon against him.

He should have felt fear. One septagem was enough to strike terror into the heart of a mage. The power of four arrayed against him should have been incomprehensible.

He did not feel fear. He felt anger.

He tensed as the spokesman summoned fire to his fingertips. It quickly became apparent this was not threat, merely illumination. Another of the Dinac-Mentà moved closer, holding out a cloth-covered tray. On it sat three silver rings, one larger than the others, glinting orange in the fiery glow.

Jorra-hin recoiled involuntarily. Where had they found another restraint cast, he wondered? The one Gÿldan had placed on Kirin was the only one known to exist.

"You must submit."

"To that?" Jorra-hin retorted angrily. Some of his power slipped his leash. The torches in the chamber flared, as though caught in a sudden squall. Many breaths were sucked in between clenched teeth. "Do you honestly believe that I would submit to such a thing at your hands?"

"It is the only way you will be permitted to leave here alive."

Jorra-hin scoffed. "Do not think I'm ignorant of your history, you who murdered the first Dinac-Mentà after they submitted to the restraint casts they had made. What madness has gripped you that makes you think I would render myself powerless before you, when you showed no mercy even to your very own founding fathers?"

There was a very long moment, filled with silence.

"I can see there is no reasoning with you," the spokesman intoned gravely. "You leave us no choice." With a flick of his wrist, he signalled to his brethren. As one, they began to chant.

Jorra-hin felt an abrupt wall of heat slap him in the face. It was like opening the door to an oven and peering inside. The seven incantations of the Septis Dömon swirled around him, combining into an oppressive force, intent on crushing him.

"Enough!" he roared, repulsing the Dinac-Mentà's attack by a force of will so much greater than theirs. In an instant, every torch in the cavern was extinguished. His presence filled the chamber, overwhelming his assailants' senses. He dispensed with spoken words and appropriated the Dinac-Mentà bond.

You will listen to me. His voice expanded like thunder in every Dinac-Mentà mind, inundating their capacity to think. In the absolute darkness, they knew only him. *You may not have imposed the restraint cast that killed Soprina Kirin-orrà DelaMorjáy, but you were the cause of its necessity. It may have been Kirin's decision to defy its purpose by saving me, but it was you that killed her. You have destroyed my love, and no doubt that of countless others. So do not think that I would hesitate to be rid of you all. Nothing would satisfy me more.*

Jorra-hin let a little wrath escape his control. Intimately connected to their every thought, he could feel their terror.

You would kill me. Indeed, you have already tried. Such are your methods — but they are not mine. I will not wade in the midden of your ways. I am a brother of the Adak-rann, and to their humble embrace I shall return, after I have fulfilled one final obligation to Amatt the Blind.

But know this: I shall be watching you. I will know if you try to seek my thoughts. I will know if you try to unleash the power of the Septis Dömon again. And if you do, there will be a reckoning!

21

Jorra-hin was a long time inside the Cymàtagé, allowing opportunity for Torrin-Ashur's thoughts to dwell on the task ahead. It held almost as much dread as facing Tsnath, though the foe that awaited them in the palace was of a very different kind; the massed ranks of Alondria's nobility. Armed with their shields of arrogance and swords of contempt, the impending confrontation would not be without its own kind of bloodshed.

The only pleasant greeting whose sincerity could be guaranteed would be Kirshtahll's. The general had gone on ahead a few days earlier to appraise the royal court of what had really happened in the north, preferably with an unexaggerated version of events. Though to any who hadn't witnessed the dramatic conclusion to the battle at Tail-ébeth, even an account carefully abridged by an Adak-rann monk would sound far-fetched.

By the time Jorra-hin eventually emerged through the great bronze doors, looking rather older than his years, it seemed to Torrin-Ashur as though most of Alondris had managed to pack itself into the People's Square. There was little enough room for anyone to manoeuvre, let alone part the way to allow a small army to march through. The far edge of the crowd was already very nearly wading in the Els-spear.

Jorra-hin was quick to size up the difficulties. He beckoned Torrin-Ashur towards him. "Come up the steps. We can reach the river via the front of the Cymàtagé."

Torrin-Ashur nodded. Jostling through the masses to get across the square would take forever, whereas the steps were clear – they were magely territory, and not even the most assertive city dweller would dream of sullying them without invitation. Once at the Els-spear, they could use the towpath to get to the bridge.

Of the thousand or more that had marched down from the north, only a small number were destined to enter the palace. Torrin-Ashur picked them out of the crowd and hustled them up the Cymàtagé steps.

At the foot of the Middle Gosh Bridge, Nash formed up the battle-thinned ranks of the Ashurmen into a squad and marched them across to the palace. The sight of them passing under the portcullis reminded Torrin-Ashur of King Althar's funeral. The scarred and dented Dendricá armour his men were wearing compared incongruously with the dignified uniforms that had been worn by the honour guard that day. He rather suspected Althar would have preferred armour to finery for his send-off. At least the dents and gouges on display now demonstrated service to Alondria, which is more than could be said for anything worn by those who had escorted his coffin. Their plumage had spoken of a rather more self-centred service.

As for the difference in stature of the men involved, the contrast could not have been more stark. The betitled of the land had vied to carry the king on his final journey. Now there was barely a highborn in sight. Given Elona's disgraced status, and his own unratified one, the only recognised noble to march across the bridge with them was Borádin.

The disparity really struck Torrin-Ashur. Alondria's mightiest had been saved by some of her lowliest. He wondered how that particular slap in the face was sitting with the elite; the most privileged having to honour the once Pressed. More than a few were going to have to swallow their pride this day.

Before striking out across the bridge, he glanced round to make sure no one had been devoured by the overeager multitude pressing in from behind. Elona and Jorra-hin were by his side. Elam and Mac flanked a figure whose identity was deliberately hidden beneath a deep-hooded cowl. Behind them came the mayor of Mitcha and his daughter, Katla, as well as some of Mitcha's council. Timerra, just back from Colòtt, marched alongside Captain Agarma, who in turn had been reunited with Elona's lady-in-waiting, a much relieved Céline. Little daylight had managed to prise its way between those two since. Close on their heels were Pomaltheus, Seth and Temesh-ai, and bringing up the rear was Borádin, ahead a squad of what was left of his men. Happy that all were present, Torrin-Ashur offered Elona his arm and escorted her across the bridge into the palace courtyard.

"Last time I came here, it was in the Duke of Cöbèck's carriage," he muttered under his breath, "escorting the fictitious Lady Rachel to Vickrà's ball. That seems like lifetimes ago now."

Elona nodded, hugging his arm a little tighter. "Considering this is supposed to be my home, I'm not sure I should be feeling quite so much the stranger. Things have changed."

"It's us that have changed."

At the foot of the steps leading up to the palace entrance, Nash rearranged the Ashurmen into a pair of escorting columns with Torrin-Ashur and Elona between them. Borádin joined Jorra-hin immediately behind them. Together they mounted the steps and entered the reception hall. There was no fanfare of trumpets, just the sound of hard boots on marble and the clatter of scabbards against tassets. Pages lined the palace walls, looking rather worried at the military invasion stomping past. Gone were the candelabra Torrin-Ashur remembered illuminating the reception on his previous visit; only daylight graced the vast hall now. It didn't seem as warm and welcoming. Probably a portent of things to come, he mused. The thought twisted his lips into a sour expression.

Elona noticed and raised an eyebrow, her reflection in one of the huge mirrors facing them drawing his attention to her glance. They both stared at their approaching counterparts.

"Ye gods," she whispered, using a few fingers to comb one side of her hair. She tucked a loose strand behind an ear. "There was a time when I'd have died of shame to be seen like this."

Torrin-Ashur smirked. "At least now you don't have to pretend to be someone you're not."

"Maybe. But I did not doff my title just to become a frump." She eyed her reflection with a very dubious frown.

Torrin-Ashur grunted. If the vision he beheld was frumpish, the world had no need of sophistication.

Just before they met their reflected selves, they turned a corner into a corridor lined with portraits and tapestries rather than gilded mirrors. At the far end stood the tall doors to the throne room. They were shut, and looked wholly uninviting.

Torrin-Ashur swallowed hard. "Perhaps we should just go home instead."

"Coward," Elona whispered, squeezing his arm. "After what we've been through, there's nothing in there that we have to fear. Besides, there's a reckoning to be had, or had you forgotten?"

No, Torrin-Ashur had not forgotten. A brief tinge of anger bolstered him.

As the doors to the throne room were pulled open by a pair of guards, a hush descended on the milling elite within. The gathering parted, opening up a way to the throne. All eyes swung towards those framed by the doors' arch.

The Lord High Chancellor announced them. It was rather unnecessary, but the gods forbid that protocol should be breached.

"Your Majesty, my lords, ladies, I present to you Princess Elona of the House Dönn-àbrah, Lord Borádin of the House Kin-Shísim, Lord Ashur of the March of Ashur, and Mage..."

"Brother."

"Brother – Hin, of the Cym..."

"Adak-rann."

"...of the Adak-rann," the man spluttered in quick adjustment. He was obviously unaccustomed to being interrupted at such a juncture.

Torrin-Ashur suppressed a smile. Jorra-hin was having none of it where allusions to his magely status were concerned.

Announcements complete, the four of them marched into the middle of the huge chamber, holding everyone's attention. Comparatively unnoticed, the Ashurmen and Borádin's men filed in quietly and spread out around the walls, unobtrusively corralling the gathering. Mac and Elam supplanted the palace guards and took charge of the doors, closing them behind the last man to enter. The hooded figure they'd been escorting remained outside. They took up station, barring the possibility of exit.

It seemed only Lord Vickrà, standing beside and just a little behind the throne, took much notice of this influx of rather purposeful-looking soldiers. His brow creased in a curious frown, Torrin-Ashur noted.

The four of them came to a halt just short of the dais step and bowed as one, Elona included; armour wasn't designed for dainty manoeuvres such as curtsies.

After a curious frown at her sister's choice of garb, Midana acknowledged them with a nod.

"Welcome." Her eyes surveyed each of them in turn, then came to rest on Elona. "I seem to recall that I gave orders for your arrest..." Torrin-Ashur tensed, just managing to hold himself in check as Midana raised a conciliatory hand, "which, if you will allow me to finish, Lord Ashur, I was about to say I have since rescinded. In light of recent revelations, as recounted to us by Lord Kirshtahll, I have issued a full pardon. Rare, considering the charge was treason."

"If friendship is treason, Your Majesty," Elona bristled, "I stand guilty. Since no help was extended to me here, I was left with little choice."

"Your meddling nearly jeopardised the relationship between the Crown and the Cymàtagé," the queen retorted, her tone sharp. In danger of appearing churlish, she softened quickly. "However, the matter is in the past, where I am prepared to leave it."

The blatantly orchestrated display of magnanimity grated on Torrin-Ashur's nerves more than a little.

Midana moved on. "Lord Borádin, you have done your country a great service, and brought honour to your house. No doubt you have been reconciled to your father?"

Borádin allowed himself a smile and dipped his head towards the queen in acknowledgement. "Indeed, Your Majesty."

The reunion between father and son had occurred many leagues north of Alondris. Lord Kin-Shísim, as Borádin would one day be known, had not waited for his son to reach the capital, but had journeyed up to meet him, such had been his eagerness to welcome him home. There hadn't been a dry eye between them when they'd embraced.

"And you must be the Mage Hin I have heard so much about," Midana presumed, her attention dismissing Borádin and flicking sideways.

"I would prefer just Brother, Your Majesty."

"But I am told you are what is called a Natural mage?"

"I have been told the same."

Clearly that was as much of a concession as Jorra-hin was prepared to give on the matter.

Torrin-Ashur watched Midana for her reaction. Her eyes narrowed for a second, but she was careful. She knew enough about Natural mages to know she didn't want to get on the wrong side of one. Especially not this particular One.

She did not dwell. "Which, of course, leaves us our man of the hour. If half the rumours I have heard recently are to be believed, Lord Ashur, you have defeated the known world all points north of the Mathians."

"A slight exaggeration, Your Majesty. We succeeded in surviving annihilation, little more."

"Oh, come, come, modesty at this juncture is unfitting. You must learn to accept praise where it is due."

Following Midana's example, the gathering began to clap. It was clearly not that heartfelt; polite taps on the backs of hands, reserved, more for the sake of being seen to be doing the right thing. Furthest from Torrin-Ashur's mind was the word *jubilant*. The trite display was galling.

With a brief glance at Borádin, who knew full well what was coming, he took a step forwards and turned slowly to scan the faces of Alondria's gathered nobility. It might have appeared as though he was acknowledging the applause, but that would have been to disregard the look on his face. With the exception of Kirshtahll, to whom he gave a respectful nod, he saw little that impressed him.

At his raised hand, the clapping quickly died down. "We did not come here for your accolades, or as a spectacle for your entertainment. We are not here for tribute, or for recognition."

"Then what are you here for?" Midana demanded. Her outrage was not in her voice, but in her eyes.

"Restitution."

A silence smothered the gathering as Torrin-Ashur's single word made a heavy landing. It was the silence of confusion for the majority, the beginnings of concern for some.

"Restitution? Explain."

"Gladly, Your Majesty."

With total disregard for the fact that he was breaching protocol by stepping on to the dais unbidden, Torrin-Ashur mounted the step so that he stood a good head taller than any of those staring at him.

"Long has the Tsnathsarré Empire been regarded as an enemy. History is full of stories concerning the enmity between our two peoples. Wars, some long and bitter, have been commonplace. But the one that has just taken place will not fade into a mere footnote in the annals of Alondria, like its predecessors, for it is unique amongst them." He left the gathering in suspense a moment, breath held, before answering the question he'd placed on every lip. "For this conflict was orchestrated by a conspiracy of Alondrians. Some of whom are here with us now."

Torrin-Ashur's glaring eye roamed the crowd. Few dared meet it. Nearly every Alondrian nobleman and politician of note was present; Kirshtahll had seen to that.

"You have proof of this, Lieutenant?"

It didn't escape Torrin-Ashur's notice that he'd just been demoted in title. That was the least of his worries.

"We do, Your Majesty."

He beckoned Elam forwards from the throne room door. Nash took over the vacated gatekeeper duties. A few more of the gathered nobles began to realise they were, in more than one sense, a captive audience.

"Your Majesty," Torrin-Ashur continued, glancing back towards the throne, "this is Elam. Though a mercenary, without pay he fought alongside us throughout the recent conflict. His loyalty is beyond questioning." He turned to Elam. "When we first met, you had only just arrived in the Northern Territories. Why was it you were up there?"

Elam addressed his reply to the gathering. "Believe it or not, I thought it would be safer than remaining in the south." The mercenary raised a philosophical eyebrow at the irony of how things had played out.

"That's because someone tried to murder you in your bed, didn't they?" Torrin-Ashur added. "And the reason for that...?"

"We-ell," Elam replied, drawing the word out as if having to think long and hard about it, "I have a theory. My men and I had been employed to take a message to a town called Ham-tak, just across the border in Nmemia."

A murmur of interest rippled around the throne room.

"We met a superintendent there called Gil-kott. I don't know what the message was – it was a sealed letter – but I'm pretty sure the attack on us after we got back was an attempt to silence us."

"Someone was trying to cover their tracks," Torrin-Ashur affirmed, "someone who would probably find it difficult to explain their interests in Nmemia, were they to come to light."

Elam nodded.

"That person is in this room?"

Elam nodded again. He stared straight at a man who had gone very pale.

"Minister Gëorgas?" Midana hissed.

Gëorgas shrank backwards. Mac, who'd been subtly positioning himself over the last few minutes, clamped his hand down on the minister's shoulder so hard that the man yelped.

"Going somewhere?" he murmured in the minister's ear.

Mac's grip negated the possibility of Gëorgas going anywhere except where Mac wanted him to go, which was directly towards Torrin-Ashur and Elam.

There was no doubt that Gëorgas had gone a little off-colour, but that didn't stop him mounting a spirited defence.

"This is outrageous. Get your hands off me!" He wriggled, trying to slip from Mac's grip. Futile, given his captor's immutable determination. "I've done nothing wrong."

"Oh," Elam shot back, cutting off Torrin-Ashur's nearly uttered challenge, "you're going to deny sending Mac and me into Nmemia, now, are you?"

"N – no," Gëorgas answered, after a moment's hesitation. He was obviously thinking hard. It was his word against Elam's, minister against mercenary, suspect versus someone whose loyalty was not in question. Even a fool could see that denying the facts would only damn him.

"So explain, then, why you sent a message to Superintendent Gilkott," Torrin-Ashur demanded.

"It was a confidential matter," Gëorgas defended, trying to sound as though he had justification for his reticence.

"It isn't confidential now," Midana growled, ending all possibility of further details being withheld.

Gëorgas had nowhere to turn. "It was a proposition for a trade agreement, Your Majesty," he blustered, putting on a bit of bravado.

Perhaps he thought there was safety in a semi-truth, Torrin-Ashur mused.

"Sent to the commander of the Nmemian border force?"

Gëorgas didn't waver. "Nmemia is a military dominated society. Who better to deal with?"

"Then why the secrecy?" Midana demanded. "Why send mercenaries to deliver your proposals?"

"Secrecy is not uncommon in trade, ma'am. It does not do to allow details to become public before deals are struck. And Nmemian territory is not safe for Alondrians. I wanted to ensure my message had the best chance of being delivered, that's all."

Which, on the face of it, sounded perfectly reasonable.

The ball seemed to have landed back in Midana's court. She glared at Torrin-Ashur, expecting him to respond.

"Your Majesty, what the minister has said is true. But not the whole truth. His message did contain the details of a trade agreement as he claims, but it was not one for the benefit of Alondria, or even for the Minister himself. At least, not directly."

Midana frowned. "Explain…"

Torrin-Ashur drew in a breath. "The deal being struck was between Nmemia and the Tsnathsarré. Gëorgas was merely an instrument of its brokerage."

"This is preposterous!" Gëorgas exclaimed, apparently secure in his belief that his position could not be refuted. "You have no proof of this."

"I do."

Kirshtahll's interruption garnered him immediate and undivided attention.

The general nodded towards Timerra, beckoning the lieutenant to join him. Torrin-Ashur's attention alighted on the ornate box Timerra had tucked under his arm.

Kirshtahll pushed his way through the gathering and stepped up on to the dais, pointing for Timerra to stand beside him.

"Alondria owes this young man a great debt. His recent bravery probably prevented us going to war with the Nmemians." Kirshtahll allowed a moment for that to sink in. "Lieutenant Timerra volunteered for a mission into Nmemia to seek out an old acquaintance of mine, a senior politician in their hierarchy, Supreme Gal Ibissam. I spared the Gal's life many years ago, and as a token of his appreciation, the Gal presented me with an ornamental dagger belonging to his family. Timerra took this with him and presented it back – as a reminder to the Gal of his debt to me; a debt I am pleased to say he more than repaid. The Gal was able to alert the Nmemian royal household to the existence of a conspiracy about which even they knew nothing."

Kirshtahll paused to catch his breath.

"You are all aware of the fact that I invaded Nmemia, risking war. What you do not know is that it was a bluff. I believed the Nmemians had no genuine desire to engage us."

"You came damned close," Midana accused. "I sent you to Colòtt to stop them from invading *us*."

"Indeed," Kirshtahll conceded. "In fact, having assembled my troops on the Nmemian side of the Great West Wall, it was only the most timely intervention of Prince Kassem that stopped battle commencing. Afterwards, it was the prince himself who told me the details of the conspiracy that had been uncovered."

"Which was?" Midana demanded impatiently.

"A deal struck between the Nmemians and the Tsnathsarré whereby, in return for creating a diversion on Alondria's western border to draw our troops out of the Northern Territories, the Tsnathsarré would guarantee the Nmemians free trade across the Inland Mäss. A very lucrative deal indeed to some."

"I don't understand," Minister Parkos interrupted. Torrin-Ashur glanced across, recalling the minister as being a staunch opponent of maintaining an army in the Northern Territories. A likely candidate for being in on the conspiracy, he considered. "If the Tsnath had made a deal with the Nmemians, what has that got to do with us?"

"As Lord Ashur has told you, it was brokered by Alondrians," Kirshtahll answered, "as I shall prove to you in a moment. After Prince Kassem and I had agreed that neither of us really wanted a war, he returned the dagger that I had sent with Timerra. The Prince also slipped something of his own into the box." Kirshtahll clicked his fingers at Timerra, who presented the dagger case forwards, holding the lid open for him. Kirshtahll extracted a piece of parchment from within the lining. "This," he said, holding it up for all to see, "is a document that Elam might recognise, since it is the one Gëorgas commissioned him to deliver to Gill-kott."

Gëorgas was looking very scared, imprisoned as he was by a barrel-chested mercenary with no intention whatsoever of granting his captive any degree of freedom.

"One man is hardly a whole conspiracy, Padráig," Midana observed, her tone now one of interest rather than indignation.

"No indeed, ma'am. But this document does indicate that others were involved. I have to confess, I do not know their names, though I know someone we could ask..."

Many eyes fell on Gëorgas. Gëorgas fell on his knees. Mac stooped to make sure he wasn't about to lose his catch.

"But that might take some time," Kirshtahll continued. "There is a quicker way."

Jorra-hin stepped forwards. The gathering sucked in its breath. Those nearest shrank away a few paces.

"This is an outrage," Parkos burst out, a shade of red displaying his anger.

Jorra-hin cocked an eyebrow, regarding the minister with uncomfortable singularity.

Parkos was not easily intimidated. "Using the Taümatha to extract the truth. That's precisely the sort of thing that went on when the Natural mages were free to abuse their powers. It's why they had to be put down."

The minister's outrage had severely dulled his tact. Unwisely so.

Orange sparks crackled at the ends of Jorra-hin's fingers. He clenched his fists tightly, suppressing the Taümatha that had been goaded forth. Not before some nearest him had witnessed what had happened. The colour drained from a few more faces.

Parkos was too far away to have seen the accidental display. "This can't be allowed," he continued to object. "Chancellor Gÿldan – do something."

Jorra-hin squinted his eyes slightly, issuing an almost imperceptible warning. Gÿldan opened his mouth to speak, thought better of it and shut it again.

Seeing salvation from that direction dry up, Parkos appealed to Midana. "Your Majesty, surely you're not going to permit this?"

Parkos clearly hadn't counted on how much Midana wanted to know who amongst her subjects had betrayed her. When it came to such things, she had very few scruples. He ought to have known that.

"Minister, I am a firm believer that confession should be voluntary," Jorra-hin said to the affronted politician. "*and by their own hearts will They be betrayed,*" he added, his gaze circling the gathering.

The quotation caused a few frowns amongst the nobles.

Jorra-hin ordered those nearest the walls to step away from them. He waited until they had complied, then lifted his hand and blew gently upon it. Out of his palm rose a diaphanous blue flame about a foot high. He tipped it sideways, allowing it to spill on to the floor like a liquid. It pooled, swelling as though fed from an invisible barrel. When it reached what he deemed to be an appropriate size, he waved his hands in a parting gesture. The flames went forth left and right.

The ethereal creation, serpentine in its movements, undulated over the marble floor, exploring the new and fascinating world into which it had been released. Like an excited hound, nose to the ground, it investigated everything. Wherever it veered, people hurriedly vacated its path.

Enslaved by his fascination, Torrin-Ashur couldn't draw his eyes away. Flecked with orange and red hues, it was as if within the flames there existed a creature, long in body, scaled, with fangs and claws and eyes that pierced momentarily. An elusive beast, it was an impression more than a vision, there one moment, gone the next, something caught only with the net of imagination, too nebulous to be snared by anything more substantial.

The fire slithered round the nobles gathered in the middle of the throne room, herding them like sheep into a pen, its flaming body the fence. Its two heads met, closing the gate to form an unbroken circle around its captives.

None within the gossamer stockade attempted to flee.

"Chancellor Gÿldan," Jorra-hin's gentle and unthreatening voice rose above the gathering, "do you know what this is?"

"If I am not mistaken, it is a magic not seen for many years. It is known as Dragon's Breath."

Jorra-hin smiled. "And could you explain what it does?"

Gÿldan paused before responding. "It caresses the innocent, but sears the guilty?" he offered, slightly unsure of himself.

"Indeed it does. Allow me to demonstrate. Minister Gëorgas…" Jorra-hin motioned for the hapless politician to come forwards. Mac had to lift the quivering wreck off the floor and practically carry the man. "Stroke the dragon's back, if you please."

Paralysed by fear, the only part of Gëorgas that moved was his arm, its animation supplied by his captor.

The moment the minister's hand entered the flames, there was a flare of red. He screamed.

"Enough," Jorra-hin intervened quickly.

There was a snigger from a number of those who hadn't yet foreseen that it would shortly be their turn.

Taking Torrin-Ashur by surprise, next Jorra-hin invited Parkos to step forwards.

"Would you care to stroke the dragon's back, Minister?"

Torrin-Ashur noticed there was a questioning frown on the minister's brow, but no suggestion of fear, other than perhaps a natural reticence to do something contrary to common sense.

Parkos stepped forwards and gingerly nipped the tips of his fingers into the flames. Nothing made him scream. He tried again, this time more slowly. His confidence grew by the second. He began to waft his hand back and forth, clearly fascinated at how he could be on fire and yet feel no pain. As his hand moved, so the beast within the flames seemed to take on a more substantial quality. For a fleeting moment, Torrin-Ashur thought he heard a sound not unlike that of a purring cat.

Jorra-hin beckoned Parkos to step through the fire. With only the briefest sign of hesitation, the minister complied. He emerged unscathed.

"The difference," Jorra-hin explained to the remaining captives, "between the guilty and the innocent. As concerns the matter of Alondria's betrayal, the pure of heart have nothing to fear."

Jorra-hin noticed Torrin-Ashur's quizzical stare. "Oh come, now,

Torrin, isn't it obvious? A difference of political opinion does not make one a traitor. Minister Parkos may have been opposed to Alondria's stance in the Northern Territories, but if he was a conspirator, he would have been wiser not to be so outspoken."

Torrin-Ashur tried not to look too embarrassed. He wasn't quite sure where to look, actually. There were clearly very good reasons why he'd never be a politician; too often the subtler things stared him in the face without him noticing.

Chancellor Gÿldan was next to prove his innocence. He stepped through the trial without any hesitation at all. He acknowledged Jorra-hin with a nod on emerging from the flames.

Gÿldan's departure opened the floodgate for those confident of their loyalty to prove themselves. As the gathering within quickly became the gathering without, the translucent beast tightened its grip, shrinking ever inwards upon the lingering guilty. A couple tried their luck, perhaps thinking they could fool their captor, but whatever magic it was Jorra-hin had conjured up, it knew their hearts. Shouts of pain and rapidly withdrawn hands declared their complicity.

When all was said and done, eleven remained with Gëorgas. Mac had abandoned his charge, his role as gaoler superseded by a rather more exotic authority.

Torrin-Ashur was surprised to see the Academy's politics tutor, Yeddir, standing amongst those remaining. Though their contact at the Academy had been limited, the man had seemed quite genuine in his concern for the wellbeing of his pupils, many of whom had nonetheless just died in the recent campaign. Less surprising was Zimm, the Minister of Finance. Like Parkos, he'd been vociferous about the cost of maintaining the army in the north.

Jorra-hin turned to face Midana. He bowed to her ever so slightly. "The conspirators, Your Majesty. Just as Amatt foresaw, '*by their own hearts will They be betrayed*'. The great prophet's last prophecy has been fulfilled."

Midana glared down at the captives, her stare failing to be met by any of those still corralled by the ring of fire.

Torrin-Ashur nodded at Corporal Silfast. The Ashurmen stepped through the gathering, drawing their swords. They surrounded the traitors.

The ethereal dragon flickered within its flames. A fleeting spectre of exquisite beauty, its reds, interspersed with shimmering hues of iridescent green and yellow, seemed to dance with joy at the lure of impending freedom. It appeared to chase its own tail as it spun round the captives. At the merest flick of Jorra-hin's forefinger, the creature streaked off towards the throne room doors, trailing flames like a hurtling comet. It passed through the solid oak without a sound and vanished from sight, leaving Torrin-Ashur wondering for a moment whether it had ever been real.

The ring of Dendricá steel that had been left its place emanated an unequivocal reality. The gathering seemed to come back on track with a collective sigh.

Midana leaned forwards on the throne. "Is this all of the traitors?"

"Not quite," Jorra-hin answered. "There is one more."

Contrary to most of the gathering's expectations, Jorra-hin stepped away, leaving the floor to Torrin-Ashur once more.

Of those in the throne room at whom the finger of guilt could be pointed, all but two had either passed through trial by combat against the Tsnath in the past few months, or trial by fire in the past few minutes. Of the exceptions, one sat upon the throne, and the other stood beside it. This realisation dawned upon everyone present. Eyes in their hundreds transfixed the queen and her fiancé.

While attention flitted between the two, Midana seemed to notice that it was not at her that Torrin-Ashur stared. She turned to Tanaséy and regarded him with uncomprehending shock.

"Tell me it isn't so," she stammered, bereft of all the usual confidence with which her position normally endowed her.

Tanaséy's reaction was masterful. "This is absurd. What, in the name of all that's holy, could I possibly have to gain from conspiring with the Tsnath?"

It was indeed a good question. One that had vexed Torrin-Ashur for some considerable time.

"I'm lord of Vickrà-döthmore. My lands lie entirely within the Northern Territories. If the Tsnath had succeeded, I'd have lost everything. How would I have benefited from that?"

Midana looked stricken. Her eyes demanded an answer from Torrin-Ashur.

"I asked myself that same question many times," he answered, pinning Vickrà with his unswerving gaze. "Your position ruled you out of my consideration for a long time. I had thought you an ally. The friendship you offered me while I was at the Academy, your assistance with my incarceration, the invitation you gave me to your ball; I was drawn in, I cannot deny."

He gave his head a single disbelieving shake.

"And then there is your position as the fiancé of our queen. Even if you had no lands in the north, you'd still one day be co-ruler of all Alondria. I could not see where the Tsnath might possibly fit into that picture."

Torrin-Ashur looked round at the gathering, his eyes travelling full circle, eventually alighting back on Vickrà.

"Only when I began to understand exactly what the Tsnath were aiming to achieve did I start to realise the true extent of our betrayal." He switched his attention to Midana. "Your Majesty, Baroness Daka had no real interest in the Northern Territories. It is an insignificant strip of land lying between the Mathians and the Ablath. No – her ambition was to use it in her quest to first become Empress of all Tsnathsarré."

Torrin-Ashur had to take a moment to recompose himself as he thought of the huge losses they had suffered, all because of the ambitions of one woman.

"First?" Midana queried, her voice now small and unassuming. "She wanted more?"

Torrin-Ashur nodded. "Daka knew she could only ever hope to retain her conquests for a short period. To truly succeed, she needed something more than just troops. She needed the *Dànis~Lutárn*, a weapon of unimaginable power. Had she gained possession of it, Daka could have achieved anything she desired. The Mathian Mountains would have offered little protection then to the rest of Alondria. With passage opened up beneath them that the seasons cannot close, and a force with no equal at her command, what would have stopped a tide of Tsnath from flowing south, all the way to Alondris?"

Torrin-Ashur's perspective fell heavily on the elite, the rich, the powerful, those who would have lost the most had these dire revelations come to pass. It created a silence that no one was brave enough to break, not even Midana.

Torrin-Ashur eventually continued, "But if Daka had achieved all that, if, gods forbid, Alondria had fallen at her feet, what then for Vickrà? His lands in the north gone, the throne he hoped to share under the buttock of an empress rather than a king? How would he benefit from that? Unless..." Torrin-Ashur held up his hand, and with it the breath of nearly everyone present, "what if the throne of Alondria was to be occupied by a Tsnath sympathiser?"

Gasps resounded about the throne room. If eyes could have shot fire, Vickrà would have been consumed where he stood.

But he was, if nothing else, a consummate politician.

He smiled at everyone before drawing his attention solely to Torrin-Ashur. "A masterful piece of conjecture, my lord, but one that that must, with all due respect, be confined to the realms of fantasy. I appeal to the good people of Alondria – what shred of evidence has been offered that has so utterly convicted me?"

Torrin-Ashur nodded. It was a fair point.

He turned to face the back of the throne room. The gathering had closed up behind him again, now that there was no mythical fire-creature stalking them. They had to part to clear a path towards the doors, which Elam and Mac opened, revealing the hooded figure they had been escorting earlier.

The figure glided towards the centre of the throne room. When the hood was lowered, long waves of auburn hair cascaded freely down. Impressed mutterings wittered to and fro. Many of those present recognised the remarkable young lady standing before them, holding their attention like a sculpted work of art.

"Lady Rachael?" Vickrà recalled in confusion.

"Yes – and no," Torrin-Ashur cut in. "The lady you see before you was indeed introduced to many in this room as the Lady Rachael San Cÿnter, from the island nation of Höarst. A deception for which I beg your forgiveness. It was for her protection at the time." He turned to the erstwhile islander. "Allow me to introduce Baroness Kassandra Daka."

Words could not have rung out more piercingly if they'd been peeled from bell towers. The shock they caused was as palpable as it was audible.

"Not," Torrin-Ashur sought to clarify quickly, "the baroness that so recently laid destruction at our door, but her daughter, to whom Alondria owes a great deal of the freedom she still enjoys."

In a move that surprised more than a few, Kassandra walked forwards and offered her hand. "Lord Vickrà, it is a pleasure to see you again. It has been a long time since you were so kindly receiving me at your ball here at the palace."

Kassandra acted as if she knew nothing of the circumstances into which she had been admitted.

Vickrà was clearly stunned. But his upbringing, at least, was impeccable. Taking her hand, he bent forwards to kiss it.

Kassandra didn't allow him to let go. Instead, retaining his hand in hers, she led him towards Midana.

"What a beautiful ring he wears, Your Majesty."

Midana, her confusion overriding all her usual demands for etiquette, glared at Vickrà.

The northern lord finally lost his confident air.

Kassandra let go of his hand and withdrew back to Torrin-Ashur's side, where she removed the remainder of her cape. This revealed, to the delight of many present, yet more of her sculpted beauty. And a certain necklace she was wearing.

Torrin-Ashur reached behind her neck and untied the jewellery, which had been temporarily secured with a short piece of string since the clasp was still broken. He took the necklace and offered it to Midana.

"What is this all about?" the queen implored, taking hold of the offering but giving it little consideration.

Torrin-Ashur was cut off by Kassandra.

"*The end of dreams for yet another,*" she said in Tsnathsarré. She offered a translation of her mother's words for the benefit of the gathering.

This didn't go any way towards satisfying Midana's desire for an explanation.

"Your Majesty, the necklace you are having there belonged to my mother, Baroness Alishe Daka. It was her most treasured possession. Until the *Dànis~Lutárn* was found, it was her only proof that it existed. My mother rarely ever removed the necklace from her person, to her it meant *that* much. But if you were to be examining them together, Your Majesty, you would see that the ring Lord Vickrà wears and the necklace my mother always wore – they are one of a kind. They are unique and they are belonging together."

Vickrà began looking for a means of escape. He found every doorway, every window, blocked by a Dendricá warrior. His chances of getting out were nil.

"Your Majesty, you must ask yourself this: with whom would my mother, an enemy of Alondria most ardent, have shared her most treasured possession?" The question was left to linger for a moment. "Surely, only one with whom she would one day be prepared to share the spoils of her conquest."

Vickrà backed away towards the wall behind the throne until he could go no further.

Torrin-Ashur and Kirshtahll advanced towards him.

"Kassandra recognised your ring that night at your ball," Torrin-Ashur intoned. "Without that, we wouldn't have known. Ironic, don't you think, that an act of friendship in extending an invitation to me ended up being your downfall? But then, I suppose, that is the nature of treachery. Enemies cannot betray you; only allies can do that."

Kirshtahll grunted with disdain. "You betrayed your queen, your country, even your own people, Vickrà. But do you know what galls me the most? You betrayed my friend, a man who had served with me for fourteen years and given me loyalty far beyond anything I deserved. You were Riagán's march lord; he considered you worthy of that same loyalty. He kept you informed of everything we did, every plan we made, everything we discovered, every secret, even our theories about what we didn't yet know. And you took all that and gave it to Daka. He died, along with thousands of others, and for what? Your aspirations towards grandeur?"

Vickrà knew he was done for. He reached for his sword in desperation.

The words *siad-ida Sèliccia~Castrà* appeared in a blur. With two hands on the hilt, Torrin-Ashur swung his blade across the front of Vickrà with such force that the nobleman's sword was smashed from his hand before it was even fully drawn. The weapon went flying. It clattered to the marble floor and spun like a scythe across its polished surface. As it fetched up against the far wall, the tip of Torrin-Ashur's blade came to rest under Vickrà's chin.

"Justice will not be so easily denied, Lord Vickrà. Because of you, I have lost my mother, my father, my brother, everything from my childhood, everything I ever knew. My home has gone, annihilated along with all my people. I've lost friends, soldiers and comrades. Were it not for the fact that I have seen enough blood shed to last me a thousand lifetimes, I'd kill you where you stand."

When Torrin-Ashur turned to face the throne there were tears brimming in his eyes. He blotted them on his sleeve. He didn't care that all of Alondria's nobility was watching.

"Your Majesty, I have only one request," he croaked, "send Vickrà back to Halam-Gräth, to his own people. They suffered because of his treachery. Let them decide his fate."

Midana didn't nod, or shake her head. In fact, she gave no indication she'd even comprehended the request. She just stared at Torrin-Ashur with unblinking eyes.

Elona stepped up to Torrin-Ashur's side and put her arm through his to lead him away. "Come," she said gently, "we're done here."

Jorra-hin, Kassandra and Kirshtahll fell in behind them as they made their way towards the rear of the throne room. Elam and Mac once again opened the doors.

Midana's voice pierced the silence before they passed through. "Elona, wait, where are you going?"

"Home," she said simply, "back to Mitcha."

"But – your duty is here."

*

Kirshtahll stopped abruptly and turned to face Midana. "Duty?" He strode back towards the dais. "Leave us," he commanded, not taking his eyes off the throne, "the Queen and I have some private business to discuss."

There was no denying him; he was capable of being a whole war all on his own. The courtiers departed, glad to have been spared whatever their imaginations told them was pending.

Vickrà and his co-conspirators were placed under armed escort and marched from the throne room.

Once he and the queen were alone, save for a few of her trusted bodyguards, who wisely kept their distance, Kirshtahll moved across to one of the windows that overlooked the People's Square. "Would you join me, m'dear."

Midana did so. In truth, it hadn't been a request, even if the term of reference had been familial.

"Do you see those people out there?"

Midana was silent.

"They are the people of Alondria. Just ordinary ones. Elona has done more for them in the last few months than you have in your lifetime." Kirshtahll paused to let his words sink in. "Do you see that army out there, the ones dressed in armour like Torrin-Ashur was wearing? A few months ago, they were just townsfolk, the people of Mitcha. Now they are the Dendricá, battle hardened Dancing Warriors, Custodians of the War Song. Equal to anything that the might of Alondria could throw at them. There isn't a single soldier amongst them, man or woman, who wouldn't give their life for Elona. Do you want to know why?"

Again, Midana remained silent.

"I'll tell you. She has endured their hardships. She has cared for their wounded, held the hands of their dying, dug the graves of their dead. She has shed tears with their bereaved. She has shared their fears and faced fate alongside them. She has even shed her own blood for them. *That* is duty."

Kirshtahll turned from the window. In an affectionate move, he put his hands on the queen's shoulders and gently twisted her round to face him. When he spoke again, it was in a considerably softer tone of voice. "Midana, *you* are the Queen of Alondria. Believe it or not, Elona doesn't want your throne. She doesn't want your power. In fact, from what I've heard, she would be content not even to be a princess. But she is what she is; the people out there wouldn't have it any other way." He paused for a moment, allowing Midana to take in what he'd said.

The queen's rare silence continued.

"Now, for the sake of this country, and for the memory of Althar, I will support you to my dying day. But understand one thing – I will not stand by and let you deny Elona the happiness she deserves."

When Kirshtahll had finished speaking, he did something no one had done for decades. He leaned forwards and kissed Midana on the forehead, just as her father had done when she was a child.

22

Milling about in the palace courtyard, Torrin-Ashur wondered what sort of encounter was taking place between Kirshtahll and the queen. More to the point, he wondered how long it would last. It seemed appropriate to wait for him, if for no other reason than that the general might have some idea about what they were all supposed to do next. They'd done what they'd come to do, and he was feeling at something of a loss now. The only plan he could think of was the usual one of last resort – find a tavern and get very drunk.

It turned out the wait wasn't to be long.

"He's coming," Elona noticed first.

She cocked her head to one side as Kirshtahll emerged from the palace and came down the steps towards them. Her eyebrows expressed her curiosity.

"What was said is between Midana and myself, and it will remain that way." Kirshtahll's tone made it clear there would be no further discussion on the matter.

Elona didn't hide her surprise, but she didn't press.

Kirshtahll spotted Borádin talking with his father and went over to join them. "I did have my doubts about this young man," he announced, clapping Borádin on the shoulder, "but it is just possible my initial assessment may have been wrong."

"No, you were right, Padráig," Lord Kin-Shísim replied with contrived candour. "He was well on his way to becoming an ass."

"On his way? No, not at all. He'd arrived in style."

"Indeed. You were quite right to dismiss him." Borádin's father did well to keep a straight face.

Kirshtahll smiled. "But things change, do they not? Now, a finer officer no general could hope to command."

A slightly embarrassed grin settled across Borádin's face. "If you will excuse me, I think Torrin wants a word." He extricated himself and made a beeline for Torrin-Ashur and Elona. "For the sake of the gods," he whispered urgently, "save me from old men talking about me. If my mother was here, she'd be trying to wipe smudges from my face with her handkerchief!"

"Aw," Elona teased, patting him on the cheek.

Kassandra joined them, no longer incognito and therefore catching many an admiring glance. Mostly from the Ashurmen, it had to be said.

Torrin-Ashur took her hand. "Thank you for what you did in there. I am in your debt."

Kassandra smiled and leaned forwards to kiss him on the cheek. "Torrin, it is I who shall forever be in your debt. Coming here was the very least I could do."

"Will you be returning to Brath'daka, now?"

"Yes. Though not immediately. The Lady Kirshtahll is coming to Alondris, so I shall be spending some time here before journeying home. I do not like the tunnels through the mountains, so I shall be waiting for the passes to clear of snow before departing."

"I don't blame you," Elona agreed, "I think one must need to be a Dwarve to be comfortable being underground for any length of time. The Old Homeland gave me the shivers. By the way, I meant to ask you earlier, how is Anna? Torrin told me about what happened to her."

A look of sadness crossed Kassandra's face. "She is being looked after as best we can. Unfortunately, I do not think she will ever fully recover."

Torrin-Ashur let out a murmur. "It was a bad business. But give it time. I'm sure with love and kindness, eventually she will be alright."

"She will have plenty of both," Kassandra nodded, "so we shall see."

"And what of your mother?" Elona asked.

"She awaits execution in Jèdda-galbráith."

"Still? Things move slowly in your country."

"Too slowly. But the House of Daka is one of prominence," Kassandra explained, "and even the emperor cannot simply execute someone of my mother's status. There must be agreements between the barons before such things can happen."

"Is there any likelihood she will be reprieved?"

"Reprieved?"

"Let off, given a lesser punishment," Torrin-Ashur revised. It was too easy to forget that Kassandra was still new to speaking Alondrian. She had learned so much over the last few months.

"No. The barons know what would have happened had my mother

succeeded in her plan. They will agree to the emperor's judgement. It is just their way of showing to Omnitas that he must consider their wishes in such matters, that is all."

The word *good* was on Torrin-Ashur's lips, but he didn't utter it. There had to be some justice served against the perpetrator of all that had happened.

Elona sighed and changed the subject. "So, what's next for a couple of redundant empire conquerors?" she asked, eyeing Borádin and Torrin-Ashur together.

"Don't forget the monk," Jorra-hin called across to them. He'd been in conversation with Chancellor Gÿldan, but made his way over to join them.

"Monk? What monk?" Borádin joked, making a playful show of looking everywhere except at Jorra-hin.

Jorra-hin gave him a sour glance.

It was in jest, Torrin-Ashur was relieved to note. "Seriously though," he said, "what *do* we do now? Fate has directed us for so long that I'm not even sure I know how to fill my own time anymore."

"Well, I know what I'm going to do," Kirshtahll interrupted, coming up behind them. "I'm going to barge my way into the Duke of Cöbèck's residence and insist that His Grace teaches me the fine art of afternoon napping."

"Geirvald is an undisputed master of that," Elona attested. "But that's a little boring for my tastes. I had something else in mind."

"Oh?" Torrin-Ashur cocked a curious eyebrow.

Elona gave him a wistful smile and took him by the hand. Instead of heading for the Middle Gosh bridge and thence to the People's Square, she dragged him sideways towards an ornate wrought iron gate, one that opened out on to a manicured garden that was just beginning to wake up to the idea of spring.

"Where are we going?"

"You'll see."

The garden extended the entire length of the palace. On the right hand side was the wall that faced the People's Square. About half way along there was an archway with a shell-shaped balcony projecting out over the Els-spear. A stone balustrade surrounded its outer rim. To this Elona set her course.

Kirshtahll and the others followed on behind, at a slight distance. Part way across the lawn, Mac suddenly veered off on a tangent. He came to the base of a tree and wrapped his arms around its trunk.

Mystified by this behaviour, Kirshtahll came to a standstill. "What *is* he doing?"

Torrin-Ashur and Elona stopped and turned to see what was going on. Torrin-Ashur burst out laughing.

"Don't worry, sir. Ex-pirates are an odd lot."

Elam cleared his throat. "It's a palm tree, General. He's always wanted one."

Kirshtahll shuddered, as though steeling himself against the possibility that such behaviour might be contagious.

Elona pulled at Torrin-Ashur's arm impatiently, dragging him on towards her goal. As they approached the little balcony, Torrin-Ashur felt that he must have noticed it before at some point. It was quite obviously designed to be seen from the People's Square. Those outside had an unrestricted view of it from across the Els-spear, and anyone standing at the balustrade could see right to the far side of the square, some half a mile in the distance.

The moment they made their appearance, a mighty cheer went up from across the water. Elona waved at the crowd, nudging Torrin-Ashur to do likewise.

Behind them, Kirshtahll spread out his arms, preventing the rest of the group from going any further.

After a few minutes of simply gazing in awe at the sheer number of people now assembled in the square, Elona raised her hand, not in another wave, but in a manner that called for quiet. Torrin-Ashur doubted that such a subtle gesture could possibly have an effect on so vast a gathering; he was utterly amazed when a hush descended.

Elona took his hands in hers and pull him round to face her. She drew herself closer to him and gazed up into his eyes, smiling something stolen from the heavens. Then she lifted herself up on tiptoes and kissed him.

For a sublime moment, Torrin-Ashur completely forgot that the world existed. A feeling of absolute wonder overwhelmed him, suffusing his heart with rapturous joy.

The leader of the Dancing Warriors actually went weak at the knees.

But it was hard to ignore the world for long; especially as it had gone berserk.

His euphoric moment was swept away by a wave of jubilation that surged across the El-spear. The noise hit with a force that was physical, the crowd managing to produce a tumultuous roar of applause that rivalled thunder. The Dendricá amongst them hammered on their shields in total disarray; no threat, no War Song to unite them. There wasn't a coordinated beat to be had. Just the sheer, unadulterated din of their approval.

Incredulous at the volume, Torrin-Ashur turned to face the crowd. Laughter bubbled up within him as he tried to comprehend how people alone could make such a clamour.

He glanced back at the others. Céline clutched Agarma's arm, tears of joy streaming down her cheeks. Beside her, Kirshtahll nodded to Jorra-hin, motioning for him to go forwards and join them on the balcony.

As he approach, Torrin-Ashur jerked his thumb towards the crowd. "Listen to them – they've gone mad!" he said, having to shout to make himself heard.

"Of course they have."

A momentary frown flashed its way across Torrin-Ashur's brow. Elona rolled her eyes skywards in exasperation.

"He doesn't know?" Jorra-hin queried.

"What don't I know?"

Elona gave Jorra-hin a nod, granting him permission to explain.

"Alondrian princesses have always announced their engagements with a kiss on this balcony."

For the first time in a while the infamous Ashur blush had a fling. It did have to battle with a rather stunned expression, but still, it managed to gain ground.

Torrin-Ashur grabbed Elona by the edges of her breastplate and gently yanked her towards him. "Engaged? I do wish people would warn me of these things occasionally."

Elona let slip one of her heart-stopping giggles, though it was largely lost to the crowd.

"Anyway, I thought you'd given up being a princess?"

Elona shrugged and nodded towards the people of Alondria. "Try telling them that."

Torrin-Ashur cupped her head in his hands and kissed her again, with no less elation than before.

It wasn't really possible for the crowd to applaud more than they were already.

That didn't stop them trying.

*

Behind, in the palace, at a window overlooking the People's Square, stood a lone figure. She had come to see what had caused the furore that seemed to have rocked the very foundations of the building.

On her head, a crown.

In her eyes, a tear.

On her lips, the trace of a smile.

A note from the author:

It is my sincerest hope that I have left you smiling.

When I first set out to write this story, I had little but an ending in mind, and one or two keystone events to underpin it. The rest fell into place as I tackled the gluing-together of what were, back then, the scantest of details. Inevitably, the story took on a life of its own, though I have to confess, if I'd known from the outset that it was going to become such a behemoth, weighing-in at a third of a million words, it is probable that I would have run away in terror shortly after page one!

What kept me going throughout the whole process, from the initial ideas, subsequent years of hard slog and countless rewrites, to the end result, was that I really wanted to tell a story the likes of which I'd enjoy reading myself. It has been fun, albeit infinitely harder than I'd ever imagined. Even now, having reviewed the manuscript so many times I could recite it in my sleep, I still find myself bound up in its drama and passionate about its characters. The latter have been my friends and travelling companions on a journey more than a decade in the making.

As for the future, well, I'm reliably informed that the archives of Alondria are full of prophecies just waiting for their moment. It is entirely possible that Jorra-hin and Torrin-Ashur may again find themselves embroiled. After all, fate is never happy unless it's sticking its oar in somewhere...

May reality only trouble you when you want it to. I try to avoid it myself.

Glossary

Alondrian and Nicián Characters

Abiatha – the name of Jorra-hin's mother.

Captain **Agarma** – in charge of Princess Elona's personal bodyguard.

Brother **Akmir** – the Adak-rann's most senior representative at the Cymàtagé.

King **Althar** – King of Alondria.

Secretary **Anton** – a mage at the Cymàtagé.

Mage **Aolap** – a confidant of Chancellor Gÿldan and infiltrator of the Dinac-Mentà.

Benhin – a young guide working the streets of Alondris.

Queen **Bernice** – Princess Elona's mother. Bernice is no longer queen, having been put away from the royal household for an indiscretion with a younger man.

Lord (heir apparent) **Borádin** – young nobleman of Alondria of the House of Kin-Shísim.

Corporal **Botfiár** – one of the Pressed's non-commissioned officers under Torrin-Ashur's command.

Brother **Brömin** – a member of the Adak-rann council.

Brother **Brosspear** – a member of the Adak-rann council, and former mage.

Lady **Céline** – Princess Elona's lady-in-waiting.

Brother **Connrad** – a member of the Adak-rann council.

Captain **Corbett** – the officer in charge of cadets at the Royal Military

Academy in Alondris.

Mage **Cosmin** – the local mage in Torrin-Ashur's home town of Tail-ébeth.

Lieutenant **D'Amada** – an Alondrian officer in Kirshtahll's Executive.

Mage **Dümarr** – Head of Philosophy at the Cymàtagé.

Brother **Egall** – a member of the Adak-rann council.

Elam – a freelance Alondrian mercenary.

Eldris-Ashur – Torrin-Ashur's elder brother and Lord (heir apparent) to the March of Ashur.

Princess **Elona** – second daughter of the House of Dönn-àbrah; younger sister to Princess Midana.

Mage **Emmett** – one of the healers at the Cymàtagé.

Emmy – the little girl Kirin is called to heal.

Etáin L'Tembarh – Lady Karina Kirshtahll's father and former ambassador to the Tsnathsarré Empire.

Mage **Flassmidd** – one of the healers at the Cymàtagé.

Fylmar – a henchman employed by Minister Gëorgas.

Gad – the head of the serving staff at the residence of the Duke of Cöbèck.

Gadrick-Ashur – one of Torrin-Ashur's ancestors.

Duke **Geirvald** – the Duke of Cöbèck.

Minister **Gëorgas** – one of Alondria's career politicians.

Brother **Gerard** – a brother of the Adak-rann.

Gil – a nocturnal opportunist.

Golan – one of the Pressed under Torrin-Ashur's command.

Guyass – a friend of Torrin-Ashur at the Royal Military Academy.

Chancellor **Gÿldan** – the Chancellor of the Cymàtagé, and thereby Alondria's most senior mage.

Major **Halacon** – an Alondrian officer in Kirshtahll's Executive.

Captain **Halam** – an Alondrian officer in Kirshtahll's Executive.

Hallvor – a young Alondrian girl – survivor from Tail-ébeth.

Brother **Heckart** – the head of the Adak-rann and leader of the brotherhood's council.

Minister **Hekdama** – an Alondrian politician and Speaker of the Assembly.

Lord **Henndel** – Lord of Sördina.

Lord **Huron** – an Alondrian commander under Kirshtahll when he faces the Nmemians.

Ida – Mac's wife.

Prince **Idris** – King Althar's firstborn son. The boy died in infancy.

Jacks – proper name **Jàckrin-àsethàsám** – a Nicián resident of Alondris, curator of the archives at the stonemasons' guildhall.

Brigadier **Jàcos** – the commandant in charge of the Royal Military Academy in Alondris.

Jess – Mac's eldest son.

Jonash – the head of the serving staff at the residence of the

Kirshtahll household.

Brother **Jorra-hin** – a brother of the Adak-rann and friend of Torrin-Ashur.

Brother **Joss** – a brother of the Adak-rann at the Cymàtagé.

Lady **Karina** – the wife of General Kirshtahll.

Katla – the daughter of the mayor of Mitcha.

Soprina **Kirin-orrà DelaMorjáy** – more usually called **Kirin**. Daughter of the Nición ambassador in Alondris, and friend to Jorra-hin at the Cymàtagé.

Mage **Lödmick** – a mage at the Cymàtagé with a seat on the Cymàtseà.

Mac – a freelance Alondrian mercenary.

Marro – Mac's middle son.

Captain **Marsisma** – an Alondrian officer in Kirshtahll's Executive.

Mage **Martiss** – a mage at the Cymàtagé, with particular responsibility for controlling who is admitted.

Massim – a lost Alondrian soldier found on the way to Mitcha.

Mage **Mattohr** – Pomaltheus's preceptor.

Princess **Midana** – first daughter of the House of Dönn-àbrah, Elona's elder sister and heir to the throne of Alondria.

Millardis (nicknamed **M'Lud**) – one of the Pressed under Torrin-Ashur's command.

Lord (heir apparent) **Mir** – an Alondrian noble and Borádin's second in the call-out with Torrin-Ashur.

Myle – the wife of Willoam.

Lord **Naman-Ashur** – Torrin-Ashur's father, Lord of Tail-ébeth and the March of Ashur.

Sergeant **Nash** – Torrin-Ashur's assigned sergeant.

Mage **Nikrá** – an ancient mage at the Cymàtagé, and one of Alondria's most respected present-day seers.

Deputy Chancellor **Nÿat** – the Deputy Chancellor of the Cymàtagé.

General **Padráig Kirshtahll** – Alondria's most senior military figure and commander of the Alondrian army stationed in the Northern Territories, with responsibility for keeping the Tsnathsarré at bay.

Minister **Parkos** – one of Alondria's career politicians and a staunch opponent of Alondria's military policies in the Northern Territories.

Paulus – a young Alondrian boy – survivor from Tail-ébeth.

Acolyte **Pomaltheus** – one of the acolytes Jorra-hin becomes friends with at the Cymàtagé.

Governor **Rakmar** – Timerra's father and Governor of Colòtt.

Mage **Rhonnin** – one of the healers at the Cymàtagé.

Major **Riagán** – the adjutant to General Kirshtahll.

Rogett – one of the mercenaries under Elam's command.

Lord **Ruther** – an Alondrian commander under Kirshtahll when he faces the Nmemians.

Sàhodd – a friend of Torrin-Ashur at Mitcha.

Lord **Saldir** – an Alondrian commander under Kirshtahll when he faces the Nmemians.

Master **Salsar** – Master of the Alondris docks.

Acolyte **Seth** – one of the acolytes Jorra-hin becomes friends with at the Cymàtagé.

Corporal **Silfast** – one of the Pressed's non-commissioned officers under Torrin-Ashur's command.

Mage **Sömat** – head of Ancient Studies at the Cymàtagé.

Symon – one of the Pressed under Torrin-Ashur's command.

Lord **Tanaséy Vickrà** – Lord of Vickrà-döthmore and cohort to Princess Mattrice.

Major **Temesh-ai** – Kirshtahll's personal physician.

Terrance – King Althar's manservant of many years.

Lord **Tiam** – Borádin's father, formally known as Lord Kin-Shísim.

Tick – one of the Pressed under Torrin-Ashur's command.

Lieutenant **Timerra** – a friend of Torrin-Ashur at the Royal Military Academy.

Brother **Tobas** – a brother of the Adak-rann.

Tomàss – one of the Pressed under Torrin-Ashur's command.

Captain **Tonché** – an Alondrian officer in Kirshtahll's Executive.

Corpsman **Tork** – part of the Alondrian Messaging Corps.

Torrin-Ashur – the second son of Naman-Ashur. His father is Lord of Tail-ébeth and the March of Ashur.

Mage **Tutt-tus** – one of the mages at the Cymàtagé, assigned as preceptor to Kirin when she is admitted for training.

Brother **Valis** – a member of the Adak-rann council.

Willoam – the man who accused Golan of attempting to have his way with his wife.

Wisehelm of Campas – a young noble Kirshtahll once chose to sponsor.

Minister **Yeddir** – the politics tutor at the Royal Military Academy in Alondris.

Brother **Yisson** – a member of the Adak-rann council.

Yngvarr – a friend of Torrin-Ashur at Mitcha.

Minister **Zimm** – the Alondrian Finance Minister.

Tsnathsarré Characters

Alber – Gömalt's right hand man.

Baroness **Alishe Daka** – a powerful Tsnathsarré noblewoman. Her lands lie just north of the River Ablath, adjacent to the Marches of Nairn, Ashur and Ràbinth.

Anna – the handmaid to Kassandra.

Bressnar – a Tsnathsarré mercenary.

Emperor **Callis** – the Tsnathsarré emperor at the time when Alondria purchased the Northern Territories.

Advisor **Döshan** – a Tsnathsarré advisor to Emperor Omnitas.

Baron **Fidampàss** – a Tsnathsarré baron and western neighbour to Baroness Daka's lands. His lands lie just north of the River Ablath, adjacent to the March of Léddürland.

Baron **Ginngár** – the Baron of Ürald, a northern province of the Tsnathsarré Empire.

Gömalt – Baroness Daka's right hand man and assassin.

Halfdanr – the head of the serving staff in Baroness Daka's household.

Jonatárn – a spy working on behalf of Baroness Daka.

Kassandra – daughter of Baroness Daka.

Commander **Këddir** – a Tsnathsarré officer under Lord Özeransk.

Advisor **Kremlish** – a Tsnathsarré advisor to Emperor Omnitas.

Michàss – the sweetheart of Kassandra's handmaid, Anna.

Minnàk – a Tsnathsarré mercenary.

Oddon – the chief cook in Baroness Daka's household.

Emperor **Omnitas** – the present Emperor of Tsnathsarré.

Lord **Özeransk** – a respected Tsnathsarré lord and military commander.

Rasmin – a Tsnathsarré fisherman, and part of the advanced party that lands in the Bay of Shallow Graves.

Commander **Scarlis** – a Tsnathsarré commander – part of Töuslàn's landing party.

Shyla – one of the cook's assistants in Baroness Daka's household.

Sörrell – one of Minnàk's mercenary commanders, left to occupy Mitcha.

Commander **Streàck** – a Tsnathsarré commander.

Commander **Tass** – a Tsnathsarré commander – part of Töuslàn's landing party.

Lord **Töuslàn** – a Tsnathsarré baron and eastern neighbour to Baroness Daka's lands. His lands lie just north of the Ablath, adjacent to the March of Vickrà-döthmore.

Baron **Ürengarr** – the Tsnathsarré emperor that succeeded Callis at the time when Alondria purchased the Northern Territories.

Dwarvish, Nmemian and Historical Characters

Amatt the Blind – Alondria's most famous and reliable prophet, who lived about twelve hundred years prior to the present day.

Mage **Cormàcc** – an ancient mage – inventor of Mages' Fire.

Superintendent **Gil-kott** – the district commander of the Nmemian border force.

Gorrack-na-tek – a Dwarvish acquaintance of Advisor Döshan, living in Jèdda-galbráith.

Mage **Holôidees** – an ancient mage – one of those involved in the creation of the Dànis~Lutárn and who stood against Lornadus.

Mad **Iffan** – Alondria's most infamous pirate of old, mentioned in the Legend of Tallümund.

Mage **Joseph** – an ancient mage – one of those involved in the creation of the Dànis~Lutárn and who stood against Lornadus.

Prince **Kassem** – the Eldest son of the King of Nmemia.

Mage **Lornadus** – an ancient mage – leader of those who tried to ensnare the Sèliccia~Castrà.

General **Márcucious** – the general in charge of the Custodians, otherwise known as the Dancing Warriors or the Dendricá.

Mage **Nickölaus** – an ancient mage – one of those involved in the creation of the Dànis~Lutárn and who stood against Lornadus.

Papanos Meiter – Master Stonemason from 232BF to 201BF

King **Ranadar** – the Dwarvish king at the time of the departure of the Dwarve Nation from the Old Homeland.

Commissar **Rolarn** – a Nmemian military commander.

Seya **Roumin-Lenka** – the Dwarvish clan leader summoned by Baroness Daka to assist with finding the Menhir of Ranadar.

Silas – an ancient mage – one of those involved in the creation of the Dànis~Lutárn.

Mage **Solautus** – one of the original Natural mages who founded the Dinac-Mentà in order to bring the Mages' War to an end, some five hundred years prior to the present day.

Mage **Yazcöp D'Bless** – an ancient mage – one of those involved in the creation of the Dànis~Lutárn and who stood against Lornadus.

Country and Regional References

Alondria – the principal country in which the story is set.

The **Great Inland Mäss** – a vast lake, almost a sea, sitting just north of Nmemia. Its northern and eastern coasts are Tsnathsarré lands. Alondria only has a very small exposure to this sea, adjacent to the Am-gött.

Höarst – an island nation lying off the coast of the Tsnathsarré Empire, with whom Alondria has limited relations.

The **Mäss of Súmari** – the sea lying south of Alondria.

Niciá – a country lying south of Alondria, beyond the Mäss of Súmari. Kirin's homeland.

Nmemia – Alondria's western neighbour. There have been wars between the two in the past, but relations between them have been relatively peaceful in recent times.

Söbria – a land lying to the south of Alondria, famed for its spicy meat dishes and other culinary delights.

The **Tsnathsarré Empire** – the country that lies to the north of Alondria. They share a six hundred mile long border with each other, defined by the River Ablath.

The **Vickrà-mäss** – the sea to the east of Vickrà-döthmore.

Alondrian Geographical References

River **Ablath** – the river that marks the border between the Northern Territories of Alondria and the Tsnathsarré Empire.

Akanu Pass – one of the principal passes through the Mathian Mountains.

River **Alam-goürd** – one of Alondria's principal rivers running south from the Mathians.

Alondris – the capital of Alondria.

Am-còt – a trading town on the southern side of the Mathian Mountains near the headwaters of the Alam-goürd.

Am-gött – a short and inhospitable strip of land at the far western end of the Mathian Mountains.

Loch **Andür** – a loch situated part way down the Alam-goürd, between Am-còt and Suth-còt.

Mount **Àthái** – part of the Mathian Mountain range.

Bay of Shallow Graves – a bay off the east coast of the Northern Territories named for its infamous toll on shipping.

Bosün-béck – a town mentioned in the Legend of Tallümund – formerly known as Sag-herron before the Hür Tribe Siege.

Bythe-Kim – a trading town on the southern side of the Mathian Mountains near the headwaters of the Els-spear.

Colòtt – the westernmost region of Alondria, neighbouring Nmemia.

Dórine Basin – a region of Alondria near the Nmemian border. Dispute over its sovereignty led to the Kilópeé War between Alondria and Nmemia some thirty years prior to the present day.

Dramm-Mastür Forest – a large forested region of Alondria lying south of the Mathian Mountains between Colòtt and Kirsh.

Dubré Marsh – a region to the south of the Dumássay Gorge.

Dumássay Gorge – the gorge formed by the Dumássay River, strategically significant because it restricts passage south from Vickrà-döthmore to the rest of Alondria. It can only be crossed via a handful of suspended bridges.

The **Easterhalb** – the name given to the smaller half of the city of Alondris, lying to the east of the River Els-spear.

River **Ébeth** – a river in the Northern Territories.

River **Els-spear** – one of the principal rivers flowing south from the Mathian mountains down through Alondria. The Els-spear flows through the middle of the city of Alondris.

Lake **Gosh** – a large lake just to the south of Alondris through which the Els-spear flows.

Halam-Gräth – the principal town of the March of Vickrà-döthmore.

Hassguard – a trading town at the northern start point of the Akanu Pass.

Hébott – the principal town of the March of Léddürland.

The **Holmes** – a district within the city of Alondris, between the First Wall and the New Wall, where many of Alondria's nobility have their city residences.

Jàb-áldis – the Adak-rann's monastery up in the Jàb-áldis Pass, high in the Mathian Mountains.

Loch **Kim** – a loch on the south side of the Mathian Mountains, not far from the headwaters of the River Els-spear.

Kimballi Pass – one of the easternmost passes through the Mathian Mountains, and the usual route for most traffic from Alondris travelling north through the Vale of Caspárr to reach Mitcha.

Kirsh – General Kirshtahll's home province.

Lamàst – a border town in Colòtt, not far from the Great West Wall.

Léddürland – the westernmost march of the Northern Territories.

Loch **Masson** – one of the larger lochs along the River Ablath, straddling the border between the March of Nairn and the March of Léddürland.

Mathian Mountains – the principal mountain range that divides Alondria across her breadth, cutting off the Northern Territories from much of the rest of the country.

Mitcha – the name of both the military camp and the local town in the heart of the March of Ràbinth. Kirshtahll's military stronghold.

Monument to Nabor – a small town on route from Kirsh to Loch Andür.

Nabor's Gate – one of the easier places to cross the otherwise treacherous River Ablath.

Nairn – one of the marches of the Northern Territories.

Nairnkirsh – the principal town of the March of Nairn.

Northern Territories – the strip of land that lies between the northern slopes of the Mathian Mountains and the River Ablath. The Tsnathsarré call it the Tep-Mödiss.

Parars Hove – a small town a few miles inland from the mouth of the Dumássay River.

Pass of Trombéi – one of the main eastern passes through the Mathian Mountains.

The **People's Square** – the centre of the city of Alondris.

Ràbinth – one of the marches in the Northern Territories.

River **Sam-hédi** – a river in the Northern Territories.

Shinn-còtt – an arid, almost desert-like region of Alondria.

Sound of Goàtt – a large inlet on the coast of Vickrà-döthmore, just north of the town of Halam-Gräth.

Stroth Ford – one of the easier places to cross the otherwise treacherous River Ablath.

Suth-còt – an Alondrian town at the southern end of Loch Andür, famed for hosting the popular Festival of Light.

Taib-hédi – a strategic town situated in the March of Ràbinth. 'Taib' is a northern term meaning 'across' or 'straddling'. The Sam-hédi runs through the town.

Tail-ébeth – Torrin-Ashur's home town, and principal town of the March of Ashur. 'Tail' is a northern term meaning 'near'. Tail-ébeth means Near (the) Ébeth.

Mount **Tatënbau** – an unusual mountain said to have been shaped by the dragon Bël-samir during the Legend of Tallümund.

Toutleth – a trading town at the southern start point of the Akanu Pass.

Vale of Caspárr – one of the few really fertile regions of the Northern Territories.

Vickrà-döthmore – the easternmost march of the Northern Territories. Lord Tanaséy Vickrà's march.

The **Westerhalb** – the name given to the larger half of the city of Alondris lying to the west of the River Els-spear.

Tsnathsarré Geological References

Brath'daka – the name of the castle Baroness Daka calls home.

Göndd – a small town in southern Tsnathsarré, not far from the Alondrian border.

Jèdda-galbráith – the capital city of the Tsnathsarré Empire.

Sèdessa Range – a region of mountainous country lying north of the Tsnathsarré Empire. Current home to the majority of the Dwarvish clans.

Tep-Mödiss – the Tsnathsarré name for the Northern Territories. It means 'below the river' (the Ablath denotes the border).

Nmemian and Dwarvish Geographical References

Dikàthi – one of the entrances to the Mathian Mines (also known as the Old Homeland).

Dörgànk – the gorge outside the city of Üzsspeck.

Hamm-tak – a border town just inside Nmemia.

Hàttàmoréy – one of the entrances to the Mathian Mines (also known as the Old Homeland).

Niliàthái – one of the entrances to the Mathian Mines (also known as the Old Homeland).

Trombéi – one of the entrances to the Mathian Mines (also known as the Old Homeland).

Üzsspeck – the principal city of the Dwarve Nation when they lived in the Old Homeland under the Mathian Mountains.

Zèet-ársh – a town about seventy miles inside Nmemia.

Miscellaneous References

Adak-rann – a scholastic brotherhood dedicated to the preservation of historical knowledge.

After Foundation (AF) – Alondrian calendar dating system – referring to years after the foundation of Alondria, 947 years prior to the present day.

Akarish – one of the Dwarvish clans.

aldar – the main coinage of Alondria.

A'lyavine – the name of the language used to control magic. Also referred to as the Tongue of the Ancients.

Before Foundation (BF) – Alondrian calendar dating system – referring to years before the foundation of Alondria, 947 years prior to the present day.

Bël-aírnon – dragon god in the old religions of Tsnathsarré, which centre around belief in a number of great dragons, the chief of whom is Bël-aírnon.

Bël-samir – the famous dragon at the centre of one of Alondria's most beloved of fables, The Legend of Tallümund.

Blacksmith of Orea – a folklore character famed for being the best armourer in the world.

Blood – a sharp tasting alcoholic concoction popular with the Dwarves.

Brock – a powerful alcoholic concoction commonly brewed in northern Alondria.

Cymàtagé – the main seat of learning for all mages in Alondria. Cymàtagé is an old A'lyavinical word meaning Hall of Mages.

Cymàtseà – the name given to the mages' council at the Cymàtagé.

Dànis~Lutárn – an ancient magic conceived in part to ensnare the Sèliccia~Castrà.

Dendricá – an ancient tribe of formidable warriors who used to live in the lands now known as the Northern Territories. Also known as the Dancing Warriors.

Dinac-Mentà – a secretive and ruthless sect of mages who see it as their duty to regulate the activity of their fellow mages and eliminate Natural mages, thereby preventing a recurrence of past atrocities.

House of **Dönn-àbrah** – the present royal house of Alondria.

The **Executive** – the group of Alondrian officers Kirshtahll relies on to get things done.

Followers of the Path – a term given to ordinary mages who take up the study of the Mages' Path at the Cymàtagé.

Grand Assembly – Alondria's main legislative body.

Great West Wall – the wall erected between Alondria and Nmemia after the Kilópeé War.

Kilópeé War – the name given to the war between Alondria and Nmemia over the sovereignty of the Dórine Basin, concluded some thirty years prior to the present day.

House of **Kin-Shísim** – one of the high noble houses of Alondria. Borádin's household.

Legend of Tallümund – a beloved tale in Alondrian literature.

Lenka – a Dwarvish clan name. Roumin-Lenka is the clan leader. Most Dwarves use their clan name as the second part of their familiar name.

lumines – a rather special flower, pod-like in appearance when closed, which glows when visited by certain insects, most notably the Giant Moon Moth.

Mages' Path – the name given to the curriculum taught to acolytes at the Cymàtagé, embodying all aspects of a mage's life. Ordinary mages are those who take the Mages' Path, which has led to them being called Followers of the Path.

Menhir of Ranadar – stone tablets, inscribed with A'lyavinical texts, thought to have been left by King Ranadar when he led the Dwarve Nation out of the Mathian Mountains some eighteen hundred years prior to the present day.

Natural mage – the term used to refer to a mage whose powers do not stem from a study of the Mages' Path. They are able to draw power from their surroundings, and are in consequence much more powerful than Followers of the Path. They are therefore targeted by the Dinac-Mentà for supposedly being dangerous.

Old Homeland – the name the Dwarves gave to the system of tunnels and caves that they excavated under the Mathian Mountains.

The **Pressed** – a term used to refer to units of men in the army assembled from slaves, debtors and petty criminals whose sentences have been commuted to military service.

sadura – a rather potent liqueur usually served warm.

Sai-raska – a Tsnathsarré toast – akin to 'cheers' – but reserved for use between warriors who have shared the battlefield.

sárccanisáe – special spherical glass-like objects used to absorb stray magic, known as Taümatha, when it is accidentally released by mages undertaking training at the Cymàtagé.

Sèliccia~Castrà – a First Dialect A'lyavinical reference, meaning War Song.

Sentinels – strange tower-like structures situated along the River Ablath.

Septagem – the name given to groups of seven mages forming the cells within the Dinac-Mentà.

Septis Dömon – the Dinac-Mentà's most sacred book, containing the seven incantations that give them their powers to overcome Natural mages.

Seya – a Dwarvish title, meaning Clan Leader (female).

Sölass~Hésporra – a Wandering Whisper – a kind of magically imbued rumour that can erase the truth and replace it with belief in a falsehood.

Sönnatt – the Dwarvish High Council.

Soprina – a Nicián title, meaning Daughter Of, reserved for unmarried ladies of noble houses.

Talmathic Dömon – Amatt the Blind's great treatise on the Nature of the Taümatha. Written in First Dialect A'lyavine. Guarded most closely by the mages of the Cymàtagé.

Taümatha – the proper name for magic.

Taümathakiya – a device, glass-like in appearance and shaped like a giant teardrop, that resides in the Adak-rann monastery at Jàb-áldis. It is used to detect significant events of Taümathic origin.

Telem-aki – a most treasured historical reference and one of the Cymàtagé's most valuable books, charting the history of the lands that eventually became Alondria. Attributed to many authors, including Amatt the Blind.

Tongue of the Ancients – alternative name for the ancient language of A'lyavine.

Torvàstos – a flat plate-shaped mushroom that tastes a little like bread if dried out.

Tsnath – a common abbreviation used by the Alondrians to refer to the Tsnathsarré.

CPSIA information can be obtained
at www.ICGtesting.com
Printed in the USA
LVHW052159230621
690929LV00015B/2464